PRAISE

From the moment you read the first paragraph of *Dorfuss Bubblebutt*, you are transported into a story that grips you page by page until the end. The vivid descriptions breathe life into a tale of love, compassion, and the classic battle of good against evil. You will find yourself rooting for a creature whose mission in life is humble sacrifice and cheering for a surefooted model of love all of us can learn from.

—Blanche Norris, Illinois, product developer

Dorfuss Bubblebutt is a magical, enchanting journey of good versus evil. Dorfuss is the Harry Potter of the cat world.

—Victoria M. Kern, Illinois, school bus driver

Cynthia Mueller takes the young reader to a world full of fun and fantasy where their imaginations can run wild. Readers of all ages will enjoy the fun-filled adventures!

—Shari R. Riddle, Illinois, transportation coordinator

Cynthia Mueller has created a wonderful book truly for all ages. She takes you on a magical adventure. You will laugh with her, you will cry with her, and in the end you will cheer with her!

—Sue Olson, Illinois, school bus driver

Mueller has written a wonderful story that reminds children of all ages that God is with us and often uses things we least expect to help us navigate through life.

—Stephanie Bolger, Illinois, early childhood teacher and daycare provider

Once again Cynthia Mueller weaves a tale full of imagination and adventure. This novel is even better than her first; full of insight into not only human nature but that of felines as well.

—Donald Abel, Illinois, retired house painter

Beautifully written, this delightful, adventurous tale of three children and their cat with magical powers is a must-read for cat lovers!

—Margaret Jarzombek, elementary school teacher

For Angel.

You will find pawprints on your heart! ♡

Cynthia Jean Muller

Dorfuss Bubblebutt

Cynthia Jean Mueller

Tate Publishing & *Enterprises*

Published by Tate Publishing & Enterprises, LLC
127 E. Trade Center Terrace | Mustang, Oklahoma 73064 USA
1.888.361.9473 | www.tatepublishing.com

Tate Publishing is committed to excellence in the publishing industry. The company reflects the philosophy established by the founders, based on Psalm 68:11,
"The Lord gave the word and great was the company of those who published it."

Cover design by Kellie Southerland
Interior design by Blake Brasor
Illustration by Cynthia Jean Mueller

Published in the United States of America

ISBN: 978-1-61566-595-2
1. Juvenile Fiction, Animals, Cats
2. Juvenile Fiction, Action & Adventure, General
2010.1.12

Dedication

Dedicated to all of my furry feline friends with whom I've had the honor of companionship: you've taught me about friendship, humor, and most important of all, love.

And also, most particularly, my youngest son, Gerrod, who one day, in an awesome, unadulterated moment of genius, dubbed one of our cats with a hilarious nickname, which became the title of this book! I love you, kiddo!

Also, a special thanks to my deceased uncle and aunt, Wayne and Betty Paul, of Laurel, Iowa. You live on in my memory and my heart. You were the only people I knew who truly brought me closer to Christ and helped me understand the Bible better. You lived your lives according to God's Word. Now I know what God's plan is for all Christians and am no longer frightened of the future.

For any reader who knows of the town of rural Laurel and other towns mentioned in this book, creative liberties have been taken to make this story work. I hope that you will forgive me for them and simply enjoy this novel!

Forever in My Heart

In memory of
my beloved puddies,
some departed and some still with me.
I will always love you!

Sammy, departed
Dusty, departed
Hobo, departed
Barney, departed July 7, 2009 (Dorfuss Bubblebutt)
& Clyde, departed
Ninja, departed February 25, 2008
Elvira
Moe, departed April 29, 2009
Larry & Curly

COMPANION

A poem by Cynthia Jean Mueller

Soft,
Warm fur,
Purr.
Silly antics,
Languorous naps,
Wild adventures.

Nine lives,
Glowing green eyes,
Fantasize.
Make my heart
Grow twice its size.

Mysterious
And magical,
Comical.
One never knows
The end of it all!

Cuddle up with me,
My solitary, warm
Comfort be.
Let's dream of far-off places,
And unknown faces.

Dear snuggly companion,
Know that until the end of time.
You've left cat hair
Everywhere,
Even in the far-reaching recesses
Of my very soul and mind.

Pandora's menacing mysteries clamor feverishly for release!

THE PROMISE

Craaack! Snap! *Oh my gosh!* Ralph Walters found himself panicking as the rung of the rickety old, dry-rotted ladder broke under his weight. In that split second, his heart was filled with angst for the well-being of his three children. He began to plunge downward, and reached out as quickly as possible to grab the remaining rung in front of him with his one free hand. But he missed it anyway, and as he began his horrid descent, a huge hole of worry began to open up in his heart.

What will become of them now? For surely he would not, could not, survive a fall from this height, and if he were somehow lucky enough to, he would be damaged for life!

He had been meaning to replace those old boards on that ladder, in fact, for the past couple of years. Yet other chores around the old place always seemed more pressing, and he had found excuses to keep putting it off. There were always so many things to keep one busy around a farm! Still, the ladder had supported him well

every single morning until this fateful one, he briefly reflected as he plunged to the floor.

As he fell, he was acutely aware of the sound of the milk-filled bucket he had been holding in his other hand clanging loudly to the ground, followed closely by a loud splash as its contents sprayed everywhere. He knew then with a morbid certainty the cattle would not receive their hay that morning, the cats in the hayloft would not get their dish of warm milk, and the remaining cows would not be milked at all. He cried out loudly with fear in the last conscious moment before his head connected with a thick, solid-wood support beam near the dirt floor. He saw it coming. Subsequently, inside of his head it felt as if an explosion had taken place—millions of blinding rays of light consumed his vision, and then he blacked out entirely.

In the early darkness of the bleak midwestern November morning, the farmer lay unmoving for the longest time until ultimately, hopeless consciousness began to surface.

The first thing he was aware of as he came to was a terrible coldness permeating his body, one he had never before experienced. His anatomy shivered uncontrollably in its shock. Although the barn always held the natural warmth from the animals that resided within, the farmer knew something inside of him was dreadfully irreparable. There was terrible, consuming pain, pounding not only in his head but in the middle of his back. Everything hurt so terribly, in fact, that it was nearly impossible to differentiate between where one pain ended and another began. After his head had connected with the support beam, he had landed awkwardly in an unnatural, twisted position, slightly on his side. Yet he could not feel his legs at all. *Not a good sign!*

His vision was terribly hazy; then it temporarily cleared as he blinked and tried to collect his thoughts. He was certain he had suffered a concussion in addition to his other untold and numerous injuries. His eyes continued to waver in and out of focus.

Ralph lay there many moments longer—forever, it seemed—as the awful coldness worsened and pervaded him from head to toe. He did not know how much longer he could stand the cold or the shivering completely consuming his body. His heart felt overwhelmed with aching loneliness for the children. He was so certain at this point he would never see them again. How horrible to be out here, dying all alone, unbeknownst to them, while they slept peacefully in their beds up in the warmth of the farmhouse. What a desolate emotion! He was so close yet so very far away from them all, it seemed, in this barn in the wee hours of the morning. He longed for them and their loving comforts, their sweet, varied dispositions, their cheerful smiles.

He glanced one last time in the only direction he could see as the blurriness again began to overtake him. He did not want to leave, yet he could feel death's omnipresence summoning him, calling to him louder and louder with each struggling beat of his heart. *Please, God*, he implored silently. *Please watch over my family. Keep them safe!*

The cows nearby complained, the majority with teats still heavy with milk.

A few of the barn cats wandered about listlessly. They yowled impatiently with protest in their hunger and anguish, wondering in their puny feline brains just what was holding up their breakfast.

An unusual-looking, longhaired, tortoiseshell-marked female cat had uncertainly watched the farmer from afar for some time. She knew somehow in her sweet little feline heart that something was horribly wrong with the poor man. She finally made her way to the broken body that lay contorted on the barn floor. She was quite awkward with her latest litter due to arrive in this world any day. Cautiously, she made her way to the kindly farmer who had cared for her all of the past years in return for her having helped to keep the barn free of rodents.

Investigating the scene before her carefully and daintily, she sniffed the straw-scattered ground, which smelled of the milk that should have been not only her breakfast but the other cats' as well. Eventually she approached the man, hesitantly sniffing his face in curiosity and concern. "Meow!" she implored. He heard the rumble of a beginning purr, and then it became a full-fledged, characteristically loud one. She cautiously rubbed her fuzzy head against his several times, worriedly, questioningly, yet affectionately.

The farmer stared hazily at her pretty, worried tortoise face, memorizing it in case it was the last mortal vision he was to behold. *Sweet Mamma Kitty*, he had called her so many times over the years as she had given birth to litter after litter of sprightly kittens in her short life. He had always felt more than a degree of affection for this lowly, loving animal. She had been such a wonderful mother to all of her kittens.

With his last ounce of strength, Farmer Walters finally, experiencing pain, shakily reached out to the loudly purring, ungainly feline form and the warmth of Mamma Kitty's long fur. It was the only heat he had encountered for what seemed like forever. He knew then that this simple yet loving creature would be the only witness to his imminent departure from this earth. His hand wavered and then briefly and clumsily connected with her velvety angora fur. He only caressed her back for mere moments, and then his hand dropped to her burgeoning belly as his strength began to wane, long enough to find himself wishing deeply for her warmth. Then his hand fell limply to the ground, never to be lifted by his own power again. His heart finally ceased its beating.

Suddenly then, in a breathtaking and wondrous sensation he had never known, his spiritual being shattered into a thousand points of light. All pain passed from him in that very moment. *Is this death?* he found himself wondering with awe. *How very resplendent and amazing! What a wonderful surprise!* He smiled a bit in final, all-consuming reverence. His soul then was rejoined almost instantaneously into what would forevermore be his eternal body.

While witnessing this unparalleled event, Mamma Kitty momentarily experienced an overwhelming sensation of fear. Her mind underwent a brief, skittish urge to bolt, and she ceased her purring. Yet something kept her hopelessly rooted to the spot. Mamma Kitty continued to observe, she the unwilling witness, from her close vantage point. An unusual light developed deep within the kind farmer's eyes just as his life ceased. Somehow it emanated, temporarily consuming and penetrating her eyes with its ethereal brightness. Yet just when her little cat mind urged her to run for safety, the fear suddenly dissipated. Next it was replaced by a deep feeling of love that enveloped her heart completely with its warmth. She resumed her heartfelt purr, her green eyes filled with wonder.

And as the farmer's soul passed into eternal life, into the light from beyond, which now encompassed him, the fuzzy, loveable face before him disappeared forever from his view.

"Do not worry, dear Brother Ralph; we will see to it that your family is cared for," he faintly heard with an echoing resonance. He then entered, walking with strong, brand-new, immortal legs, the great beyond. He witnessed the angels heralding their welcomes to him and saw the glorious vision of the renowned pearly gates. And his wife, parents, infant son, and so many other dear ancestors and acquaintances who had long since passed were all there. They waited for him with welcoming smiles, and ultimately he knew only an all-encompassing peace. He vanished, smiling gratefully with a fresh, love-consumed heart into eternity with them all.

THE WALTERS FAMILY

The year was 1958 and the setting Laurel, Iowa. Farms like the Walterses' were legion throughout the state, which was known for its picturesque, rolling hills with vast green fields covered with crops. Lovely streams ran deeply between the hills, and barns and farmhouses were scattered here and there, most often miles apart.

It was common for farms of this type to be passed down from generation to generation, just as the Walters farm had been. The land Ralph had owned was vast, and plopped directly into the middle of it was an ordinary-looking, two-story white farmhouse. It sat at the top of a scenic hill and was graced with your standard covered, homey-looking porch that stretched across the front. A regular-looking red barn with a large hayloft door near its peak resided a short way down a slight incline more toward the road. Several outbuildings, including sheds and silos, were scattered here and there all around it. A windbreak of tall junipers screened two sides of the property from the road with gaping holes like those of missing teeth here and there. One or two had died away years ago, providing brief glimpses of the homestead to passersby.

Ralph had inherited the farm from his parents, who were blessed with three children. Ralph was their only son and the youngest.

The eldest, his beautiful sister Ruth, married right out of college and moved to Davenport. She had always possessed a friendly, outgoing personality and longed for big-city life rather than the rural life she had grown up knowing. He'd rarely seen her since she'd married. Ralph always loved to tease her when they were younger that since she had been born first, she was the one who had gotten all the good looks.

His other sister, Hilda, was the middle child.

Hilda was a rather unattractive spinster who lived several miles away within the boundaries of the tiny town of Laurel. She had never had a taste for farming, so the farm had gone to her brother when both of their parents passed on at a relatively young age. Ralph was more capable anyway of undertaking such a responsibility. Without a husband, managing a farm would have been impossible for Hilda.

All three siblings, born and raised in the Depression era, learned at an early age to make do with what they had and to scrimp and save their hard-earned pennies. That was typical of folks who grew up during those hard times.

Ralph finally got married in his late twenties to a sweet woman named Edith Morley. She was twenty-five. As was typical in that day and age, they thereafter wasted no time starting a family.

Ralph had never been particularly attractive himself, but he was of good, strong, farmer stock with blotchy, reddish-brown, thinning hair, green, slightly-crossed eyes, freckles, and barely noticeable buck teeth. His appearance had not bothered Edith in the least. At her age, and in that time, she was grateful to have a man like her husband show an interest in her, especially since she was supposedly already past her prime. It relieved her from her secret worries that she would waste away the remainder of *her* life in spinsterhood. The selection of available men in this sparsely populated region had never been wide. And Ralph was a good, loving man, which was all important to her. She knew he would make an excellent husband and provider. She had been born and raised on a farm also and loved the life.

As he aged, Ralph's eyesight began to deteriorate rapidly. He wore coke-bottle-lens glasses that did nothing to enhance his appearance. He also, in his ever-advancing years, put on a good deal of middle-aged spread due mainly to Edith's wonderful touch in the kitchen. Even though he was a man of short stature and husky build, he was still taller than his sweet little Edie.

Edith Walters had been a kind and loving wife. She had a fair complexion and dark hair and was petite. She and Ralph grew to love each other dearly over the years. With each child she bore, she put on more than a little weight herself. Still, she had a pretty face and a cheerful disposition that were conducive to raising a family well.

Edie and Ralph's first child, Jonathan, was a handful of a boy from the minute he started to squirm in his mother's belly. Rambunctious and full of energy, the terrible-twos stage his parents endured with him seemed interminable. Blessed with his father's red hair and complexion but his mother's good looks, he was also a bright, studious child. Jon loved to learn new and different things. He was built large for his age, taking after the men in his mother's family. By the time he turned four, he was out and about on the farm by his father's side, helping with the chores on a daily basis.

When Jonathan began school, he became a trial for his teachers, however. His intelligence quickly exceeded what the teachers taught, and he often became bored. There were times when he threw tantrums in class. He also developed an unbecoming fondness of calling the other students cruel names. Frankly, he became somewhat of a bully due in part to his size.

Ralph and Edie's second child was another son, born approximately two years after his brother. They named him Joseph. He was born with his mother's dark hair and pale complexion but was sickly, unfortunately. He passed away soon afterward, much to his parents' despair. He seemed to be such a mild-mannered child in comparison to his brother, and of course, on the farm, sons were always much needed and welcome. At the tender age of two and a half weeks old, the dear child's heart simply gave out, and his parents buried him with deep misery. Their sadness over his loss and the emptiness he had left behind was unbearable for months.

Again, approximately two years later, Edie gave birth to their third son, and they proudly named him James. James also had a sweet, calm disposition, as had his departed brother. Again, he possessed the darker hair and silver eyes of his mother but the stature and looks of his dad. Eventually, the loss of poor Joseph began to seem a sad but distant memory.

Three years after the birth of James, a daughter finally made her appearance, much to the joy of both of her parents. They named her Jenna. With flaming red hair and bright green eyes, she was the apple of her parents' eyes. Hereafter, Edith would have a lovely daughter to dress all up in frilly feminine whatnots and help her around the home too.

As Jonathan grew up, he settled down somewhat, but he remained bored and dissatisfied with school. He loved to take apart motors and other moving gadgets and put them back together again. He amazed both his parents continuously with his seemingly natural mechanical and handyman skills. Things Ralph had no idea how to repair and would have thrown out on the trash heap way out in the back forty, Jonathan would somehow stick back together with mere baling wire and chewing gum. He would have whatever it was up and running again in no time.

Edie's old wringer washer stopped working one morning. The young Jonathan took it apart with a wrench, tinkered around inside a bit, and then put it back together again that same afternoon. The next morning, Edie was proudly and with much amazement using it again. This earned Jon the nickname *Wrench*, which his father used with pride whenever Jon attempted a usually successful repair.

As James aged, it became apparent to both of his parents that he did not possess the intelligence of his older brother. In fact, his folks were fairly sure that James, at the age of four, was simple. Still, he had always been a sweet child with a kind and loving temperament, and he was such a joy to have around. He loved to help his mother in the kitchen, making small snacks when he was younger. And as he grew older, he too joined his father and brother in helping with the chores out and about on the large family farm.

Something about James simply touched one's heart, and the animals on the farm were able to sense it too. His baby sister, Jenna, learned at an early age that he was her best friend in the whole wide world. James had a way with living things that was obviously a gift from God, at times apparently being able to read their minds. He would cradle creatures in his arms if they were small and pet them gently or quietly hug and stroke the larger beasts, speaking softly to them in a language of his very own.

James possessed a particularly helpful touch with animals about to give birth. He was able to calm their temperaments and help them relax to better ease their pain. The two horses the Walterses owned absolutely loved James. In his presence, they calmed almost immediately if they were feeling skittish or upset, as did all the other beasts and birds on the farm.

Jenna grew into a sweet and sassy little girl who loved to tease and be teased. She always doted on her brothers, particularly James, who was, of course, closest to her in age. She absolutely adored her parents. She was the light of all of their lives. Jenna liked to spend some time of her own helping out with the animals on the farm and especially liked the kitties. They were so warm and cuddly, and when they purred, she would lie down with them in the hayloft and drift off to sleep.

Approximately four years after Jenna's birth, Edie began to experience what she first believed to be morning sickness. Excited at first about the prospect of yet another sweet child, her anticipation waned when her illness became more and more violent and gradually began to last most of each and every day. Pale and thin after weeks of this experience, Ralph finally overrode his wife's objection to doctors and called in old Dr. Jones from town to examine his deteriorating wife.

After scrutinizing Edith at home and not being able to come up with an explanation for her ill health, Dr. Jones suggested a brief stay for her at the hospital in Marshalltown some fifteen miles away. Perhaps, he advised, the doctors there would be better able to examine her and recommend a treatment with the fancy, new, more advanced equipment that small-town doctors just did not have access to.

While at the hospital, however, Edie's health deteriorated even further. Several days later, with her husband waiting anxiously at her bedside, an older surgeon entered the small, private room. He gave Ralph the worst news of his life. During an exploratory surgery, cancer had been found, and it had already metastasized extensively throughout his dear wife's body. Edie only had weeks or perhaps days of her life left.

She never left the hospital. Throughout everything, the kind minister's wife from Laurel had let their children live at their home in town, caring for them lovingly and never once complaining. Ralph's sister Hilda had helped with their care somewhat during this time also, but because of her job, her assistance was sporadic.

Edie's funeral was a dark and melancholy event. Even with the relative isolation of farm families' lives, she had been well-known and loved throughout the small community. Friends and neighbors from all over the area were in attendance.

After Edith's death, Ralph was lost for months. He went through his daily chores, sure enough, albeit in a haze. Kind women from the church stopped in biweekly to help clean house and prepare meals. But life was just not the same for him anymore. What was he going to do? He could barely even look at his children once she was gone, since they were constant reminders of the wife he would never see again.

In the daytime, there were numerous mementos of his departed wife just about everywhere he looked. And at night—well, at night, the bedroom was just lonely and empty and cold without her. Her warm, soft, comfort in the night was never to be again, and he cried silent tears for many, many dark hours.

Finally, after months of this desolate funk, one hot summer's day, Ralph was shocked into dealing more directly with everyday life and paying better attention to his family members who still remained.

The children were swimming in the deep pond down by the creek when Jenna's swim skirt became caught in a submerged tree branch. Ralph had not even realized they were down there. He only found out about this near loss of yet another beloved family member when the boys came tearing across the yard, dripping wet. They ran up to the house yelling for him.

In his arms, Jonathan held a loudly wailing, flailing, and terribly frightened Jenna. Only after she calmed and the boys were able to relay their horrid tale to their father did Ralph sit down and take a reality check of his life.

If her brothers had not been able to untangle her from that awful branch and sweet Jenna had drowned, I would not be able to go on! Thank you, Lord, for saving her! he prayed silently. And even though dear Edith was now in heaven, he felt sure she would never have forgiven him for his foolish slight.

Thereafter, Ralph made it a point to be the best possible father to his children. He paid attention to their whereabouts at all times, helped as much as he could with their schoolwork, and even learned to prepare a few simple meals. Gradually, both he and the children began to deal better with the loss of his partner and their mother, and things began to return to some semblance of normal. Things went well with the somewhat tinier family for the next three years.

And then Ralph died as well.

SPINSTER HILDA

Jonathan, who'd grown into a strapping, handsome thirteen-year-old, was the one to find his father that fateful morning. He realized he had overslept for school and that Ralph had not come into their rooms to wake them all in his usual jovial manner. His brother and sister had slept in as well! When he awoke on his own, he faintly heard sounds of the cattle mooing in the barn. That seemed rather odd to Jon. Usually they did that only when it was time to be fed or milked.

After searching the house and not finding his pappa, he made his way out to the barn to give his father a hand, for certainly he must be out there. Perhaps he was just running a little late with things that day or something.

He was not at all prepared for the sight of his deceased father lying twisted and broken near the base of the ladder leading to the hayloft. It was patently obvious upon observation that one of the top rungs had broken. The splintered remnants of it were all that remained.

"Pappa!" he cried out in shock, quickly running to his father in the hopes that he might somehow be able to help him. Ralph's body was stone cold, however, and it was obvious Jonathan's help had arrived much too late. "Pappa!" he cried out again, and finally his face crumpled with realization. Next, he only cried, sitting down on the dirt floor of the barn and cradling his father's head in his lap for what seemed like forever.

Ultimately, of course, he was forced to gather his senses as the cows persistently mooed louder and louder yet. They were obviously in pain from the fullness of their teats. Jonathan slowly trudged back up to the house with a heavy heart and tears streaming down his cheeks anew and met his awakened brother and sister.

"James, Jenna, Pappa is dead! There was an accident in the barn, and it looks like he fell! The hayloft ladder is broken!" he rasped out, his freckled face streaked with dirt and tears. He breathed tremulously.

His siblings were stunned and disbelieving at first. Jenna initially accused Jonathan of lying and then ultimately broke down bawling. James, after shedding quite a few tears himself, finally suggested to his brother, "We should go get Pappa then and bring him up here to the house at least." As simple as James was, he had always had a lot of common sense where it counted.

His brother and sister finally agreed with deep sadness, and all three of them made their way down toward the barn, hearts heavy with disbelief and grief.

The minute they entered the barn, Jenna began to howl even louder. She could not bear the loss of her dear pappa! Her two older brothers began to cry again too. Jenna was so upset that she refused to leave the barn when the boys began to lift their father into one of the smaller farm wagons that Jon had brought by with the tractor. Instead she opted to pet Mamma Kitty, who had found the tearful trio. Jenna stubbornly leaned against a bale of hay and pulled Mamma Kitty onto her lap, squeezing her tight enough to make the poor, pregnant cat let out a sharp meow of protest. Then with compassionate realization of the poor cat's predicament, she eased up on the hapless feline just enough to calm her and began petting her furiously so she would stay.

Tears streamed down her pretty little face as she waited in disbelief for many moments longer for her brothers' return. It had been good judgment for the boys to leave her there as she wished. By the time they reappeared after laying Pappa on his bed up at the house, she had calmed considerably. She was petting Mamma Kitty and only crying softly now.

James went over to his sister and sat down beside her, putting a comforting arm around her and pulling her to him. Absently, he too petted the cat. "Won't be long before she has her kittens," he stated dully.

Jonathan leaned against the railing of the cattle pen with his arms folded in front of him, staring into space. In all their shock and grief, there really was not much to say.

Eventually, however, the cows began protesting so loudly the boys were forced to take care of their needs, and after a while, Jenna joined them too. Working did seem to ease their shock and grief somewhat, and somehow they took care of everything that had to be done. All the years of helping their father around the place had certainly paid off. There was no question as to what needed to be done, and they took care of it all with looming and increasing heaviness in their hearts.

When they finally arrived back up at the house, it was late in the morning. They all knew it would be useless to try to attend school that day. The bus was long gone. None of them felt like going anyway. What would they do now, and who would take care of them?

Their late mother had no family at all in the area, and the only relative they did have nearby was their aunt Hilda in town. She had never had children, of course, and had never been particularly interested in or seemed to care about any of them. She hadn't helped much when Mamma had died. Should they call her? Or perhaps the closest farmers a couple of miles down the road? At least the Stahls had a few of their own children.

Jenna, feeling rather useless and hungry just like her brothers, decided to make them all a simple breakfast of oatmeal, scrambled eggs, and juice. Luckily, her mother, and later her dad had taught her well, and she handled the chore deftly.

While they all went through the motions of eating yet barely tasting anything, they discussed again whom to call. They finally decided on Aunt Hilda. She was kin, after all, and close, and should be notified of her brother's death if nothing else. If she was not interested in caring for them, perhaps she could help them contact their other aunt, Ruth, who lived far off in a city near Illinois. They knew they had cousins there if Aunt Hilda didn't want the responsibility.

Later, they telephoned their aunt Hilda. After expressing her initial shock and then grief at the loss of her only brother, she apprehensively agreed to come and care for them while funeral arrangements and such were taken care of. She hinted perhaps she could stay longer if things worked out. She did not sound pleased at all and did not really promise anything specific. Hilda bluntly answered Jonathan's numerous questions while she tried to figure everything out in her head that would need tending to.

Hildegarde Walters had inherited a relatively substantial amount of money from her parents since Ralph had gotten the farm and everything that had come with it. With that, she had purchased her tiny two-bedroom house in town. It would not be big enough to contain three children. Also, she owned quite a few priceless antiques. She was particularly fond of ornate lamps. Many of her antiquities also had belonged to their parents, and she had no desire to watch them be destroyed by tiny hands or silly antics. She decided it would be in everyone's best interests if she stayed with the children at the farm, at least for a while.

Unbeknownst to anyone in the town, Hilda had developed quite an interest in the occult. When patrons were sparse at the library, she covertly studied carefully several of the library's books on the subject. She had also secreted away to her home several old, outdated volumes on witchcraft over the years that patrons had apparently not shown any interest in.

Prim and proper librarian by day, she privately considered herself to be a witch. She had even tried, albeit unsuccessfully, a few of the easier spells in her spare time at home. She intended to keep trying. Perhaps she only needed more practice.

The lone librarian in the small town, she had always been very withdrawn, not very friendly, and not comfortable around large groups of people.

Hilda had rather sharp, unattractive features and dark, thin, stringy hair with a whisper of a wave she could never seem to do anything with. Thus, she always kept it severely pulled back from her face in a very tight knot. Rather tall for a woman and quite thin, except for an uncharacteristically large posterior in proportion to the rest of her body, she was also mostly flat chested and angular in a way that matched her severe face. As her age advanced, she began to develop the beginnings of a dowager's hump. Men never paid her any attention. The older she became, the more she realized that she actually preferred things that way.

Dealing with people in general had usually not been a problem for her at the tiny library. There, she maintained a strict code of silence and professionalism in her domain and only spoke to others when necessary. She had always been proud of the fact that she had never missed one single day of work. Few of the townspeople even knew her very well. She did not attend most social events, including church. Only when necessary, she ventured to the small mercantile in town to pick up her usual staples and then retreated to the library or her tiny home.

Hilda owned a rather old, rickety black Oldsmobile that she tooled around town in and used to visit Ralph and his family on the farm from time to time. It wasn't the nicest car anymore, but it was efficient, mimicking its owner. Most of the time, though, it stood next to the library or in her driveway. The town was small, and often in nice weather, she left it at home, preferring to walk to accomplish her errands.

Hilda had a rather comical walk. She bandied about town, leaning forward on skinny legs, with ample posterior jutting out rudely as she made her way about town, as if to compensate for a strong wind. Yet, again, her walk was efficient, with quick steps and no effort wasted. Many times, she could be seen carrying her black umbrella on a perfectly nice, sunny day. It suited her, though, since her moods tended toward the dark and forbidding, just as her mode of dress did. Her face usually held a sour, dour expression. Her outfits, like her hair, were severe and without much color and at least ten to fifteen years out of style.

After she hung up the phone with her nephew, she went into her tiny bathroom. Hilda glanced into the small mirror to wipe away the remnants of the tears that had uncharacteristically streaked her face. She was not prone to crying!

Why, poor Ralph was only forty-two! How sad for him to pass away so young and how awful for him to leave three young children behind, particularly for me, anyway. Hilda did not care much for children. Rather, she had always barely tolerated them.

In Laurel, parents paid attention to what their children were up to, and generally they were very well behaved in public. It was still a time when children respected their elders and adults believed that children should be seen and not heard. Hilda, particularly, had always agreed with this edict.

Wiping away all remaining streaks on her face, she observed it with dismay. *I am not getting any younger myself*, her gaunt reflection reminded her cruelly. *Forty-five already with no marriage prospects in sight. Never have been and probably never will be!* It was just as well, she supposed. She was a loner and had become comfortable with that brutal reality.

Still, when women of substantial beauty came into the library, she resented them for making her feel even more unworthy than usual. Deep lines had begun to carve their way around her eyes and also her thin mouth, which was often puckered into a disapproving prune. As she aged, brown age spots had appeared on her face. The skin on her neck had begun to sag and lose its tone, wrinkling and creasing unattractively whenever she moved her thin head this way or that. Her eyes were still a pretty shade of olive green, as

Ralph's had been, but her eyesight had deteriorated. She wore small, wire-rimmed glasses with bifocals that blurred their view. Her thin, almost bony hands were also covered with age spots.

She had angular eyebrows and high cheekbones, which might have been attractive in a severe way if she weighed a few more pounds. But underneath them, dark hollows had begun to develop, reminding her slightly of a denuded skull.

When she had been a young woman, Hilda's brunette hair had held the prettiest red highlights that were especially apparent in sunlight. However, as she grew older, they faded away and then disappeared entirely around the time she turned thirty. At the present, her hair was just a dull shade of dark brown with large streaks of gray forming here and there. A particularly intense gray streak had formed in the deep widow's peak on her forehead. She fingered it absently for a moment.

Finally, shrugging at her useless and pathetic reflection, she reached over to the tiny corner table in the Victorian-style bathroom and selected a small, dark hat with netting from her hat tree. She placed it on top of her unflattering hairstyle and shoved a hatpin through it, securing it firmly to her hair. She'd best make her way over to the farm and see about the children, and planning a funeral, come to think of it again! *It just doesn't seem real!*

Hilda wiped away the beginnings of new tears as she efficiently packed a small bag, put on her dark wool coat, got into her black Olds, and tooled off in the direction of Ralph's farm. The rickety thing chugged, clattered, and puffed away, blowing black smoke now and then while rolling jerkily on the gravel road that led toward the home she had grown up in.

No More Pappa to Tuck Us into Bed

When Hilda arrived at the farm, Jonathan met her outside to help her carry her small suitcase into the house. His expression was somber, as were the other children's. Not much was said by any of them. After putting away her items in the spare downstairs bedroom, she asked Jonathan if the chores had been taken care of for the day. He nodded, adding that he would see to it the evening ones were handled shortly.

After spending a few quiet moments in Ralph's and her deceased sister-in-law's room upstairs, reminiscing and grieving his loss anew, Hilda went down to the desk in the parlor and attempted to telephone the local funeral establishment to begin making arrangements.

The nosy operator on the other end of the party line was persistent in her questions about Ralph and his family, and Hilda finally told the irritating woman to shut up and connect her to the funeral home.

Jonathan and James headed out to the barn to take care of the evening rituals for the animals. Mamma Kitty was giving birth to her kittens. After the chores were completed, James stuck around in the barn for a long time, helping her and speaking to her soothingly in his mumbo jumbo sort of way. She didn't care that his words made no particular sense; they calmed her and made things easier, and she appreciated that.

Up at the house, Jenna began moving about in the kitchen half-heartedly, opening up some jars of homemade chicken soup that one of the kind ladies from the church had left for them months ago. She set out a loaf of bread and some butter and applesauce to accompany it. She wished to herself that she had learned more about cooking in her short lifetime. The simple meals she did know how to prepare were not going to go far. Everyone would be sick of them in no time!

Hilda droned on and on in the parlor with the funeral director for what seemed like forever.

Jonathan came back inside and put some dirty clothes in the wringer washer. *I might as well learn how to do things around here*, he realized, seeing how he was suddenly man of the house!

When their dinner was ready, Jonathan went out to the porch to ring the dinner bell to call James up to the house.

James arrived in an excited mood, loudly announcing that Mamma Kitty had already birthed three kittens and probably still had several more to go. He proudly proclaimed that as soon as he had eaten he would go back outside to help her until she was finished. Everyone else at the table continued eating and barely heard him. They were all disinterested about the goings-on with Mamma Kitty in their grief and internalized questions about the future. After all, it was only a cat James was bellering about, and they had many more important things on their minds.

After dinner, the mortician showed up in a large, dark hearse to transport Ralph's body away. Jonathan cried quietly while Jenna became very upset, screaming that the man was not to take her dear pappa away. Hilda had done her best to restrain the understandably upset child. Hilda didn't like it any more than the children, but she knew things should be taken care of quickly before the body began to smell bad and the foul odor enveloped the entire house. James was fortunate enough to miss this dreadful event, since he had already ventured back outside to help Mamma Kitty out in the barn.

The funeral director began to drive away. Jenna's keening became almost unbearable as she watched the car roll slowly down the drive. Jonathan picked her up in his arms and tried unsuccessfully to console her while she kicked and squirmed and fought against his grip.

Suddenly Hilda snapped, shouting at the both of them, "Contain that child, for heaven's sake! That insidious noise is enough to drive a person insane!" Glaring at them each with a hideous, contemptuous look in her eyes and pruning her lips in disapproval, she placed her hands on her ample hips, appearing formidable with her considerable height in comparison to the two of them.

Both of them stood there, wide-eyed, gazing back at her for a moment as they tried to take in what had just happened. Neither of their parents had *ever* yelled at any of them! Jenna silenced immediately, and body shaking, with tear-stained face, she surveyed Hilda unbelievingly, her lower lip still trembling. The poor child breathed raggedly in a vain attempt to immediately calm her tiny nerves. Finally, after several awkward moments of silence, Jonathan strode off toward the staircase and up to Jenna's bedroom with her arms still wrapped around his neck.

Moments later, in Jenna's bedroom, Jonathan hugged her as he set her down on her bed, and she began to cry again. After long minutes and more of her tears, she began to quiet. She asked Jonathan then, "Why was Aunt Hilda so awful?"

Jonathan just shook his head, not sure himself. Finally, he shrugged, telling her, "Maybe it's just 'cause she's upset about Pappa's death too." Jenna continued to stare at him, wide-eyed and full of unspent tears, her body trembling and breath still ragged.

"Well, kiddo," he finally said, standing and patting her awkwardly on the head, "you'd best get dressed for bed. It's late, and I think we are all worn out! You should try to get some sleep now."

Jenna nodded and then quickly stood to hug her big brother before he left. She felt closer to him that night than she ever had. "G'night, Jon-Jon!" she said thickly, wiping at her eyes. Jonathan shyly hugged her back. Then he left her to get ready for bed himself, mostly because he did not want her to see the fresh tears that had sprung to his eyes and get her started up all over again. Aunt Hilda probably would not stand for that, especially right now.

He entered his and James's shared room and started getting into his pajamas.

Soon, James was bursting through their bedroom door, announcing loudly and proudly that Mamma Kitty had birthed eight babies. One had been stillborn, but the rest were seemingly healthy. The last one to have been born, however, had been a runt. James seemed concerned about that one, saying he would keep an eye on the poor little thing.

Then he noticed that his older brother had not commented much. He suddenly realized with overwhelming, renewed force, Jonathan's sadness about their beloved pappa. Jonathan was already climbing into the upper bunk. James started to change into his warm winter pajamas too, and the grief began to overtake him anew also. "What's wrong, Jon? Are you missing Pappa too?"

"Well, of course I am!" was his brother's blunt reply. And then, "A man came and took him away while you were out there playing with dumb cats! Pappa's gone!"

James crawled into his lower bunk after turning out the dim bedside lamp. He said nothing further to Jon, sensing it would be best not to. He lay there for what seemed to be the longest time. Jonathan also seemed to be having trouble getting comfortable up above him and was shaking the bed frame and James's lower mattress. James lay on his side in silence, watching things take shape in the darkness with the dim moonlight making its way through the thin curtains on the two large windows of their room. *No more Pappa to tuck us into bed or kiss us goodnight anymore.* Mamma had been gone for quite some time by now, but he found himself missing her more than usual again this night.

Jonathan was thinking similar thoughts above him. Also, now the disturbing thought that he was going to have to grow up *real* fast struck him. All of them would, actually. *What are the three of us going to do, especially if Aunt Hilda doesn't want us? No more childish pranks or troublemaking*, he realized with a bit of dismay. *I am going to have to be the man of the house, at least temporarily, and that will include taking care of my brother and sister too.* He knew James was not overly intelligent and that it would be his own job to do all the thinking for the three of them for quite some time. And then, of course, there would be the daily chores and animals to worry about too.

Thinking back to Aunt Hilda's sharp treatment of them earlier, he was worried about what the days to come would bring. He knew she was not used to having children underfoot. With an uncomfortable, gnawing sense, he began to realize that what he and Jenna had witnessed earlier was Hilda's *true* personality just beginning to come to the surface. When Pappa had still been alive, she had always treated them with indifference, thus none of them had ever gotten to know her very well.

It was a long while before he was able to settle down and get to sleep; hours, it seemed, after he finally heard James quietly sob himself to sleep. Ultimately, James began to snore loudly. *No more Pappa to tuck us in!* The loneliness and silence that followed that revelation was almost unbearable.

Downstairs in the guest bedroom that had been her parents' room when she was a child, Aunt Hilda had begun to perform her bedtime preparations as well. She was distracted, however. Between each step of her nightly ritual, she paced back and forth in the large room.

Not only was she deeply upset about her brother's death, but she was equally dismayed about *her* predicament besides. *I do not like children; I know that with absolute certainty now that I have responsibility for three of them! I will have to do some serious thinking about what I am going to do about them now!* She knew she would also have to move more of her own personal belongings to the farm, at least temporarily, while she resolved everything. There was also her job at the library. Perhaps she would need to hire a person or two to help around the farm here and keep an eye on the children too.

Certainly, Ruth, way off in Davenport with her husband Tom and four nearly grown children, would not want three additional children to tend to at this point in her life! And, after all, Hilda had not communicated with her for years. They had never gotten along particularly well. *In fact, I do not intend to telephone Ruth now either!* she ruminated with spite.

Hilda, as a teen, had always been envious of her sister's beauty, and as they both grew into womanhood, their differences became even more apparent. Ruth was an open, friendly young woman and leaned toward big-city life. Hilda was comfortable remaining in the relative obscurity of Laurel, knowing the life there already. *But I am not about to once again play second fiddle to my audacious, gorgeous sister. To heck with Ralph's possible wishes! And he left no will behind! How dare he do this to me!*

She was all alone. Except for three kids now! Frankly, she had been more than a little afraid of striking out all on her own in her youth with no man to take care of her. And unfortunately for Hilda, one had never materialized.

She finally crawled into one of the twin beds in the room, reached out to turn off the bedside lamp, and slid down into the sheets to get comfortable. Sleep for her as well that night turned out to be a long time in coming. Finally, mercifully, she succumbed to its welcoming silence.

Spring's Renewal

On a cold, windy, and rainy November morning, Ralph Walters's funeral was held at the tiny town church. The burial followed in the small cemetery on what was usually a pictorial hill just outside town. The gloom of the day, as well as everyone's spirits, eradicated its usual beauty. Many folks from miles around attended that day despite the miserable weather that only added to its desolation.

The children were subdued during the entire thing, hardly speaking at all. Only once did Jenna talk to her brothers through her tears while they all took shelter together under one of Hilda's large, black umbrellas that flailed about in the wind. "Look, Jon-Jon, the sky is crying for Pappa too!" Jenna stated in a whisper.

Jonathan glanced up at the dark clouds through the rain as they rolled rather menacingly across the sky. James said nothing while he gazed skyward; perhaps the grief had finally overwhelmed him also, as it had his brother and sister three days earlier. Reality had struck.

Thanksgiving was only days later, and it passed, more or less ignored by Hilda along with the children, who had no idea of how to go about preparing a Thanksgiving feast anyway. They did not even attend church for the holiday this year, as they always had in the past. Hilda, who had never appreciated church and always avoided it like the plague, did not suggest it, and they did not bring it up either.

Hilda did have a slight knack in the kitchen, however. As the days continued to pass, she began taking over the breakfast and suppertime meals. Then the children only had to fend for themselves at lunchtime. That was easy enough for all of them, since they only needed to prepare their own sandwiches and other snacks to either take in their school lunches or eat on the weekends.

During the weekdays and on Saturday mornings, Hilda was gone at her job at the library, and for her, it was a welcome respite. In the evenings, however, she came back to the farm tired and irritable from working all day. She routinely behaved distantly toward the children. They had come to accept this. There had been no further rude outbursts from their aunt, and they were grateful. Perhaps, they reasoned to themselves, her testiness with them on that fateful evening after Pappa had passed away had only been her own grief speaking out.

Hilda hired a woman to come in twice a week and clean and tend to the laundry during the days, while she worked at the library and the children attended school. A kindhearted farmer named Harvey Jensen, who lived just down the road and also helped out at other area farms, was also paid to come by twice a day to see to the heavier aspects of farming.

Mamma Kitty's kittens were growing and no longer had their eyes shut. The runt, a funny little tortoise-marked thing that looked rather like its mama, had grown some but was still much smaller than its brothers and sisters. The rest of the kittens were marked more ordinarily. There were a couple of orange tigers, one black kitten, and three tabbies, one with socks and white chest and tummy.

James continued to tend Mamma Kitty daily, treating her special in his own way since she was still a brand-new mama in his mind. He also paid special consideration to the runt, feeling sorry for the poor thing and giving it extra attention and love from day one. The tiny, warm ball of fur seemed to return his affection too.

As the kittens grew, James identified the sexes of all of them. Three were female, and four were male, the runt included. Most of them by then appeared to be longhaired like their mother. Jenna also began making frequent visits to the new kitties. She had always loved them so! Petting the cats helped distract her from her troubles, and she was grateful. She had already named each and every one after characters in the Bible. Jon was so busy with chores around the farm that he did not pay much attention to the cats. After all, James had been taking care of them anyway.

Weeks passed, and Aunt Hilda began moving more and more of her own possessions from her house in town to the bedroom she had claimed as her own. She had the extra twin bed in it removed by Harvey and stored away up in the attic. In its place she had him install a large, dark, low table. It was virtually covered with curious, odd-looking items and candles and big, menacing-looking books. The door to her room was always kept strictly shut and locked at all times, and not even the cleaning woman was to go in there, she proclaimed in one of her more talkative moments.

Hilda evolved the rather gloomy habit of always keeping the shades drawn in her room. When one happened to walk by as she was coming out of there, it gave a person the unnerving, shivery sense of the atmosphere of a mausoleum. And, of course, nothing could ever be seen through her window shades from the outside of the house either.

The children obeyed her edict to stay out of her bedroom; they still had not warmed up to her any more than she had to them. They sensed that it would not be wise to cross the woman. Yet there was something about the secretiveness of it all that mystified them and made them somewhat curious.

They began to gossip about their aunt outside during the daytimes while taking care of the animals. Something about the woman and her room was creepy, they all agreed. Jon nicknamed her Brun-Hilda, after some book he had read about witches in school around Halloween time, and James and Jenna snickered a little at that. He also enjoyed calling her Prune-Hilda, referring to her constantly pruned and disapproving expression. In fact, he'd begun calling her names so often that he had to remind himself on numerous occasions when she was near that those were *not* her names.

All three of the children were pleased that she was not around full-time. Dinner was usually conducted silently and efficiently, as was breakfast. In the evenings, after cleaning up following the suppertime meal, just after her bath, Hilda locked herself away in her room. And at times an odd incense odor found its way through the cracks around her door and into the hall outside of it.

After their nightly baths before bedtime, the children developed a habit of spending time all together in the boys' shared bedroom. They talked, sometimes for hours in their loneliness. They brought up a few pictures of their parents from the living room and parlor below and situated them in various places in their rooms. All three of them had become much closer since Ralph's death, and they shared all their thoughts and feelings openly. With the photographs there, they somehow felt as if Mamma and Pappa were still with them, watching over them.

Hilda was always busy in her dark bedroom downstairs doing God only knew what, and she ignored them completely at that time of the night.

One evening, Jenna whispered to both of her brothers in the darkness from the overstuffed chair nearby. She routinely cuddled in it with her blanket and teddy bear, and this particular evening, she reminded her brothers that it was almost Christmastime. Aunt Hilda hadn't even mentioned it or done anything to decorate the house at all. The boys, having both been so busy with their own jobs around the farm as well as their schooling, hadn't really even thought about it either. But Jenna was correct; Christmas was only days away, and Aunt Hilda hadn't brought it up. Snow was on the ground and had been for weeks.

"She's probably too busy down there with her magic potions and wicked spells or whatever the heck she does down there!" Jon blurted out loudly. Then he suggested, "Maybe she could conjure us up a decorated tree!"

His sister and brother, amidst snickers, shushed their older brother promptly. Soon they whispered quietly again, discussing whether they should do anything such as cut down a small tree and possibly carry it up to the bedroom so Santa could come. Or, they wondered if they should present the matter to Aunt Hilda.

Finally, Jon remembered that the Christmas tree stand and a few ornaments were stashed somewhere down in the cellar, and he promised to look for them in the morning. He also agreed that the next day he would look into cutting down a small evergreen from somewhere on the farm. He was sure there would be something suitable around.

"I'll talk to the old prune about it tomorrow," he told his brother and sister just before they all dozed off. "If she doesn't want it set up in the living room, we'll put something small up here."

His siblings seemed content at hearing this, and Jenna headed drowsily off toward her adjacent bedroom to cuddle up with Mr. Teddy in her warm bed.

True to his word, Jon came across all the Christmas fixings the next day and talked to Aunt Hilda about it also. The woman seemed irritated, vague, and distracted but finally relented. That afternoon, Jon brought in a handsome pine tree, secured it in its stand in the living room, and added water. The children merrily spent the next hour or so decorating it.

Only nights later, Santa showed up, bringing a few small items for each child. Aunt Hilda had, with some distaste, opened her tight purse strings long enough to purchase some much-needed clothing items for each of the children from the general store. That was how she justified the uncharacteristic expenditures to herself. A fancy, colored lollipop was included for each of them also. They all cried out in delight upon discovering those!

Jon's shoes had been tight for weeks, so he received some nice, new, heavy work boots with room to grow. James got a warm winter coat since he had outgrown his old one. Jenna acquired two new pretty dresses.

The kind proprietor at the general store, having known the children for years, had helped Hilda with judging sizes and such and had been the one to suggest the lollipops. He had always been fond of the Walters family.

Ultimately, the children had a pleasant Christmas. They joyfully opened their gifts despite Hilda's dour expression and avoidance of the ritual. Then Jenna and the boys baked sugar cookies, complete with colored sugar sprinkled on top, and served them with the dinner Hilda prepared that evening.

Things were pleasant enough until after the dishes had been washed and put away. Then Hilda, keeping true to form, sullenly retired to her room immediately following the meal and her bath.

Later that night, in the boys' room, the three children whispered together again. Mamma and Pappa were discussed, and all three still missed them so greatly. Christmas without them seemed empty. Aunt Hilda had tried, in her own joyless and unexcited fashion, they supposed, to make it at least relatively nice, but it just hadn't been the same.

Weeks passed and then months. Signs of spring began to appear here and there. Chickens began to prepare for their nesting and so did the ducks, laying eggs and hoarding and guarding them in secret places.

The snow began to melt, and green buds started to swell on the trees. One of the horses was with foal. Mamma Kitty's kittens were all over the place. They were more than four months old. Mamma began to roam again, probably in her own preparations for another litter. Although she still cuddled with the growing kittens at night, her work with them was complete.

As the weather warmed, Jenna began to play outside more often, and she and James delighted in playing with the kittens every day. They had grown greatly by that time, and their eyes had been open for months. Their personalities were developing also. Frisky, furry, and cute, they skittered about the barn, barely avoiding injury at times when they deftly sidestepped the large cattle's hooves with their feline athleticism. The runt Jenna had dubbed *Matthew* weeks ago also had grown considerably and was barely smaller than the rest of them by now. He had also acquired a voracious appetite!

Jenna and James particularly liked little Matthew. He was so loveable and cuddly, just like his mother, with his long, soft fur. He just loved to purr, and very loudly at that! His little green eyes were slightly crossed, which made him rather goofy looking. His tiny fangs protruded a little way out of his mouth and over his lower jaw, giving the appearance of buck fangs and adding to his overall silly countenance. With his comical tortoise markings besides, his appearance was quite hilarious yet just plain adorable.

As the kittens grew, their legs became long and gangly and their antics bolder.

Jon became annoyed one weekend morning. James and Jenna were playing with the kittens over on the other side of the barn and not helping him take care of the feeding or milking at all. He kept working irritably, saying nothing to them. He slammed things around as he milked the cows. *Why do I always have to do everything?* he wondered silently with vague anger. Yet he managed to contain a small smile despite himself when a kitten performed a particularly hilarious stunt and his brother and sister giggled in response, not far away. He was glad to see his sister and brother seeming happier, and he had begun to feel more cheerful also. He set a full bucket of milk off to one side as he continued to fill a second.

Without warning, the full bucket suddenly tipped and splashed in his direction and even startled the poor cow he had been milking into a loud, surprised moo! of protest. Glancing toward the mess and feeling even more irritated when he realized that the tortoise-marked kitten had done it in an attempt to reach the milk, he swatted the stupid cat away. It protested with a sharp meow! and took off running toward the welcome and much safer haven of the other two children.

Jon finished milking the agitated cow, speaking to her soothingly to calm her down, and then picked up the only full bucket of milk there was and left the cow pen. Setting the bucket down and folding his arms over his chest, he admonished his brother and sister in a raised voice. "Keep those stupid cats away from the cows when I'm milking them! That idiot, dorfuss of a cat spilled an entire bucket of fresh milk, wasting the whole thing!"

He pointed angrily toward the guilty culprit, who had already completely forgotten his just-moments-ago escapade. The ridiculous cat was heartily and busily having his tummy rubbed by Jenna, rolling to and fro on her lap with no shame, and purring loudly enough for Jon to hear him from a dozen feet away.

"Matthew's not a dorfuss!" James protested loudly. "Look how sweet he is; all he wants is to have his tummy rubbed and to get fed!"

"Well, he's not going to get fed if he keeps spilling his breakfast! Keep the stupid dorfuss away!" Jon stated bluntly again. The cat stopped rolling around momentarily, as if recognizing that he was the subject of conversation. He stood up on Jenna's lap next and gazed at Jon with his ridiculous, crossed green eyes, head cocked slightly, and fangs protruding stupidly. Then he apparently forgot whatever it was that had briefly interested him, lay back down, and resumed his loud purring and gyrating.

Now, Jenna joined in with James's protest as well. "Don't call my kitty a dorfuss! You're a dorfuss!" she hollered at her older brother.

Jon finally grew tired of this pointless, name-calling argument, which was obviously going nowhere. He headed back toward the house with the remaining bucket of milk, muttering under his breath all the way. Jon had never particularly cared for cats, and that stunt in the barn was an excellent example why!

Days became longer, and the nights began to warm up also. Harvey Jensen had been busy getting the fields all tilled and planted as summer approached.

Flowers began to bloom, bees to buzz, birds that had flown south for the winter returned, and the whole farm was alive with the promise of warm breezes, lazy summer days, and hot summer nights to come.

One warm, late spring night when windows were left open, Jenna failed to come into the boys' bedroom for their nightly ritualistic chat. The two boys lay there for a time, talking quietly between themselves. James began to drift off to sleep, and Jon still had not seen his sister. *Perhaps she is upset about something*, he decided, and finally he climbed down off his bunk to investigate.

His worries had been unnecessary, however. When he peered through the darkness into her room, he found his sister sound asleep in her bed. She was cuddled with that dorfuss cat, conked out too in all of his buck-fanged glory. Jenna's Mr. Teddy lay on the floor off to the side of the bed, looking bereft and forgotten. A picture of their parents situated on Jenna's nightstand seemed to call to him in the dimness. An inexplicable sense of peace permeated the entire room, and even Jon felt it. Within seconds, it began to calm him as well. He had intended to toss the cat outside, but suddenly it didn't seem quite as important to do so.

"Hummph!" he snorted once he went back into his and James's shared room. He startled James from the sleep that had already begun to claim him in Jon's brief absence while he climbed back into his top bunk.

"What's wrong, Jon?" James managed thickly.

"Oh, not much! Your sister just has that dorfuss cat in bed with her, and they are both sound asleep!" Jon replied with grumbling irritation. "Just watch. Now that cat will use our rug for its toilet in the middle of the night or something, and then our room will stink too, just like that dorfuss!"

"Oh, quit calling that cat names. And he doesn't stink either! If Matthew makes her feel happy, then he can sleep with her all he wants. He follows her all over the farm and keeps her happy. At least she doesn't seem as upset about Pappa being gone as she used to!"

"Why are you calling that cat a human name anyway?" Jon argued back. "Matthew! What a stupid name for a cat! Animals should have animal names, and his is Dorfuss! If she thinks she can have him sleep in there with her, then I should at least be able to name the stupid thing!"

James was too tired to argue at this point, and with his simple mind, he had never been much good at it anyhow. He was already beginning to feel sleep calling him yet again and yawned and rolled over and relented, simply saying, "Fine. G'night, Jon."

A muffled grunt was the only reply.

DORFUSS BUBBLEBUTT

In the weeks that followed, summer came into its full-fledged glory. School was out, much to Jon's delight, and there was always a lot to be done on the farm. There would also be plenty of time now for relaxation and playing.

The vegetable garden Edie and Ralph had always tended was tilled and then planted by the kind and patient Harvey, who showed little Jenna what to do to take care of it. It became her proud task to tend every day, and she was thrilled when the very first seedlings sprouted.

Soon they would have fresh vegetables to grace their table! James enjoyed helping his little sister with the gardening too. Harvey also worked up a small patch right up by the front porch of the house and sprinkled some zinnia seeds throughout. Within days, they too had sprouted and were reaching for the warm sun rapidly. It wouldn't be long before butterflies would be visiting them! Jenna had come across a small statue of a cherub in one of the sheds, cleaned it up

with soap and a scrub brush, and set it amongst the zinnias. Her new flower garden looked adorable!

Much time was spent by the children down by the pond, swimming and horsing about. This new summer, Jenna watched while the boys swam around in there for the first time. They repeatedly dove in deeply, removing sticks, branches, and any other items that might create a hazard for their sister's, as well as their own safety. Sometimes the kids carried their fishing rods down there, dug up worms, and caught blue gills and the like.

Jenna completely gave up on calling her beloved cat Matthew. He didn't even answer that name, much to her resentment at her brother Jon. But call the cat Dorfuss and he came running immediately. He followed her everywhere, even to the pond.

Jenna had protested vigorously about this rude name at first, mad at Jon for insisting that this insulting name belonged to her pet. Jon had persisted, however, and somehow ultimately it stuck and seemed to suit the cat anyway.

Aunt Hilda became weirder and weirder throughout all of this, talking to the children less and less and more and more to herself. She was now spending even more time, if that was possible, holed up in her depressing room. When she wasn't at the library or preparing meals, she was in there, and sometimes odd noises could be heard coming from inside. The children didn't ask many questions, though. When they did, they were consistently rebuffed by a rude, angry woman who contemptuously informed them that her business was none of their business!

Other than that, Hilda rarely spoke to them at all. It was lonely not having Mamma or Pappa around anymore. Hilda made a very poor substitute. At least they were still able to stay in their own home, though. And they were well fed. Because of this, they were mostly appreciative and never complained to Aunt Hilda.

With June came the June bugs and the lightning bugs too. The children created their own entertainment. Evenings were spent by them running about the yard at dusk, holding glowing glass jars full of the luminescent creatures and searching evermore for additional ones to add to their already abundantly full jars. Jon poked a few holes in the lids with a hammer and nail. At bedtime, they set these jars on the nightstands next to their beds and watched the insects crawl around inside and glow for hours.

The glowing from the jars softly illuminated the photographs of Mamma and Pappa well into the night, making their parents appear as if they were somehow watching over them. The June bugs outside would see the lights through the window and buzz annoyingly against the screens in an attempt to reach the evasive glimmer. Windows were left open at almost all times in the summer. Iowa summers were hot and humid, and the upstairs of the house in particular was often sweltering.

Dorfuss the cat climbed up onto the porch every evening, squeezed though a slit in one of the screens, and slept with Jenna each and every night. Jon still did not really appreciate this and protested loudly and often about the cat sleeping in her bed. But mostly he just protested out of habit; it was the routine thing to do in order to annoy his little sister. Dorfuss was quite large by then and didn't have much growing left to do, only some filling out that would come with age.

He was different from his brothers and sisters, a little clumsier than they, and with his comical markings, catty-whampus eyes, and buck-fangs, he *was* a dorfuss, Jenna supposed after a while. The cat was no longer a runt; he had been well fed and loved. He was, by that time, the biggest of all of his siblings, maybe even scarcely overweight. He was also the most affectionate, loving cat she had ever known. She loved her big puddy-tat! When he purred, his eyes took on the most soulful, full-of-adoration look Jenna had ever witnessed in an animal's eyes. He would gaze directly into her eyes as he rumbled away. That he loved her back was patently obvious. Dorfuss followed her everywhere, much to Aunt Hilda's chagrin besides Jenna's brother Jon.

Hilda became agitated every time she discovered the cat in the house. Animals were meant to live outside. Houses were for *people.*

One hot Saturday morning, the festering woman discovered Dorfuss taking a nap on a lower shelf in the relative coolness and shade of the dark pantry. She chased him outside furiously, wielding a broom.

The children were sitting outside in the beautiful sunny day next to the well pump on the raised concrete slab encircling it. They were merrily blowing large soap bubbles from big, crudely fashioned plastic rings with wire handles that Jon had made for them. A large, old, shallow oil pan filled with dish detergent and water sat before them. A pair of brilliant tiger swallowtails drifted past on their way to visit the zinnias, unnoticed by the cheerful children.

The children were startled suddenly from their lazy reverie as the screen door abruptly flew wide open, slamming hard against the side of the house.

First, a terrified-looking Dorfuss emerged, soaring clumsily out of the opening. His feet flew askew in an attempt to gain some traction, and his crossed green eyes were dilated in fear.

Ridiculous Aunt Hilda then followed in close pursuit with an enraged, wild look in her eyes. She screamed loudly at the poor animal, with her dark skirts billowing crazily behind her, holding her broom high and flailing it insanely about. The cherub statue tipped over, harmlessly landing in the grass. At that point, the children became alarmed as not only Dorfuss but the irrational Hilda appeared to be heading straight for them. The butterflies that had been gracefully soaring over the zinnias quickly scattered for safety.

Dorfuss bounded toward the kids gawkily, panic evident in his emerald eyes. His only thought at that moment was of escaping the crazed harpy who pursued him with vengeance as she swatted at his fuzzy rump madly with the broom. It connected once finally with its target, just a bit. In fright, the poor cat leapt into the air in haste and with a loud screech. He then landed haplessly into the oil pan with a big splash. Soapy water and bubbles flew everywhere, scattering the children at the same time.

"Serves him right!" Hilda screamed at all three of them with craziness filling her eyes. Still, she held the broom aloft and waved it high into the air. "Keep that disgusting, moronic, flea-bitten animal out of this house! He needs a bath; even he knows it!" she hissed, pruning her lips into a disapproving pucker and pointing a long, skinny, twisted finger in the feline's direction. Her hand shook in her frenzy. "Look at the simpleton, just sitting there in that soapy water, looking exactly like a fool! What kind of cat does that anyway?"

Dorfuss gazed back at his nemesis with a crazed look of fear, apparent even now in his own catty-whampus eyes. His fangs protruded out of his mouth, like those of an idiot. He gazed at her in terror from his soapy-water haven. A large, glistening bubble shimmered atop his furry head, quivering, as he was, and then it burst. The cat blinked at this but otherwise never attempted to move.

"Ummm, sorry, Aunt Hilda," Jon finally managed, wiping soap bubbles off his legs and barely managing to contain a grin. "We didn't know he was inside." James and Jenna remained silent but wide-eyed, not wishing to irritate their aunt any further.

Finally, having lost her thunder and most of her rage, Hilda realized there really wasn't anything left to say. "Well, see to it that it doesn't happen again!" she finally spewed out lamely, only then comprehending just how foolish she probably appeared. She muttered and stomped her way back inside the house, the broom now only trailing limply from the anorexic-looking hand behind her. Her ridiculous and out-of-proportion posterior was the last thing the children and their cat viewed before the screen door slammed shut.

"Sheesh!" Jon muttered, being the first one to break the silence. "Crazy old Broom Hilda, wielding her broom after stupid old Dorfuss Bubblebutt here! Why, she was almost flying! A witch with her broom! That was hilarious!"

"Stop calling my sweet kitty names!" Jenna protested.

Dorfuss remained stupefied and terrorized, with his rump firmly situated in the bubble-filled oil pan. Finally, Jenna stooped to pick him up, holding the wet cat against her and wiping the bubbly, soapy mess from him with her free hand. "At least help me clean him off!" she scolded her big brother. He only surveyed her and the ridiculous cat sheepishly, still barely containing the roar of laughter struggling to break free at any moment.

James picked up a nearby bucket and ran some water into it from the well, and Jenna held her beloved cat as far away from her as she could. James carefully rinsed Dorfuss's long fur, speaking softly to him in an effort to calm the feline. Jon stood nearby, chuckling to himself, his face a rosy smirk and his entire body quivering with humor. The dumb cat protested somewhat, complaining with objections of howling meows! His body dangled limply while he kicked, swinging to and fro from underneath his front legs, by which Jenna was supporting him.

Finally, all traces of soap were rinsed off, and Jenna set the hapless cat down. The poor thing scurried off to hide underneath the front porch and lick the wounds of his injured pride.

Jenna glanced up, scarlet cheeks matching her red hair. She was enraged at her older brother, who was by then laughing loudly and with very little containment at the preposterousness of the entire event.

"Dorfuss Bubblebutt!" he proclaimed loudly and proudly at his poor little sister. "Dorfuss Bubblebutt!"

"Stop it, Jon! *You're* the dorfuss!" she yelled back at him angrily. Then, with heightened temper, she approached him, shoving him without success even though she mustered all of her tiny might. She yelled out with a loud, hurt expression, "You're just a great big jerk!" She next ran tearfully inside the house, the screen door slamming once more with a noisome whack.

James began to laugh at what had happened also. He too had a boy's sense of humor, and the more he thought about it, the more hilarious the whole event had become in *his* mind. Soon he and his brother were rolling around on the grass, smacking at each other with silliness and the camaraderie and familiarity brothers have with each other.

"Broom Hilda and Dorfuss Bubblebutt!" they repeated loudly and goofily over and over, laughing 'til their sides felt as if they were about to burst and finally wearing themselves out after much of that.

Inside the house and upstairs, Jenna held her thin curtains aside and watched angrily for a long while from the vantage point of her bedroom window, furious with both of her brothers. After time, however, she settled down and lay on her bed with Mr. Teddy. Ultimately, she too could see the humor in it all. Particularly, Aunt Hilda had acted outrageously ridiculous.

Eventually Dorfuss slid through the slash in her window screen, somehow knowing his adored mistress was up there, and joined her. All seemed to be forgotten with him. The only remnant of the ludicrous scene of earlier was his still slightly damp fur.

Hilda, however, downstairs in her morbid bedroom not long after the incident, was still fuming, her lips a pruny pucker. *Those two boys rolling around out there on the front lawn should be ashamed of themselves*! She had observed them through the screened door shortly after the incident. Having never possessed a sense of humor, she could not see anything funny in any of it at all. She had also heard the brothers call her Broom Hilda and hadn't appreciated that either. And, above all, nasty critters belonged outside!

She then lit a couple of candles and some incense and leaned over the low table, searching through the stack of books on it. She was still trying to accomplish a small spell but had not yet been successful. Perhaps if she tried a different one, she decided. Perhaps there might even be one within the heavy volumes to help her extinguish the life of that revolting, numbskull cat! She cackled to herself a bit. *Perhaps…*

THE WITCH WITHIN

That evening, Hilda retired to her quarters immediately after the supper dishes were washed and put away. The children went to play outside. The day had been an especially hot one, and the evening was sweltering still. Evening chores were performed. After a short stint down by the pond, where the kids swam to cool down and then fished for a bit without success, they became bored. With Dorfuss Bubblebutt in tow, they headed back up toward the house.

Spying their empty lightning bug jars at the corner of the front porch as they approached it, they decided to once again chase the hapless, luminous creatures around the yard and catch more that night. July was just around the corner, and there would not be much time left before the glowing insects disappeared until the next summer.

Soon dusk fell, and the lightning bugs began their ageless, nightly routine of glowing brightly while suspended in the dark air in their search for mates. Dorfuss began scurrying around the yard playfully after them too, jumping gawkily into the air and swatting

at the luminescent insects. The three children ran with glee around the yard and then into the orchard to the north of the house, giggling loudly. Periodically they pointed new ones out to each other in darker areas of the yard and then chased after them. Eventually the little group worked its way to the back of the house near Aunt Hilda's bedroom.

A strange light glowed from within her room, through a hole toward the bottom of one of her shades, quite apparent now that the darkness was full.

Curiosity soon got the better of the three of them, and they abandoned their jars and approached the window with caution, attempting to keep as silent as possible so as not to alert her to their presence. Hilda's windows were open also, even with the drawn shades, in a meager attempt to release the day's heat into the night's welcoming and relative coolness.

The odor of incense loomed heavily around the windows, and Jon peered first into the hole in the shade.

What a weird vision he was to behold!

There, stooping over the big, circular table in the center of her crypt of corruption stood Aunt Hilda dressed very darkly and strangely. She was moaning and chanting and moving, bent over a large, glowing glass ball situated in the middle of the table. It emitted a queer blue light from its depths. A large book sat open underneath her, and she was concentrating heavily on its contents.

Incense protruding from a small, strange-looking receptacle near all of this glowed dimly. Eerie blue smoke wafted slowly up and away from it. Clusters of candles burned brightly in different areas of the room, casting an odd, quivering glow of light throughout the room and onto the ceiling. Hilda repeatedly waved her hand over the radiating ball, creating surreal shadows on the ceiling above while she murmured the same, strange verse over and over.

Finally, James and Jenna grew impatient and poked their older brother, wishing to view the sight seeming to completely entrance Jon.

He relented, letting James peer through first, and then finally Jenna got her turn too.

Afterward, silently, they gaped at each other with terrified eyes, wondering what the heck their aunt was up to inside her mysterious, eerie sanctuary. Each one stared through the hole several more times.

Dorfuss, who had remained scurrying about in the orchard attempting to catch fireflies, eventually tired of this and realized that his adored Jenna had disappeared. He loped off in search of the children. Soon he discovered them around the back of the house, hovering in a cluster, and ran blissfully toward the object of his affection.

As he approached the open window, however, the cat became alarmed. With a sense that animals possess and humans do not always immediately grasp, he felt the presence of evil. He pressed his ears flat against his fuzzy head, crouching low, and then he began to growl slightly.

With wide, emerald, crossed eyes, Dorfuss continued to utter the guttural rumbling noise. Jon became afraid Hilda might discover their group, and he attempted to kick the stupid noisy cat away from underneath his feet.

Jenna then swatted at her brother, terrified of making any noise but wanting to stop him from kicking her cat. She reached for Dorfuss, who uncharacteristically backed away from her and hissed menacingly and intensely at her several times. He swatted at her with a pawful of nasty, razor-sharp claws. He backed away more from the children as quickly as he possibly could, ultimately turning and running for cover into some thick bushes up toward the front of the house.

Finally, afraid of being discovered by the old harpy, the children crept away from the window and ran to the relative safety of the opposite side of the house, far away from Hilda's room.

"What do you suppose she's up to in there?" Jon spoke first, shaking nervously. "I told you she's a witch! I just knew it! There's something *just weird* about that old bag!"

James nodded in agreement, still trying to rid himself of the creepiness pervading his core as he viewed the odd scene. "Jon is right!" he finally said, looking to his little sister for validation to see if she was also in agreement.

Jenna stared up at her brothers in wide-eyed astonishment, feel ing terribly worried and scared about the whole thing. Her stomach was in tumult, squirming with revulsion at the depravity she had just witnessed. "I wonder just what she's trying to do in there!" she finally exclaimed. "Do you think she's conjuring up evil spirits or something? I read a book at school last year about some witch, and that's what she would do! And then sometimes she would try to cast horrid spells on people!"

"I don't know," Jon said, finally speaking again after having thought the whole thing through for a few more minutes. He too was experiencing a sick, writhing sensation inside that he was having a hard time shaking. "I can't believe she could be Pappa's sister, though. How could he ever have a sister that is so creepy? What a crazy old hag! Insane Broom Hilda!"

"You don't think Aunt Hilda would try to hurt us, do you Jon-Jon?" Jenna suddenly asked her older brother in a small voice, finally raising the question no one was courageous enough to give voice to before then. They all were becoming more frightened by the minute. "What if she really *is* crazy?"

Jon, only wishing to mollify his little sister and James also, who was wide-eyed and looking very worried too, finally said, "Awww, heck no. She's just a weird old lady, that's all! She hardly even talks to us. I don't think she even knows we're here most the time! Don't you worry about her!"

But James and Jenna didn't share their brother's seeming optimism, and frankly, secretly, neither did Jon himself. He still felt uneasy about what the three of them had witnessed and planned on watching the old biddy much more closely from then on.

EVIL SPIRITS OF THE NIGHTTIME

The darkness of the approaching night seemed to hold evil spirits. The three decided to go to bed for the night, into the welcome safety of their bedrooms.

Firefly chasing had somehow lost its appeal, and they all scooped their glowing jars up and began to head inside. Even the cherub statue by the front porch seemed to observe them all in the darkness with a creepy, almost luminescent gaze.

Dorfuss followed Jenna inside and up the staircase while Jon muttered in disgust about the annoying cat still sleeping with his sister.

"Shut up!" she commanded in her tiny voice, scooping up her almost-instantly purring, furry cat into her arms. She then strutted with haughty irritation into her bedroom with the creature and slammed her door behind her.

Not much later, she was changed into her pajamas for the night, as her brothers were, and she knocked on their door and then entered their room with Dorfuss following along just behind her.

"Oh, would you get that stupid cat out of here?" Jon continued to taunt, not really minding the cat's presence all that much anymore. It was just so amusing to aggravate his little sister!

"Shut up, Jon!" Jenna retorted once again. She climbed up into the overstuffed chair, and Dorfuss jumped up onto her lap. He resumed his loud, rumbling purr and began rolling about on her lap in order that his tummy and every other feline square inch might get scratched.

The dumb cat was so huge that he barely even fit on Jenna's lap anymore, Jon observed with mild amusement. He relaxed and watched the whole absurd scene from his vantage point atop his upper bunk, chuckling a bit and lying flat on his stomach with one leg dangling over the edge.

James lay on his back in the duskiness with his hands folded underneath his head, mesmerized by the faint glow from the fireflies in the jars as they reflected dimly off the ceiling.

Dorfuss tired momentarily of his petting and purring, and he rose from the comfort of Jenna's lap to stretch and then began to groom himself. Jon swung his dangling leg lazily at the cat. Dorfuss jumped off Jenna's lap in annoyance and down onto the floor.

While the children worried and talked softly about their crazy aunt, Dorfuss sat on the floor and cleaned and groomed himself fastidiously. The cat paused now and then and looked right at them all at times, as if he were perhaps taking in and understanding their conversation.

Grooming finally completed, he again jumped back into Jenna's lap. Then curiosity got the better of the cat, and he leaped onto the night table to observe the glowing insects inside the jars for himself.

The light from within the jars reflected eerily into the cat's goofy eyes, illuminating them peculiarly. Everything about this night was taking on the weirdness of Aunt Hilda's earlier unknown-by-her performance.

James scrutinized the cat, glimpsing its glowing eyes, and shivered slightly.

The cat, finally bored with the spectacle within the jars, sat up and turned his back to the wall and gazed with shining emerald eyes back at James.

Suddenly then, James realized Dorfuss was sitting next to the photograph of Pappa on the night table. All at once, he peered more closely at first the cat and then the image of Pappa in the picture. *Why, in the darkness of the bedroom, the resemblance between the two is amazing!* James sat up jerkily, awestruck.

"Look, you guys!" he said with astonishment. "Dorfuss looks like Pappa!"

"Oh, don't be stupid, James!" Jon retorted loudly, sitting up himself. He glanced at the photo and the cat yet couldn't see any resemblance at all. *How ridiculous!* he thought.

Jenna got up from the comfort of her chair off to the side of the table to see for herself what James was talking about. *Why, James is right. Dorfuss does look like Pappa!* she thought, experiencing a surge of excitement. "He does too, Jon! James is right! Look at them!"

Jon just laughed at the both of them, refusing to look anymore. Maybe they were foolish because they were both so much younger than he and still had their childish imaginations to contend with. He didn't know or care. Besides, his younger brother wasn't very bright; he knew *that* for sure. He laughed loudly at the absurdity of it all and finally just shrugged, telling them both they were nuts and pronouncing it bedtime.

After arguing with them for several minutes more, Jon shooed his sister and her annoying cat into their room and the waiting haven of her bed.

Sleep eventually came to the three, but they were restless, uneasy slumbers, haunted by images of dark, fleeting, evil specters. Throughout the night, the children were frequented by images of what they had witnessed in Aunt Hilda's room, and they spent it tossing and turning often.

Hours later, Jenna awakened to discover Dorfuss gone from her bed. Moonlight streamed through the windows of her room, and a slight breeze ruffled her transparent curtains. The wind seemed to be picking up. She searched her room and then her brothers' quietly in the darkness while they slept but to no avail. Perhaps Dorfuss had gone back out into the night, she finally decided sadly.

With a still-lingering fright over the night's earlier events and fresh memory of her haunting dreams, she was not about to wander out into the darkness to search for her comforting kitty. She stood in front of her window and gazed longingly at the hole in the screen for several moments longer, wishing Dorfuss inside. It was not to be. She could hear coyotes howling far off in the distance and closer, the hoot of an owl. Jenna shivered; these sounds only added to the ominous feeling of this night.

Finally, she gave up, grabbed Mr. Teddy from the nearby toy box, where he spent most of his time nowadays, and crawled back into the welcome, cool softness of her bed. Cuddling the bear close to guard herself from any evil that might lurk nearby, only minutes later, she returned to sound sleep.

Dorfuss sat in the slight breeze, high up on the opposite end of the cool roof of the porch, and gazed up at the full moon beaming down upon him from above. An overall uneasiness had dwelt within the feline all night long. Sleep evaded him. It was a night for wandering and roaming, of that he was certain.

The wind whipped up without warning, and the smell of rain suddenly filled the breeze, a sure sign a storm was on its way. Crickets and other nocturnal noises filled the nighttime everywhere, adding to the suspense of the darkness and calling to him. Something wild was in the air. He too had heard the coyotes in the distance and the owl closer, somewhere within the orchard, he guessed.

Instinct kicked in, and finally he jumped down from his perch onto the ground. He began to investigate the farm's vast grounds. He headed first toward the barn and then much later moved into and sniffed around in the orchard, chasing mice. He climbed a craggy tree in the moonlight, his feline image silhouetted in the perfect, shining orb, and gazed upon their darkened farmhouse some distance off. Then the rain-filled breeze whipped up again.

The full moon disappeared suddenly, now covered by thick, dark clouds, and the rumble of thunder could be heard in the distance. Soon the thunderous rumbles increased as the wind picked up even more. Then lightning lit the grounds up as if it were daytime, resulting in a booming crash moments later. The storm was getting closer.

Inside the house, Jon, restless from his dreams, suddenly woke as a consequence of the loud clap of thunder. He rose quickly and closed all of the upstairs windows, including his little sister's. He peered through the darkness at her, wondering briefly if the noisy storm might wake her, but still she remained sleeping soundly. The wind was whipping the curtains around the windows wildly, and he was forced to push them away from his face several times in order to shut and latch all the panes.

Outside, Dorfuss chased a frightened mouse as it scurried about in panic. The thunder had terrified that tiny being as well. Suddenly, Dorfuss found himself at the back of the house for the second time this night, near Hilda's bedroom.

He was reminded yet again of the depravity he had sensed there only hours earlier. He hesitated and considered bolting. The smell of stale incense still hung heavily near her window in the air outdoors. But then curiosity got the better of him. The wind was not nearly as strong on this side of the house.

Perching on his two hind legs, he balanced the upper half of his body against the window ledge with his front paws. For the very first time, he peered with his keen nighttime cat vision through the hole in the shade and into the frightful dungeon of doom that horrid woman spent most of her time in. He could hear the old biddy snoring loudly, sawing away into the night. Thunder crashed with a roar another time, almost causing him to tear away for safety. But still he was intrigued enough in an odd, fearful way to investigate further.

He was worried for the children he watched over and had heard and understood their earlier conversation. He wished to witness for himself just what it was that had entranced and frightened the children and himself so intensely before. Once again, the sense of evil that stole over him much earlier began to pervade his senses.

The candles in Hilda's room had been extinguished. Yet the eerie blue light from the glowing glass ball the children observed earlier still radiated dimly in the dark, as if it had a life of its own. It almost seemed to gaze back at him. Dorfuss shivered involuntarily. The incense clipped into the burner had gone out on its own hours ago, but the acrid stench of it still hung in the air inside, reaching the cat's nostrils and tickling the back of Dorfuss's throat. Odd, dark forms within the room were indistinguishable in the night, yet something caused the hair on the back of Dorfuss's neck to prickle and stand straight up. His tail bushed out hugely.

The cat's ears again pressed back flat against his head, and he growled lowly. He sensed he would have to do something about this situation. He felt a pang of anxiety growing within his quickening heart. *My sweet Jenna, who loves me so dearly, and her brothers will not be safe here.* He knew that with certainty. *The woman is deranged, and I will have to protect the children from her.*

Hilda stopped snoring for a second, sputtered and coughed loudly, and then rolled over and resumed her cacophony.

The evil in the atmosphere seemed to intensify. For a split second, Dorfuss could have sworn he saw a pair of red, hideous eyes glaring back at him from the other side of the window ledge.

Suddenly, lightning flashed brilliantly and blindingly, followed by a thunderous boom. It seemed to crash from directly overhead. The cat instantly backed down to the ground, shrieking loudly and then scurrying and hissing into the night. His own utterances echoed about, frightening him even further. He bolted skittishly and ran to hide beneath the bushes at the side of the house.

Only then was Hilda disturbed within the confines of her den of depravity. She had totally disregarded the crashes of thunder up 'til then. Temporarily, she rolled over in her bed, tossing a bit and muttering about the idiocy of cats; then she resumed her snoring presently.

Evil spirits loomed within her dreams, flying corruptly about in her head and beckoning her. They invited her to summon them and let them wreak their havoc at will if only she were to release them. Shadowy and horrid images writhed about amidst glowing embers radiating from diabolical niches. Who knew what ungodly spirits resided within? Twisted hands beckoned to her, reaching out from their glowing, menacing grottos. They called to her in hideous voices. The approaching storm did nothing to alarm the old harpy; it simply enhanced the insidiousness of the torturous dreams she was already so deeply enjoying.

Hilda became restless in her distorted reverie. She smiled slightly and cackled in her sleep at the notion she was indeed getting closer to raising these demons from the captivity of their purgatory. She would have to keep practicing these spells; she knew that with certainty, for she felt she was becoming more proficient. Perhaps soon she would release these spirits, and they would then be her slaves, at her beck and call, to grant her every evil wish.

There was an eerie calm outside for a weird, hushed moment just before the storm. Dorfuss, in his sanctuary beneath the bushes, heard Hilda cackling with his keen, feline sense of sound. For the second time that night, the fur on the back of his neck prickled, standing stiffly aloft, and his tail bushed hugely with fright. He plastered his ears against his head, shrieking loudly anew. Then he hissed and scampered off, scurrying quickly with all his might up the trellis and onto the roof of the porch.

It had all been in vain, he realized. The window with the holey screen was shut, as were all of the others. He was locked outside, at least for the rest of the night! He pawed unsuccessfully for several moments, meowing loudly. Then the wind whipped up again, this time with ferocity! Lightning lit the sky, flashing almost in strobe-light effect, quickly followed by the expected deafening thunder.

Scurrying back down the trellis as quickly as he had climbed up, the terrified cat reached the ground just as the first huge plops of rain began to fall. Then the sky opened up, letting loose a torrent of rain. Lightning flashed again. Not wasting a moment, he shot like a bullet toward the welcome dryness of the waiting barn and the warm, soft comfort of his siblings and Mamma Kitty, reaching it before the resulting thunder could resound.

A New Sense of Purpose

Dorfuss slept restlessly while the storm continued to thunder and roar outside in the night. The wind howled, the rain pounded, and lightning flashed relentlessly. He cuddled with his siblings and mother in the hayloft in the barn. Throughout the night, he was consistently and inexplicably haunted in his dreams.

Time and again, he experienced the vision of a man falling from a ladder, breaking his back, and ultimately dying in the barn only a short distance away and just down the ladder from where he slept. Heights had never bothered him; he was a cat, after all. But to a man, this would surely be not only a terrifying height but experience besides, he supposed. After some time, this repetitive conception began to terrify him as well.

Later, the dreams evolved into visions of himself, it seemed, peering into this dying man's eyes. It was as if he were observing a strange light develop and shine from within them and then radiate

into his own eyes, penetrating his very being and filling his heart with an unusual sensation.

What is all of this? he wondered as he thrashed about, disturbing his siblings. He finally aggravated one of them enough to cause the other cat to hiss at him and then give him a sound swat across his nose.

Dorfuss awakened enough to move away from the pile of soft, warm, furry bodies. The night had cooled considerably. He stretched out again in the comfort of the hay and then attempted to sleep some more. It was still the dead of the night but past the time when he normally felt like roaming. And the rain still pounded outside. He knew he did not like to get wet. The constant drone eventually helped him to relax, and he drifted off to sleep again.

Next, his dreams were focused on his earlier encounters outside Hilda's windows. The children were not safe; he remembered. Wicked cackling noises and the sight of red, glowing, evil eyes were intermingled with the quaint, sweet visions of Jon, James, and Jenna, all sleeping safely in their beds. Evil spirits seemed to swarm above the children in their sleep, as if hovering and waiting for the right moment to perform their corrupt deeds. *How much longer will they be safe?* Again, he found himself restless, and his nightmares nearly woke him as he flailed about.

Nonetheless, eventually he fell into a deep sleep even again, and this time, he felt more soothed. He had finally gotten some time to absorb everything and mull it through somewhat. *I will watch over the children,* he assured himself in his dreams, *and do something about that insane old biddy while I'm at it!* He wasn't yet sure what, but just resolving to take care of the problem had a soothing effect.

Dorfuss slept better then until just before dawn. Then, in repetition, the image of the man plunging to the dirt floor of the barn began to overtake his dreams. It was more complete this time. In slow motion, he heard the man cry out and watched him hit his head. He felt the man's pain as his head connected with the solid-wood beam and then the barn floor. He experienced a terrible coldness seep throughout the man's entire body, as if it were his own, as he lay broken and twisted in the dirt.

He could interpret the man's thoughts and feelings. He knew the horrible isolation he had felt in the ensuing moments, the terror of the farmer's predicament, and his worry about the future for his three children. He could even see the man's *children's* faces.

Dorfuss again began to move wildly about in his sleep. For now he realized those faces were just slightly younger versions of the three children he had come to know and love so deeply in his short existence. The children!

Now, many of you probably have a preconceived notion about life after death. We all have heard that if we lead good, true lives, we will spend eternity in heaven. We have also heard that doing the opposite will lead to condemnation. Ralph had been a good, virtuous man, and the rewards of heaven had awaited him.

And although animals possess no souls, a miracle of sorts *had* taken place. For somehow, in the fraction of the instant that Ralph Walters's soul had shattered into a thousand points of light that fateful November morning, something had gone awry. Just before it rejoined the man's new, forever body, a tiny shard of that soul had entered Mamma Kitty as she watched on. Her heart had then been consumed by love, overflowing its boundaries. Ultimately, that love had penetrated Dorfuss's tiny, unborn kitten body that lay closest to her heart within the safety of her womb.

The angels that had carried the man off to heaven to spend eternity with his loved ones had granted their father his final pleading wish, an absolute miracle: that his children would be cared for in his absence.

And Dorfuss, willing or not, *was* that miracle. He could see it now, could feel it, and in his dreams, his heart seemed to grow within him at that very moment until it almost felt as though it would burst. No wonder he felt different, even to himself, from the other cats! He wasn't like them, not really that much at all! Oh, sure, he had a feline body and all of the agility that went along with being a cat.

However, his mind and heart knew and felt so much more than those of other cats. There were things he wanted to see and do, things ordinary cats could never conceive of! He was much more comfortable around people, especially the children.

Sweet, calming sleep enveloped him ultimately as his thoughts centered then on the children, blessing him finally with tranquil, welcome peace of mind. His dreams felt different that time: warming and soothing and reassuring. Peace had come to him at last.

Finally, the dawn of a new day began, and the roosters in the chicken shed began to crow. Dorfuss awakened, feeling well restored despite his unusually restless night and experiencing a brand new sense of purpose and being. The other cats around him stirred as he moved but remained asleep, at least for the moment. Dorfuss rose and stretched.

Quietly, he made his way over to Mamma Kitty, who was still sleeping soundly in the early morning light. He loved her so. *She has given me this wonderful miracle of my life!* He licked her affectionately on her head for several moments while she shifted and sighed and then began purring softly in her sleep.

The sun was shining brightly. It beamed through the open hayloft door, and he walked over to it, basking in its warmth. He surveyed the barnyard and farmhouse before him. The roosters crowed proudly by the chicken shed as they did every morning, strutting about with heads held high, announcing the brand new day.

Rain glistened on the leaves of the trees, on the surface of the grass, and just about everywhere else. The sunlight caught the moisture, creating a multitude of rainbow-hued prisms all about and making the landscape before him appear to be enchanted. The grass, having soaked up the abundant rain throughout the night, had lost its faded, wilted look of the day before. It looked lush and green as an emerald! Large puddles occupied low spots in the long gravel driveway, reflecting the new morning light in their still, mirrorlike depths. Magic and glory seemed to fill the air, and the dark and ominous sense of the night before seemed but a distant memory.

Absorbing the grandeur of the new morning, Dorfuss felt as if his life held new purpose and promise. Of what, he was not quite sure, but with happiness in his heart and a spring in his step, he made his way down from the hayloft and outside into the fresh air of the new, cool morning. He listened to the cheerful sound of birds chirping happily. On the long driveway, he paused to take a drink from a large, crystal-clear puddle, lapping up the fresh, new water with relish. As he finished drinking, the water stilled, reflecting his furry face from within as cleanly and sharply as a brand new mirror.

Dorfuss was taken aback. He realized, just as the children had stated the night before, that indeed he looked quite similar to the man he had dreamt nightmarishly about for most of the night. *So I do look like their pappa*! James was right! He peered once again into the still water. The resemblance was uncanny. Uncanny indeed! *Well, why not!* he decided after a few moments. He felt like Pappa and knew all of his thoughts, feelings, and desires. He might as well look like him too!

Dorfuss was instantaneously consumed with pride and held his furry head high. He strutted up to the house; then, with agility, he climbed up the morning-glory-covered trellis. It bloomed freshly and brilliantly with brand new blossoms in the welcoming light of the new morning.

Then he waited patiently on the coolness of the porch roof for Jenna to awaken and let him into her room. He loved her and her brothers. He would see to it that their pappa's wishes were fulfilled. He had been given an unusual gift—three priceless ones at that! He would not let them down!

FOURTH OF JULY FIREWORKS

The next few days on the Walters farm passed by relatively tamely. Although Aunt Hilda still spent the majority of her time at home in her room doing weird things, she avoided the children and they her.

Not much more was said amongst the children about the strange things they had witnessed Hilda doing that awful night in her room. It all still frightened them even now, but they tried to put it out of their minds.

Dorfuss shadowed them everywhere they went, even more than he had before, as if he were watching over them all somehow. Jenna and James were comforted by that. Jon, however, still found it humorous to consistently ridicule the outrageously unusual-looking feline. He stated that he wished the dumb cat would go away forever whenever he got underfoot.

On the Fourth of July, Jon dug out some old bottle rockets and ladyfingers he had been saving just for the occasion. His father had purchased them for himself and James just the summer before.

Since it was a national holiday, Hilda was not required to work, and therefore, she had grumblingly stayed home. In her consistency, she stayed hidden in her sanctuary of soullessness most of the day, poring over her spell books. She only emerged now and then to prepare a meal or take care of a little laundry or other required daily task.

The children spent the majority of the afternoon way out back behind the house, near the cornfield, lighting the little ladyfingers, much to Aunt Hilda's resentment.

In the darkness of her room, as she was putting the finishing touches on the newest spell she had been practicing, the intermittent, loud popping noises were interrupting her concentration. She felt ready to go outside and scream at the little brats. After all, they were on the side of the house where her bedroom was. There really was no special reason why they had to play with those noisy firecrackers back there, except for the relative openness of the area in comparison to the rest of the farmyard.

Not wishing to interrupt her work, however, she continued to put up with the distraction in the utmost hope that very soon the children's supply would run out. Then they would be forced to move on to some other form of entertainment. Now, vainly seeking renewed concentration on her spell, another cluster of ladyfingers popped loudly, and she allowed her mind to wander to the events of a few days earlier.

She had been replacing returned books on the large shelves at the library. Suddenly, a handsome, middle-aged salesman ventured into the building, carrying his briefcase filled with its large supply of book-order magazines.

Hilda was bewildered when he introduced himself to her. The usual, rather elderly man who had stopped by monthly for the same purpose for years was nowhere in sight, she noticed.

After introducing herself as Miss Walters to the dashing man in return, with unusual shyness, she then asked him, "Where is Mr. Rutherford?"

"I'm very sorry to have to tell you this, madam," the nice-looking man informed her piously, "but our dear Mr. Rutherford has passed away, God rest his soul! I am here in his stead. I do hope that you don't mind." He leaned against the countertop she spent most of her time behind and observed Hilda with a tinge of flirtatiousness, a twinkling sparkle in his cheerful blue eyes.

"Well, n-no sir. Of course not!" Hilda stammered, experiencing an odd thrill within her heart she had not known in years.

For approximately the next hour, they both pored over his book catalogues, enjoying cups of coffee. Activity at the library had been slow that day, and Hilda soon found herself procrastinating with the task she normally would have efficiently rushed through with old Mr. Rutherford. *This new salesman is very attractive! And he seems to be paying unusual attention to me!* Which was something she just was not used to at all. In fact, this was the kind of gentleman her sister, Ruth, would have been able to snare without any difficulty—way out of Hilda's league!

As she sat across the table from him, stealing glances at the becoming silver sideburns and speckles in his dark, full head of hair, she realized she did not remember his name! *What did he tell me? What is the matter with me?* She was having a great deal of difficulty even conversing with the man.

Too soon the task of ordering new library books for the month was over, and with regret, Hilda stood to shake the impressive gentleman's hand before he left. She was thrown off guard when an unusual current of electricity passed between them in that short instant when their hands connected. What was the matter with her? Had he noticed it? Apologizing profusely to him, she did not want to let him leave until she knew his name.

The nice gentleman chuckled slightly, offering it without hesitation to her again, "Thames Fulton at your service, madam! Well, I'll be off now and look forward to seeing you next month!" With another twinkle of his merry blue eyes, he doffed his hat at Hilda and turned and proceeded out the front glass doors.

Hilda was left bereft and standing in his wake, feeling regret immediately at his absence and all of the things she should have said to him but hadn't.

After he was gone, she ran through that short hour over and over in her mind. *Just how many books did I order from him anyway? Why, I have absolutely no idea!* With panic, she opened the drawer near the bottom of her large counter and took out the strongbox containing the funds for the library. She received monies on a quarterly basis from the town hall.

Hilda counted the money carefully, and then feeling assured there should be enough to cover whatever foolishness she had just committed, she returned the box to its place down below. Normally she was miserly with the library funds, so there was an ample amount of money within the box. Relief passed through her.

She only had to wait until next month when he showed up with her orders and a brand new supply of catalogues. *A whole month! How ever will I survive?*

She stopped off at her home in town briefly after work that day to tend to a few small things that needed attention around the place. She watered the few lonely houseplants sitting in the bay window in the lovely living room. She looked around at the attractive antiques inside her small dwelling with regret, wishing she could return to the peace and comfort and beauty that welcomed and called to her. This was her home. She missed it!

Hilda wandered momentarily into her bedroom and found herself rummaging through her closet, looking at the few clothing items still remaining, hanging forlornly from their hangers, as if abandoned. *Nothing attractive in here*, she observed absently to herself. The emptiness of her life, as well as the ugliness of her wardrobe, seemed to smack her full force in the face with its overwhelming obviousness. She was suddenly consumed by the desire to do something about her appearance, something she was not at all accustomed to! *How could I have not noticed all of this before?*

In her distraction, she made her way over to the lovely antique dresser and peered into the graceful oval mirror hovering over it. "Hummph!" she snorted in response to her reflection.

The handsome gentleman had obviously been blind, or perhaps he was just a cad. *What could he possibly have seen in me anyway? His attention to me was most likely only an evil ploy to sell me as many books as possible, and it worked! How foolish of me to have been swayed by his attentions!* she ruminated as she gazed at her wanting reflection.

Nonetheless, she lingered at the dresser longer, observing the few dainty items sitting upon it. A lovely, softly pink-tinted hurricane lamp sat at one end on an intricate doily. On a mirrored tray in the center of the dresser dwelled an antique comb, brush, and hand mirror set. Behind it, up against the mirror, a beautiful antique jewelry box was situated, containing items of jewelry her mother had left behind. Hilda never wore any of the beautiful pieces. They always appeared garish in contrast to her somber clothing. At the other end, there was a matching doily graced with several bottles of perfume she had not used in years. They resided underneath a tall, ornate hatpin holder containing many ornate pins, again left behind by her mother and far too fancy for her. She enjoyed their intricate beauty but never wore them. Hilda fingered the prettiest perfume bottle absently. Surprising even herself, on impulse, she hurriedly picked it up and sprayed some of the delicate fragrance on her wrinkly neck and bony wrists.

Then, feeling extremely foolish at her vain attempts to feel even remotely feminine, she snorted again and blushed brilliantly. Quickly, she made her way out of the bedroom and house with her face attractively rosy in its unaccustomed hue. *I am just a foolish old biddy!* she told herself.

Back at the farm, she was again startled out of her daydreams by the sound of more firecrackers. *Confound it all anyway!* she thought with irritation. *Why were children even invented? They are only a nuisance!*

Leaning back over her book of spells, she again attempted to push her daydreams out of her mind and resume concentration on her current spell. At the top of the page staring back at her, the chapter name called out to her in large letters: *Poise, Beauty, Intelligence, and Articulating with Eloquence. Well, I could certainly use all of those characteristics*, she ruminated.

Even though she was extremely intelligent, she felt lacking in the skill of portraying it with poise and confidence. Perhaps this spell would help her attain what, at this moment, seemed like the impossible. Just maybe she would then be confident enough to portray herself well when Mr. Fulton returned next month. *Thames! What an attractive name!* Hilda found herself beginning an involuntary blush. She fought it back. Then, coming to her senses as more firecrackers popped in the distance, she blushed uncharacteristically and fully.

Shaking her head to regain her judgment, she resumed her careful study of the spell. Soon, however, she became distracted again with the memory of that short, sweet hour. Hilda leaned forward and reached for the stack of her other spell books. Riffling through them, she finally found the one she suddenly felt herself drawn to.

Quickly, she paged through it, her breathing at a newly quickened pace. She stopped when she came to the chapter she sought. *Attaining Heretofore Unrequited Love*, it was titled. Setting it aside, she placed a paperweight upon it to keep it open. When she was through with her current spell, she would begin to work on that one.

Out back, near the cornfield, Jon, James, and Jenna realized with great disappointment that all of the ladyfingers had been used up. Jon had kept the bottle rockets hidden upstairs in the bedroom as a surprise for later in the day. He gleefully headed toward the house to search for an empty glass pop bottle and then get the rockets and bring them outside.

After clattering about in the pantry for several moments, he rejoined his brother and sister, who were sitting and sunning on a couple of large boulders that had been pushed out of the field ages ago during cultivation.

James and Jenna squealed with delight when they discovered Jon's armload of bottle rockets. They had not realized any had been left over from last Fourth of July. Their attention centered on those then. They resumed their celebrations, placing their sticks into the bottle, lighting the ends of the rockets, and watching them soar skyward over the cornfield.

Even Dorfuss seemed uncharacteristically interested in the strange objects. Though he kept his distance, he sat nearby and watched the children play joyfully, content just to remain near them. The rockets were not nearly as noisy as the ladyfingers had been.

The bottle rockets were nearly finished up, and Jon lit one more. For some reason, it sputtered as if to fizzle out. Then suddenly it popped loudly, and with a brilliant flashing light, it knocked the bottle sideways before it blasted off.

Straight through the window screen and into Hilda's bedroom it shot, propelled by an unusual force. The three children watched, first in horror and next apprehension at what Aunt Hilda's reaction would be if she discovered the rocket in her room!

Sure enough, the sparkling, disappearing end of the bottle rocket was closely followed by a loud, terrified scream from the old hag. Then much banging and clattering about could be heard as she attempted to escape the awry, sputtering, and sparkling object while it ricocheted in abandon around her room, knocking various items over.

All of the noise was quickly followed by a short period of stunned silence while their aunt presumably came out of whatever cover she had dived for. The three children gazed at each other with worry. As expected, Hilda began to scream loudly and throw out curse words between each bellow.

Suddenly, the window shade was torn aside, and Hilda's angry, red, and contorted face shrieked at them from her place on the other side of the ripped window screen. "What's the matter with you stupid little brats? Take those disgusting noisemakers somewhere else! In fact," she hissed at them upon reconsidering for just a moment, "get up to your rooms for the rest of the day! You are all grounded!"

Hilda placed her hands on her rotund hips, her mouth puckered disagreeably into a prune. She observed these objects of her displeasure for just a few moments longer with a wild look of fury in her eyes, her wrathful countenance surrounded by her gray and dark brown disarrayed hair. Then she let go of the ruined window shade and disappeared. Soon she resumed banging about and cursing in the confines of her room in an attempt to restore it to some semblance of order.

The three children wasted no time obeying the crazy woman, fearful of what she might do if they failed to listen. They quickly ran upstairs and into their bedrooms, slamming their doors shut for safety.

Dorfuss remained outside. He had been terribly startled when the rocket burst from the bottle only a very short distance past his face and toward the house. He immediately shot into the cornfield in order to escape the wrath of the sparkling, hissing object. He huddled in the safety and relative silence of the shady corn even now, waiting for his tiny heart to resume a more normal pattern of beating. His eyes remained large and round as saucers for a long while in the sanctuary of the field.

Evening approached, and a disgusted and raging Aunt Hilda began dinner preparations. As she clattered and banged about in the kitchen, attempting to whip up something edible for their meal, everything kept going wrong. She was still very angry at the thought of the mess in her bedroom and her ruined spell. *Will I ever be successful?* She was beginning to doubt it, and her fury increased. If steam could have billowed from her ears, it would have. Soon the beef stew she had been warming over the stove began to smoke and stink in the telltale sign it was ruined.

Angrily, she reached for the pot without thinking, picking it up without a potholder and burning her hand quite soundly in the process. Clumsily and in pain, she immediately tossed it into the sinkful of soapy dishwater other dishes had been soaking in, causing the water to hiss and spew everywhere, including onto Hilda.

While she cussed and caterwauled down below and ultimately ran cold water over her throbbing, burned hand, the three children huddled upstairs in Jon and James's bedroom, worried about their fate. They could hear their crazy aunt down below. *What will she do to us now?* they all wondered.

Dorfuss, hearing all the noise and cursing emanating from somewhere inside the house, decided to investigate to make sure the children were okay. Stealthily, he crept from the cover of the cornfield toward Hilda's window to peer inside. *Well, no doubt about it; the noise is not coming from there.* The door leading out into the hallway appeared to be soundly shut. With the curiosity of any normal cat, he stood on his two hind legs and gazed through the torn screen at the disarrayed scene inside.

Candlesticks and books and other odd-looking items were strewn about in the dimly lit room. It appeared from Dorfuss's vantage point as if there had been a couple of small fires from tipped over candles the old hag had been forced to extinguish. *Good thing the house didn't burn down,* he mused absently.

As he observed the biddy's crypt of corruption through the still brightly shining light of evening and the torn window shade, he noted with relief the sense of evil pervading the room the last time he had peered in did not seem quite so heavy.

Curiosity then got the better of him, and he hopped up onto the windowsill and slid through the large gash in the screen. He told himself it would be wise to investigate and make sure there was nothing that could possibly pose a danger to the children lurking about.

Dorfuss wandered about the shadowy room for a bit, sniffing cautiously first one item and then moving on to the next. In time, he jumped up onto the large, low, round table. In the center of the table, the big magical ball suddenly began to glow brightly blue, as if somehow sensing a presence. This unexpected occurrence startled the large cat into backing up slightly. And that's when three tiny white mice observed him and began scurrying around frantically in a large, covered pickle jar! Being a cat, he began batting ineffectively at the glass in a vain attempt to reach the wildly moving mice whilst they ran round and round, counterclockwise, on the inside. Fear was apparent in their tiny pink eyes while they attempted vainly within the circular vessel to escape their natural enemy.

And round and round outside the large jar Dorfuss moved, still unsuccessfully attempting to break through while he jumped and pounced and batted his paws against it.

Finally, in one huge attempt of force on the part of the large cat, the heavy bottle tipped, teetered, and fell over, bashing into the magical glass ball and shattering it in a glittering explosion. The lid popped off the jar, scattering the mice in their frenzied attempt to escape their nemesis.

Dorfuss followed one of them across the tabletop in full, instinctive feline pursuit. As he pumped his rear legs wildly, he knocked over vials and test tubes full of odd liquids, jars containing frogs, and all sorts of weird, unknown objects and powders in a loud clatter. In his frenzy, they all became mixed haphazardly together as he homed in on his prey. When finally he had nearly grasped the mouse, he accidentally dragged his tail and paws through the disarrayed mess of spilled items.

A lit candle, its flame burning brightly atop an ornate brass holder, tipped over, holder and all, landing near the open book. It caused the edge of a page to suddenly begin to glow and smolder. Almost instantly, the aged and yellowed page burst into fire near the cat's tail, prompting Dorfuss to let out a loud screech as he jumped in bewilderment just when his paws were closing in on the mouse.

Without warning, thousands of bright lights suddenly surrounded the cat as he eagerly grasped at his prey, filling the entire room in a wondrous splendor. At the same time, hundreds of Dorfuss's cat hairs were released and rose from his body, filling the miraculous light and also glistening in the magical aura that surrounded him. That startled Dorfuss even further, causing him to lose his grip. *What's happening?* he found himself wondering with fear. His grip loosened, and the terrified mouse escaped in the cat's momentary confusion, running off to hide someplace safe from his natural predator.

Dorfuss, finally coming to his senses, realized the fire would need to be put out and quickly if he was to prevent it from causing the house to burn down.

Strange apparitions floated and dipped around him mystically in the sparkling lights, having been released from their torturous prison of the magical glass ball. Entities shadowed even his mind whilst whispering odd, murmuring aphorisms. Dorfuss became momentarily wide-eyed with fright. He gazed at the enormity of the Pandora's boxlike scene playing out before him. But he soon collected his wits. He knew what he needed to do.

He screeched and meowed loudly and banged about as he swatted at the nearly flame-consumed page. The ruckus was loud enough for the festering Hilda to hear it from the nearby kitchen.

As he batted with all his might at the small fire, he read the title just as it began to disappear forever from view. *Poise, Beauty, Intelligence, and Articulating with Eloquence*, it proclaimed in large print just before being devoured by the combustion. It occurred to him suddenly that he could read! That was a first!

Furiously, Hilda swiftly stormed back into her room, forgetting for once to shut the door behind her as she took in the ridiculous scene. There was that imbecile cat of the children's in her room! Hers! *What the heck is he doing in here, and why, oh why, with everything else that has gone awry on this horrible day, is he in here now?*

He had messed up everything she had so carefully restored to the tabletop after the children's bottle rocket had gone askew! Her beloved magical ball had tipped over, and the glass was shattered and destroyed. Her white mice were nowhere in sight. All of her vials containing secret potions and powders had been spilled and scattered. Some of the liquids had splashed onto her precious spell books, and one of them was on *fire*!

Flying into another rage at the awful injustice of it all, Hilda became insane with anger. She began picking up and throwing anything and everything she could get hold of at the terrified cat without any regard for its worth.

Dorfuss, fully aware that the crazed harpy was near and in hot pursuit of him, forgot completely about the burning book. He dodged a large, hurled brass candlestick and ran between the legs of the crazed Hilda in an attempt to escape, tripping her and knocking her off balance as she heaved another heavy object. The first of his nine lives ended in that moment as the brass candlestick narrowly missed his poor, patchwork-designed furry head.

The crone hit her head on the edge of the table as she fell. She lay dazed on the floor for several moments afterward as the cat ricocheted his way out of the room. He ran straight away up the stairs and began clawing frantically on Jenna's door. In no time, his precious girl opened it and let him into the waiting haven.

Down below, Hilda recovered after a couple of minutes, holding the side of her head that had connected with the tabletop as she struggled to her feet. A sharp pain stabbed inside her brain, throbbing and sending a blinding light flashing into her eye. "Confounded, moronic cat!" she muttered angrily to herself, swearing that never again would that stupid animal be allowed inside the house.

The flame-consumed book was still cheerfully burning. The flames were spreading, complete with merry popping sounds, as if to mock her. Suddenly, she was aware of the urgency of the situation. She grabbed her pillow from the nearby bed and pummeled the fire repeatedly until it lived no more.

Of course, after that, her pillow was ruined too, and finally she gave in to the tears that had threatened for several minutes already. She threw it to the floor. The force of it smacking against the floor propelled its fluffy down feathers into the air, scattering them everywhere. Gracefully, they floated aloft throughout the room. Plopping her middle-aged body onto the bed in utter defeat, she sobbed and caterwauled and beat her fists repeatedly onto the mattress at the injustice of it all. All of her several months' worth of work, ruined in only a few short hours. It was not fair! She hadn't even been successful with a single spell to this day!

Actually, however, she had achieved an indirect sort of success; she just didn't know it yet. And the results of it had not benefitted her in the least. For when Dorfuss had pounced on the mouse, all of the potions had mixed together, culminating in a successful but unknown mixture of never-to-be-discovered-again proportions. The resulting magic had surrounded and permeated the cat, and various unleashed spirits had been set free within the room, unbeknownst at that particular moment to either of them.

Hilda continued to wail noisily for hours on end. Poise, beauty, intelligence, and speaking with eloquence would most likely never be hers! Or love! Oh, how would she ever be able to lure the unsuspecting, handsome Thames into perhaps actually becoming interested in her? And it had all been just within a hair's breadth of her grasp. *Oh, Thames! This just is not fair!*

Plan of Action

No one got dinner that night. The children heard all of the commotion down beneath them from the vantage point of their rooms. They knew it would not be prudent to disturb their aunt, who had obviously gone out of her mind.

Unknowing of what Dorfuss had done to further compound their problems, they resignedly talked quietly and worried for hours before going to bed with their stomachs all growling away. Dorfuss slept, cuddling with Jenna very closely all night long.

The next morning, unable to stand their hunger any longer, the children tiptoed downstairs in the early morning hours. Quietly, they poured themselves repeated bowls of boxed cereal from the pantry until their hungers felt satisfied, eating them in careful silence.

Jon and James ventured outdoors to take care of the daily morning chores. Jenna went back up to the safety of her bedroom until Aunt Hilda left, working on a coloring book on the floor. Dorfuss watched over her protectively from his comfortable perch on her bed. Soon Aunt Hilda was up and off to work in an irritated huff without preparing any food or saying a word to any of them.

Later in the day, Jon attempted to go into Hilda's room in order to observe for himself the wackiness inside. The door was locked obstinately. He went around to the back of the house, hoping his aunt had been foolish enough to leave the back window open in the heat, but it too was latched solidly shut.

With resignation, he informed Jenna and James that the three of them should hold a meeting at the pond in the afternoon after their daily swim and decide what to do. Jon, in particular, did not feel safe at the farm with Hilda around any longer. A heavy, odd sense seemed to saturate the house and outbuildings as if something evil lurked about. Dark corners now seemed creepy instead of ordinary, and he did not know why.

After lunch, the children cleaned up the breakfast and lunch dishes themselves. They then headed down toward the pond wearing their swimsuits and carrying their towels, a jug of water, and a box of homemade cookies. It was a very hot July afternoon. The sun was sweltering in the humidity, and locusts busily sang their characteristic, buzzing cacophony from the shelter of the large trees.

In the shade of the crooked willows down at the pond, things were slightly cooler, and the water looked refreshing. Things seemed light and peaceful out there. Dragonflies soared about above the surface of the water and sunned on cattails toward the marshy end of the pond. Water skaters skittered across the glassy surface, causing rippling designs to spread out in tiny, repetitive waves. Despite the depressing mood filling the atmosphere at the house, the children soon began to cheer up in the outdoors and enjoy the otherwise perfect midsummer day.

Dorfuss, of course, true to form, followed them down there. He stretched lazily under the coolness of the largest willow on the soft green grass beneath. First, he groomed his patchwork-design fur, and when that was complete, he lay down and relaxed, easily enjoying the glory of the afternoon. Jon ignored his presence while James and Jenna petted the loudly purring thing for several minutes before surrendering to the cool promise of the waiting water. As the ridiculous creature purred, he gazed at his mistress with large, soulful eyes that appeared to be brimming over with love. A look of unadulterated content was on his furry face.

Finally, Dorfuss began to snooze, and the children headed for the refreshment of the sparkling water. In no time, the three were laughing and splashing about, and the horrors of Hilda were temporarily forgotten. Eventually, however, they became tired and dragged themselves out of the water to enjoy their cookies and cool water in the shade near Dorfuss.

Dorfuss still lay in the shade of the willow, snoring away soundly. Jon shook his head at the pathetic creature. Then, after glancing at his brother and sister, he announced that it was time for them to devise a plan of action.

"What do you mean, Jon?" little Jenna implored.

"I mean, we need to figure out what to do to get away from Broom Hilda! She is evil; that is obvious, and I'm afraid she may try to hurt us if we stick around much longer!"

"So," James stated bluntly, "you think we should run away?"

"Well, yes, if that's what it takes for us to be safe. Yes, I think we should!" asserted Jon.

Jenna's shocked, green eyes opened wide, and she immediately began to bawl loudly at the prospect of this awful suggestion. She was afraid in her tiny heart of what might become of all of them if they ran away. "No, please, Jon. We just can't leave! I can't leave Dorfuss behind and Mr. Teddy and my soft bed! I like our house! Please don't make us leave!"

Jon's heart softened somewhat at his sister's obvious turmoil. He considered things for a few moments and then said, "You could take your stupid cat if he's that important! He follows us everywhere anyway! And Mr. Teddy too!"

Jenna continued to howl.

The loud wailing of his adored Jenna awakened Dorfuss from his nap. He stood and stretched unceremoniously and then walked over to his girl and rubbed against her in an unembarrassed display of feline affection. The girl's crying began to diminish. She reached out to hug Dorfuss to her while he surrendered to her for her comfort. Purring loudly again, he observed with an odd, almost intelligent and interested look in his eyes, as the conversation taking place before him continued. His fangs protruded stupidly.

James piped up again, irritated with his brother for even suggesting such a crazy thing. Even with his simple mind, he knew running away could pose many more dangers than staying put in a situation they already knew. "Jon, you're stupid! What are we supposed to do about food, where are we going to sleep at night, and where are we going to run away to? Huh?"

"Well, I haven't quite figured all of the details out yet," Jon confessed sheepishly. He was surprised at James's sudden display of unaccustomed wisdom. "But I think we should try to find our aunt Ruth in Davenport. Pappa talked about her once in a while, and he always smiled when he did. I think Broom Hilda never even told her about Pappa's death and that's why she didn't show up at his funeral! She's got to be better than crazy old Broom Hilda; she's just got to be!"

"But how will we find her house? She's got to live at least a hundred miles away from here!" Jenna pointed out. Then she began to wail loudly again.

"It's quite simple, actually! I will show you! I know where she lives!" said a new and unknown voice with an oddly eloquent English accent.

Astonished mouths abruptly dropped open as all three children realized the voice belonged to Dorfuss!

"Well, what do you say then? Should we give it a go?" Dorfuss asked as he proceeded to continue rubbing against the stunned Jenna. Suddenly, hundreds of cat hairs began floating aloft around the furry cat, creating an aura around the feline and glistening as they drifted lazily in the light breeze of the sunlit day.

"Dorfuss can talk!" Jenna proclaimed with loud abandon. Jon remained stupefied, unbelieving even then, while James stood suddenly and began jumping about happily. Soon Jenna joined him, and the two of them began whooping it up.

Finally, Jon had seen enough of this nonsense. Looking directly at the ridiculous cat, he said, "Okay, Dorfuss, tell me. How is it that you are able to talk? You are a stupid cat, nothing more! Stupid dorfuss bubblebutts *don't talk*!"

"That's *Sir* Dorfuss, if you don't mind! You *must* be respectful!" the cat reprimanded and then continued. "Well, actually, you see, it was *all* rather accidental, as I happened upon your Aunt Hilda's witchcraft in progress last evening. In the confusion, I spilled and knocked over a few items, and somehow, I believe, a few of her spells managed to rub off onto me!" The cat held his head high and cocked it sideways in a mocking manner.

"Incidentally," the tortie continued, "you would be wise not to presume that *you* know everything or that *I* am simply an ignorant specimen of the feline persuasion! Looks can be quite deceiving, you know!"

Jon continued to sit dumbfounded as the cat went on. "I do believe, that just as your aunt Hilda's magic spell book was being consumed by fire, which by the way, *I* was brave enough to attempt to extinguish, I did read on the open page of the spell she appeared to be working on: *Poise, Beauty, Intelligence, and Articulating with Eloquence!* Apparently, not only am I newly gifted with the ability to read, I can also now speak with elegant intelligence! All due, I'm sure, to that horrible harpy you so fondly refer to quite often as Broom Hilda! Furthermore, as for the poise and beauty part of all of it, well, was there ever any question about that?" In emphasis, Dorfuss posed his fuzzy body proudly, as if to prove beyond a shadow of a doubt that his magnificent, absurd feline silhouette a la buck fangs were beautiful and that he held it with poise.

Finally coming to his senses, Jon stood and began muttering to himself while he absently brushed off the legs of his cut-off jeans. "Well, if this isn't the most ridiculous thing I've ever seen or heard! I'm surrounded by idiots! First we have crazy Broom Hilda back at the farm, chanting and moaning in her locked bedroom all hours of the day and night and attempting to unleash evil spirits! And now we have a stupid talking cat, the evil spirit she managed to unleash!"

"Um, excuse me, Jon," Dorfuss ultimately cut in. "But I do believe the simple act of a cat having the gift of speech would rule out your claim that I am stupid! Moreover, I am most certainly not evil! I was sent to watch over all three of you, and that deserves appreciation! Please do not refer to me in such a disrespectful manner any further!"

With that, the cat finally strutted off into the underbrush, head held high, his absurd feline body moving in an arrogant, offended stride at his wounded pride. The last thing the three astonished children observed before he disappeared was his ample, patchwork posterior and matching goofy tail, also held high.

"This is all your fault!" Jon finally proclaimed, yelling at Jenna loudly and staring at her with accusation. "If you hadn't insisted on bringing that stupid dorfuss of a cat into our house, none of this would have happened at all! Now, we have a cat that thinks he can boss us around!"

"Oh, shut up, Jon! Dorfuss is right! He's not stupid! Besides, if he knows where Aunty Ruth lives, then maybe he can help us get there. He would keep us safe. I just know it! He has always watched over *me*!"

James finally cut in, saying, "Would the two of you please stop arguing? There's nothing wrong with Dorfuss being able to talk. I talk to him and the other animals around here all the time! Besides, Dorfuss looks like Pappa, and he said he would watch over us all! That's all I need to know!"

"Oh, Dorfuss does *not* look like Pappa, and he is a cat! He is not capable of watching over us, protecting us, or anything like that! The only thing cats are capable of is chasin' varmints! Both of you are as stupid as he is!" With that, Jon angrily stomped off toward home without his sister and brother.

When he reached the house, the screen door was hanging slightly open, swinging and creaking about in the barely discernible breeze, as if it had not latched properly when they left earlier. The cherub statue stood sentry nearby, seeming to glare at Jon with seething hatred as he reached for the door handle. He shivered involuntarily. He was going to dump that thing out in the back forty in the pile of all their other useless junk one of these days, he vowed. *Lately it seems as weird as Aunt Hilda!*

Jon strode inside, letting the lightweight door slam shut with a smack behind him as the old spring on it protested with a loud groan. He was still more than a little irritated by all of the happenings of the last twenty-four hours. Then there had been this new revelation involving an imbecile cat!

With a storm brewing in his eyes, he took a clean glass out of the cupboard next to the sink and turned on the tap and filled his glass with water. Once it was full, he turned around and leaned against the counter, still trying to collect his thoughts.

Something moved in the parlor on the other side of the doorway, catching his attention and startling him a bit, and he looked closer. There was Dorfuss, sitting on top of the desk. He gazed at Jon with glowing green eyes, sitting next to the telephone with the address book spread wide open next to him on the glass top.

Having calmed down somewhat, Jon finally became curious as to just what the cat was up to now. He approached Dorfuss, who jumped down onto the floor and moved to the corner of the room, fearful that Jon was still angry with him.

Jon momentarily forgot all about the cat as he peered closer at the open address book. There, open to the proper page, was his aunt Ruth's address and telephone number, plain as day.

Astonished, he gazed momentarily at Dorfuss, who stood observing him right back, fuzzy head slightly cocked and goofy fangs glistening. "Well, what do you say, Wrench? Do you believe me now?" the cat calmly inquired.

Runaways

After Jon's encounter with Dorfuss in the parlor, his attitude was more subdued. He tended to be less critical when it came to the cat. He had gained a new, although skeptical, respect for the silly animal. When Dorfuss spoke, it was only in the children's presence and only when he deemed it absolutely necessary. Most of the time, he appeared to be simply a stupid cat. That made the minor miracle of his intelligent speech seem impossible and ridiculous most of the time, especially to Jon.

Several days passed quietly on the farm, with Aunt Hilda barely acknowledging any of the children. When they did manage to catch her glance, it was filled with a glaring, insidious hatred. Hilda would come home from work, go into her den of iniquity, and slam and lock the door. Low, odd, chanting noises and incense odors would then soon follow. Meals were now totally ignored by her, and the children had to fend for themselves.

Jenna took daily care of her gardens, keeping them weeded, sometimes with James's help also. She already had some green beans, and her tomatoes were looking ready to ripen soon.

However, when she weeded her zinnias in the tiny flower garden next to the front porch later that week, an uneasy feeling crept over her. She hadn't realized it at first, but without thinking, she glanced up at the cherub statue. For a split second, she could have sworn that it was staring right back at her with a menacing look in its concrete eyes. Then, as quickly as she thought she had seen it, the evil countenance disappeared, and she wondered if she had only been imagining things. She was left with a brief chill and shivered for an instant before trying to shake it off.

Dorfuss was sitting nearby in the shade of a large oak tree, sleeping. Jenna quickly finished her work in that small garden, yet the uneasiness remained with her. She was glad her beloved cat lay nearby. She hadn't noticed many cheerful butterflies around the flowers lately. Perhaps the statue had been scaring them off as well.

The children whispered quietly in the boys' bedroom until very late almost every night, making plans for their escape if it were deemed necessary. All three of them were apprehensive over the prospect of being on their own for approximately one hundred miles with no adult present to look after or care for them and keep them safe.

In addition, in the daytime, they were no longer spending as much carefree time outside. Something seemed to be lurking just about everywhere they went, making them feel uneasy, but they couldn't quite put a finger on what it was. It was similar to the uneasy sensation of being watched by something that one can't see. Perhaps they *were* being watched!

Dorfuss spent all of his time with the children of late, not speaking often, but instead serving as their much appreciated but silent sentry. He too sensed the odd depravity that seemed to hang in the very air.

Then, a few evenings later, while the children were preparing soup and sandwiches for their dinner, Hilda began ranting and raving within the confines of her anteroom of animosity again. The children grew wide-eyed in fear as noises of items on the other side of the wall breaking and crashing ensued, as if she were throwing things around in there. Suddenly, in red-faced rage, she emerged from her bedroom, slamming the door hard against the wall. Hilda burst into the kitchen with a scream and hurled a large brass candlestick in the general direction of the children.

Instead of striking the children, who scattered, it knocked the hot pan of soup off the top of the stove. The liquid inside had nearly reached boiling point. The force splattered the juice, meat, noodles, and carrots everywhere. Jenna barely managed to get out of the way of the scalding liquid in time.

Before the crazed Hilda emerged from her room, Dorfuss had been sleeping close by in the pantry again. Lately he felt it pertinent to remain near enough to protect the children but out of the demented Hilda's sight. He was aware of her dislike of animals in the house, that particularly being him. He awakened immediately when the maniacal ranting began.

Peeking cautiously around the corner of the doorframe, he observed the mentally unbalanced harpy emerge from her funereal fortress, screaming a bunch of unintelligible nonsense and grasping the large, heavy candlestick holder in her gnarly fingers.

As she hurled it in the direction of the children, Dorfuss flew up into the air at the crazed woman, claws bared. For a split instant, within her eyes, as he hovered over her just before making contact, he observed the red, evil glow of a demon.

Hissing, baring his teeth, and growling, he no longer cared about his own safety. The children were at the forefront of his mind. With a vengeance, he attached himself to her face, hair, and clothing like Velcro.

Enraged, Hilda swatted and pounded on the courageous beast in an effort to remove it and its painfully sharp claws from her body. She screeched in pain. Finally, she grabbed hold of the cat and began pulling at him.

Ripping fabric sounds could be heard, along with Hilda's wild bellering. The children cowered all together in the corner of the kitchen, crying and pleading with their aunt to calm down.

Suddenly, in a horrific burst of energy and rage, Hilda pulled Dorfuss free, and with her surging adrenaline, she threw the poor cat directly onto the still-burning flames on the stove.

The second of his nine lives escaped him then. Dorfuss hissed and flailed and clawed in fright and pain as the fur on his backside began to catch fire.

"Meeeoooowwww!" he screeched in distressed terror. Awkwardly and speedily, he gained his footing on the burner grates and was off the stove and out of the room in an instant, leaving behind the odor of burnt cat hair.

The three cowering children were again the focus of the lunatic woman. With still glowing red eyes, she glowered at them, breathing heavily. Her hands were balled into tight, angry, bony fists.

"Who was in my room, getting into my possessions?" she shrieked maniacally.

None of the children had been in there, of course, since Hilda always kept it firmly locked at all times. Perhaps the woman really was losing it.

"Well, answer me!" she raged.

Finally, Jon spoke up. He was not only frightened but also angry. "None of us have been in your room, Aunt Hilda! How could we have been? It's always locked up! Even the outside window is locked!"

"How dare you! So you *have* been trying to break into my room then, haven't you, you incorrigible brat!" she accused, pointing a menacing, spindly finger his way.

There was no way for the children to win this type of argument. Their accuser was behaving in such a deranged manner that they would never be able to talk sense with her.

And so, up to the safety of their bedrooms they fled, in the same direction Dorfuss had previously taken cover.

Fortunately for Dorfuss, the injury he sustained from the flames on the stove burner was very slight, consisting mainly of burnt fur. He and Jenna both comforted each other to sleep that night.

Bright and early the very next morning, as soon as Hilda left for the day, Jon took it upon himself to attempt to repair the old car down in the dark, musty garage. Pappa had used the car only for emergencies. It occurred to Jon that he was probably capable of driving it if only he could get the old jalopy running and keep it that way.

During the days while Hilda was busy returning books to shelves and checking new ones out, Jon tinkered around with the antiquated motor, being careful not to take too much of it apart. He did not want it to be obvious to Hilda that he had even been in there working on it. After all, she always parked her car just outside the door.

Once or twice, while adjusting various things inside the engine compartment, he became uneasy, feeling chilled. The hair rose on the back of his neck, as if evil lurked somewhere nearby. Then, as quickly as the sense overtook him it disappeared, and he shrugged it off. *Probably just my apprehension about the journey ahead*, he reasoned.

In the days following Hilda's demented rage, Jon also tried several times to telephone their aunt Ruth but with no success. He was distressed because he did not know for sure if the information was even correct anymore.

It had been written in the old address book for years and had faded with age. Maybe he was even deciphering the number incorrectly. Perhaps the phone number had changed. Possibly, his aunt and uncle were working, and their children were at school, and there was no one home during the day. So many unknowns and uncertainties!

In the evenings, it was impossible to attempt to use the telephone with crazy Broom Hilda lurking about. She would probably take a belt to all three of them if she knew what they were planning.

He fiddled with some hoses connecting to the engine; the clamp on one seemed a little loose, and he tightened it.

Over and over, Jon attempted to start the old car after adjusting this and turning that but to no avail.

After several days of his vain attempts, one afternoon, Dorfuss jumped up onto the roof of the car and just sat, merely watching Jon's movements for the longest time. Jon was in a dour mood and ignored him.

Again, Jon attempted to start the engine but was not successful. He went back to making adjustments. While doing so, he made a mental list of all that still needed to be done before he and his brother and sister could be on their way. *If only I could get this aggravating old heap up and running!*

Most of their preparations had by then been completed. Jon had rummaged through the attic just a couple days before and produced several old and rather musty but serviceable sleeping bags and two large duffel bags. While he was up there in the darkness moving things around, he could have sworn that just for an instant he had seen glowing red eyes observing him. He felt the presence of evil, just as he had observed in Broom Hilda's eyes a few days before when she appeared to have gone nuts. But then the vermilion apparition vanished as quickly as it had appeared. With his heart beating at a quickened pace, Jon finished his search successfully and got out of the dim attic. He tried to put the incident at the back of his mind and concentrate on his present task. Yet the foreboding sense did not want to leave him. And he wished the stupid cat sitting on the top of the car would disappear as well.

Quite some time later, Dorfuss yawned, stood, and stretched on his lofty perch then inched his way over to the front end and jumped down onto the edge of the hood with a plunk. He peered into the cavernous opening next to Jon, startling the concentrating boy. "Is there gasoline in the tank, Wrench?" Dorfuss finally asked politely.

"Well, of course there is. That was the first thing I checked!" Jon retorted indignantly.

"Yes, I'm sure you did, but you've been trying to start this car over and over for several days now," the cat offered, "and I'm sure that has used some gas up! You've made quite a few necessary adjustments without success. Maybe you should check the gas level again or simply try adding some more!"

Jon snorted at the cat with contempt. "If you know so much about all of this, then why don't you fix this stupid car yourself! You think you're so smart. Prove it!"

Dorfuss refused to be goaded and stood his ground. "Check the gas tank, Wrench," he commanded quietly. "Perhaps the gauge showing you the level is incorrect. After all, many other things were out of proper adjustment."

Irritated fully, Jon felt like smacking the annoying cat, but instead he managed to contain his temper. He compressed his mouth into a thin line. "Fine, if you promise that after I do it and try to start this thing again, you will leave me alone in here! You are messing up my concentration!"

"No problem, Wrench. If I am wrong, I will do as you wish and leave you to your unending chore in peace!"

Exasperated, Jon searched around the garage for the gas can, but he could not find it. While Dorfuss waited patiently, he dug and banged around in the large pile of junky tires and other unidentifiable objects of all sorts and found nothing. Then, frustrated, he swung open the door to the small, dark storeroom in back. He reached for the chain pull to turn on the overhead bulb but could not find it either.

Jon was about to yell at Dorfuss in fury when his frustration suddenly turned to fright. Just as his eyes began to adjust to the darkness of the old closet, for just the flicker of an instant, he was once again confronted by a pair of glowing red eyes observing him back. They blinked. That was accompanied by a steadily building hissing sound, which sent chills down Jon's spine. Why, those were the same eyes he had observed occupying Aunt Hilda's when she had gone crazy just the other day, he recalled remotely, and just like what he had seen in the attic. The eyes vanished as suddenly as they had materialized. Then a force resembling an icy, windlike sensation writhed and escaped past him with a whooshing sound, nearly knocking him over.

Jon took in a quick breath. *What on earth was that?*

Dorfuss, still sitting on the edge of the car, sensed the depravity immediately. His emerald eyes widened, he plastered his ears back against his head, and then he began to growl under his breath, at first almost imperceptibly. Swiftly, the nearly invisible, wraithlike form with vermilion eyes swooped past him too, still hissing. Dorfuss hissed back and raised a pawful of menacing, razor-sharp claws.

Then the catlike instinct of the ages—to valiantly pursue its enemy no matter what—took charge of the feline. Dorfuss sprang high into the air with athleticism, claws bared and swiping.

It was all in vain. Grasping and clawing at nothing of substance while he hissed wildly, the large cat fell swiftly to the ground with a thud. He screeched as he hit the hard dirt floor. He stood and shook his long fur off, the fur on his back still sticking straight up and his tail still puffed up hugely with fear.

He and Jon stared at each other in mutual fright and bewilderment for a moment or two.

"I thought I saw something like that up in the attic the other day," Jon finally confessed. "Whatever it was had red, evil eyes too. But then it just disappeared before I even had time to decide if I had imagined it or not!"

Dorfuss collected his thoughts. "Yes, I have observed similar things once or twice myself. The other day when I messed up your aunt Hilda's precious spell, I accidentally broke her magical glass ball. It seems to me when that happened, something corrupt escaped the confines of the glass. Strange, ghostly apparitions began floating and dancing round and singing to me. I regret to say I believe I may have accidentally caused evil spirits to escape! Perhaps one of them has possessed your aunt! That would be the only logical explanation for her deranged behavior the other day."

Dorfuss paused and considered for a moment and then returned his green gaze to Jon's. "It is not safe to stay here any longer, dear boy. We must leave, and soon! It is very important to get this car running!"

Jon couldn't argue at all with that. He continued to tremble. Hesitantly, he turned back toward the darkened closet. Jumping a bit this time, he reached for and finally located the short chain pull for the light and gave it a yank. The small bulb glowed dimly. Jon sighed with relief. There was the gas can, way in the back corner. He grabbed it. It was quite heavy and nearly full. *Yes!*

Quickly, Jon returned to the car and poured the precious liquid into the gas tank, and then he tossed the empty can aside. He got into the car and tried again to fire it up. It sputtered and spit for a bit, protesting after having sat for so long without being used. The entire car rattled with sluggishness and shook with the force of the motor straining to turn over.

Jon's heart began to sink when the battery began to sound as if it were quickly losing its remaining power, and he glanced through the windshield at Dorfuss with defeat.

Dorfuss was hanging valiantly onto the shaking old contraption. Jon observed as the cat suddenly quirked his tail oddly, pointing it and one of his paws directly at the motor. Then the furry cat began to purr loudly, more loudly than Jon had ever heard him purr before. Jon could hear it above the racket the old engine was making. An aura of glistening cat hairs appeared to lift and circle the absurd cat, surrounding him momentarily. His green, slightly askew eyes glowed just for the briefest time while they stared at and appeared to will the old engine to fire up.

"Try it again, Wrench!" the distinguished cat commanded.

Jon's heart filled with hope, and he complied in amazement, turning the key and pressing on the gas pedal. The motor coughed, and the exhaust pipe fumed and belched a huge puff of black smoke. Then suddenly, the old jalopy began to run!

Looking out at Dorfuss rather sheepishly, Jon apologized, saying, "I don't understand! The gauge said it had half a tank!"

"Well, so much for mechanical devices, Wrench," Dorfuss said calmly. "You yourself know they always seem to need repair. I helped it along a little, however. It is time to get your brother and sister. We now have a mode of transportation. We should be on our way!"

Jon shut the motor down in an effort to conserve what little gas the car's tank did have. He then hurried toward the house to get his brother and sister, with Dorfuss following closely behind.

Finally, he couldn't stand it any longer. "What was that thing you just did with your tail and hair?" he asked the cat.

"Just a bit more of your aunt Hilda's magic that I got into, I'm afraid. I seem to have acquired a few trivial magical powers from her, in addition to my gift of speech. I have been trying them out here and there, and maybe with practice they will develop even more.

Why, two days ago, I managed to vaporize a pesky fly! The varmint wouldn't leave me alone! Most of the time, whatever I try fails, however. I really have no idea what I am capable of. Yet these unwelcome powers may come in handy on our journey, and I am grateful for whatever I have been blessed with."

Jon didn't reply; he just gazed at the cat with bewilderment as they made their way to the house. He had encountered many animals in his lifetime on the farm, but this one exceeded everything his wildest imagination could ever have concocted! He would never have admitted it to his sister or James, but this cat was highly unusual, if nothing else.

The bedrooms upstairs were alive with disarray and commotion in the ensuing half hour. The children packed any remaining items necessary before leaving their home and their wicked aunt behind.

While packing, Jenna tucked a small photograph of her parents and her Mr. Teddy in her items in one of the bags. Tears filled her green eyes as the prospect of leaving behind everything she loved began to loom large in her mind. "Promise me, Jon, that someday we will come back!" she implored as a large tear escaped one of her fear-filled eyes and rolled down her rosy, freckled cheek.

Jon, not wanting to promise much of anything right now, merely grunted at his little sister. He too was overwhelmed with emotion and his own fear of the unknown and did not wish to let it show.

Jenna wiped the tears away and said nothing more.

James glanced at his brother and sister while he packed with apprehension also. He had not voiced his concerns, but the prospect of them all being on their own had him very worried, just like his brother and sister and Dorfuss.

A short time later, downstairs in the kitchen, they made up a bunch of sandwiches. They also packed apples, oranges, cookies, and other snacks to help them survive their journey. Then they ate a quick, large lunch before hitting the road.

Jenna balked, claiming she just was not hungry. Her poor little stomach was tied into a knot of nerves. Her brothers, though, along with Dorfuss, encouraged her to at least eat a sandwich right then so she wouldn't become hungry moments after they were on their way.

Soon, duffel bags full of clothes and food, all of the money from their piggy banks, and their sleeping bags and pillows had been tossed into the trunk of their pappa's old car, which Jon had restarted and pulled up in front of the house. The children hovered wistfully in the kitchen entryway for a few moments, gazing out at the chugging old vehicle just yards away and experiencing growing trepidation. They gathered what they knew could be their last look ever at the only home they had ever known.

They had been through so much these past few years. First, they had lost Mamma. Then Pappa had tragically died. Now, they were going to be losing their home besides. It was an awful lot for children so young to have to bear.

Finally, Dorfuss prodded them along, reminding them that their aunt would be home in only three short hours. "We should be well away from here by then so she cannot find us!" he asserted wisely.

What could the children do but agree? It was time to leave. Perhaps they would never return again. Hopefully they would.

And so, with tears in everyone's eyes, they slowly made their way down the long gravel drive in the sputtering, chugging old car that had belonged to their parents. It too seemed hesitant to depart the beloved farm.

Silently, they watched with anxiety and foreboding as their beloved home disappeared from sight in the dust the weather-beaten tires kicked up from the gravel road. Then they turned their faces away and looked forward, each secretly and hopefully assuring himself that everything would be all right.

Traveling on the Road

Unfortunately, the rickety old car did not stay running for very long. Not only was it low on gasoline, but only eighteen short miles from their beloved farmstead, the motor overheated. With steam pouring hotly from the radiator, Jon thought it necessary to pull the car into the drive of an abandoned farm. They left it there, hidden behind a hazardously leaning barn. Unknowingly for them, it was probably the wisest decision they could have made at the moment, as it would be weeks before the broken-down vehicle would be discovered back there.

With the children watching hopefully as the sky began to cloud over, Dorfuss tried his best to wield his magical tail, cat hair, and paw at the motor while purring loudly. Apparently, however, the old device had turned over for its very last time. Nothing came of his efforts.

When Aunt Hilda arrived at the farm, distracted, at her usual time of approximately four thirty in the evening, she vaguely noticed the garage door open but did not think much about it. Something *did* seem different and out of sorts to her, though.

Carrying a few packages, she entered the old homestead and found it to be alarmingly quiet. After making her way through the house and not finding the children and then wandering about outside on the vast grounds of the farm and still coming up empty-handed, she began to become worried.

Hilda was rather ashamed of her behavior of several days before, had taken a few days to mull it all over, and was hoping to make things right between them all somehow that evening. She was not sure just what had possessed her that evening.

After her rant, she had returned to her room and discovered her missing crucible sitting right in plain sight, almost as if to taunt her! It had been obvious then that neither the children nor their cat had disturbed anything. She then began to question her own sanity. She shook off her recollections of several days past and returned to the present.

Her new magical ball had arrived earlier that day at the post office. She had picked it up with growing excitement, even remembering to thank the kindly gentleman behind the countertop.

Then Hilda even stopped briefly at the general store and picked up some fresh staples for their dinner. She was planning to prepare something delicious for them all in a conciliatory effort.

Making her way back up to the house from the direction of the barn, she finally realized the garage was empty. Then it suddenly struck her! *Why, Ralph's old jalopy is gone! How on earth?*

Instantly she realized what had happened. Jon had always been a tinkerer. Hadn't Ralph given him the boy a nickname of some sort? What had it been? Screwdriver? Socket set? Wrench? That was it! Ralph had often referred to Jon as *Wrench* due to his knack for being able to repair almost anything! And now, apparently, Jon had by some miracle gotten Ralph's worthless old car up and running!

When she had surveyed the children's bedrooms shortly before coming outside, she noticed a bit of disarray in them but disregarded

it at first. After all, children were notorious for making messes. They wouldn't be normal if they didn't mess things up.

What if the children have run away? But where could they possibly be headed? There was nowhere for them to go, at least around here. Not unless they had only ventured on down to the next farm just a few miles down the road.

Becoming rather anxious, since the children *were* her responsibility, after all, she went back into the house to locate her handbag. *I will drive to all of the closest farms and see if anyone knows of the children's whereabouts,* she decided.

Unfortunately, even after spending a couple of hours driving around to check with all her neighbors, she came up empty-handed. At each farm she stopped at, nice people came out to greet her, always looking for a new person to chitchat with due to the relative isolation of farm life. Needless to say, they had all been very hard to get away from. None of them had seen the children, however. It was by now after seven o'clock, and the sun would be setting in only an hour or so.

Hilda finally headed back toward the farm with increasing angst, now knowing with an ever-mounting certainty that the children had, indeed, run away.

Arriving back at the lovely old farmstead, she noticed immediately that no lights were on inside the house. That was not a good sign. The garage, of course, still sat empty and forlorn looking, mouth gaping wide, as if it somehow missed its old, beaten-up resident.

The chores! Naturally, the children had not done any of them either. Hilda, of course, was dumbfounded as to what needed to be done. She had always relied on the children and Harvey Jensen to tend to all of that. She would have to telephone Mr. Jensen first thing in the morning if the children did not materialize soon.

She wandered back up to the children's rooms, which remained quiet and empty in the darkness. This time, she noticed all three of their pillows were missing—a sure sign that they had left. After all, they would have taken some of the comforts of home with them.

Hilda went to bed that night full of worry and sorrow at the way she had behaved toward the children. The more she thought about it all, the guiltier she felt. Of course, it had been all of her fault they had left. She hadn't spoken a civil word to them in days. She knew they were terrified of her. What else would possibly have caused them to go?

Lying alone in her twin bed, she gazed through the soft moonlight illuminating her room at her new glass ball. Perhaps it would hold some secrets to the children's whereabouts. A bit of hopeful excitement began to surge through her.

Hilda rose from her bed and hovered over it, waving her hands, her dowager's hump higher than her head. She proceeded to murmur strange chants and odd incantations as it began to glow, first a dim and then somewhat brighter, blue. She waved her spindly fingers over the receptacle, willing it to reveal to her any clue it might have regarding the children's location.

First, Hilda observed just a flicker of a glimpse of strange, glowing red eyes peering back at her from within. She shivered involuntarily at the evil that seemed to reside inside and then fill her room but only for a brief instant. Then the eyes disappeared.

Presently, the dim outline of a run-down farmhouse came into view within the glass. *But that could be one of many different abandoned farmhouses in the area*, she reflected. Over the years, as families died off or simply moved away and new tenants had failed to replace them, their surrounding lands continued to be planted by other area farmers. Old houses would stand empty, their barns and silos used only for sporadic storage, alone and forgotten in the vastness of the state known as Iowa.

Technologies had improved over the years, of course, and it was now possible for any farmer who was willing to farm much greater acreage than in years past. This old, white house within the glass orb could belong to any abandoned farm in the area. Not much to go on, of that she was sure. However, it was a clue and one she would have to notify the police of in the morning if the children had not returned by then.

She felt it prudent to be patient for the moment and hope for the children to return of their own free will. She did not wish for news of Ralph's children's disappearance to become public knowledge, particularly if it was not necessary.

Just as she began to wave her hands over the glass yet again, the red eyes appeared once more. This time they brightened, and a hissing sound emanated from within the orb's depths. More frantically, Hilda waved her skinny fingers over it in a hurried attempt to vanquish the unsettling apparition.

Instead of doing her bidding, the eyes broke past the boundaries of her glass ball and rushed directly toward her, hissing sinisterly. With a force she could only feel, they seemed to smack her directly in the face. Hilda was knocked off balance and landed very hard on the bedroom floor on her bulbous rump.

She sat on the floor a few moments, temporarily dazed and apprehensive besides. Finally, she gathered up her composure and courage and hauled herself up off the floor. Cautiously, she approached her magical ball, yet instinct now told her to keep her distance. Either this new one was more powerful than its predecessor, or her powers were becoming stronger. *Just what kind of evil lurks within?* she wondered. *Perhaps that was the demon that possessed me just a few nights ago when I unleashed my temper on the children.* She trembled a bit involuntarily. Suddenly, she felt vaguely unsettled at the idea of playing with a fire she did not fully understand. Dare she try to unleash it again, or should she destroy all of her works right now before things became more than she could handle?

She knew not what to do. She felt more than a bit of excitement at the hopeful thought that she had finally achieved a victory of sorts with her witchcraft. Something had definitely been released and appeared to be waiting for her to give it some kind of command. Yet she was unsure of just how to proceed. She resolved to search her spell books the next day for the meaning of the red eyes' appearance.

She paced a while, and then, feeling unsettled even still, Hilda finally returned to her bed. Eventually she drifted off into a vaguely tormented sleep. Throughout the night, the red glowing eyes continued to haunt her in her dreams relentlessly, and she slept in uneasiness.

The children made use of the abandoned farmhouse for their shelter that evening, scooting in one by one through a broken basement window.

Their entire group was despondent about the apparent loss of their mode of transportation, but Jon promised to look the motor over again in the morning.

During the night, severe thunderstorms pounded the area, and the children hovered together in fright in their sleeping bags with Dorfuss nearby, all together in a first-floor room. None of them slept particularly well. The dilapidated structure groaned and creaked throughout the night against the strain of the fierce winds. The thunder and lightning was terribly scary at times, sometimes sounding as if it had actually made contact very near to the old house. And of course, everyone felt vaguely uneasy in the unfamiliar surroundings and worried that marauding creatures might enter the old house through the broken windows and, at the very least, disturb their sleep.

Dorfuss, instinctively nocturnal, slept now and then but with an always watchful eye on his three charges. During the night, he briefly observed red glowing eyes hovering up in the darkest corner of the room, watching him and seemingly waiting for something he did not understand. Then the eyes faded away.

Dorfuss was glad to see them disappear. The children were his responsibility now, and he took that responsibility very seriously. He did not enjoy the glowing eyes' insidious company.

Miles away, Hilda tossed and turned in her bed repeatedly in restless response not only to her unsettling dreams but also the thunder, lightning, and wind. It occurred to her when she awoke that the children could possibly be outside somewhere in the nasty weather and helpless against its fury. She willed herself not to worry. Yet that thought continued to nag her with persistence throughout the night, even in her demon-haunted dreams. The glowing eyes also pestered her, more persistent now. An odd, detached voice seemed to accompany them, taunting her with mysterious achievement of a victory she did not fully understand.

Hilda awakened earlier than usual after a full night of tossing and turning and encountering vague nightmares, even in the hours approaching dawn. When she opened her eyes in the grayness preceding the morning, she realized she had a pounding headache.

Then, instead of merely being upset that the children had run away, she comprehended now that morning had arrived that she was downright angry. For one thing, she had barely slept all night. *How could they do this to me? And what will people think when they find out?* After all, everyone in the area knew just how secluded a life she had always lived. Anytime she was around other folks in public, she was openly gossiped about for being her usual, odd, antisocial self. She had no friends, no one to confide in. Certainly the townspeople wouldn't take very long to put two and two together and realize the children had left the only home they had ever known because of her. *How dare they do this to me!* Her reputation had never been top-notch, and now it would probably suffer even further.

And then, suddenly, she was struck with another horrible thought. *Why, what if Thames finds out?* She certainly couldn't allow *that* to happen.

She vowed right there and then to set to work on improving her spells in an attempt to frighten the children into returning. Hilda contemplated a while. What if she were able to cause some evil spirits to work their corrupt wills on the children's surroundings? Would it be possible to do that?

She lit a few candles in the early morning darkness, fumbling around briefly and knocking one on its brass stand over, barely missing her new glass ball. She muttered to herself, cursing under her breath. She couldn't see her own eyes, of course, but if she had looked in the mirror just then, she would have discovered them again occupied with a wicked, glowing, bright red hue.

Quickly, she paged through her spell books, searching for something that would scare the children half to death. Perhaps, if she could locate just the right one; she was sure she had seen something like that in one of these books recently. She continued to rapidly flip the yellowed, time-worn pages of the huge volumes.

There it was! *Possessing Inanimate Objects with Demons!* Perfect.

Quickly, she read through the instructions. It was her wicked plan to cause ordinarily inanimate objects—such as trees and houses and even plants—to become alive with corrupt dispositions and work their perverted wills on the children. *This could be quite advantageous*! She cackled wickedly as she prepared the necessary items to perform her dastardly scheme.

Hilda cackled again. A few doses of terrifying, screaming trees, plants, rocks, or whatever, and the children would most likely tuck tail and run straight back home. Once they returned, she planned to punish them all harshly. She would see to it they received double the chores. Perhaps she would have them repaint the farmhouse, for starters. *Let's see them pull this one again!* she ruminated, smiling sardonically as she worked.

She began her evil chanting, muttering unintelligible incantations over and over and progressively louder and louder. Her magical ball began to glow a bright blue, a good sign. She peered deeply inside as she continued chanting and watched demonlike forms beginning to resurrect and move about inside. She became hopeful, and her chanting frantically escalated.

Suddenly, her bedroom filled with innumerable desolate souls willing to do her bidding. Incandescent lights sparkled and swirled between the dark apparitions, and Hilda was in her glory. Finally, something appeared to be successful.

Simultaneously, her conflicted heart became consumed with the evil into which she had delved, and right there and then, it began to harden. Her conscience abruptly began to shrink and fade and be replaced by the small but already strengthening voice of the corrupt spirit that had taken it over. *To heck with those incorrigible brats!* she mused. If she wasn't successful in convincing them to return home, perhaps she could perpetuate some tragedy to befall them instead!

She cackled, overwhelmed with the thrill of the knowledge that at last she had been successful. Overjoyed, she completed the corrupt spell, clasping her bony hands together and caterwauling in joy as the lost souls swarming around her began praising her as their new master and imploring her to give them orders. She willingly complied.

THE VASTNESS OF IOWA

Morning dawned with overcast skies. The outside temperature was much cooler than it had been the day before. Luckily, the children had packed light jackets and long pants, and they changed into them then. They only had brought along a few changes of clothes for each of them and would have to make do with what there was for the remainder of their journey. Perhaps they would get lucky enough to find a stream to bathe in and wash a few items of clothing when necessary. So much was still uncertain at this point.

They sat in the relative warmth of the abandoned house, snacking on cookies and oranges for their breakfast. Soon their sleeping bags were rolled up, and everything else was packed back into the duffel bags. It was time to be on their way.

Dorfuss had already gone outside to check the car innards and perhaps catch a small rodent for his breakfast.

In the increasing daylight, as they left through the creaky front door that had been locked, James discovered a small, moss-covered statue of a frog sitting nearby, almost concealed by an overgrown evergreen bush, right up next to the front porch. He pointed to it to show his sister, knowing that she liked statues and had the cherub one standing in her little garden back home. She giggled a little, wishing aloud that she could take it home with them and place it in her flower garden alongside the cherub. Jon admonished her, saying they had enough to carry already. Reluctantly, she knew she had to agree, and they began to walk away.

Suddenly, all three children looked back at it, as it had just appeared to move. "What are you three looking at?" it demanded immediately with glowing eyes rapidly coming to life. They seemed to bore into the children's souls. The representation scowled at them with malice. Then, as quickly as it had begun to move, it resumed its statuelike appearance, shaking all three of them to their core. Did they actually see what they just thought they had? Jenna screamed and ran, heading toward their old car. Her brothers followed closely, also frightened.

Jon tried to start the car back behind the barn again with near desperation, just to make sure that it was hopeless. Sadly, that morning, he found he couldn't even get the aged, tired motor to turn over. Jenna and James poked around in the gravel near Jon for a bit with sticks, became bored, and finally went and sat up against the dilapidated barn under the welcoming shade of a tree. The temperature was rapidly becoming hot for so early in the day, and soon James and Jenna removed their jackets and stuffed them into the duffel bags.

As Jon kept tinkering, he became certain that the car's battery was either dead or something else within its workings was seriously wrong. Unfortunately, the only tools he had brought along with him for their journey were his pocketknife and an old flint for starting fires. Not of much use where the car was concerned. And thoughts of that creepy frog statue were bothering him. He only wished now for them all to be on their way. *Where is Dorfuss at anyway?*

As if summoned, Dorfuss appeared, making his way out of some scrubby brush near the dilapidated old barn. Unfortunately for him, he had come up empty-pawed and was still feeling very hungry, but he did not complain to the children. It was his duty to see these three children to safety, and perhaps soon he would find something to satisfy his hunger. He jumped up on the car next to the open hood and tried quirking his tail and pointing his paw at the stubborn motor without any success.

James then told Dorfuss of the unusual encounter with the statue.

Dorfuss jumped back down onto the ground, contemplating everything for a moment. *Might as well tell them*, he finally concluded. “Yes, I believe you, James,” he said. “Several times recently, I have had similar things happen to me. I believe some of your aunt Hilda’s evil spirits that were released have been following us. I only hope they wish us no harm. I have been watching them closely and will continue to do so,” he promised valiantly.

Suddenly, the tree they were all standing underneath began to sway and bend terrifyingly. The children looked up, first in surprise and then with horror and fright, as they realized that the tree had also sprouted an evil face. It glared at them with wickedness filling its glowing scarlet eyes.

Its branches suddenly began to grow longer, and the maple writhed, reaching out to grab at the children with contorted, vicious arms, and wooden, clawlike fingers. The possessed maple just missed Dorfuss’s tail as the children grabbed their belongings hurriedly and took off for safety. *Anywhere else* was fine. The children and Dorfuss rushed away, screaming at the top of their lungs.

They didn’t stop running until they were exhausted, approximately two miles down the road. Jenna stumbled a little and skinned her knee, and she began crying. She declared to Jon and James she wanted to go back to their home and farm now!

They all stopped for a few minutes to inspect Jenna’s scrape. Jon told Jenna firmly they were *not* going back. He reminded her that what they had just encountered was only more of Hilda’s evil and the

farther they all got away from that woman—and the sooner—the better. James had to agree with Jon. Dorfuss did also. Dorfuss began rubbing against Jenna's good leg, purring loudly. Eventually, she crouched down to pet him and then wiped her tears away. She knew, even though she was very small, that her brothers and Dorfuss were right. She reinspected her knee. The minor bleeding had already nearly stopped.

Without a car now and frustration and apprehension looming large, they continued on their venture, this time on foot, down the hilly, gravel road. They headed in the same direction as the previous day. Disappointment nagged at them, however. With no car to make things easier, they would be forced to walk and carry all of their belongings, and their journey would be much more difficult and a lot longer.

As they traveled along the gravel road, from time to time, a vehicle could be seen far off in the distance. As it approached, the children scurried into the cornfields for cover. Jon was not comfortable letting anyone notice them, at least not until they were relatively far away from home. Once, during the morning hours, they even saw a police car rolling slowly down a crossroad nearly a mile away. Quickly, they took cover in the nearby field.

Noon approached, and the children rested under the shade of a tree along a fence row. They all gladly changed into cooler clothing and finished the remainder of the sandwiches they had prepared just a day before. Their food supply was already beginning to run dangerously low. The sky clouded over, and they continued and watched, hoping the skies would not open up once more. It was terribly humid.

Dorfuss disappeared into the field for a short time while they ate, catching and eating small, unsuspecting critters for his sustenance and finally satisfying his own hunger to some degree. Perhaps that night for dinner, he hoped, he might be able to snare a squirrel, rabbit, or other larger creature, and they could all enjoy some fresh, cooked meat.

Later, in the heat of the midafternoon, the sun came out again. The humidity of the day became sweltering, and with the sun, the heat intensified. The moisture from the rainfall of the night before was now evaporating from the dirt of the fields and hung in the air thickly around them. The children became too hot to continue, especially poor Jenna, who was also beginning to become terribly thirsty. Heat had always bothered her more than it had ever affected the two boys.

Not knowing what to else to do, Dorfuss volunteered to remain behind with Jenna resting next to him along the same fence line, which they had continued to traverse after eating their lunch. Jon had decided earlier it would be a little safer for them, as they would be out of sight of any people in passing cars who might see them walking along the roads. Certainly, there would be a creek, stream or pond somewhere along the way, they reasoned.

Finally, a mile or two farther along the fencerow, the two brothers discovered a small, merry creek running cheerfully through a grassy clearing. It sparkled with crystal-clear water. Nearby, a stand of tall trees created a welcoming, shaded area. They knew then that this would be where they would all spend their night. In this vibrant, green clearing, there was even a bit of a welcoming and soothing breeze! Jon remained behind to collect firewood while James traversed the seemingly endless distance in the thick humidity with a cup full of cool water back to where Jenna had stayed behind with her beloved cat.

Eventually he reached her. She was sleeping soundly in the shade of a small, scrubby tree, with Dorfuss watching over her protectively. Dorfuss gazed up through questioning green eyes at James and then whispered to him, "This poor child is exhausted. You and Jon would be wise to find a place for us all to settle down for the night. I don't believe she can go much farther!"

James set the cup on a nearby rock and reached out to stroke the furry head reassuringly. "Don't worry, Dorfuss. Jon found a little shaded clearing only a mile or so up the fence line. He's getting firewood together right now!"

Dorfuss was reassured. He nudged Jenna's childish face with his own fuzzy one, touching her with his chilly wet nose. Soon the child began to stir. When James presented her with the cup of water, she gladly drank it. She was still irritable at having been woken from her nap in the sweltering heat, however, and fussed and argued with James all the way to where their older brother was.

Jon by then had gathered together a hefty pile of firewood from underneath the grove of trees, used his flint, and a small fire was merrily beginning to blaze. Smoke wafted up from the flames for several brief moments and then vanished as the fire burned off the moisture that remained in the wood.

Dorfuss disappeared into the tall grass. James joined his brother in the search for more firewood. Jenna sat in the welcoming shade, recovering from the heat and her dehydration and drinking more refreshing water out of the communal metal cup they would all share for this journey.

The trepidation of the day before and also this morning was finally beginning to fade for everyone in the group. Now that they had found this cheerful, welcoming, and refreshing place to spend their night, their perceived misfortunes were beginning to take on the brand new feel of a marvelous adventure. They began to experience anticipation for the three of them to discover many exciting, and unknown things.

After drinking several cupfuls of cool water from the creek, Jenna began to feel better. She also joined her brothers in the search for firewood.

Eventually, Dorfuss appeared with a fat, dead rabbit in tow. "It was nothing!" he offered modestly as the children cheered at the prospect of eating a warm meal.

Jon soon had the hapless creature skinned and cleaned. He crafted a small spit out of some green wood from the surrounding trees with his pocketknife. They would all enjoy some hot, campfire-roasted meat for dinner tonight, Dorfuss included!

Later, after their tummies were full, they took turns washing the sweat and dirt of the day off in the cold, refreshing water of the stream. Jon was glad he'd had the foresight to bring along two bars of soap and some old towels for their journey, as were his brother and sister when they discovered the items.

That night, as the stars shone brightly and protectively over the tiny group, they all slept soundly in their sleeping bags, cradled gently by the long, softly wafting grass. They lay surrounding the dwindling fire, with Dorfuss nearby gazing silently at those stars, always their guardian and protector.

By his calculations, now that they no longer had a vehicle, they probably had ten to twelve days left to travel as long as all went well and they stayed on course. He would have to keep a watchful eye on the direction they traveled. He knew they should keep heading east. Eventually it would be necessary to adjust their direction when they came close to their destination.

As he himself began to drift off into a welcoming sleep, he thought cavalierly, *Never fear; Sir Dorfuss is here!* For the remainder of the night, he dreamt of himself as a furry, cross-eyed, buck-fanged hero watching over and protecting his three charges with valor, always their victorious guardian and protector. There was absolutely no doubt in his mind that he would be successful.

SHADOWS IN THE FOREST

The next morning, the three children and their cat awoke bright and early to the sound of birds happily chirping above them in the small stand of trees. They had all slept peacefully. The brightness of the morning promised them all a cheery, sunlit day. Dorfuss had slept cuddled next to Jenna all night, both of them atop her sleeping bag. It was too warm all night long for either of them to feel the need to crawl inside of it. And it was already becoming quite warm outside this morning.

As the children snacked on the remainder of cookies and apples they had brought along, Jon worried at their lack of meal prospects. He felt they should probably seek out a town soon in order to restock things. Perhaps Dorfuss would be kind and lucky enough to find them another small animal to roast that evening. He could only hope. They would not get far with no food and very little to drink.

While they ate, Jon told them all about his plan. After thinking back to the previous day, he felt they should all try to get to sleep early in the evenings and rise early enough in the mornings to beat

some of the heat each day. In the afternoons, when the heat was at its most intense, they should attempt to find shelter of some sort and a place to settle in each evening. Jon appointed Dorfuss chief food catcher, which Dorfuss proudly accepted, head held high with his accomplishment and green, silly eyes and buck fangs sparkling.

Soon all the food was polished off. Jon still felt vaguely hungry but said nothing. Their small breakfast would just have to be enough for now. They rolled up and repacked all of their belongings and soon began to resume their journey along the fence line of the vast field.

As they trudged along, bluebirds and red-winged blackbirds fluttered about, chirping cheerfully, completely at home in the fields and surrounding meadows. Occasionally, the children came across a small stream and took refreshing drinks from the sparkling, clear water. Now and then, Jon developed a sense that something was watching them, however ridiculous that seemed. *What could there possibly be way out here in the middle of nowhere, surveying our movements, except for perhaps the wild creatures that live here?* He banished the thought from his mind.

Toward late afternoon, finally, at one such oasis, Jon ran ahead of the rest of the group. He climbed a large, grass-covered hill that some cattle were grazing on, and then came running back down toward his brother and sister, proclaiming loudly that a forest appeared to be some distance off.

They all followed Jon back up. They briefly rested in the shade of a large oak tree on the hilltop, enjoying the tender breeze that wafted about there at the slightly higher, unobstructed elevation above the fields. They watched as the cattle munched on the long green grass, enjoying their pasture. The grass flowed and swayed gently in the breeze. The bovines made a quaint picture against their soothing green backdrop, way out there in the middle of nowhere. The sweet odor of manure drifted past occasionally in the faint draft.

Jenna made herself comfortable on the grass alongside her beloved cat and began to ruffle his fur. He immediately began to purr. He gazed up at her now and then with all-consuming adoration evident in his large eyes.

James lay back in the soft grass, bending his elbows and supporting his head with his hands as he gazed at the puffy, lazy white clouds drifting slowly overhead. He then observed the large tree trunk bent slightly over them as his sister and brother sat on each side of him, gazing at the cows.

Without warning, just as the morning before, in the enormous trunk, an angry face resembling Aunt Hilda developed. Momentarily, it frowned and scowled in seeming disapproval at the unsuspecting group. It pruned its lips. James blinked his eyes, unbelieving for the moment as he attempted to focus and make certain the odd face wasn't just the result of an overactive, tired imagination. The eyes of the face blinked back in astonishment temporarily. Then they began to glare evilly, and James whispered to his brother and sister, "Jon, Jenna, look above at the tree trunk! There's a face up there, and it looks really angry! It looks just like Aunt Hilda! Do you think she can see us? It's just like that tree at the farm yesterday morning!"

The formidable mouth opened and began yelling angrily, "Why are you sitting in my shade without my permission? Why, I ask you? Stay out of my shade! It's mine! Leave it alone! Go home to where you belong and leave me in peace, I say!" it thundered wickedly.

Instantly startled, all three children leapt to their feet. That same moment, the cattle grazing calmly on the panoramic hillside heard all the frightful noise emanating from the tree. They were jolted into a stampede, mooing frantically, away from the angry oak. Dorfuss hissed in dread and began backing away, fur raised on the back of his neck and tail puffed out wildly. Out of instinct more than anything, hundreds of glistening cat hairs surrounded the air around him. Dorfuss raised his paw and quirked his fright-enlarged tail.

Uncharacteristically, he began purring thunderously. His green eyes glowed, beaming directly at the infuriated visage. The huge tree trunk bent, swayed, and backed away in dread, not expecting this sudden change of events.

"No!" it screamed at the cat, its own fright evident in the wooden countenance. Then the face resembling their aunt began to shrink and finally fade away, all the while emitting distraught screeches.

Finally, it was silent. The tree returned to its former, quaint position, and the pasture to its previous calmness. The cattle had disappeared, but otherwise, the entire area was still again, as if nothing out of the ordinary had ever happened!

The three children observed this with astonishment.

Then Jenna picked Dorfuss up and hugged him to her with relief and pride. "Oh, thank you, Dorfuss! You are our hero!" she said with joy. "Thank you so much for saving us!" She gazed at Jon with an I-told-you-so look, mocking her older brother. Jon remained silent but gaped at the ridiculous cat with newfound respect. James stood nearby, astounded beyond words also.

"See, Jon," Jenna finally pronounced. "Dorfuss *is* our hero again! He saved us from the horrible tree!"

Jon could do nothing but mutter, but deep inside, he suspected his sister was right. Perhaps Dorfuss *was* somehow the embodiment of their departed father and Hilda's magic all rolled into one! He most likely would never know for sure. Still, to annoy his sister, he brushed with feigned irritation at all the cat hair that had come to rest on his clothing.

James also said nothing but had to agree with his sister. Dorfuss *was* one special cat.

Dorfuss sat back down next to Jenna and quickly resumed his former, rumbling state. He needed no praise. Keeping the children safe was the only reward important to him. As usual, he gazed deep into his mistress's eyes with utmost adoration.

Jon watched all this and snorted under his breath, scoffing to himself. Now, the silly cat appeared to be just that as he rolled back and forth with no embarrassment whatsoever at the ridiculous picture he made while Jenna petted him. *Cat or hero?* he wondered. *Nah, just a dorfuss!* he concluded.

Eager to get away from this place, lest another wicked spirit make itself known, they resumed their seemingly endless trek, plodding along in the ever increasing heat of the day. After time, Jenna began to complain again. The heat was getting to her once more, and of course, she was hungry. Her brothers were also hungry; they just hadn't been giving voice to their discomfort.

Finally, they all reached the welcoming shade of the forest, nearly two hours after Jon had viewed it from the hilltop. They appeared to be in complete wilderness, with no signs of civilization anywhere around. Jon conferred with Dorfuss while James and Jenna began to scavenge for firewood, staying close by each other. Dorfuss affirmed to Jon that they were all indeed still traveling in the correct direction and that they should stick to the course they were on. In a short time, enough firewood had been discovered for Jon to start a fire. He sent his brother and sister off together in search of more so they could keep the fire burning all night long. Jenna complained, telling Jon it was hot enough already, but he insisted they bring more firewood along. Soon, she relented and rejoined James a short distance away.

Dorfuss again disappeared into the thick underbrush, scavenging for something that could suffice as a meal. Wildlife was abundant there in the woods, and it was not long before he returned with a squirrel. Jon began to prepare the squirrel while Dorfuss again disappeared, returning shortly afterward this time with another rabbit, like the night before.

Jon distractedly petted the furry cat later while the two small animals roasted over the fire. The smell of cooking meat made both of their mouths water in hunger while they watched it sizzle away. James and Jenna returned soon, gushing happily over their discovery of a large stream not too far off and a thicket of wild blackberries, full of ripe ones to boot.

Jon secretly said a small prayer. Certainly something was watching over the three of them. Perhaps there was a God after all. He had often wondered about that.

After they joyfully shared in the roasted meat, they all went off to the cluster of wild blackberries and ate their fill. Jon admonished them, saying they should save some for the morning's breakfast, which they then did.

Nighttime had begun to fall. With it, the cheerful daytime noises began to disappear and were replaced by the sounds of coyotes howling far off in the distance and owls hooting. The children began to experience fear at the new and strange noises.

"Don't be afraid, guys." Jon reassured them as best he could. "I read once that those creatures we are hearing now are afraid of fire. As long as we keep the fire tended, we should all be fine. That's why I had you collect so much firewood. I will get up now and then during the night and add more wood. He glanced at the pile they had gathered and deemed it sufficient for the whole night.

Dorfuss amiably agreed to wake Jon occasionally so he could add more wood. Soon all of the sleeping bags had been unrolled, and sleepy heads sank deeply and comfortably into welcoming pillows. All three of them were exhausted, and soon they were sound asleep.

The night wore on. Occasionally, Dorfuss, ever watchful and aware with his keen senses of sight and sound and cat instinct, awoke to an odd noise or sense and then nudged Jon. Jon tiredly rose, added a few logs to the dying fire, and quickly resumed his position on the ground in his sleeping bag to nod off to sleep again.

Several times during the night, shadows of unidentifiable forms moved about in the distance, and Dorfuss remained very still, observing from afar and trying not to draw any unnecessary attention to the small group.

Once, however, not far from them, he observed a detached, glowing red eye, not unlike the obviously evil pair he and Jon had encountered just days before in the garage.

The fur on Dorfuss's neck started to prickle characteristically. He began to growl under his breath while the frightful, wraith-like apparition hovered briefly with apparent interest over the three innocent children.

Dorfuss finally stood and bared his teeth, buck fangs glistening weirdly and green eyes glowing in the dim light cast by the fire. A low, barely discernible growl escaped his throat. The light in his eyes intensified, and he returned the wraith's glower with equal ferocity.

Somewhat put off, the specter hovered and bobbed a few moments more, as if it sensed Dorfuss's unknown power over it. It almost appeared to have an inquiring look about it. Next, the expression changed to one of seeming dejection. It blinked. Then, as quickly as it had materialized, it disappeared into the blackness of the surrounding forest.

Dorfuss did not sleep the remainder of the night. He felt uneasy about the appearance of another evil form near them in the woods. Quite definitely, some of Hilda's corruption had followed them. *What am I to do about it? Is there anything I can do about it?* He surveyed the forest in the darkness around them all. The glow from the burning fire cast distorted, moving shadows against the surrounding trees in the blackness. Some of them appeared oddly and frighteningly contorted into twisted forms and faces, almost like the one they had seen on the oak tree earlier in the daylight. The thought of the crazed Hilda entered Dorfuss's mind again. *Hopefully the old biddy has not been overly successful with her magic! Who knows what awful things might befall us if she becomes more proficient?*

Dorfuss spent the remainder of the night surveying their surroundings keenly, listening for any odd noises. Throughout the long night, several glowing pairs of vermilion eyes presented themselves, floating aloft toward the outskirts of their encampment, but they did not attempt to approach the cat. He surveyed them with interest and fear. Yet they kept their distance and ultimately faded away into the depths of the inky night. A bit of satisfaction stole over Dorfuss. Apparently, those evil specters were afraid of him as well. He would have to make certain to keep things that way.

As the nighttime wore on, nothing else of interest made itself known, but Dorfuss was nonetheless not entirely assured. Evil had followed them on their journey, of that he was certain. He would have to find some means to eradicate it.

Meanwhile, back at the farm, Hilda paced nervously about in her sanctuary of the soulless 'til the wee hours of the morning. The sheriff's office had telephoned her earlier in the day when she was at the library working, but they informed her they had neither found a trace of the children nor Ralph's old car. They had thoroughly combed an area within ten miles of their farm, they told her apologetically. That was all they could offer for the time being.

In the late afternoon when she had arrived home from work, her magical ball only revealed rolling cornfields and tranquil pastures, certainly nothing of distinction. Once, she observed within the orb a hilly meadow with cows grazing on it and the forms of the children sitting under a large tree. She then commanded the spirits within the magical orb to do their dirty deeds, just as the morning before, and scare the daylights out of the children. However, that little ruse was only temporary.

For, much to Hilda's surprise and disappointment, she observed the wily cat rebuff the evil face in the tree with some magical powers of his own. *How on earth did that happen?* she wondered with dismay. *Perhaps when the stupid feline got into my magical necessities, somehow my magical powers rubbed off. Is that possible?* She did not know, but she was certain of what she had seen within her magical glass orb, and she was not at all happy about it.

If that darn cat is able to overcome my wicked spells with his own magic, the children will probably never return! And how then will I explain myself to Thames if he hears about the children's disappearance?

Again, she wondered vainly just where the children were so she could call the sheriff's office back and let them know something of substance. She gazed deeply into the glass ball again and only viewed more cornfields, streams, meadows, and an occasional forest. She snorted in disgust. *The whole state of Iowa is mostly cornfields and meadows with forests and waterways scattered here and there! What I need is a landmark of some sort, a building of distinction, perhaps, or a sign naming a town.*

She paged recklessly through her spell books in the unsuccessful search for a spell to help her locate someone. *Nothing! Worthless spell books! Stupid enchanted ball! Idiotic magic tricks! Nothing ever works! Except for that damnable cat! Perhaps I should just toss all of this stuff in the trash!* She snorted once more in frustration and abandoned her low round table for the time being.

Morning came with a slightly overcast sky. *Perhaps the heat will not be quite so bad with the clouds,* Jon reflected as they took turns down at the stream bathing and packing up their camp. He only hoped it didn't rain. The fire was still smoldering but would not be of much use to them this morning. There was nothing to cook.

Dorfuss searched in the underbrush for quite some time for an edible critter while the children packed and bathed but came up empty-pawed. Jon finally stomped the embers of last night's fire out the best he could, making sure the still glowing campfire would not set fire to anything else. He realized there would be no substantial breakfast for any of them this morning.

After their camp was packed up, the children stopped at the stream briefly to eat the delicious wild blackberries they had saved last evening before beginning their hike this day. They were all grateful for the foresight to save some from yesterday for that morning. Overnight, a bunch more had ripened up. They ate until every last one of the ripe berries was gone.

Then they resumed their journey. There was no doubt traveling would be more difficult with tree roots and dead branches and occasional rocks jutting out of the ground. They would have to watch their steps carefully to avoid injury. Nasty little things such as poison ivy and oak abounded and would need to be avoided, which Jon pointed out to them whenever he happened to come across any.

Nonetheless, hiking through the forest turned out to be a welcome respite from their ventures along cornfields the last couple of days. In the woods, it was shady, and even though there was no breeze, it was much cooler than the humid fields had been.

Lunchtime passed, and no one said anything about the lack of food. They all knew there was nothing they would be able to do about their hunger until Dorfuss or they themselves came across something edible. They kept their eyes open for berry bushes but did not have any further luck. The crystal-clear stream water kept their thirst quenched adequately, however, and they were appreciative whenever they came across a small brook. Onward they trudged, using Dorfuss's keen sense of direction as their guide.

In midafternoon, they again happened upon a good-sized stream. Glad to have a reason to take a break, they all took turns with the metal cup and sat on some large rocks on the water's edge. They removed their hot, sweaty socks and shoes and immersed their feet in the cheerful, refreshing water. The water where they sat was deep, and Jon noted with interest that there were some relatively large fish swimming about in it.

"Dorfuss!" he prodded the cat. "How about snagging us a few of those fish? Do you think you could manage that? We sure could use a bite to eat right about now!"

Dorfuss, himself experiencing annoying hunger pangs, jumped onto a dead log partially immersed in the water. He began a watchful, concentrated wait for a fish to swim close enough for him to snag it. Fish would make a delightful meal for him and the children. The cat could already taste them, and his stomach began to groan in anticipation. He swiped at several without much luck. His stomach growled in protest at its hollowness.

Finally, in frustration, he bent his tail and pointed his paw at the teeming fish below. The fish only appeared to ignore him. With irritation, he began to purr loudly. Suddenly, the water creatures snapped to attention as his emerald eyes pierced the waters below with his concentration. Now, they all swarmed directly beneath him, almost as if they were begging to be caught. It wasn't long before he had one and then two.

The children were thrilled. "Yes!" Their stomachs were also crying out in hunger.

Jon took the two Dorfuss had snared so far and began to clean them. He instructed his sister and brother to search for firewood to cook their dinner over. Excitedly, they dashed away into the woods, taking care to keep each other in sight. Meanwhile, Jon managed to collect several pieces himself. Dead limbs were in abundance deep within the woods. It wasn't long before a good-sized fire was snapping and crackling happily in a small, grassy clearing near the stream. There, the temperature was much cooler due to the rushing water. The children and Dorfuss were refreshed. By the time Jenna and James returned with extra wood, Dorfuss had managed to catch three more fish. One, a catfish, was very large.

"Dorfuss, how can we all thank you?" James asked, ruffling the furry and ludicrous yet dignified head. "Without you along, we would be hopelessly lost and starving besides! Thank you so much! You are our magical cat! Dorfuss the wizard!" he quipped. "You pick the fish you want since you caught them all!"

Dorfuss looked exceedingly proud, but, even so, selected the smallest one for his dinner.

Jon handed his brother and sister green sticks, which they impaled their dead fish upon, and they held their awaiting dinners over the fire to roast with anticipation.

After the fish had roasted over the fire, everyone smilingly and very thankfully filled their stomachs. They debated for a bit whether it would be wisest to stay there for the remainder of the day since they had found a food and water source or carry on for another hour or two.

They all voted unanimously to stay put. It was so refreshingly cool right there. They were all exhausted, and this had been the first decent meal they had eaten all day. Perhaps they would be able to catch a few more fish before bedtime if Dorfuss were so kind as to perform a bit more of his magic. The children all gathered additional firewood and then unrolled their sleeping bags.

"All right then, guys," Jon proclaimed. "I say tonight it's early to bed, and then we try to get up bright and early in the morning so our amazing Dorfuss can snag us all a few more fish. Then, after breakfast, let's get an early start again."

The other children agreed. This camping-out thing wasn't so bad after all, especially when they were all well fed.

In the evening, they took turns bathing while the others collected firewood. Shortly before dark, Dorfuss managed to catch three more fish. They roasted them, savoring the smell and splitting the smaller meal between the four of them. It would be enough to help them sleep well through the night. They were very thankful for Dorfuss and his amazing ingenuity and Hilda's magic that had indirectly given him this mystical gift.

Later that night, as the fire crackled nearby, Dorfuss slept cuddled with his darling Jenna. She had already fallen soundly asleep some time before. He purred loudly, content to be in the warm circle of her arms.

Dorfuss chuckled softly to himself, observing her sweet, slumbering face. It appeared almost angelic in the soft glow of the firelight. "I may not be your daddy, sweet thing, but I *am* the closest thing there could possibly be," he whispered to her with affection just before contentedly dozing off himself.

Hilda paced nervously in her haven of havoc that evening. No telephone call at all from the sheriff's office today! She was not at all happy about the lack of development in their search for the children. Just before she left the library, she telephoned them and reached a bland-sounding gentleman on the other end of the line who didn't seem to know much of anything about her case. She hung up angrily after speaking with him. *Obviously he is not at all concerned about my missing niece and nephews!*

She fidgeted nervously and then consulted her magical orb. What could she do, she wondered, to cause the children to return home? As she waved her gnarled hands over it and it returned to its odd blue glow, she viewed the sight of them roasting in merriment what appeared to be fish over a campfire. *How do they know how to do all of this?* Of course, she remembered that Jon was handy. Certainly he was old enough now to be at least relatively responsible and crafty about things.

Suddenly, it struck her. *Wild animals should be plentiful in the forest! Also, they would be attracted to the smell of cooking food! Perhaps I could convince my conjured spirits to work their charms on something menacing. But what?* Then, she was inspired. Coyotes were abundant in Iowa. Surely there were dens of them roaming about within hollering distance of the children.

As a child, Hilda had experienced a frightening encounter with one of the wily creatures herself. She had been wandering about in a meadow near the farm, picking wildflowers. She had never forgotten the frightening event or how the animal bared its teeth and growled at her with a horribly menacing expression, and in broad daylight at that! She picked up a nearby broken tree branch and swatted at the awful creature until it finally tucked tail and ran. After remembering her horror of long ago, Hilda cackled wickedly. Her evil ploy was a perfect idea.

So she began waving her hands over her enchanted ball, willing the demonic spirits within to do her bidding. She sniggered evilly as they began to whisper to her in encouragement, promising a late-night visit to the children involving terrifying coyotes. She ranted and raved insanely, like the blithering idiot she was rapidly morphing into. Any conscience she had previously possessed was steadily proceeding to wither and fade. Evil had indeed been victorious.

Ultimately, she shrieked with joy, thanking all of her captive demons for their willingness to help her. She admonished them to be certain that the event was terrifying so the children would be convinced to return back to the farm.

Her mind was beginning to become blurred regarding the distinction between good and evil. *For certainly*, she reasoned to herself in her demented state, *bringing the children home is important. The end justifies the means. If they return to me in a timely manner, I will be able to demonstrate to Thames my wondrous, compassionate motherly skills!* And deep within her magical glass, the tortured spirits beckoned to her, willing her to join them.

Hilda's mind was twisted into something base that perhaps had no hope of redemption. Even at this early stage of the game, she did not realize what she was delving into had a point of no return. With her mind skewed so irretrievably, perhaps she had already crossed it. Only time would tell.

Sometime in the middle of the night, the howling and barking of coyotes echoed not far off from the little encampment. The children awoke to the frightening noises and instinctively lay motionless in their sleeping bags, eyes opened wide and terrified.

"Coyotes!" Dorfuss whispered to them all in warning. "Jon, you should probably add some more wood to that fire. If those beasts discover us, a roaring fire could be the only thing that keeps them at bay!"

Jon complied hastily and then scooted back down into his sleeping bag. The fire was snapping and sparkling brightly very soon.

Unfortunately, the hungry coyotes did not seem to be deterred. Perhaps they smelled the remains of the little group's dinner, for soon their noises became louder and more persistent.

Jenna began to cry, cower, and tremble within her sleeping bag. James did likewise. Their little party had no shelter and no way to protect themselves if the coyotes decided to attack! What should they do? What could they do?

And so they lay, quivering within the frail safety of their sleeping bags. Jon finally decided someone would have to take the initiative. He bravely arose, this time carefully sliding a rather long log out of the fire.

He could see a pair of glowing coyote eyes. They were a mere fifteen or twenty feet away. A second animal was just behind the first. Jon walked a few feet in their direction, courageously jabbing the large, glowing end of the log at their faces and hollering at them to get away. One of the animals began growling and barking brazenly and viciously at him, baring deadly-looking teeth. The eyes of both animals began glowing a deep, penetrating red, and it was obvious they both had malicious intent.

Again, Jon poked at the undeterred pair. A few sparks flew from the glowing embers on the log, drifting lazily above the smoldering weapon before disappearing into minute wisps of smoke.

Undaunted, one of the animals took a bold step toward Jon, snarling and baring its fangs.

Completely surprising Jon, Dorfuss suddenly sprang with abandon at the closest coyote. He grasped onto it with his sharp claws, tearing into its muzzle and soft, unprotected nose. The angry, hungry animal swatted back ineffectively with a large, clawed paw. It grabbed Dorfuss by the fur with its teeth, whipping its large head and throwing the feline soundly against the trunk of an enormous tree with a loud thud.

Stars appeared before the dazed cat's eyes. Luckily for Dorfuss, and the children also, this was only the third of his nine lives spent.

He stood shakily at first, recovered, and then again, knowing he had no time to waste, flew at the face of the same coyote, attaching himself to it soundly. Valiantly, he swiped again and again at the dog's face while the animal began to yelp and then tried to back away. The other vicious coyote remained, however, hovering dangerously close by and growling lowly and menacingly with its fangs bared intrepidly. Then Jon attacked it, clubbing it soundly against the side of its furry head with the smoldering log. Embers scattered everywhere, including into the animal's eyes.

Immediately, that coyote lost its boldness and began to run off, yelping as it went along. It faded away into the depths of the forest. Jon again raised the glowing club at the remaining animal. Instantly, the object of Dorfuss's wrath lost interest, and the cat let loose his grip and dropped to the loamy, leaf-covered ground. That beast soon followed its companion into the darkness of the woods.

"Whew!" Jon exclaimed, breathing hard and shaking violently once the imminent danger had passed. "That was a close one! I hope we don't have to be in this forest much longer; there are too many deadly creatures about! What would we have done if the second one had attacked? We wouldn't have been able to hold them off!"

James and Jenna agreed tearfully. Everything that had just taken place was seriously sinking in, and they were terribly frightened and worried the coyotes might return.

Jenna began to sob loudly now that the immediate threat from the coyotes was gone. "Jon," she wailed, "I wanna go home! Take me home, please!"

Jon finally took Jenna onto his lap to calm and comfort her.

Dorfuss was still dazed from having had the wind knocked out of him, and his ribs felt sore, as if they had been bruised. It hurt him to breathe. He went down to the water's edge to take a calming drink and try to settle his nerves. Jon was right. He knew that with certainty.

Frankly, Dorfuss had begun to wonder if the whole running away thing had been a good idea. He was fearful for all of their safety. However, he did not voice his opinion, afraid of making the kids upset all over again. Instead he turned and addressed all three of the children. "Well, you know, the only option we have for the rest of the night is to stay here. I will keep watch. I am too wide awake now to do anything else! Jon, the best thing you could do is make this fire as large as possible. That will be the only thing that will keep creatures of that size at bay. I will awaken you now and then to add more firewood."

Eventually the children all calmed sufficiently to attempt a return to sleep, with Dorfuss's watchful eye always over them. When the children were sleeping, in the dead of the nighttime the red glowing eyes returned, as if they waited for something. Dorfuss stood and brazenly swatted at the wraith. He glared at the red eyes with fierce, glowing green ones in return. Eventually the evil apparition hissed in frustration and finally faded from view.

THAMES FULTON

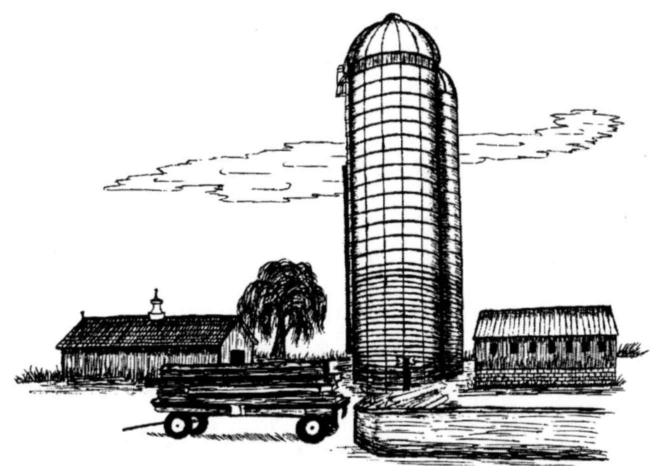

Hilda Walters was working busily at the library the very next day. Out of the blue, Thames Fulton reappeared at the library's front desk, which proudly displayed a nameplate proclaiming, *Miss Walters, Librarian*. Hilda was nowhere in sight.

She was preoccupied, going through the library's books studiously, checking to see which ones had not been checked out for long periods of time. She also was sorting through more popular but worn editions to decide which ones might need replacing in the not too distant future.

Always one to be prepared, she knew the attractive salesman should be due to make an appearance for book orders again within a couple of weeks. Best then to begin the arduous task of carefully going through all of the books so she could better get her order put together.

Worries about the children's disappearance nagged at her while she continued to work, but here at the library, it was a different world, her world. She put them from her mind as best as she could.

She did feel vaguely guilty for their obvious actions and knew deep within she had been the sole reason for them. But it was a relief in many ways not to be burdened by the little brats at the same time. Still, she felt she should keep working on her spells in order to persuade them to return. She had after all reached a small level of victory.

Earlier that morning, as she gazed into her magical ball while preparing for work, she observed vicious, doglike forms near a campfire. *Does that mean that the children have been attacked? I only wish I knew!* She waved her hands frantically over it for minutes longer. The confounded orb gave her nothing more after that brief vision, and she became angry when it refused to divulge anything further.

A part of her wished the children would never return, and another part of her wished that they would so she could at least pretend to Thames she made a loving maternal substitute. They had been gone more than four days, however. The uneasy thought they might never return nagged at her viciously. She still worried intensely that even though she did not know him well yet, Thames might find out and be repelled by her. She had already found herself obsessing over him on more than one occasion.

Hilda was way in the back of the library, contemplating the lousy job she had done caring for the children and the ineffectiveness of her spells, in a small, musty-smelling room where discarded books ended up until they were sold at the annual town bazaar in the fall.

Suddenly, through her distracted concentration, a boisterous and friendly-sounding hello rang out. She had believed she was all alone in the large building. That particular day had been especially slow, hence her decision to begin her annual purging and replacing of the library's inventory.

Swiftly, she strode to the front of the library to find herself astonished anew at the sight of the handsome, familiar salesman. She quickly sifted through her memory, trying to determine just how many weeks had passed since this object of her obsession took her order last month. *Why, it hasn't even been quite three weeks!* she realized.

"Well, hello!" she greeted him, so astonished at his early materialization that she temporarily forgot her shyness.

"And a cheerful hello to you too, young lady!" Thames Fulton greeted her, his blue eyes twinkling merrily.

Hilda drew in a sharp intake of her breath. *Young lady?* she thought! She actually caught herself smiling back and then quickly composed herself, not wishing to appear schoolgirlish. Yet she could barely contain her excitement. There was just something about his crooked, handsome grin and the crinkle of crow's feet around his eyes when he smiled that made her want to swoon. *Why, I have never been so overcome by anyone in my life!*

Then her shyness began to return as she brushed off her somber dress and ran her hand over her hair in a vain attempt to smooth it. The back room *was* rather dusty, and she had no idea just how unkempt her appearance was at the moment. Finally, she mustered up the courage to continue their conversation. Hopefully she would be able to keep him in her company for as long as possible.

"So, what brings you to this neck of the woods so soon?" she asked him politely.

Thames chuckled and rather apologetically told her, "Well, I know I *am* rather early for the month. I received your entire order already and felt you would be thrilled to have it delivered early. I do hope this is convenient for you."

Not wanting him to leave, Hilda agreeably replied, "Oh, yes sir. That would be wonderful! It's just that I was way in the back of the library in one of the storerooms sorting through books, and I probably look a mess." She laughed nervously, fingering an errant strand of hair, then recovered. "So you already have all of my new orders? What a pleasant surprise!"

Since Hilda's spell for endowing herself with the gift of eloquent speech had been unsuccessful those few weeks ago, she was poring over books on the subject in her spare time at the library. She often had a lot of free time here since this was such a small town. She felt her studies had been at least moderately advantageous.

"Well then, if you wish, I will go outside and retrieve the boxes containing your orders. I shall return momentarily," Thames replied. With a quick nod and lopsided grin, he headed toward the glass doors.

While he was busy outside unloading her order from the trunk of his car, Hilda remained for a short time behind her desk, completely lost as to what to do. Then she began to pace nervously. *What an incredibly handsome man! Mmm, mmm, mmm!* Involuntarily, she blushed. All at once, the question of what she must look like again popped into her mind.

With haste, she strode into the small ladies' powder room toward the back of the library and flicked on the light. She peered into the tiny, time-worn mirror over the old pedestal sink. There were a few smudges of dust on her face, and she quickly brushed them off. Her hair *was* slightly disarrayed with a few strands loose here and there in front of her ears forming soft, curling tendrils.

There was, however, no time to comb it all out and pin it carefully back up into its severe knot. In haste, she quickly wet her hands and was about to attempt to pat everything carefully into place. Suddenly it struck her that the loose strands added some femininity to her otherwise severe appearance. She changed her mind. This would just have to do, at least for now. *Perhaps I would be wise to consult the local beautician about a new and more feminine hairstyle*, she pondered for a moment.

She wiped her hands off on the tiny towel next to the sink and hurriedly made her way back to the front of the library. Just in time too, as Thames had a large stack of boxes waiting just outside the heavy doors. She would just have to help him by holding those doors open for him.

Gratefully, he returned just as she reached them, carrying the last few boxes. She opened the door quickly, and he brought the first batch in. She helped him with the rest of the boxes in the same manner.

"Thank you so very much, dear madam! You are so very kind!" he praised her, taking her blushing face in with what appeared to her to be not only gratefulness and admiration but *interest*.

Hilda blushed even more fully, if that were possible. She was not at all used to this kind of attention. She only hoped this dear man would be at least moderately understanding with her when she informed him she was not yet ready to place her next monthly order.

Once everything was inside, Hilda helped Mr. Fulton place all of the boxes on one of the large, heavy library tables. Then they proceeded to open them all up.

"Oh yes!" she responded in delight while examining each and every new book. "How very lovely!" she exclaimed at one volume in particular. It was a gardener's delight of horticulture containing virtually hundreds of brilliantly colored photographs with various types of flowers of each and every imaginable variety known to exist.

Thames continued to attentively cut the boxes open, finally reaching the last of them.

In particular, Hilda observed there was one small package he had taken care to place off to the side several times while the larger boxes had been opened. He then carefully opened that one, handing a small, exquisite, leather-bound volume of poetry to her hesitantly. Hilda watched him raptly. *Why, the man almost appears to be just as shy as I feel at this moment! What could have brought that on?* she wondered in amazement as she reached for the offered book.

"Dear madam," he then said to her, uncertainly, "I do hope that you will not object, but I have a gift here for you. I also hope I do not seem too forward and you will accept my meager offering. I did so *very* much enjoy our last visit and am obliged that you were not upset with me when I came in the place of your former salesman. Some of my other new customers have not been as eager to embrace the burden of working with someone new. People come to depend upon seeing the same friendly face month after month and year after year and do not always trust newcomers. I am so happy you accepted me so easily. Last month, you placed the biggest order I took in for the entire month! This is my thanks to you."

"Oh, don't be silly, Mr. Fulton. You are by no means a burden!" she returned delightedly, blushing again like a teenager. She examined the charming volume of poetry, carefully flipping through the brand new pages. "My, my, this is *exquisite*!" she concluded with awe, speaking softly and then, with a shy smile, nervously making eye contact with him.

"I only hope *you* will be patient with *me.* I am not yet ready with this next month's orders. Actually, I was just beginning to compile a list today, which is the reason for my appearance, but it will not be ready for probably a week and a half! I do hope you are not too upset."

"Why, no, not at all, dear lady, and there is certainly nothing wrong with your appearance! I hope you will accept my offered gift. You seem to me to be a woman that admires quality things and also one that would appreciate the gentleness of poetry. Am I correct in my assumption?"

"Yes, and I will accept your gift!" Hilda finally replied. She had always enjoyed the peacefulness of poetry, and this volume appeared to contain some *love* poems. She hoped his only purpose was not trying to butter her up for another large order. With his easy access to purchasing books, most likely at a hefty discount, poetry books such as this one were probably a dime a dozen for a salesman. And perhaps he *was* only a slick, polished salesman. Hilda did have to be careful with the money she was allotted each month for new orders. After all, last month, she had spent approximately two months' worth of her allowance from the village hall.

Both of them seemed to lose the ability to speak for a moment. They both gazed into each other's eyes, dumbfounded temporarily. Finally, Mr. Fulton recovered while Hilda felt as if she would faint. She was in love—no ifs, ands, or buts about it.

"I do hope you will call me Thames, Miss Walters," he then offered with uncertainty. "I also hope you will enjoy your new book of poetry. If you don't mind my asking, what is *your* first name?" he inquired, glancing pointedly at the plaque bearing the name *Miss Walters* on her desk.

Hilda stammered, her mind racing for a moment as she collected her thoughts. *Why, what is my first name, anyway?* she wondered wildly before it finally came to her. "Hilda," she managed, shaking her head a bit to clear it of its fog. "Hilda Walters!" she added more assuredly.

"Well, Hilda Walters, would you consider joining me for lunch at the nearby diner on this fine day?" Thames grinned shyly.

Hilda stared at him in wonder and disbelief.

"I would be so very honored!" he continued, even more uncertainly than before and a bit more quietly.

Hilda couldn't believe her ears. *This lovely man is asking me to accompany him to lunch! In a public place!* Why, she was certain to be the gossip of the entire town with a development such as this. Everyone in town knew her, or rather of her, since she wasn't overly friendly. They also knew she was a spinster, always had been, and probably always would be. To be seen in public with a handsome man such as Thames—why, it was almost unimaginable! She wasn't sure she would know how to behave properly. She certainly didn't want to end up being an embarrassment to the poor man, or herself, for that matter.

Yet if she refused his generous suggestion, she would have only herself to blame when her life continued on in the same boring, lonely vein it always had before. *Is that what I want?* Until Thames had made his appearance in her life, she had always thought so, having grown complacent with what was, but now she was no longer sure. After all, being in his presence was so very thrilling that to refuse this generous offer right now would be to certainly condemn herself to her usual life of empty bitterness and regret.

Suddenly, she just knew she would have to bite the bullet, overcome her shyness of men and public places, and take him up on his offer. And so, trembling from head to toe, she appreciatively and nervously replied, "Yes, Mr. Fulton, I too would be quite honored!"

They walked together the two blocks down to the only restaurant in town, past the quaint, shady park and a few small businesses, chatting about nothing in particular along the way. Hilda was beginning to find Thames very easy to talk to.

Ethel's Diner was very tiny, with just one long countertop containing a row of dining stools lined up along the customer side and half a dozen small tables with chairs surrounding them just past. Since it was the only eating establishment for miles, evenings and weekends could be fairly busy. Right then, however, the place was nearly deserted, except for one lone waitress, a cook somewhere in the back, and a couple of elderly gentlemen enjoying their daily lunch together there. They peered at the odd couple as they were seated through inquisitive eyes and thick glasses.

Nonetheless, to Hilda, the whole town might as well have been present, as she was certain the gossip would immediately start to fly. By nightfall, if not before, everyone in the area would know she had been seen dining with a handsome stranger. The thought of it all made her so nervous that she contemplated bolting.

However, she managed to contain herself as she and Thames subsequently made small talk. The waitress brought them glasses of water, took their orders, and hovered nosily, finally disappearing. After she had gone in the back, presumably to place their order, Hilda wondered repeatedly just what she had ordered anyway.

Soon their soup and sandwiches arrived. Thames asked Hilda all about herself. Nervously, she filled him in on the bland details. Her life had not been much, she reflected. No men, no husband, no children. Her entire adult life had consisted of briefly attending a small women's college and then becoming the town librarian.

She told him of her tiny house in town, her beloved antiques, and of her brother's passing and how she had been taking care of her nephews and niece out on Ralph's farm. She mentioned she had never married due to the slim selection in the area, which in many ways seemed plausible to Thames. She did not remark, however, on the fact that Ralph's children were missing.

Other than that, she did not participate in town activities and did not attend church. Therefore, she had no activities or hobbies outside of her librarian work to tell this wonderful man about. All she could think about was what a dear man Thames was, feigning interest in her obviously empty and boring life. And she was not about to tell him of her interest in witchcraft. Suddenly, just the thought of having delved into something such as that made her blush with shame. Thankfully, Thames probably just thought she was blushing at him.

After a nervous pause, they went on to discuss Thames and his life. His had been an active, full one in comparison to hers. He too had attended college and graduated with honors in Ames and also been married once. He had met his wife, who had worked as a teacher, in college. He was now a relatively recent widower of less than two years, had adored his wife, and had three grown children and several grandchildren to boot. Hilda was practically beside herself with glee at this new revelation but contained it well. Not only was this dear man exceedingly attractive, he was also exceedingly available and letting her know it!

His life was still full; he saw his children often and adored his grandchildren, who called him Gramps. Hilda had to chuckle a little. Thames seemed so youthful to her that it was difficult to imagine him as a grandpa. He seemed glad to hear about her caring for her deceased brother's children. He complimented her on having taken on such a monumental task on her own and told her he was glad to know she enjoyed children. She did not comment about her actual dislike of the little absent vixens. Reflecting on them while Thames continued to speak, however, she realized she had never really even taken the time to get to know them.

Before either of them knew it, they had consumed their meals. Then both were left aimlessly sipping away at rather unwanted cups of coffee. Neither of them wished for the conversation to end just yet. However, eventually their conversation did begin to wear thin, mostly due to Hilda's nervousness.

Finally, she looked at her watch and suggested it was time for her to return to the library in case any patrons had shown up in her absence. The morning had been so slow, however, she doubted to herself that anyone had come by during the lunch hour.

So Thames paid for their meals while Hilda stood next to him and blushed repeatedly, wishing she had discovered the magic that could cause her to disappear at will. The waitress observed the pair of them openly. Thames, noticing the waitress's unusual interest in the two of them, was nonetheless gracious, handing the unduly curious woman two dollars for her *extraordinarily* attentive service, which he pointed out with emphasis while thanking her.

The waitress actually had the grace to appear embarrassed at the indicative comment. *Certainly, the minute we are out of sight that twit will pick up the telephone and begin spreading the unusual sighting of Hilda Walters—with a man, no less—all over town,* Hilda worried.

Back at the library, Hilda took Thames's offered hand as he bade her farewell with a promise to return within the next two weeks for her order. He reassured her it would be absolutely no trouble for him to do so. "I only live in Des Moines, you know!" he reminded her.

When their hands touched, that warm current of electricity passed between them, momentarily catching Hilda completely off guard. She stammered and fussed and probably looked totally ridiculous as she told him goodbye in turn. Completely astonished at this new turn of events, she waved briefly as he backed away in his car. Then hastily, she made a mad dash into the library, heading for the comfort and safety and nothingness of the empty building and her equally empty life. It *was* what she knew, after all.

A Town by the River's Edge

In the forest the next morning, the children awakened to the cheerful melody of birds heralding the new day. The sun was shining brightly. The menacing sounds and shadows that encompassed the area throughout the hours of darkness had disappeared, along with the frightening coyotes. The children felt completely safe now that a new day had presented itself.

Dorfuss did not mention the glowing eyes he had witnessed in the darkest hours of the last couple nights. After the fright the coyotes posed, he did not want to worry the children any further. He had never gone back to sleep after the beasts had run off. He knew his uneasiness would continue to haunt his heart for hours that day.

He resumed his position on the log overhanging the stream and performed his magic of obtaining food for the small group while Jon added more wood to the smoldering fire. Dorfuss was not really com-

fortable with his magical gift but decided that as long as he used it only for the good of the children, he would accept it for what it was.

James and Jenna searched nearby for additional wood to cook their breakfast with. The fish were active at this time of the morning. Soon Dorfuss snared four relatively good-sized ones for their breakfast. Once, he actually fell into the water when he narrowly missed a quick one while the children laughed at his predicament.

Undaunted, he held his fanged face high, taking his place on his perch once more, dripping away and ignoring their teasing laughter. He vigorously shook the water off his long, luxurious fur. The children all knew cats did not like to get wet, and his pride was injured. Perhaps it was due to his anxiety about their safety from the malicious spirits that had presented themselves several times on this journey. *The children have no idea just what I am going through, after all!* He had already lost three of his nine lives since all of this started and did not wish to shorten his lifespan any further! He also felt an incredible responsibility to them all and their deceased father. *If I die, what will happen to them? Will they be safe? Will they ever reach their destination?*

He remembered again the dying man from his dreams, the children's father. The children's safety had been their father's parting wish. Jon seemed to be fairly adept at survival, but he was, after all, not even fourteen yet. And the children, having been raised in such a remote, quaint existence all of their lives, were so innocent. They had absolutely no perception of the evil that existed in this world or its abundance.

Within minutes of his unplanned dip in the cold, rushing water, Dorfuss snagged two more fish with his hooklike claws. He carried them in his teeth over to Jon, who was pleased to see them. Jon ruffled Dorfuss's tortoise-marked and still-damp fur in thanks and again let him choose his fish. After cleaning, he and James and Jenna held the fish over the flames, two each pierced through forked sticks, and they turned their bounty occasionally as they roasted.

When the cooking was complete, they ravenously consumed their delicious breakfast in minutes, sharing the spoils. All three of them thanked Dorfuss for all of the food he had provided for them.

While they ate, Jon secretly contemplated that if it were not for the cat and his atypical magic, they probably would all have starved by now and instead been meals themselves for the coyotes. He shuddered again at the fresh memory and resolved to see all of them out of the woods as quickly as possible. He also decided it would be prudent to keep an eye on their wonderful and very helpful feline friend.

Afterward, within a short time, camp was torn down. The fire had mostly burnt itself out. Jon ground the embers around with his shoes, scattering them into the dirt and extinguishing them the best he could.

Soon they were all on their way.

The day wore on. Jon and Dorfuss both decided it would be a good idea to stay with the stream and perhaps follow it to an area town. Many towns existed along waterways. No more coyotes or other threatening beasts made appearances, thankfully. After a while, the children became encouraged by the cheerfulness of the day. At some points, the woods appeared to be thinning out; then they would return to thick forest.

As they hiked along, the stream began to widen. Afternoon approached, and the children and Dorfuss all were becoming hungry. No wild animals were in sight, however, and once more, the woods appeared to be thinning out. They kept going, encouraging each other. Eventually they decided to take a cooling break by the water's edge on the hill leading down to the water. As they sat by the rushing water, they thought they heard something. It almost sounded to them as if people were conversing nearby.

Dorfuss looked around, always uneasy. Something did *seem* different, as if civilization were approaching. Perhaps there were people nearby! He began to investigate, sniffing the ground thoroughly.

The noise appeared to emanate from behind a large rock, only a few feet up the embankment, he deduced as he sniffed the ground for clues. Dorfuss jumped up onto the rock and gazed downward.

Near the base of it, in a loamy spot that looked to him to always be shady, were dozens of large, moving, dome-shaped mushrooms. They were all endowed with faces and appeared to be arguing with each other. They also resembled the horrid Aunt Hilda! Then they noticed the furry cat peering at them.

"Hey, what do you want?" one of them demanded rudely. "And why are you nosing into our business anyway? Gerdo here keeps looking at me, and I told him to stop! Now, *you're* looking at me! I want *you* to stop! Stay away from our rock!" the mouthy one insisted. "Go home!"

Dorfuss stammered in bewilderment, never having encountered talking mushrooms, or speaking plants of any kind for that matter, before. However, he remembered the dreadful events involving trees in recent days that were still fresh in his memory.

The children, in their curiosity, joined him and were equally astonished by the odd, chattering fungi. Finally, in a moment of pure genius, Dorfuss asked the toadstools, "Would you perhaps have directions to the nearest town or know how far away one might be?"

It was the mushrooms' turn to look astounded. They began to gossip loudly amongst themselves in wonder, talking ever louder over each other while the children and Dorfuss gazed on in amusement. Likewise, the curious fungi had never heard of talking cats!

Finally, another of them spoke, saying, "Just keep following the stream for only a few more miles! Civilization is not far away!" Then the mushrooms resumed their arguing, bending to and fro from their stems attached firmly to the ground. They banged their silly heads against each other, as if fighting. Malodorous gases appeared to escape the rounded heads, leaving a weird, greenish aura surrounding them.

Jon looked at Dorfuss, about to laugh. "We haven't had lunch yet!" he suggested to the cat very loudly so the mushrooms could hear. "Maybe we should just eat these great big, juicy-looking mushrooms here!"

James and Jenna began to giggle as they peered at the comical sight.

"No!" the toadstools all exclaimed in fear, cowering as they bent toward the ground yet ineffectual at their efforts to disappear.

"We are poisonous! Anyone who eats us will die!" the mouthy one asserted. "Who wants to be first? I hereby offer to the first one bold enough to ascertain what I say is true, my neighbor Gerdo here!"

"Hey!" the mushroom referred to as Gerdo retorted angrily. "Speak for yourself!" He angrily flailed his puffy mushroom head at his neighbor, bumping into him firmly. Green fumes radiated from the irritated visage in a cloudy poof.

"Do you mind?" his boisterous neighbor questioned him in mounting rage. "Give me some space, would ya?" Back and forth the angry heads bent, twisted, and clubbed at each other. Effluvium burst in greenish billows into the surrounding air.

Dorfuss just shook his head. Something *did* smell odd, and it also was beginning to make him feel sleepy at the same time. "Well, kids," he finally said with an exaggerated yawn, "we should all be on our way."

The children all chuckled agreeably and followed Dorfuss up the hill. They began making their way throughout the mossy woods once more. They hadn't gotten far, however, when they realized they were all were feeling tired even though they had just rested.

Jenna was the first to succumb to the poisonous gases the mushrooms had emitted. Rubbing her eyes and making them terribly red, she quickly became whiny and informed her wayward group she needed a nap right then.

"No, Jenna! A town is nearby! We need to be on our way!" Jon told her firmly, and then he himself began to yawn widely. Turning around to ascertain just where Dorfuss and James were, he observed with astonishment them both already lying on the ground where they had only been standing just moments before, snoring away with their mouths agape. Then it was *his* turn to black out.

The children and Dorfuss experienced restless, haunted dreams while they slept off the poisonous gases. They flailed about in their sleep while the daylight dappled gently onto their unaware faces in the filtered sunlight streaming through the tall trees. Precious time was being wasted while they were oblivious to everything around them.

Eventually, however, the poison they had all inhaled finally began to wear off, and Jon, being the largest of the group, awakened first.

He shivered as he stood and stretched, uncertain for a few moments of his whereabouts or circumstances. Then he remembered the mushrooms. He surveyed James, Jenna, and Dorfuss lying nearby, themselves just beginning to regain consciousness. James let out a moan, and Jenna rubbed at her eyes. Dorfuss began rolling from side to side, and then finally he stood, tottering, and shook himself off. He stretched a long, feline stretch, accompanied by a huge, buck-fanged yawn.

He was not at all inclined to spend another night and waste even more time in these frightening woods. Unsavory spirits and odd dangers seemed to be pursuing them all, and he longed to see a return to civilization. His mind felt thick and hazy, as if he had been drugged.

It wasn't long before James and Jenna rose also, feeling similarly groggy. Dorfuss staggered as he attempted to overcome whatever poisonous fumes the mushrooms had secreted. If anything, he had gotten the worst of it, since he had stood closer to them than the children had. He was smaller than them too and would naturally be affected to a greater degree than the children because of his size. His eyes were crossed worse than usual, and he went about blinking in an attempt to regain his focus. His ever present fangs sparkled in the sunlight that dappled onto the ground through the tall trees.

Jenna reached down and patted him on the head, asking him, "Are you all right, Dorfuss? You look awfully woozy!"

Dorfuss shook his head in an attempt to clear the murky fog from it. "Yes," he said finally, reassuring her, "I will be okay. However, I really should do something about those insidious mushrooms back by that rock! I certainly wouldn't want them to spread or affect anyone else!"

Dorfuss headed back over with care to the large rock where the cluster of mushrooms resided. As he neared, he could hear the puffy heads arguing again. *Or perhaps still*, he mused silently. The

children began to follow him over there, and Dorfuss hesitated. He warned them to keep their distance this time so as not to re-succumb to the same fate. They listened, agreeing with their protector, and remained at a safe distance. Dorfuss approached the poisonous mushrooms, began to purr, crooked his tail, and aimed his paw at the unfortunate fungi.

"Go away! Leave us alone!" the mushrooms bellowed with obvious fear while they bent and twisted and stretched wildly in a futile attempt to escape the cat's magical wrath. "We possess better magic than you!" they claimed, still arguing and fussing the entire time and bopping against each other.

"Stop that, Gerdo!"

"No, you stop it, you idiot!"

"Get out of my space. Leave me alone!"

"Owww!"

Dorfuss wanted to chuckle at the ridiculous scene playing out before him but felt it prudent not to remain. Once more, a virulent green vapor began to form over the evil-infested toadstool heads. *Perhaps this little comedy routine of theirs is their way of persuading their victims to remain long enough to be affected by their venomous vapors!* he decided. Dorfuss just shook his head. His eyes glowed brightly green. Then he waved his paw over the cluster of ridiculous fungi and popped them like bubbles, watching as one by one, they burst and quickly shrank, screaming in vain protest the entire time. A stinky green cloud that previously hung over the evil parasites vanished in a *poof*. And then they were all gone.

The children were appreciative yet had to laugh a little at the silliness of the talking mushrooms. Jenna asked Dorfuss if he had ever seen talking mushrooms before, and he only shook his head and told her no. He knew they were most likely the result of more of Hilda's perverted magic. He only hoped that none of Hilda's rather terrifying Pandora's box escapees would prove to be deadly to their tiny group.

Only about an hour later, a rather large, worn-out-looking building appeared in the distance. Finally they reached it, only to discover that it was a shed containing dry-rotted, stacked lumber. One side of it was covered with a vegetative patch that appeared to be moving.

"Careful, guys, this is poison ivy," Dorfuss warned. "It also appears to have been enchanted by our nemesis, the wicked Hilda." The little group expediently moved back and away from it as long tentacles of the bright green vines reached toward them futilely. Despite the ominous poison ivy, the ramshackle building was an encouraging development, as it could only mean they must be approaching a town or even city.

James was walking just behind the rest of them. Suddenly, he vanished. It took Jon only a moment or so to realize he didn't know just where his little brother had gone off to. In fright, he began calling for James. Then Jenna and Dorfuss, both equally afraid, also began calling James's name. The little group backtracked. Muffled noises could be heard coming from somewhere deep within the ground.

"Here, Jon! Over here!" Dorfuss prodded, discovering first where James was by making use of his keen, feline sense of sound. He splayed his claws and frantically began tearing away at the long grass from a particular area on the ground, finally revealing a gaping hole deep in the grass, approximately a foot wide.

Then he leaned his furry head down in, calling for James. Without the long grass muffling James's replies and calls for help, they were easier to hear.

"What happened, Dorfuss?" both Jenna and Jon frantically inquired.

"I believe there is an old water cistern underneath the ground here, children. It would make sense!" Dorfuss said, glancing toward the lumber shed just a short distance away. "James has fallen inside! We must do something quickly to get him out!"

Jon began searching the ground in a frenzy, looking for a long branch or something else sturdy that might be used to pull James back up to safety. Nothing! Nearby, he noticed, stood an old metal water pump. *That certainly will be of no help*! "Dorfuss, what are we going to do?" he yelled.

About ten feet below the ground, James was submerged to his chest in cold, fetid-smelling water. He splashed about and hollered in the dimness, struggling vainly to climb up the slippery, mildew-covered sides. Then he slipped right back in. He could see Dorfuss above, clinging to the earth at the yawning opening, calling to him with equal agitation.

Up on the ground, Jenna and Jon frantically continued to search for something they could use to pull their brother out of what most certainly would become his watery grave without some kind of miracle.

Jon finally made his way over to the lumber shed. He peered into the shadows within. Miracle of all miracles, there were several ancient, large coils of rope hanging high up against the back walls above the stacked lumber. After climbing up onto the large boards quickly, he retrieved one of them. Vines of moving poison ivy reached toward him, grasping at the air. He did the best he could to avoid it, but the rope was heavy, and he struggled with it. The vines brushed up against one of his arms just as he began to back away. Jon barely noticed them. *If I get poison ivy, I'll just have to deal with it later*, he figured.

He made his way back over to the spot Dorfuss still marked with his furry little body, continuing to hover over the gaping hole. The cat spoke to James in a reassuring voice while the boy remained splashing agitatedly deep inside, crying out to all of them. Dorfuss promised they would all help him get out. Jenna stood nearby, crying and worrying.

Inside the cistern, James became increasingly terrified, for up in the darkest corner, two vermilion eyes had appeared, and they beamed evilly at him. "Dorfuss!" James yelled then. "Get me out of here! There are two really scary eyes in here watching me! *Get me out of here!*"

Jon successfully managed to tie one end of the rope up into a large loop. He tested it the best he could for strength. He did not notice the red, blistered welts that were beginning to form where he had brushed up against the poison ivy. Then he proceeded to lower the heavy loop into the well while Dorfuss continued to urge James to calm down. Next, Jon left a few feet of slack and wrapped the other end of the rope around the rusty pump, several feet away from the hole. It had proved to be helpful after all. "Jenna," he implored, "hold onto this and stand on this end of the rope so that it doesn't come unwrapped. We need to get James out of there!"

Jenna hastily complied while grasping onto the small metal structure. Her face was streaked with dirt and tears. Jon lowered the rope even more. Finally, the loop of the rope reached James, who grasped onto it thankfully.

"James, put your legs through the rope, and we will try to lift you out! Let me know when you have them through!"

James was shivering from the coldness of the water and also sheer terror but finally managed to comply. "Okay, Jon," he called to his worried brother with a quivering voice. "I'm ready now. Please hurry and get me out of here; these eyes are hissing at me now!" Sure enough, in the darkness, they had approached him, glaring evilly. With obviously sinister intentions, they began emitting frightening, seething noises. Then they started to cackle at him in a low, victorious tone. Perversely, they circled the terrified, shaking boy.

Dorfuss, from his vantage point at the mouth of the hole, witnessed the awful happenings for himself. He began to become angry. *I am fed up with this magic of Hilda's*, he thought, disgusted. In the shadowy cavern, James still dangled precariously from the rope, nearly frightened out of his skin, while sinister eyes continued homing in on the terrorized boy, snickering and screeching with insanity. Dorfuss had seen enough.

As Jon and Jenna watched on up above, Dorfuss once again began to rumble loudly. The children were familiar by now with this precursor to their cat's initiation of the wondrous magic he possessed. A nimbus encircled his furry body. His eyes began to glow brightly green. He crooked his tail and pointed his paw at the evil eyes.

Down below, the horrifying eyes realized their impending fate. Too late, they screamed, "Nooooooo," as almost instantly, they erupted into sparks and burst into two tiny balls of flame. Like whirling dervishes, they spun and then sputtered. In seconds, the flames of the evil spirit had burnt out, never to terrify another living soul again.

"Hurry, Jon," Dorfuss urged. "Pull your brother up to safety!"

It was no easy task, but once James had settled down, Jon began using all of his weight, leaning backward in order to propel his brother back toward the surface of the ground. Dorfuss joined in, sinking his claws into the heavy fiber and ground. Jenna remained on the other end of the rope, keeping it firmly in place. She still looked terrified but stayed at her post, willing James to make his appearance above ground soon.

Unfortunately, the combined strength of Jon and Dorfuss was not quite enough. Jon finally called down to James. "You're going to have to climb up the rope yourself, James; we are not strong enough! We'll keep holding the rope steady. If there was enough room for you to fall in, you should be able to crawl back out just fine! When we can reach you, we will help pull you out!" Jon deftly took the slack of the rope and wound it around the metal water pump.

James heard his brother up above. He was now most of the way out of the water, but still, he continued to swing precariously while his lower legs hung in it. Many times over the years, James realized, he had climbed the rope leading to the hayloft in their barn for fun. Relief passed over him then. He knew he could do it. Slowly, he shimmied his way up the thick rope. Finally, he reached the grassy edge. Grasping onto the surface with his hands, he kept his legs firmly twined around the rope.

Jon ran to the edge of the hole while Dorfuss and his sister stayed put a few moments longer, keeping the rope in place. Leaning down with a helping hand, James's hand grasped onto Jon's extended one. Relief flooded everyone's hearts simultaneously as Jon finally pulled his brother to safety.

All was well again for the moment.

Everyone sat in the cool grass a safe distance from the old cistern in relief, recovering from agitated breathing and the terror they all felt.

James viewed the rest of his party through tear-streaked eyes and a dirt-stained face. As his breath resumed a more normal pace, he glanced gratefully at all of them. "Thanks, guys. We make a great team!" he managed.

Jenna got up and went over to James and hugged him to herself with all of her tiny might. "James, thank goodness you're safe!" she exclaimed.

And everyone felt the same as she.

"Well, children," Dorfuss said, "we'd best be on our way. It is encouraging to have encountered a structure of some sort out here. I do believe if we resume our journey posthaste, it won't be long before we make our way out of this forest. And it won't be any too soon for me either!"

Revitalized by that prospect, the children all agreed. They began to pick up their pace as the forest continued to thin out. By now the stream had sufficiently widened to the point that it could probably be called a river. The water churned deeply, it appeared. They observed increasing areas of rapids, combined with small waterfalls within the water, as they traveled along.

Without realizing it, Jon began to rub at his arm often. It had begun to itch just terribly.

The little group came to a cluster of blue flowers waving strangely back and forth. There was no breeze. Jenna, marveling that their brilliant shade of blue was beautiful and so bright that it almost hurt her eyes to look at them, skipped her way over to the flowers to observe them. As she approached the blooms, lovely, surreal-sounding voices could be heard singing and beckoning to her softly.

Dorfuss was lagging behind the group, staying alert in case any more underground traps lurked below the vegetation on the ground. When he noticed Jenna dash ahead, he became alarmed. "Jenna," he warned, "get away from those! Flowers do not sing, just as mushrooms do not talk! It can only be another poisonous, evil trap! Apparently, your aunt Hilda has been very busy on this particular day!"

Immediately, Jenna's eyes became filled with fright. She realized Dorfuss had to be right. She dashed back toward the safety of her family just as a weird, purple haze began to develop and loom over the blooms.

Back at Dorfuss's side, she gasped in astonishment. She was glad she had escaped the poisonous cluster of blooms before they caused her any harm. "Oh, thank you, Dorfuss! It's just that they were so very pretty!" she said apologetically.

"See, dear girl, it is best to stay away from unusual things no matter how enchanting they might be! We have *most definitely* discovered that on our journey! Stick close to us, for it is the only safe way. After all, sweet child, if James had been any greater distance behind us earlier, we might never have discovered him," Dorfuss admonished her gently.

The small group pressed forward on its journey as the afternoon began to wane. Jon's poor arm became seriously swollen, and the itching was beginning to drive him crazy. Finally, he loudly complained about it. Dorfuss took a look at it.

"What have you gotten into, dear boy?" he asked Jon.

"Oh, it's probably nothing, Dorfuss. Remember the poison ivy back on the lumber shed?" he asked as a wave of nausea struck him. "Well, when I found that coil of rope, I couldn't avoid it. It was almost as if it were reaching for me! But I've had poison ivy before, and it never showed up this fast, nor did it move and try to grab me on its own! And, my stomach is beginning to hurt really bad too."

"Yes, I remember now," Dorfuss replied to Jon. "Let me try to help you."

Dorfuss announced to their whole party that it was time to take a break, and they all sank to the cool ground to rest. Jon's legs had become shaky in just mere moments, and his stomach contracted with pain.

Dorfuss stood next to Jon, whose skin was beginning to turn positively green. And, of course, he began purring loudly and raised his large paw just over Jon's arm. Jon was feeling extremely ill. His stomach began to lurch and roll violently.

Dorfuss crooked his tail, and while he observed Jon's affliction with glowing green eyes and pointed his furry tail and paw at the large, nasty-looking welts, they swiftly began to shrink and fade away. Jon was left with a mild aftereffect of tiredness, but he had been miraculously healed. He glanced at Dorfuss with pure appreciation.

"Thanks, Dorfuss. I don't think I would have been able to go on much longer." He patted the proud feline on the head.

They all rested for a brief while more. Swiftly, Jon began to recover; just as quickly as the poisonous illness had stolen over him, it was gone. *No doubt haggy old Broom Hilda's been up to her tricks again,* he mused.

Soon the group of children and their cat resumed trudging through the forest. Eventually a large water tower could be viewed hovering tall above the trees. The children gasped. Dorfuss did too, and everyone became excited. If there was a water tower only a short way off, that meant there was certainly a town nearby! There just had to be!

They began to run toward it, thrilled. Soon they were all out of the forest. Directly in front of them sat a winding gravel road. A one-lane bridge spanned a relatively wide branch of the river just up the road, certainly leading to somewhere. A large, grassy area loomed off to the side of it. It was obviously a small park lying on the outskirts of whatever town they had reached. A short distance away and over the stream nearer to the river, a large, old stone railroad bridge hovered over the waterway. It stood high and was attractively arched underneath. The fork of the stream connecting to the river could be viewed sparkling below, running merrily through it.

Near the stream that threaded its way along the edge of the park, there waited a large, welcoming pavilion. Half a dozen picnic tables sat under its beckoning shade. Not far from the pavilion stood several stationary grills. "One of those just might come in handy later," Dorfuss offhandedly pointed out. Several more picnic tables were scattered around the open grounds.

A small, push-type merry-go-round, a couple of seesaws, and a large swing set lay within shouting distance of the pavilion. Behind the swings, there was a large sandbox area. Not far off, a baseball diamond was situated with two small sets of bleachers behind the batting cage.

The little group had indeed reached civilization!

The gravel road wound its way along the edge of the park and led uphill in the direction of the water tower. Closer to the tower, a fair-sized flagstone building stood; it was presumably part of the water works.

No other people were in sight. Everyone in the little group was exhausted. It was late afternoon. For a bit, they merely sat in fatigued joy in the shade of the pavilion, collecting their thoughts.

Jon suggested to no one in particular that when they finished resting, they should see where the gravel road might lead. The bounty from their three piggy banks was still hidden safely in his pocket. He was hopeful they would come upon a small store or restaurant where they could either purchase themselves a decent meal or some supplies of food at the very least.

After discussing this all, they decided it would be easiest to stash their duffel and sleeping bags under some large bushes up near the bridge while they explored the area. Hopefully up at the top of the hill, they would soon come across a town. Then they could search for some means of obtaining food.

Dorfuss broke away from the group to survey the cool, refreshing water, lap some up, and look for fish also. Here, in the smaller stream, the pickings looked small and probably not worth his effort to catch. However, the river ran just past the bridge and around the bend. He made a mental note to check it out when they came back this way to retrieve their belongings later. The pavilion, after all, would at least provide a roof over their heads during the night in case of rain.

Soon everyone was rested sufficiently enough to feel ready to traverse the gravel road and discover whatever might lie ahead. They resumed walking, climbing the slight incline leading up to what they all hoped was a town. Soon houses began to come into view. The sounds of children happily playing outside in the beautiful day were abundant. The first houses they came upon were near the railroad tracks—just small bungalows. Some looked timeworn. But as they trudged along, the houses became larger and finer. Some very elegant Victorians finally made an appearance. They were large and graceful with big, beautiful, well-tended yards and gardens.

Soon, they could see what appeared to be a business district in the not-too-far-off distance. As they neared it, it became obvious this was the town's tiny downtown area, much like the one they had known back home in Laurel. And, much to their relief, there was not only a small-town diner but also a mercantile! Along with that existed a used furniture, clothing, and whatnot store and a small gas station. Next to the gas station, there sat a small bank. Other than two cars at the gas station and one in front of the diner, the quaint downtown appeared to be mostly deserted. At the gas station, a customer came out the front door, got into his car, got the motor started up and rumbling, and drove off.

In front of the bank, there was a small park bench. Jon motioned the small group over to it, where they sat while he removed their money from his pocket so he could count it out. Now was the time for them to make some major decisions. They would have to spend what little they had wisely, which, for them, probably meant eating at the diner was not an option.

He discussed this carefully with Dorfuss and also his sister and brother, who all came to the same conclusion. They all felt the wisest thing would be purchasing food at the mercantile. They would buy easy items that could be used to prepare sandwiches and the like and some fruit and maybe some cookies and crackers for snacks. Items such as those would be just like what they had started their journey with and should keep for a couple of days and transport well. Hopefully they would continue to be able to supplement these staples with Dorfuss's help when he performed his useful magic, snaring wild game and fish for them all to cook up. So far, their appetites had been satisfied relatively well.

Before going into the tiny store, Dorfuss made an announcement. He held his head high, tail erect, and body proud. "I just wish to suggest that we take care not to be noticed too much now that we are in public and in plain view! After all, if someone happens to recognize us or has heard the story of three missing children and their cat, they could become suspicious and notify the police! Then we would most definitely be shipped back to Laurel and, inevitably, Horrible Hilda the Hun! After everything that woman has put us through, especially this past day, certainly none of you wishes for that!"

The children had not thought of that, perceiving they were safe from scrutiny now that they were so many miles from home. Dorfuss estimated they had probably traveled thirty-five to forty miles. But they agreed with him, not wishing to face the wrath of Broom Hilda in the event they were discovered and forced to return to their home.

And so when they entered the tiny mercantile, the two boys conducted their business as efficiently as possible. Quickly, they selected a few items, paid for them, and left the store. Dorfuss remained outside on the bench across the street with Jenna, waiting for them.

Briefly, they wandered around the small town afterward to see what other undiscovered things it might have to offer. Other than more houses, a skating rink, a cluster of large grain silos, and a couple small factories, there didn't appear to be too much in the area. So they ventured back down to the park below the water tower, using it as their compass to make their way back. They looked forward to eating at the waiting picnic tables and perhaps taking shelter there for the night. It was quiet, away from curious human eyes, and seemed to be their best prospect.

By then it was early evening. Back at the farm, Hilda went about surveying the events of the children's day through her glass gazing ball, still hoping for clues to their whereabouts. With envy, she observed Dorfuss *speaking* with some magical mushrooms she had conjured up to halt their journey! The foolish fungus had seemed bent on fumigating the hapless party with poisonous gases, following her orders. *But how is it that I am only moderately successful with my magic when that ridiculous cat seems to be so lucky with his? And how on earth has he procured the gift of speech, and seemingly eloquent and articulate speech at that?*

Then suddenly it occurred to her. Why, when that dullard cat snuck his way into her room the evening of the Fourth of July, he made a mess of all of her liquids, powders, and other ghoulish accoutrements. And her spell book *had* been opened to that spell on acquiring the gift of eloquent speech! She remembered now. She had wanted to impress Thames. That had to be it! That was the spell she had worked on so vainly just before the blasted cat broke into her room. Somehow he had found just the right formula by hapless accident, which was something she had never been able to accomplish, even with precise written instructions!

Soon the lustrous orb revealed to her the dreadful scene involving James's fall into an ancient cistern. *Certainly, I did nothing to cause that!* she reflected. However, this was a curious and rather encouraging new development. Hilda grinned wickedly with anticipation. If James was currently trapped, why then, all of their little group would be forced to stay put! She continued to gaze into her magical ball's depths only to become discouraged as the scene progressed. Of all things, she was astounded to witness Dorfuss vaporize an evil spirit threatening the younger boy while he was trapped! *Why, that confounded cat actually destroyed one of my subservient minions! How dare he!*

Her dowager's hump was beginning to ache from the continued strain of leaning forward to view the events of the day. She tilted her wretched head this way and that to relieve the stress and aching muscles in her neck. Grossly irritated, Hilda continued to watch just a few minutes longer in the hopes the glowing orb would reveal more of its secrets.

She began to become frustrated. How dare the preposterous cat! All of her hard work and the long, wasted hours of concentration, not to mention the expense required for accumulating all of the necessary items to conjure up her spells. And just to have a stupid, nosy cat, in a skittish frenzy, ruin everything for her and accomplish magic for *himself* instead! He had broken her first magical ball that night also, releasing all of the evil spirits she had been so close to enslaving as *her* minions. *Why, who knows what other special powers that preposterous ball of fur might now possess?*

It wasn't fair! Why didn't anything ever turn out in her favor? Oh, why?

She rubbed at her sore neck for long moments with her skinny fingers. In a mood of defeat, she plopped her generous derriere on her bed roughly. The mattress groaned under the sudden, straining weight, squeaking loudly in protest. Hilda took one last glance at her table of corrupt equipment and observed her three small bats hanging upside down in a tiny, covered fish aquarium. They slept peacefully with not a care in the world. She plunked her face into her downy pillow and began howling with despair. *If only I had not a care in the world!*

How disgusting! A dunderhead cat had been able to accomplish what even she, an extremely intelligent human being, had not! And she had thus far not been successful in convincing the children to return home. Would she ever be? With tear-filled eyes, Hilda began pummeling her pillow. She vowed she would somehow get even with the ridiculous-looking feline.

Evening approached in the quaint little park. The children talked cheerfully while making up a stack of sandwiches and setting out apples and cookies. Then they stashed the remainder of their food in the shade on the hill with their other possessions. And it was a good thing they did so, for while they sat eating, people suddenly began showing up at the park. It wasn't long before it became obvious to the children and their cat that a little league game was going to be taking place there that very evening. The quiet gravel road became busy with cars. Dust was raised as their owners slowly rolled along the gravel road, searching for a close place to park. Children on bicycles showed up, as well as many pedestrians. The tiny park began to become noisy.

Soon lots of families were present. Many children ran around, taking turns playing on the swings and merry-go-round and see-saws. It really was a nice little nook, a delightful combination of both nature and family-oriented park. Nearby at the stream, a couple of teenage boys settled on the grass with fishing rods and bait, apparently uninterested in viewing their little brothers' game.

Jon expressed concern to Dorfuss as the crowd began to grow that perhaps they would be recognized by someone. Dorfuss surveyed the entire scene. He decided the children should have no trouble whatsoever blending into the rest of the families with children as long as they appeared to fit in. And it wasn't long before a cute blonde girl, approximately the same age as Jenna, approached her and asked her to play. Giggling, the two girls headed in the direction of the swing sets.

Jon and James decided to go watch the baseball game. Dorfuss was eager to escape the noise and haphazardly scampering children's feet. He went to go rest in the same bushes up near the bridge where the children had stashed their supplies. He *was* tired from his overall lack of sleep. He knew the children should remain safe enough for the time being with all of the cheerful families around. This would be as good of an opportunity as any for him to catch up on some much-needed shut-eye.

The little league game really turned into a fun game to watch. The score remained close for the majority of the time it ran. Near the end, the team that had lagged in score for the entire game suddenly began to catch up. Everyone began to cheer wildly. Jon and James rooted for the underdog, and when the game was finished, they had won!

Afterward, it wasn't long before families began packing up their lawn chairs, blankets, and other items they had brought along. Nor was it long before all of the cars parked along the roadside began to disappear. Dusk was rapidly approaching. The three children who remained waited quietly in the pavilion until all of the vehicles and other people were gone. Then they retrieved their duffel bags and sleeping bags and began to settle in for the night. Dorfuss awoke from his snooze, came out of his protected hiding place, and joined them. It had been a long and trying day, and they were exhausted. Their baths would have to wait until morning.

The picnic tables were hard, but while the game had still been in full swing, the children noticed clouds moving in across the sky. Dorfuss also saw the gathering darkness of the clouds drifting in. Everyone decided it would be best for each of them to choose a table in case it chose to rain. That way, they would all be up off the ground, and their sleeping bags and other personal items would remain dry. They took care to place their duffel bags on top of one of the left-over tables.

It turned out to be a good thing they had such foresight. During the night, a steady, calm rain did develop. The little group, however, remained safe and dry under the shelter of the large roof of the pavilion.

By morning, the rain had nearly ceased and was reduced to only a light mist. The temperature also dropped considerably during the night.

Again that morning, Dorfuss volunteered to attempt to catch more fish for their breakfast. The children eagerly agreed. They were helpful in their own way, contributing too, each of them picking up small bits of firewood in the brush skirting the railroad tracks. They planned to make use of one of the park grills if Dorfuss was successful.

Presently, Dorfuss disappeared as the sun began to emerge. With it, warm rays of sunlight shone upon them brightly, indicating it wouldn't be long before the day turned into a scorcher. With Dorfuss off hopefully finding them their breakfast, they decided it would be wise to take turns bathing while the others searched for firewood for the grill.

Soon Dorfuss returned with five fish of an acceptable size, looking very pleased with himself. The children were appreciative and patted their beloved cat on the head and ruffled his fur while he purred. In the end, it really didn't matter what they ate as long as their stomachs were full and their thirst satisfied. The stream took care of that for them.

When they began to pack up their items, Dorfuss pointed out that during the night a train had stopped up on the bridge. The children had seen it there already but hadn't thought too much about it. Their only concern was that someone might notice them all alone down in the park. Yet they had not encountered any other people since last evening. They all glanced upward at the bridge again now. Smack dab in the center of the bridge and in the middle of a long string of cars sat what appeared to be an empty boxcar with its doors thrown wide open.

Dorfuss announced, to no one in particular, that now that their breakfast was over with, he was going to investigate!

While he was gone, the children finished packing. No one at all happened by while they gathered their belongings. Since the town was so small and their travels through the forest had taken up a good deal of time, there was no good reason for the children to stay. It was time to be on their way toward Aunt Ruth's. At least at this small, unknown place, they had been able to replenish their food supplies for a time, gotten a good night's rest, and eaten their fill of a delicious breakfast. They were just finishing up with bathing and packing when Dorfuss reappeared, looking satisfied with his furry self.

"That boxcar up there on the bridge is indeed empty except for a couple large mounds of straw!" he proclaimed, his furry countenance held high. "And, the train is pointing in the proper direction that we wish to go! It is my belief we would be wise to attempt to hitch a ride on it! After all, we could all use some rest, and certainly this would help cut our travel time much shorter! We have food supplies now, thus eliminating for the time being anyway, the need for me to hunt for small wildlife or for us to have to explore other options! Well, what do you say?"

Happily, all three children began jumping up and down with delight. Dorfuss jumped proudly up onto the picnic tabletop between them all and strutted back and forth in a self-indulging manner with his buck-fanged head held high. He was so very taken with his own intelligence and innovation at the moment that he neglected to pay attention to just where the tabletop ended. He slipped and clumsily fell off. With typical feline recovery, he landed on all fours, appearing embarrassed. The children could do nothing but laugh at the silly cat's antics. Jenna picked poor Dorfuss up and hugged him to her. He instantly began purring loudly, his gawkiness and chagrin of just moments before totally forgotten.

"Well, what do you all say then?" he questioned between his loud rumblings.

Jenna placed him carefully back down on the ground and ruffled his fuzzy head one last time. Then all three children looked at one another and Dorfuss and exclaimed, "Let's go!"

With anticipation, they grabbed their belongings and began to make their way up the steep hill leading to the tracks. Luckily, there were plenty of small tree trunks and branches of bushes to grab hold of to ease the steep and rather difficult upward hike. Soon they were scrambling safely to the inside of the boxcar. They got themselves comfortably situated in the ends of the car, away from the doors. Now, they only had to wait for the train to begin to move.

Unfortunately, being at the whim of the train's conductor and also the train's schedule, it was several hours before the train resumed its journey. Presumably, several cars at the far end were being loaded with goods down at one of the small town's factories or perhaps the grain silos. Periodic clanking noises could be vaguely heard in the distance. Once in a while, the boxcar they waited in lurched a bit. Finally, slowly, the train began to creak, and then ultimately it began to roll along the tracks. In a few miles, its speed had picked up. Eventually it was rolling along at a comfortable pace.

The breeze wafted through the open doors, which everyone took care to stay a safe distance from. Jon tested the doors, and they moved open and closed with ease. If the weather became cooler or the rain started up again, and also probably during the night, he knew they should close them at least most of the way, which he wisely suggested. But for the time being, it just felt good for all of them to sit back on their unrolled sleeping bags in the soft straw. It was welcoming to relax and enjoy the fresh air and their effortless travel for whatever time the steadily rolling train provided. Hopefully they would reach Davenport sometime soon!

The landscape was interesting and colorful. They watched it pass by while sitting inside the boxcar, chatting amiably and enjoying a picnic lunch of sandwiches, apples, and cookies.

Jenna lay with Dorfuss on her unrolled sleeping bag. As miles passed, everyone inside the boxcar began to grow sleepy with the constant lulling motion of the train. It was good to know they were all safe and would be able to cut a good deal of time off their arduous trip. Dorfuss felt he had adequately met all his requirements thus far and was reassured the children were being well cared for. Their pappa would have been proud!

ON THE WRONG COURSE

Afternoon eventually passed into evening. Again, for their suppertime, the children assembled sandwiches and supplemented them with apples and cookies. Jenna gave Dorfuss a few slices of lunchmeat to munch on. The train was plodding along at a steady but relatively slow pace. Just when it began to pick up to a fair speed, it would slow, coming to numerous stops in various small towns. Then they would all be delayed for a time, as the conveyance was presumably loaded up or unloaded with more goods from other factories.

With the small group so tired from their long travels on foot over the last several days, they were content to doze and let the train do its work in guiding them to their destination. Their empty boxcar remained ignored by the train staff, being so close to the end of the long string of cars. No one discovered them.

In the late afternoon, dark clouds rolled in, blocking the sun out

and making the time of day seem later than normal. Eventually, after they were done eating, it began to rain, and Jon rose and pulled the train car doors shut most of the way in order to keep the moisture out.

Dorfuss was exhausted, not only from all of their travels on foot, but also his accepted but added burden of responsibility over the children. It felt so good to relax and enjoy the smooth, lulling ride the train provided and lie in the comfortable straw in the car and doze with Jenna at his side.

Unfortunately for him and the children also, he did not realize the train began to change its course. Instead of heading east, which it originally had been traveling when they left the quaint park near the river, it slowly shifted direction and now was heading north.

No one noticed the change of course. And so, unknowingly, the little group huddled in the train car unwittingly as it plodded along.

Darkness was approaching. After they finished eating their picnic supper, Jon opened the door on one side of the car and gazed out at the dreary scene passing by before him. The rain was coming down heavily and only green, rolling countryside could be seen. It all looked pretty much the same as the rest of Iowa, Jon reflected as, in the distance, fields and farms passed them by, one by one. He watched as an old-fashioned covered bridge came into view and then soon disappeared from sight.

From time to time, they continued to pass by or through a small town only to have it quickly disappear. Finally, the train seemed to be finished with its numerous stops for loading. Hopefully they would reach Davenport or someplace near it soon and the train would come to a stop so they could all disembark. For now, however, they would have to be patient.

Nighttime fell. Not knowing how much farther the train would take them, Dorfuss suggested it would be best for everyone to permanently settle in for the night. No one had a problem with that. They were already sleepy. When the motion of the train ceased, surely they would awaken. Then they could easily pack up their few things and resume their travel on foot. Jon only hoped they would not have to walk terribly far on foot in the dark before finding safe shelter.

Dorfuss awoke in the middle of the night, dreaming that his fur was becoming wet. He experienced an odd sense that something was out of sorts, and he was being watched. He stood and stretched long and shook himself, feeling vaguely disoriented at their change in surroundings and the vibrating, constant motion of the train. Something really did not feel right to him.

He looked around in the darkness of the train car. He noticed one of the cars' doors was open wider than Jon had left it earlier. No wonder he was getting wet! Perhaps one of the children had risen sometime during the night and opened it. Just then, near to the open door, over in the corner in the darkness, something began to glow eerily red. A single eyeball hovered aloft in the blackness. *And here I thought I had taken care of those nasty things once and for all!* Closer to Dorfuss it began to move with an odd, questioning look about it.

The fur on the back of Dorfuss's neck stood up straight in response, and his tail puffed out hugely. Out of instinct, Dorfuss began swatting at the vaporous apparition, which seemed unruffled when presented with the cat's razor-sharp claws.

Finally, with a look of what Dorfuss perceived to be defeat, the lone eye began to fade. It blinked and floated its way toward the car door that remained wide open. Dorfuss pursued it, resolving to chase it away once and for all. He began hissing angrily and swatting vainly, feeling vaguely victorious at the wraith's apparently easy surrender. Then he began to purr loudly and crooked his tail. Without warning, the train car door slid open even farther, seemingly of its own volition, as the glowing eyeball hovered next to it. Near the doorway, the floor was wet. As he began to raise his telltale paw toward the menacing eye and continued to move cautiously toward it, Dorfuss slipped and suddenly lost his balance on the wooden floor. His back quickly hydroplaned. The vermilion eye evaporated.

Dorfuss screeched out an astonished, "Meeeoooowwww!" His body skidded and went into a wild tailspin. Before he was even aware of what happened, he was hanging precariously by his two front paws and protruding claws while his backside dangled and swung over the moving railroad tracks. He glanced down with terror-filled eyes. The tracks were passing under him swiftly and menacingly! His suspended body was pelted fiercely by large plops of cold rain. The radiating eye reappeared and hovered near Dorfuss's own, again with a questioning look. Then it faded away into the rain and mist outside.

Jon and James both awakened at Dorfuss's startled cry. They quickly darted over to the open car door. There, Dorfuss was frantically attempting to scramble back up into the train car but without success. Soaked to the bone, he again attempted to propel his large feline body back up into the moving car, only to have his rear feet slip and fall and resume dangling.

Dangerously, he was clinging to life by only one sharply clawed paw. Yet he managed to keep his composure, cautioning Jon, who was leaning toward the unfortunate cat with an outstretched hand. "Careful, Jon. Do not stand on the wet floor! Lie flat and then grab hold of me! James, lie on the dry part of the floor and then hold onto your brother's legs! Quickly!" Dorfuss finally managed to anchor his other paw into the wet wooden plank again.

Dorfuss gasped for breath from his exertion and terror. Lives four and then five were passing before his very eyes as yet again he almost lost his grip. *I must not leave the children! It is not yet time! I have not delivered them to safety!* Desperately, the cat clung to life with his claws as Jon lowered himself carefully to the floor of the train car, and James stabilized Jon by holding on firmly to his feet.

Laying flat on his stomach, Jon reached out to grip the wet cat under its two front legs. "There, Dorfuss, you're safe! Now push with your back legs as I raise you up! I have you, and I won't let go. I promise!" Victory was evident in his voice.

Dorfuss scrambled madly with his drenched back legs as Jon began to raise the heavy cat up and back into the safety of the train car. In moments, Dorfuss was back inside, panting raggedly from the fright of his close calls with death.

By then, of course, all the commotion had woken Jenna, who scrambled to her feet just in time to see Jon and James safely haul her beloved puddy back into the train car. "Oh my gosh!" she worried. "What happened?"

Jon and James glanced at each other with questioning eyes. Neither of them was sure what had possessed Dorfuss to get so close to the open door in the first place, or how the door had opened so widely, for that matter.

Finally, Dorfuss settled down enough to explain to them what had happened. Quickly, Jenna stooped and picked up her beloved cat, holding him close to her and ignoring his wetness. She took him over to her warm, waiting spot on the straw and began to pet him. She reached into one of the duffel bags and drew out a towel and began to dry him off, speaking soothingly to him as he relaxed and eventually began to purr loudly. After time, everyone drifted back off to sleep.

Throughout the night, however, Dorfuss slept restlessly. Images of evil crimson eyes haunted his dreams, along with the vague, lingering premonition of doom he could not quite put his paw on. Something was not right. He could feel it.

Several times during the night, Jenna awoke to find her cat flailing about next to her in his sleep, apparently reenacting his earlier nightmare in his dreams. Each time, she drew him to her, held him close, and spoke reassuring words to him in a whisper. And each time, he relaxed and returned to soothing, welcome slumber.

Back at the Walters farm, in her garret of debauchery, Hilda gazed into her magical ball. She observed a freight train and, in the darkness of a boxcar, a glowing vermilion eye. It seemed to see her also through the magical conveyance, staring brightly and appearing to bore directly into her soul. It approached her within the orb, stared menacingly, hissed loudly, and then disappeared from view.

On her side of the glass, she experienced a frigid chill traveling up her spine. She started at the vicious apparition's apparent threat toward her and backed away from its glowing radiance with her heart pounding wildly. It spoke to her within her mind. *You will never be my master,* it taunted.

Attempting to shake away her feeling of apprehension, she absently wondered, *Where are Ralph's children anyway*? Obviously they were on a train, but where? And where could they be headed?

Then shrugging her shoulders and dismissing the thought of the abhorrent imps and the evil lurking in her room, her foreboding suddenly vanished, and she conceived a sudden and new inspirational thought. Within her twisted mind, she was not aware of her own deepening corruption. Her distinction between good and evil had nearly slipped away. *That eye was calling to me, inviting me to join it, not threatening me!* she assured herself. *I must make use of this apparition and turn it into my slave!*

Her heart swelling with hope at the perceived invitation, she leaned over her spell book and paged her way to a chapter called *Conjuring up Evil Spirits: The Art and Ultimate Mastery Over Them.* As she gazed upon the timeworn pages with deep concentration, she was unaware that her own eyes also reflected an evil, glowing red light.

In the early morning, the children and their cat awoke to the screeching of metal wheels as the train engineer far ahead of them pressed on the brakes. The train began to slow, and in his eagerness, Jon rose and pulled one of the doors wide open to look out. They were approaching a large town; he could see it in the distance. Excitedly, he encouraged everyone to hurry, and they began to pack up their things so they could disembark quickly when the train came to a stop. Not only were they eager to complete their journey finally, but they did not wish for their stowaway status to be discovered.

None of them had any idea how far they had traveled since the day before, but they were sure it had been a great distance, as they had been rolling along at a fairly steady pace throughout the night.

The rain had let up overnight. With the brand new morning, there were just lingering, thick clouds. Hopefully they would dissipate as the day advanced.

The train chugged slowly to a stop. The children finished rolling up their sleeping bags and gathering all of their items together while

Dorfuss hopped gratefully down onto the still earth. His frightening experience of the night before lingered in his mind, and he was very glad to be on all fours on solid ground.

He sniffed about on the dirt while he waited for the children to join him. Something didn't smell right. Soon they were at his side. Dorfuss gazed around, taking in the large city before them. Something still seemed out of sorts, but he wasn't sure just what it was. Hopefully they had reached Davenport, and it would simply be a matter of how many miles or perhaps only blocks they would need to walk to find their aunt Ruth's house. Then the children would be safe to live their lives out happily ever after, and his mission would be accomplished. But what was the gnawing sense telling him something was terribly wrong?

He shook it off, thinking he was worrying foolishly. He was certain the stress of their adventure had begun to take its toll. The little group began to venture out of the large rail yard they had ended up in, situated on the outskirts of the city. Rows upon rows of trains stood on rows upon rows of tracks. Some of them crawled along slowly, emitting chugging noises, clinks, and loud groans as they moved backward or forward while cars were added or removed. Apparently this was not only a train station but a switching hub as well. It was a noisy place indeed.

Soon the children were running along excitedly with Dorfuss following closely behind. They neared the edge of the rail yard. The loud whistle of a nearby train sounded, frightening them all. They ran around the end of yet another long stationary train and right into the path of a swiftly oncoming engine the unmanned train had blocked from their view.

Again the whistle sounded loudly as the train engineer abruptly viewed three children and a cat crossing tracks not twenty feet in front of him. Quickly, the children scurried across, barely escaping the large engine's front scoop. The left metal wheel of the train barely missed the cat. As the large scoop moved over Dorfuss, he could feel the vacuum emanating from the rapidly turning wheel as it passed just a hair's breadth from the end of his tail. A powerful, suctioning vortex attempted to pull him in, nearly successfully.

Dorfuss's adrenaline kicked in at the last possible safe instant, and he screeched and sprinted in terror away from the rapidly moving engine. Life number six disappeared swiftly as he dashed madly away from the large, moving conveyance in wide-eyed countenance. *I do not like trains*—of this he was now extremely convinced!

"Well, it's best we all get away from here!" Jon exclaimed with relief after observing Dorfuss's near-fatal encounter. "Dorfuss, you have had too many close calls with trains for my comfort!"

Dorfuss only glared at Jon. *What does Jon mean anyway, for* his *comfort? What about my comfort!* He had almost forgotten what comfort felt like anymore. *But, after all*, he reflected, *this was all my idea!* He had suggested their train ride yesterday and even this trip itself days ago, so he really had no one to blame but himself.

Well, best to put it out of his mind now that he nearly had the children delivered to safety. And certainly once they got to Aunt Ruth's any expenditure of his remaining lives should be totally unnecessary.

Finally, they reached a chain link fence and walked along its length until they found an opening. Then, after climbing a hill, they reached a street and headed upward into the large city that lay in wait not far off. They had nearly reached their destination and suddenly were all in a joyous mood. Soon they were crossing a large bridge spanning a wide body of water.

Cheerfully, Jenna began to skip alongside the prancing Dorfuss, watching the huge river flow past underneath them all, on its way to some unknown place. Finally, having reached the other side of the large expanse, suddenly all three children and the cat stopped dead in their tracks. Directly in front of them, next to the road, stood a large sign proclaiming the city name of Waterloo! Underneath it, a smaller sign said, *Cedar Falls, eight miles*. They were not in Davenport at all!

Shocked, they stood helplessly, gazing up at the sign. Their hearts fell. Waterloo! A waterloo indeed! Where on earth had they ended up, anyway? Dorfuss stood silently staring at the sign with abject hopelessness. So that was what had been subconsciously nagging at him for hours. The last twenty-four hours had been entirely wasted, and there they all were, miles and miles northwest of their destination. Rather than head straight toward Davenport as they had hoped, their hapless group had been thrown at least a hundred miles off course and were nearly as far away from their destination this day as they had been six days ago! With the clouds covering the sun yesterday evening and obscuring the moon all throughout the dark night, there had been no certain way to determine which way the train was traveling. Even right then, the clouds hovered thickly above them, blocking out the sun and almost seeming to laugh at the tragic four.

Dejectedly, they hung their heads as they made their way into the hustle and bustle of Waterloo. They would have to replenish their stock of food, which was nearly gone. By the time they came across a store and purchased food and ate, they would have lost at least a couple more hours! They would also be required to spend extra money on food. All of their troubles up to now had been for nothing!

Silently, they walked on, each with his or her pensive thoughts as they mulled over the past six days and all of the treacherous moments they had survived. Would they ever make it to their destination, or would fate intervene and finally extinguish them all? Would Hilda's evil unleashed spirits be successful and capture them all somehow or send them to some incomprehensible doom?

Or, even worse, would they be recognized by someone, discovered, and sent back to the corruption and rage of Aunt Hilda herself? That, perhaps, could be a fate even worse than death, they realized. And so they plodded forward, knowing that to give up would only mean a return to their former precarious situation with the delirious Broom Hilda.

The Bewitched Garden

Days passed with the children and their cat stopping briefly here and there in tiny towns along the way. The hapless group was now traveling southeast. They had their daily routine down to a science: get up early, travel until midafternoon when the heat was most intense, and then find a place to settle down for the night. There, they would make a fire, cook their food, bathe, prepare for bed, rise early again the next day, and repeat the cycle all over.

The Iowa landscape was rolling and unchanging. Here and there, they passed farmhouses sitting way up from the roads on hilltops. They traveled past green, grassy fields full of grazing cows mooing softly as they fed. They traversed lovely old covered bridges now and then, totally oblivious to their antiquated beauty.

Occasionally, a tractor or car approached. The children took cover in the fields until the vehicle was safely out of sight. Eventually, the vehicle lumbered slowly past, finally disappearing on the

endless gravel roads. With the typical dust raised on the dried-out roads, approaching cars could be viewed from miles away, and it was easy enough to take cover before the unfortunate foursome could be discovered by a passing motorist.

The weather since they left Waterloo had been dry and hot, typical of late July. There had not been a drop of rain since the day of their fateful ride on the train. Even with the lack of ground moisture, however, the humidity in the air was so thick each day that one could practically slice it with a knife.

By then, everything they did seemed rote, and the children, resigned to their fate and despondent, barely spoke to each other anymore. Even Dorfuss seemed depressed, rarely conversing with them, feeling guilty about their misadventure involving the train. Now their journey would certainly take at least a week and a half longer than it might have had the train been destined for Davenport.

From time to time, their group reached tiny towns along the way, replenished their food supplies, then were on their way soon enough. And so it went for many days and nights while they made their way to Aunt Ruth and what they hoped would be safety at last.

Luckily for the entire group, Dorfuss was successful in magically obtaining abundant wildlife for many of their meals, helping them stretch their dwindling supply of money. And with the dry spell, they didn't need any shelter from the weather. They didn't experience any further encounters with large, fearsome wildlife either.

However, there were plenty of other terrifying episodes all along the way. Hilda had been very thorough. Very late one dark night, a swarm of angry bats pummeled them all, awakening them in fright as they lay sleeping under several trees that formed a protective grove near a pasture.

The creatures hissed angrily upon discovering the strange beings amidst their habitat. They awakened the children and Dorfuss from sound sleep.

The fearsome bats screamed and hissed angrily and glared treacherously at the little group with glowing purple, unseeing eyes. They darted swiftly here and there, smacking headlong into all of them, using their speedy wings and radar senses in the dark. Poor Jenna was terrified when one of the creatures became temporarily tangled in her hair, causing her to scream out shrilly.

Finally, the triumphant Dorfuss intervened, wielding his razor-sharp claws at a particularly malevolent but small cluster. He injured a couple of them badly enough to instill fear into their tiny hearts and send them scurrying aloft into the safety of the trees above.

Jenna underwent such a fright from the bat attack that even many nights later she experienced trouble settling down to sleep. As they traveled along, there were many additional scary episodes involving screaming trees and objects with Hildegard Walters-type faces.

Back at the Walters farm, Hilda had not yet given up on her magical ventures. She still was attempting to work her wiles with the evil spirits within her new magical ball. Yet there persisted that annoying little voice at the back of her mind. It told her in no uncertain terms that Thames Fulton would never approve if he discovered the evil into which she had attempted to delve. *Oh, how would he ever find out?* Hilda pondered and then snorted.

Then too she was becoming increasingly distraught over the reality of the children's disappearance. *Not because I miss the three brats! It's just that they have been missing for some time now! What has become of them? And what if Thames were to find out they have run away from me?* She was experiencing qualms over that. He may have heard about the whole thing already and put two and two together. *I simply cannot allow that to happen!* This had all become a terrible quandary.

She was still furious about the ridiculous feline's unexpected but undeniable success with *her* magic. She knew the children had taken the disgusting beast with them and that he was implementing her sorcery for the greater good of the small group. *Well, good riddance in regards to the wretched cat at least! I'm glad the idiotic furball is gone from the farm! After all, who needs him anyway?* But what about the children? Without them here at her side, she would likely never have the opportunity to convince Thames how motherly she could be! There would be no one to demonstrate that falsehood with.

If only she felt more adept at dealing with children. But to Hilda, they were as foreign as men had always been. She had always been such a loner. Finally, she dismissed all of her worries, resolving to not let them get the better of her. *To heck with the children! If they don't want to be with me, who am I to change things?* Why would she want to anyway? She preferred the peace and quiet they had gifted her with these past couple of weeks. *I also don't care what Thames thinks!*

The image of the beloved Thames once again appeared in her mind. *Oh, Thames!* She *did* care! She had glanced at the calendar at the library earlier in the day and knew he was due to return to take her new order soon! *I can hardly wait!*

If only *she* could accomplish something of worth with all of this nonsense. Sure, she had managed to frighten the children and their dunderheaded feline a time or two. But it had just not been enough.

Yet somehow the insipid articles called to her even then. She gave in to the incessant, harping voices in her mentality and stooped low over the table, her dowager's hump protruding rudely.

She reread the chapter named *Conjuring up Evil Spirits: The Art and Ultimate Mastery Over Them.* Feeling certain of her knowledge of the spell's instructions afterward, she glanced deeply into her magical ball. It sat looking dusty and forgotten on her table of useless witchcraft items. Without warning, it began to glow, as if it sensed her renewed interest. Hilda moved closer and dusted the glass exterior off and then peered once more into its murky depths.

Eventually, deep inside, there materialized the vision of the three children and their flea-bitten cat walking along a small-town street. Soon the little group chanced upon an enchanting Victorian home and paused to gaze at its welcome gardens. This home in particular stood out. It was slightly larger than the rest and Victorian in its styling. It was graced with a small wraparound porch and beautiful gardens all throughout its picture-perfect yard. Hanging pots in the shade of the welcoming porch overflowed with brightly colored flowers.

Hilda seized her moment, willing the spirits within the ball to beckon the children into what she hoped to turn into a corrupt, spirit-infested trap with the spell that lay before her. Wildly, she waved her spindly fingers over the orb as she chanted a demonic verse loudly over and over several times.

Jon, James, Jenna and Dorfuss had just stopped at the nearby general store to replenish their sandwich supplies and other staples they'd relied on throughout their arduous excursion. They were all hungry.

No one appeared to be home in the park-like yard. The place seemed to call to them, so the children ventured cautiously into its welcoming shade, hoping for a few moments of respite from the intense heat of the day. It was dinnertime, and they were all hoping to find shelter or someplace private for the night ahead within the next couple hours.

In the very back portion of the yard and well away from the house, birds could be heard chirping serenely. The gardens were stunning. There, a tiny wishing well resided, surrounded by brightly colored flowers and a small stone path leading up to the well itself. Several butterflies floated blissfully and soundlessly over the cluster of brilliant blooms.

There was also a delightful stream at the back border of the yard, and it merrily sparkled and bubbled, creating a soothing sound as the water made its way to heaven knew where. Spanning the little stream was a small, arched stone bridge. An ornamental tree bent crookedly over the bridge, shading it with its thick leaves. Surrounding the area around the bridge were many colorful flower gardens with much delightful concrete statuary throughout.

Near the bridged garden stood an iridescent glass gazing ball perched on an ornate concrete pedestal. Jenna was immediately enchanted and stopped and peered into the glass, viewing her own reflection. It resembled a large bubble about to burst. She touched the delicate glass gently and then stood for long moments observing the reflections of everything surrounding it, including her own.

At the farm, Hilda became temporarily startled at the sudden vision of the precocious Jenna, who seemed to be gazing right out of her mystical orb at her! Entranced, the little girl whispered something, fingering the delicate glass again. A person with a softer heart than Hilda's might have felt a surge of love and adoration for the girl in that instant. She only experienced spite.

Why, there's that ludicrous cat again! Everyone appears to be safe. All three of the kids look a little worse for the wear, rather smudged and dirty, Hilda ruminated.

Not far from the children and cat, a Victorian-style birdhouse stood with many compartments for nests. Birds fluttered around it and chirped happily.

Jenna lost interest in the gazing ball and merrily skipped over to join her brothers as she heard them extracting their eating items from one of the duffel bags.

The children glanced once more up toward the beautiful house, hoping no one was at home to notice them trespassing. Things seemed very peaceful and quiet in the back of the yard, and they were some distance away from the lovely homestead. They began to settle themselves on the placid bridge. They set down their bags and were preparing to make sandwiches and remove their other food items and metal cup from one of the bags.

In Hilda's room, the picnic view faded and evil eyes and countenances returned. They could be viewed swimming around in the orb. They festered and taunted, becoming excitable. Hilda became consumed not only with their wantonness but also by rage. So eagerly did the spirits cry for their freedom that they began to pound furiously on the interior of the magical globe.

Obeying their unrestrained cries for liberation, Hilda resumed the wicked chant from the spell book. Soon her eyeballs began turning up into her head, and her body began deranged gyrations. She was a being possessed!

Shadows of murky apparitions began floating wispily through the glass, escaping the vitreous surface effortlessly. They surrounded and began to twirl around the wicked woman as she chanted away.

Hilda's view in the orb changed back to the charming picnic scene. She gazed at the image with resentment and hatred building inside her, like a volcano preparing to erupt. She abrasively screamed out the next wicked passage of the spell.

Suddenly, where the children were, the delightful birds ceased their cheery chirping. There was a dead silence. The butterflies on the flowers suddenly soared into the air and scattered. The atmosphere of the quaint area became thick with inexplicable corruptness. Then wild chaos broke loose.

Without warning, all the garden statues came to life. They ominously glared at the unwelcome trespassers with wicked, belligerent eyes. They moved toward the children with swift, angry steps.

"Trespassers!" the statues yelled while picking small sticks and other objects up off the ground and wielding them like weapons. An innocent-looking cherub held a small garden shovel, and a pixie-like elf the matching pronged rake. Their guileless appearances belied the hatred existing in their eyes. They marched headlong toward the group of children, who scurried as quickly as possible to repack their items before leaving.

The gazing ball in the garden began glowing oddly. Jenna, who only moments ago had been transfixed by the luminescent bubble of glass, noticed it first, and she whimpered and pointed shakily at the evolving scene inside. Within it there appeared two gleaming red eyes that seemed to bore directly into the children's very souls with their hatred. Hilda's angry, red-faced visage soon completed the picture as the vermilion eyeballs became her own. She cackled wickedly at them, a look of pleasure filling her demonic eyes. The children backed away, terribly afraid of the evil Hilda and wondering if she knew where they were.

One particularly large yard ornament had appeared to be an amiable-looking woodsman clutching an ax. He'd stood smiling placidly under a large, ancient oak. Violently and without warning, the newly possessed statue began swinging the concrete weapon wildly to and fro, heading straight for Dorfuss. The expression on its face changed from one of near laughter to complete, ugly loathing. With a powerful swing, the statue hefted the weapon directly at Dorfuss's neck, barely missing it and temporarily pinning the creature's fur instead to the ground. Dorfuss screeched and clawed ineffectively at the concrete woodsman. Then the contemptuous figure lifted the concrete ax crazily and swung it once more, nearly separating the poor cat from his tail as he struggled to dart away.

Hilda chortled evilly as she watched, willing the woodsman to kill the cat.

Dorfuss recovered swiftly after the seventh of his lives evaporated. In anger, he took off running swiftly after the insane statue, his claws and buck fangs bared, hissing. He swiped his menacing claws repeatedly at the representation. Summoning his magic, Dorfuss began to purr and raised his paw and crooked his tail. Sparkling cat hairs that must have numbered in the hundreds created a halo effect around the feline. His emerald eyes began to glow, and suddenly the statue's attitude changed. It screamed in fear and suddenly froze into position, ax held high, as if it had never moved.

Hilda pruned her lips and glared in dissatisfaction. The cat's magic had overruled her own! "I'll get you yet, you detestable ball of mange!" she shrieked at Dorfuss.

Having rendered it impotent, Dorfuss believed, he turned away from the concrete woodsman in an attempt to rejoin the children. He gazed with malevolence and hissed at the maniacal features of Hilda's within the gazing ball, baring a pawful of deadly claws. Mocking him, Hilda raised her gnarled, skinny fingers and hissed right back. She guffawed nastily at her recipient of spite, finding sick humor in taunting him. Then, the horrid woodsman again sprang to life and came after Dorfuss one more frightening time. He scampered away from it without delay, meowing loudly in distress.

The children finally had the last few of their items stuffed into one of the duffel bags. Before they even picked it up, troll-like gnomes began crawling out from underneath the bridge.

"Intruders!" the miniature forms screamed. The likenesses bent down and began picking up and hurling little round pebbles from the stream bed. They pelted the children and their unwelcome feline with the stinging rocks. Dorfuss returned protectively to their sides. All the while, the gnomes chanted angrily, "This yard is ours; you'll not get far! The stream that flows belongs to us!" Their eyes glowed red with seething hatred. More smooth pebbles flew the children's way.

Nearby, next to where Jon was putting the remainder of their possessions into one of the duffel bags, the concrete form of a coiled snake suddenly sprang to life. It hissed vilely and almost effortlessly moved toward them very rapidly, its forked tongue quivering menacingly.

Without preamble, while the statuary terrorized the children, those same forms seemed to gaze directly into Hilda's eyes through her bewitched ball in her sanctuary of doom. Their expressions were almost accusatory, as if to remind her, *Well, this was what you wanted, wasn't it? Your conscience has been blinded!* She could hear their evil voices within her mind. Her eyeballs rolled upward into her head. She was a being possessed. Hilda was unaware that the irises of her eyes had somehow changed when they resumed their normal positions in her eye sockets. They were now an insipid, grayish-white color. For just an instant, in her enmity, Hilda was momentarily blinded in sight, just as she already was in conscience.

The unfortunate group in the enchanted yard began to make its way as quickly as it possibly could out of there. They were almost home free, or so they thought. Just then, the back door of the house swung open suddenly, slapping against the side of the house. Out stepped a wizened, frightening old woman. She possessed wild eyes whose irises were so pale she appeared to be blind. Her white hair and clothing were in disarray. She was holding a broom, and she held it high above her head, shaking it insanely. It was as if the woman herself were now possessed by the horrific Broom Hilda.

The crazed woman screamed at the children wildly, "Noooo! Leave me alone! Stay away from my possessions!" She paused as if to hear instead of observe through her useless eyes whether the intruders in her garden had obeyed. Then, after somehow determining they were all still there, she resumed her crazy ranting. "Stay out of my things! You have no right to be here! Leave me alone! Trespassers! Trespassers! Wilbur, call the police!"

Hilda, over her table of magical accessories tore vainly at her eyes in an attempt to remove whatever evil force had temporarily gripped them. She screamed, "No! Leave me alone! Get out of here!" at whatever had transitorily possessed her vision. Then, with no explanation, her vision returned, clearer and more vivid than it had been in recent memory.

Dorfuss and the children were so terrified they literally flew out of the yard with their belongings in tow and down the hill toward the tiny stream. After all, the last thing they needed was attention from the police! Hilda gazed at the children's quandary through her magical orb via the garden gazing ball, smiling victoriously and shrieking wildly. The children could hear her horrid, maniacal laughter as they departed the bewitched garden. They pumped their legs as hard as they could, and soon they were well away from the frightening house with the magical yard, presuming falsely that everything would be okay down by the stream.

Suddenly, enraged faces materialized on the sides of the tree trunks, and the rocks on the ground formed infuriated visages of their own. Everything surrounding the frightened group began hollering and swaying wildly.

"Encroachers!" they too claimed. The terrified children and their startled cat wasted no time evacuating that place also. The group erratically ran on and on, struggling to catch their breaths. Behind them, seemingly endless screaming and haranguing continued. Ultimately, with the distance the little group finally managed to gain between them and the horrid place, the noises began fading away, much to everyone's relief.

While Hilda observed all of these marvelous new events taking place, deep within, she secretly laughed. She knew with certainty her magical powers were becoming stronger. She was particularly proud, realizing the children had observed her wicked face and evil merriment through the glass of the innocent-looking garden gazing ball. She congratulated herself as she cackled wickedly. The only irksome remnant was the knowledge that she had been unsuccessful in exterminating the vermin cat.

The loathsome corruptness was now at her command, waiting to receive further instruction and willing to be instructed fully in order to accomplish a Pandora's plethora of yet unknown, abhorrent, and insipid achievements.

Now, if only I can manage to make all of the spirits my subservient minions, then I will have complete power and rule over each and every one! She began to screech with joy at her marvelous achievement, laughing wildly and finally collapsing onto the bed beside her magical table. Turbulently, she flailed her limbs and body about in twisted, demented pleasure.

Her caterwauls of joy echoing from the house were so loud that Harvey Jensen, walking the grounds of the barnyard some distance away as he performed the nightly chores, paused to listen for a few moments. He shook his head in astonishment and perplexity. *Why, I can hear her plain as day through the open windows*! *What is wrong with that warped woman anyway*? He could see lights on inside and wondered for some time afterward just what the old harpy was up to in there. He had never liked the unattractive biddy much and only shook his head as he proceeded with the chores, choosing to mind his own business.

Eventually the unfortunate four put enough distance between themselves and the festering, magical place that they realized they were no longer within the town. Instead they found they had inadvertently ventured out into the middle of a large cornfield, tall with ripening corn.

Yet, the adrenaline rushing through their bodies still did not slow. Everyone in the group continued to run without direction into the vast cornfield. They became separated from one another in the process. Jenna's tiny legs wore out first. Gasping for breath so hard she felt her small lungs might burst, she finally collapsed onto the ground amongst the protective shade and welcoming peace of the tall corn. She huffed and puffed and allowed her breathing to return to normal. Beads of sweat streamed down her face while she waited for the others to join her, not realizing they were all well ahead of her.

Dorfuss, possessing the natural agility of felines, scampered into the towering corn in an entirely different direction, far ahead of the rest of the group. It seemed there for a bit that everywhere they turned, evil presented itself in the most startling and terrifying manner. The malevolent Hilda's face materializing and cackling at them from the iridescent gazing ball had frightened the daylights out of him. Even now, he was wary that something wicked would next materialize in the field of corn. So he continued to run. *No doubt we have just experienced Hilda's debauchery at its worst,* he surmised.

James ran out of steam next, but by the time he realized they had all become separated, he too was well apart from the rest of his group. Not knowing which direction to turn, he slowed to a walk to catch his breath.

Jon continued sprinting on his strong, swift legs, barely even noticing the tall stalks of corn. As he flew between the towering plants, the leaves brushed and slapped haphazardly against his face and arms, cutting him now and then as he ran swiftly between them. He barely noticed them at all. He kept running, foolishly hoping everyone else was keeping up.

He finally reached a large, grassy clearing. There, the breeze was wafting gently over a calm, prairie-type clearing. Off to one side, several ancient, scrubby trees were scattered about, providing a cooling shade. In the shade of one of the taller ones, a rickety old shed stood. Gratefully, Jon doubled over and stopped to catch his breath, his lungs feeling as if they were on fire. Presently, his breathing began to slow, and he stood and surveyed his surroundings more carefully.

And that was when he noticed the old, beaten-up tractor with connected, dilapidated wagon sitting at the edge of an apparent junk heap. They were most likely castoffs from whatever farm whose fields they were *now* trespassing on.

Inside her repulsive bedroom, the minuscule speck of reason Hilda still possessed began to condemn her deep within her mind. It pronounced its judgment upon the evil she had wished and forced upon the innocent children. It stabbed at her withering soul. After her brief moment of victory, she bolted upright on her mattress, her conscience and the reality of her situation getting the better of her finally. What would Thames think of her if he discovered the children had run away from her? It would be patently obvious that she was unsuitable as a mother or a mate! And that would be the death knell for any possible relationship with him.

As far as the fate of the preposterous feline, she still intended to exterminate him. But she realized she wanted Ralph's children safe and preferably back home with her in order to use them all to her advantage. Perhaps then she could even introduce them all to her beloved Thames. She was sure he would fall in love with them, even if she herself was incapable of that emotion toward the young people. And she was certain she could at least fake the emotion for a while in order to lure him into possible marriage. If only the children would leave her a substantial clue of some sort so she could bring them home! Anything!

The following half hour in the cornfield was terribly upsetting for the children and Dorfuss, when they realized they had separated. Jenna was the hardest to ferret out. She was nearly inconsolable afterward. Dorfuss, with his instinct for searching things out, was invaluable in locating everyone once they all realized what had happened. Disastrously for all of them, the corn was over six feet tall. Once they lost their senses of direction and caught their breaths, it was tempting to wander and try to locate the others. That only added to their difficulties.

All in all, it was a very harrowing evening. Not to mention Dorfuss now having only two remaining lives left. That did not bode well with him, and he began to hope the old wives' tale about cats having only nine lives was nothing more than fiction.

However, everything that took place that awful evening turned out to be a blessing in disguise because the maniacal and frightening events of the day had ultimately led them to this place.

Hilda and Thames, Sitting in a Tree

Two days later, Thames Fulton made another appearance at the Laurel Township Library.

Hilda was sitting behind her desk, discreetly eating her lunch when he arrived. *Thank goodness I was almost finished*, she pondered as she shoved the remainder of it deep into the dark cubbyhole underneath her desktop where she kept her lunchbox.

She greeted Thames, taking his offered hand briefly and experiencing anew the electric current that seemed to pass overwhelmingly through both of their bodies whenever they touched. Hilda honestly didn't think she would ever get over the previously unexperienced thrill. *And at my age*! *Why, I should be ashamed of myself!* she thought, but she also knew she wasn't.

For the past couple of weeks, in Thames's absence, Hilda had made visits to the local beautician. The nice woman patiently instructed her on the subtle application of makeup, which Hilda

had never bothered with before. She carefully helped Hilda conceal her age spots and suggested a softer, fuller hairstyle for her to help soften the angular lines of her thin, severe face. Once the woman gave her the flattering haircut, Hilda soon implored the woman to also remove the gray from it.

Of course, rumors were already flying all about town that Hilda was perhaps seeing a gentleman, although no one was sure just who he was. They only knew he most definitely was not from the immediate area. And her first trips ever to the local hairdresser more or less confirmed the rumors.

Hilda also had driven to nearby Marshalltown, visiting one of the few high-end clothing stores for miles with the purpose of updating her wardrobe. She purchased several new dresses in lighter, softer colors and fabrics than she had worn for all those years as a spinster. Before she exited the department store, she passed the perfume and jewelry counters. On a whim, she also purchased two new bottles of fragrance and some conservative jewelry. She was not used to vanity and felt vaguely guilty at even these small indulgences in herself. Too much change too soon was not her style. Therefore, she chose the more conservative jewelry and not some of the much prettier pieces on display.

So when Thames finally arrived, it was with a demeanor of tremendous pleasure that he greeted her that day.

Hilda's hair now softly framed her face, curling in becoming layers around it. It was cut considerably shorter than it had been before. It also was now tinted an attractive shade of medium auburn with the bold gray streaks taking on almost a strawberry blonde hue. She was wearing a fashionable dress in a light olive shade that complimented her eyes, making them stand out attractively. Tiny olive-shaded earrings graced her earlobes. She also appeared to be wearing the faintest touch of makeup, and her skin positively glowed. She looked years younger than the last time he had seen her and also a bit more confident. And she even seemed to have lost a bit of weight in his absence, perhaps five pounds or so.

So presently, he and Hilda spent several minutes poring over her new book orders, which were considerably fewer than they had been the previous month. That mattered not a bit to him, however, since he was pleased just to be in the dear woman's company.

Too soon, though, their business was finished, and each was left pondering what he or she could possibly say or do to prolong their visit. A patron approached Hilda's desk, ready to check out several books, and Hilda quickly took care of the man. Thames stood nearby, watching Hilda as she worked professionally, and again he secretly admired her improved appearance.

The customer exited the library, and Thames approached Hilda once again. "Well, I guess I'd best be on my way then," he pronounced hesitantly as Hilda looked up with dismay into his eyes. He could see instant regret in them, and he wavered. "On second thought," he offered, "would you care to have lunch with me again? Is the library too busy today, or do you think we could sneak away for a few short minutes? I did so enjoy our last visit together!"

Hilda, delighted at this new invitation, completely forgot she had already eaten and immediately accepted his offer. At the noon hour, the library typically was never very busy. Gratefully, she accepted his generous offer and locked the building up, and they traversed the short distance to the café.

That day, there were several more patrons inside the eating establishment than there had been the last time she and Thames ate there. The cheerful talk taking place inside right before they walked through the door came to an immediate, embarrassing hush as everyone took in the unusual sight before them.

Hilda Walters was *indeed* seeing a man! And a handsome one at that! How extraordinary! Everyone watched curiously as the waitress seated them, handed them menus, and hovered nosily for a few extra moments than necessary. A small child blurted out through the uncomfortable silence, "What's wrong, Mommy?" and was immediately shushed by his meddlesome mother. The woman blushed and glanced away from the couple and back down at the food on her plate.

Quietly, Hilda and Thames chatted while they waited for their food. Soon, it was brought out to them, rescuing Hilda from her momentary lapse in conversation as she struggled for something intelligent and eloquent to say to this dear man.

After time, the other patrons resumed their conversations, albeit less noisily than before, and Hilda's nervousness began to ease. She and Thames continued to chat quietly during their meal.

Thames asked her if she would be available to perhaps take in dinner and a movie in Marshalltown with him one night the coming weekend.

Astonished and overjoyed at the same time, Hilda didn't know what to say. Then, after mulling it over for a few moments, she accepted his offer. *A date? Me? With this lovely man?*

Toward the end of their meal, as they sat enjoying cups of coffee, an elderly gentleman approached. Hilda knew of him well already. Old Mr. Horton used to own the granary before he retired and then sold it to his younger nephew. Often, he came into the library to read the newspapers. He was there on almost a daily basis. Now, he was widowed with not much to do. He had always been a nosy individual. He had become even more so recently, mostly due to boredom with his retired life.

Mr. Horton said hello to Hilda, and then he waited for her to introduce him to the stranger. Of course, Hilda felt uncomfortable about this, but she awkwardly complied, introducing Thames as her book salesman.

Mr. Horton hung around several meddlesome minutes longer, asking friendly but prying questions about Mr. Fulton's life. He yakked on and on in a boisterous, know-it-all tone about inconsequential information and meaningless happenings in his own life. Thames, wishing to speak only with Hilda, quit contributing to the conversation. Finally, the old man realized he had overstayed his welcome and bid them both a good day. He went and seated himself back at his own table with his daughter and grandchildren. Soon the entire table full of people he was dining with was gazing Hilda's way and gossiping and snickering without restraint or embarrassment.

Hilda blushed brightly when she recognized this and then looked at her watch distractedly. Thames watched on, becoming disgusted at the behavior of all of the strangers in the restaurant around him.

In his offended state, he decidedly glared at the elderly Mr. Horton, who finally had the sense to notice Thames's derision and appear to be ashamed at his behavior. Quickly the old man rose. Blushing profusely, he directed the remainder of his family toward the cashier. They paid for their meal hastily and left.

Thames and Hilda remained a bit longer when Thames suggested they order dessert. Hilda was stuffed but did not wish to shorten her visit with Thames. So she said nothing and kept right on eating. It was a relief for them both that the Horton party had gone on their way.

All too soon their desserts were finished, and Hilda glanced nervously at her watch again. It really was time for her to be getting back to work. Rarely did she lock the library during the daytime, and here now she had done it twice in as many weeks!

She and Thames began to slowly make their way back to the library, passing the small park that had been vacant earlier. There, on one of the small benches under the shade of the large trees, sat old Mr. Horton and his daughter.

Her two children, a son and a daughter, were swinging merrily back and forth nearby. They observed Hilda and Thames and began to giggle. Then, without hesitation, they yelled out loudly as they swung to and fro, "Hilda and Thames, sittin' in a tree, k-i-s-s-i-n-g!"

Hilda was profoundly embarrassed and blushed crimson, quickening her pace. What was poor Thames to think? And really, the manners of those disgusting Hortons! *They ought to be ashamed of themselves, all of them!*

As they hurriedly walked away from the little group in the park, neither Hilda nor Thames ever heard the adults reprimand the children for their reprehensible behavior. Instead they heard low chuckles from the adults.

Soon Hilda and Thames arrived back at the library. The weather was inferno-like, typical of the near end of July, but a warm breeze gently moved Hilda's shorter hair attractively about her face. She glanced at Thames hesitantly as he stood near the library door, unsure of what to say.

Finally, he uttered, "Um, well, I will see you Saturday then."

"Yes, Thames, that would be very lovely," Hilda replied and smiled, unsure of herself. She was thrilled about their impending date. Yet she was sorry to have him leaving so soon already, and vague regret was apparent in her voice.

Not mentioning the embarrassment of just a few minutes earlier, Thames smiled, took Hilda's hand and squeezed it in a reassuring manner. He told her he would be by to pick her up from her home around four o'clock Saturday evening.

All too soon, he was gone. Hilda nervously unlocked the library and went back inside to finish out her day.

THE FAIR PARADE

The next two days, the children spent their time on the outskirts of an unknown stranger's farm near the large junk pile. It was a bone yard of many broken-down pieces of farm equipment left to rust and eventually return to the earth. Jon investigated the run-down shed and found some old tools, an oil can, and also a gasoline can still nearly full. Immediately, he took it upon himself to attempt get the rusty old tractor up and running.

They spent their days resting in the shade of the nearby trees, playing in the area, and sleeping in the dilapidated old structure at night. Jon gave Jenna and James the chore of cleaning out as much of the mess as they could from inside it that first evening, and it served nicely as their shelter while they remained. He also instructed them both to search for firewood and other tinder while he worked.

Dorfuss reassumed the role of head food catcher, hunting most of each day. He was resourceful at coming up with many small critters for them to sustain themselves with. A cheerful stream wound

its way through the valleys of the hills nearby, providing them with water for drinking and freshening up.

It was nice for all of them to have a couple days of break and catch up on some much-needed rest. There still had not been any rain. It was now the first day of August, and everything was very hot and dry.

Jon spent many hours both days partially disassembling the old motor, using parts from other broken-down things as replacements, and then putting everything all back together once he had discovered the underlying mechanical problem.

During the afternoon of the second day, Jon attempted to get the rusty old tractor started. It groaned, fussed, and complained for several minutes, but finally, with a loud backfire and puff of dirty smoke, it began to chug slowly. The whole tractor shimmied and shook, but minutes later, the chugging ceased, and the engine began to run smoothly.

"Ha ha!" Jon yelled in excitement. His heart leapt. "Yes!"

James and Jenna had ventured down to the nearby stream earlier to play with crayfish and minnows while he worked. Only Dorfuss remained behind, coaching him on from time to time and calling him the affectionate name *Wrench*. Dorfuss was sitting nearby in the shade of a scrubby tree. When the tractor engine began to jangle and clang, he arose, stretched, and walked over and stood by Jon.

"Good job, Wrench!" he praised the boy. "You know, you turned fourteen just a couple of days ago by my calculations! This is definitely a cause for us all to celebrate! I will go search out some wild game for our dinner and try to make it extra special for all of us."

Jon ruffled the furry head, and Dorfuss headed off into the tall grass and disappeared from sight.

After the cat was gone, Jon thought about what Dorfuss had just said about his birthday. He had completely forgotten it, as did his brother and sister, it having been on July 29. Then he shrugged his shoulders, realizing he really didn't care. He had more important things to worry about and tend to these days. It struck him forcefully that he was becoming a man. Filled with new realization of his accomplishment, he stood tall and raised his head proudly. *I feel like a man!*

He puttered with the engine for a while longer and then shut the tractor down, knowing it would be best to conserve what fuel the tractor held, although the can in the shed was almost full.

It wasn't much longer before James and Jenna returned after having become bored with alarming the stream's varied critters. His heart singing, Jon told them of his latest conquest. They jumped up and down with gladness at this turn of events. They could resume their journey with another vehicle to help them along. Traveling would be much easier for them now.

Jon informed them the first thing next morning they would be on their way. They were all thrilled. Since the dreadful experience they had endured two days ago, they had not encountered any further terrifying forms, but that did not mean they were not lurking about somewhere close by.

That evening, the tiny group enjoyed two freshly caught rabbits, courtesy of their beloved Dorfuss, roasted over an open fire. Their stock of food was nearly gone and they would need to purchase more soon. But due to their new mode of transportation, they should reach another town in a short time.

The next morning, they were all off bright and early, heading in the direction Dorfuss guided them. Jon drove the tractor, and Dorfuss, Jenna, and James were his grateful passengers. One axle of the wagon was bent a bit, and the going was rough. The wagon bed heaved up and down with each turn of its old wheels. Still, this new mode of travel was quicker and easier than the endless walking had been.

Toward afternoon they were thrilled to see they were approaching another large city. They were so glad to see something different from the endless hilly farm fields that had occupied the majority of their quest. They pressed on as the city drew ever closer, and eventually they reached its limits. There, looming large in front of them, was a huge sign proclaiming, *Cedar Rapids*. The children began hooting and hollering when Dorfuss informed them they were nearly halfway to Davenport.

They made their way on into the city, which seemed to be unusually full of hustle and bustle and noise. There, they discovered it was the Friday of the beginning of the annual county fair, which was always marked with an elaborate parade.

Marching bands, floats, and different processional groups proceeded past them. Church groups, boy scouts, and women's groups paraded past. A group of war veterans carrying flags marched by, looking very proud and saluting the crowd. Excitement over the impending county fair was prevalent. Politicians from the area were also participants. They drove past in fancy convertible cars, waving at prospective voters. Before the little group realized what happened, a kind police officer directed them into the parade as well, assuming they were a part of it.

Hundreds of onlookers lined the sidewalks, some sitting comfortably in lawn chairs in the shade, others cheerfully standing despite the heat. They were waving small American flags patriotically and cheering and waving to everyone participating in the procession. Likewise, the participants were all waving back. Astonished, the children all realized they were now in a parade!

Then the contagious excitement of the event caught on to even them, and they began to wave back at the onlookers. Jovially, they shouted and raised their arms in greeting as the crowd cheered at them, believing they were indeed intended participants in the parade. The tractor passed by numerous stores and buildings and homes, and the parade seemed endless. Eventually it passed the town square and gazebo, where cameramen from newspapers were set up behind the crowds, taking photographs of the happy event. Reporters for the papers were interviewing contestants and participants in both the parade and the fair and were expounding upon all of the wonderful events to take place.

Past the cameras the procession continued with the wagon in tow. The children and cat observed the waving throng as they drove past, waving joyously in return and shouting the entire time. They never realized what had just happened.

Saturday night took forever to arrive, it being the much-anticipated evening of Hilda's big date with Thames. She spent the afternoon at her little home in town, bathing carefully and pressing a brand new, elegant dress she had saved just for a special occasion. She had been so completely absorbed the past couple of days with their impending date that for once she had forgotten all about her witchcraft.

She spent meticulous time applying her makeup, trying, as the beautician had instructed, to make it appear as natural as possible. She styled her new hairdo, pulling at it this way and that in order to make it just perfect for Thames. She applied hairspray too liberally. Then she spritzed herself with one of her new, very expensive fragrances. Last but not least, she put on a lovely set of rhinestone earrings with matching necklace that had belonged to her mother.

She stepped back from her dresser mirror to admire her reflection. *It is certainly different from that of just a few short weeks ago*, she reflected. She had lost almost ten pounds, and her large rump had diminished significantly because of her persistence.

She still had not received any news regarding the children, but for that night, it was just as well, she supposed. At least this way she wouldn't have to worry about returning to the farm that evening to take care of anything.

Thames picked her up from her house in town at four o'clock sharp. Hilda was incredibly nervous on the twenty-minute ride into Marshalltown and didn't say much. Thames noticed her quietness and reached over and took her hand in reassurance while they drove in silence.

They enjoyed a lovely meal at a classy restaurant in the large town and then went and saw a picture show at the theater. It was a fascinating movie about a woman. Two men vied for her attention with unrequited love on the part of one. It ended sadly, and Hilda was forced to dab at her eyes several times before they walked out of the dark theater. Thames smiled a little, touched to see her so moved.

All in all, it turned out to be an enjoyable evening. When he took her home, he walked her to the front door, kissed her gently, and bade her good night. Hilda was almost overcome by the kiss and practically swooned right then and there.

Later, at her small, antique-filled home, her mind ran over and over the events of the evening and how thrilling it had all been for her.

It was the middle of the night before she was able to drift off into a semblance of sleep. However, she kept waking and reliving their entire wonderful date.

Monday morning, bright and early at the library, Hilda was busily setting all the area weekend newspapers out for library patrons to read, as she did every Monday. She had just laid the Cedar Rapids one on the table next to others when something familiar caught her eye.

There, on the very front page in a large black and white photograph, were Ralph's three children and that nonsensical cat of theirs! Jon was driving a beaten-up old tractor, pulling along a crummy wagon. In the wagon were standing James and Jenna both, along with the cat. He was proudly holding his ridiculous furry head high, buck fangs sparkling for the whole world to see. All three of the children were waving happily at a throng of people, apparently participants in some parade!

Hilda's heart skipped a beat, and swiftly she picked the paper up and began scanning the page.

The headline over the large photo proclaimed, *Linn County Fair Parade Takes Place*. A smaller caption underneath the photo stated the town had experienced a lovely dry day of typical August weather for the parade. Her eyes moved to a long article underneath the photograph, outlining the various events and goings-on that were to take place during the fair.

The reporter for the article detailed a pie bake-off that was to take place the very next day, which was now two days past. Hilda continued to scan the article for clues.

The children! What about the children? There was absolutely nothing in the paper about the children except for their photo.

Still, it was at least somewhat of a clue to go on. She was certain this development was important enough to telephone the sheriff's office and give them an approximate location of where to search.

She only wished she knew if they were planning to stay in Cedar Rapids permanently or perhaps already lived there. *But who would they be living with? They have no relatives there! And where did they obtain the tractor and wagon*? So many unanswered questions! She would be sure to give the police the photograph when they arrived so they not only had descriptions of the missing children but also the tractor and wagon they were using.

TWISTER

The children did not remain in Cedar Rapids very long. It had been Friday afternoon when the parade had taken place. They traveled on through the city and to its outskirts before the daylight began to dwindle. Unfortunately, the tractor was not overly speedy, but their new mode of transportation was welcome. They stopped at a grocery store in town and restored their food supplies, so they were well set in that department for at least the next few days. Jon also made sure the gasoline tank of the tractor was filled to the brim before they set off again.

Luckily for them, that evening they came across a vacant factory building and took shelter there for the night, parking the tractor and wagon behind it and well out of sight.

Saturday morning, they set off bright and early, making their way slowly in the direction of Davenport. The day was nondescript, much like so many of the past ones had been. They all knew they had

at least several days of travel ahead of them, even with the advantage of the tractor and wagon.

Sunday was a bright, cheerful day and everyone was glad it was not quite so hot for once. Yet, with the dryness the area had experienced for the past couple of weeks, any sort of breeze kicked up lots of unwelcome dust from the roads, especially when they took the gravel ones, which they preferred. Jon still insisted they stick to those whenever possible so they would be less likely to be discovered.

They plodded along, and toward the afternoon they came across another vacant farm whose house had been razed, but the barn still stood, solid as could be. Several pieces of ancient farm equipment were stored inside but that didn't faze the children any. They set up their sleeping bags in the hayloft and parked the tractor and wagon inside, down below with the rest of the farm equipment.

Monday morning dawned with dark clouds rolling in from the west. The day was decidedly hotter and muggier than recent ones. Jon surveyed the ominous clouds often as the group rolled along on the gravel road. He figured they only had an hour or two before the storm reached them.

Sure enough, shortly before they were ready to stop for a lunch break, the wind suddenly whipped up. Bursts of cold air, mixed with the decidedly warmer air, whorled around them feverishly. A farm could be viewed only a mile or two up the road, and Dorfuss felt it would be best for them all to make an attempt to reach it.

Thunder began to rumble loudly, followed by a sharp, bright streak of lightning only a short span away. Frightened, poor Jenna began to cry and wail as James took hold of her arm, talking to her soothingly in an attempt to calm her. It seemed to be taking forever for them to reach the farm way in the distance.

Huge drops of rain began randomly plopping here and there, and the temperature began to plummet swiftly. In the area west of them where the storm was rapidly building, the sky was beginning to darken perceptibly, turning a sickly shade of green. Strobes of lightning escalated, followed by deafening claps of thunder. Jenna began to cry harder.

Jon started to worry silently. This was tornado weather; there was no doubt in his mind about it. He thought back to years earlier. One time, on their own farm, such a storm had passed nearby. Pappa had warned him then about storms such as these. Jon pushed down on the gas pedal of the tractor with his foot as hard as possible, willing it to move faster, without much success. Instead the motor chugged and rattled louder than normal, and bursts of black smoke belched out of the exhaust pipe. The tractor lurched a bit and then continued on. At least, he noticed with relief, the farm in the distance *was* getting closer.

Glancing back in the direction of the storm, however, his heart leapt with fear. The sky had darkened even more, almost to the point of resembling nightfall. A funnel cloud had begun to form in the distance! The wind began to blow even harder. Blue lightning dissected the sky, followed by a terrifying crash of thunder.

Finally, their hearts pounding, they reached the driveway of the farm. Lights were on inside the house, so someone was most likely there. Jon decided for the moment it wasn't important whether someone might recognize them. He only wanted to make sure they all reached safety before the storm hit.

He parked the tractor as swiftly as possible, up close to the house. They all grabbed their belongings at Dorfuss's instruction and ran as fast as their legs could carry them up to the front stoop. Wildly, they pounded on the door in the hopes someone would let them in, in order for their little group to seek shelter in the storm cellar.

The wind whipped up even stronger, and their ears all popped, as if suddenly they were within a vacuum. All at once, Dorfuss literally began floating in the air before them. Debris from the farmyard began to raise and lift in an unexpectedly surreal scene. Dorfuss's legs stiffened and his claws stuck out in a futile attempt to anchor them to something, *anything*, and he cried out in fear. Jon reached out and grabbed the cat's fear-puffed tail at the very last possible instant before he became sucked away up into the sky from them and disappeared forever.

Eight lives gone now, Dorfuss worried as shingles began lifting from the roof of the house and barn. The barn, which was yards away from the house, began to groan and sway, almost as if it had sprung to life, and the children held onto the welded iron porch railing and pounded on the door of the farmhouse even harder.

"Hello?" they yelled. "Is anyone in there?"

Finally, a middle-aged farmer appeared behind the glass window, opened the door swiftly, and without asking any questions, urged them all to get inside.

Surveying with fear himself one last time the wild weather building up rapidly outside, the farmer quickly shut and latched the front door and hurriedly ushered everyone down the basement steps and into the storm cellar.

Wide-eyed with anxiety, everyone huddled together without speaking and waited for the horrible storm to do its deadly deed. Dorfuss was literally shaking, as was Jenna, and she gathered him ferociously onto her lap as she cowered in the corner of the cellar. Perhaps they could comfort each other. Neither Jon nor James gave voice to their fears, keeping them restrained inside.

The very foundation of the house began to strain and groan. Everyone heard nightmarish reverberations of objects blowing and banging about outdoors; structures bending and twisting. The storm continued to relentlessly rage on and on around the farmhouse.

The farmer glanced at the children now and then with equal fear in his eyes, wondering just what was happening to the beloved farm he inherited from his parents, and they from theirs.

Finally, the weather sounded as if it had calmed, the groaning of the ancient house began to diminish, and clattering of articles blowing and banging around outside subsided.

Almost reluctantly, they left the safety of the storm shelter and slowly made their way back upstairs in order to view for themselves the damage the violent storm had wrought.

Gazing through the numerous windows on the front porch with despair, they all took in the horrid sight of the devastation the storm had left behind. The barn had collapsed on one side, and the roof of it hung, precariously teetering off the remaining undamaged end of the structure.

Several small outbuildings, such as chicken coops and the like, sustained severe disfigurement. The children's rusty tractor lay bent and twisted at least fifty feet closer to the barn than they had parked it, obviously unsalvageable. Their wagon was gone, nowhere in sight; presumably, it had been sucked away and completely destroyed by the storm.

"Oh no!" Jon exclaimed, the first of the entire hapless group to speak. The middle-aged farmer, who was not much of a talker anyway, only removed his hat from his head, took his handkerchief from his pants pocket, and wiped his brow with it. He gazed morosely at the mess before him. The rain had diminished to merely a slow sprinkle. The farmer reluctantly ventured outside to survey the damage to the house while the children remained inside, observing the devastation in despair.

"What are we going to do now, Jon?" James whispered while Jenna stood nearby, resuming her earlier tears and holding Dorfuss so close that he meowed sharply and flailed his legs in protest.

"Well, guys," Jon stated flatly, "looks like we're back to walking again unless one of you can come up with a better idea."

Jenna's crying escalated into loud bawling. Then Jon lost his temper. "Jenna, you're going to have to cut it out! Stop crying *now!* This is bad for all of us, you know, not just you!"

Jenna was startled enough to quiet immediately. She whimpered a bit, setting Dorfuss down, and the cat was glad. She began wiping at her eyes and her body shook as her nerves began to settle. She realized her big brother was right and felt sorry for making things worse for all of them.

Presently, the farmer returned to the inside of the house after surveying the damage the storm had wrought. A large section of the roof of the house had been pulled apart, and he reflected he would have to attempt to place a good-sized tarp over it soon. The gutters hung distended from one corner. Other than that, thankfully the house itself remained relatively untouched. *Hopefully my wife will return home soon*, he thought.

She had been visiting her sister's farmstead several miles away, and he was more than a little worried about her well-being since the storm had hit. *She should have been back by now.* He stood inside the doorway, gazing outward at the mess in the barnyard for several more minutes and willing his wife to return safely home. Then he finally spoke for the first time to the children.

"Where are you children from?" he asked with concern more than anything.

"Oh, we are just staying with our cousins a few miles up the road," Jon answered, thinking fast. "We were helping them move that tractor and the wagon that used to be there."

"The Nielsens' old place then?" the kind farmer queried.

Jon shook his head yes while Jenna and James remained silent. They had learned much over the past few weeks, and knew they needed to be careful not to give away too much information. It was likely the farmer knew many other families in his area well, just as their parents always had.

"Well," the farmer suggested to them, "you'd best be on your way there so your folks don't worry. Certainly, they'll be afraid for your safety in the aftermath of that storm!"

The children nodded and thanked the kind man for providing them with sanctuary, and then they were on their way.

As they walked along the road, they couldn't help but notice the debris scattered everywhere. The corn in the fields had been virtually flattened to the ground in spots, creating whorled patterns. What damage it hadn't sustained from the wind had been taken care of by the torrential hail and rain that accompanied it. The roots of many tall stalks had loosened from the ground with the moisture, and the long, narrow leaves appeared to be almost pulverized from the beating the hail inflicted.

A car approached them on the road. A middle-aged woman drove past them slowly, heading in the direction from where they had just come. She briefly surveyed the group of children and also the storm-wrought damage and then continued on. The flattened fields would not have provided any cover for the little group.

"What are we going to do now, Jon?" James asked him.

Jon only shrugged his shoulders in exhausted defeat. He was frustrated and heartsick. It seemed every time they were lucky enough to obtain a mode of transportation, something went awry.

Dorfuss finally spoke, telling the children they would just have to try to find a train station somewhere and perhaps buy tickets to their destination of Davenport.

Now, Jon lost his temper. "Oh, don't be stupid, Dorfuss! I'm not going to fall for that again! Next, we'll end up in Timbuktu or Siberia or something! That's all we need! And where would we possibly find the money for train tickets? We barely have enough left now for more food!"

Dorfuss conceded to Jon he knew they were indeed low on money. "Perhaps, though, dear boy, we could stop at one of these farms along the way and help them clean up their mess for pay! Train tickets can't be too terribly expensive. The distance we still need to travel is probably fifty miles or so now. If we keep walking, certainly we should come across a town with at least a small depot! It would definitely be worth a try! Let's see what we can do! In fact, perhaps we should double back to the farm we were just at and see if that kind farmer would consider hiring us for a couple of days until we get some money saved up. It would not only help us but him besides. He did seem like a very nice man."

Jon was still annoyed, but he knew Dorfuss's suggestion was probably the best that any of them could come up with. James suggested they all eat their lunch right then. Since everyone was so hungry, they took care of that, sitting on a large, flat rock at the edge of a field in the nearby ditch, assembling sandwiches. A dark look resided on Jon's face, but he said nothing more while they ate. He *was* getting fed up with all of the walking they had been subjected to. Inside, he knew well that Dorfuss was right! When they were finished with lunch, without any further argument they all turned around and went back to the farm where they had taken shelter from the storm.

They knocked on the farmhouse door with much less fervor than the previous time. A kind-looking, older woman holding a dish towel answered their knock. Apparently the farmer's wife had returned in their absence. When Jon told her what they wished to do, she replied, "Well, Kenny is somewhere about the place surveying all of the damage. Why don't you try to find him and see what he says? We are all alone here, and he would most likely appreciate your kind offer!" She smiled at the small group of children kindly and curiously. "Just where are you children from?"

Jon quickly told her the same story he had told the kind farmer earlier: they were cousins of the people from the farm just up the road and were only visiting.

"Oh!" the woman replied hesitantly, surveying the bags they carried with a hint of disbelief. She evaluated the odd-looking Dorfuss, who remained standing behind the rest of the group with a questioning look in her eyes. She then instructed them again to find her husband.

They wandered about the vast barnyard. The barn appeared to be a candidate for a bulldozer. The small outbuildings didn't look much better. They finally came across the old farmer, who was muttering angrily and tossing debris around behind the grain silo.

Jon told the other children to keep silent and let him do the talking. He approached the farmer and told him they would all be willing to help him and his wife clear up the disastrous mess. He offered all of their services to him for two dollars each a day.

The farmer muttered to himself for a few more minutes while surveying the mess the silo was in. He grumbled some more and finally accepted their offer. He went off to search out the wheelbarrow. The chickens were scurrying about and clucking wildly, completely lost and out of sorts, their coop totally destroyed.

Dorfuss took off into the surrounding fields to survey the area, as well as roust up a lunch for himself.

Eventually the old man returned to the children with a rusty wheelbarrow and offered to bring up his tractor and wagon too so they could begin to haul some of the mess away. The farmer instructed them to save all the loose bricks from the silo they could find and then put the rest of the debris in the wagon. The children immediately set to work.

The afternoon passed, and within a few hours, the children had stacked a good-sized pile of bricks just yards away from where the silo stood. Two wagonloads of debris were already removed and thrown on the junk pile way out back. Jon drove the load there with James in tow. They surveyed the junk heap in hopes of coming across another lucky find but came up empty-handed.

Both boys struggled to set a large roof section from one of the smaller outbuildings on the heap. Suddenly Jon stepped back, taking another look at it.

"You know, James, if we lean this against that and the other corner against something else, we could fashion a small lean-to for us all to spend the next night or two in. What do you think? And here are some old boards we could use for the floor!"

"Sure, Jon. If that's what you think would be best, it's fine with me!" James agreed.

So they carefully set the roof section off to the side. They would return later that evening and get everything all set up.

Dorfuss followed the children around for a while, mainly to keep an eye on them. Eventually though, he realized they were perfectly safe. The farmer seemed to be a very kind man. Even though the wife was rather obnoxious, deep down inside, Dorfuss also sensed she was a good person. Neither of these adults would let harm come to his charges.

Dorfuss began to meander around, having a lack of interest in the tedious chore the children had undertaken. He knew he would be completely useless in that department. He followed James and Jon out to the pile of debris once.

Eventually he began investigating the empty outbuildings that had not been totally flattened. He wandered from one to the next, finding nothing particularly intriguing.

Toward the outer perimeter of the barnyard just before the fields began, stood a large, sturdy-looking concrete-walled building whose only apparent damage was a slightly disfigured roof. One end of it had lifted a bit, most likely from the strong winds of earlier in the day. There was a small hole in the other end next to the chimney. That possibly had not even occurred when the twister had wreaked its havoc earlier.

The front of the building had large, sliding doors typical of many outbuildings on farms. Most likely this was a storage building for tractors and other farm implements, he deduced. One of the sliding doors was open a few feet, and Dorfuss decided to go in and investigate.

It was dark inside. Sure enough, another tractor dwelt inside, along with a plow, a seeder, and a reaper. Over by the wood-burning stove was evidence of a long-ago, accidental fire. The sunlight of the day shone brightly through the hole in the roof, providing enough illumination that Dorfuss was able to make out most of the hulking objects stored inside. Dust wafted through the beam of sunlight, sparkling a bit. Near the chimney sat a mechanic's tool bench with different tools lying on top and hanging on the wall behind it.

Dorfuss continued to wander, feeling rather bored. He had gotten used to the busy days he had spent with the children as they traveled along and was no longer used to sitting still. *Perhaps I am only restless.* He *was* looking forward to reaching their destination. Their trip seemed to be taking forever.

Without warning, he experienced that creepy sensation of being watched. Swiftly, he wheeled around, gazing into the darkness back and forth and around him. A single red, glowing eye appeared behind the large tractor, where the room was darkest. Dorfuss immediately went into protective mode, as fear raised the fur on the back of his neck and caused his tail to puff out hugely. Displaying incredible bravery and growling with bared buck-fangs for effect, he advanced on the apparition, daring it to approach him.

Reaching the phantom, he displayed a large, deadly paw adorned with sparkling razor-sharp claws. After pausing a moment to emphasize their deadliness, he sliced them through the air where the spirit hung suspended. It backed off temporarily. The eye encompassed an appearance of sorrow first, and then it adopted a questioning air. *Apparently, this specter is not easily dissuaded,* Dorfuss realized. He had encountered it several times before, he was sure.

Again, Dorfuss whipped his deadly claws through the space the eye occupied. "Go away, evil one!" he demanded. "Leave me be! I am not afraid of you!"

"As you wish, Master," was the apparition's sad reply. The eye blinked morosely and began to turn away from the cat and fade at the same time.

"What do you mean, *Master*?" Dorfuss demanded, astounded that such a being might address him in such a subordinate manner.

The faded eye began to take on a brighter, more hopeful glow with apparent, renewed interest.

"It's very simple, Master Dorfuss Bubblebutt! You are the one who released me from the grotto of spirits dwelling within the magical ball of Broom Hilda! Remember when you knocked it over and broke it? How you were momentarily surrounded by numerous specters?"

Dorfuss reflected for a moment. He remembered the events of that disastrous day quite well. Indeed, when the glass ball had shattered ghostly spirits had surrounded him, calling to him in indecipherable, beckoning voices that had frightened the daylights out of him.

"Yes, I remember," he finally replied defensively to the questioning eye. "What could that possibly have to do with me now?"

"You are the one who released me, Master. Therefore, it is my duty to serve you either until you discharge me from my servitude to you or the sad day that you leave this earth forever!" the eye informed him humbly. "Why, then, when you are the one who released me from my prison, do you continue to turn me away? I am very grateful for what you did for me. It was a nightmarish existence, dwelling in the darkness for so very long!"

"I want nothing to do with Hilda's evil!" Dorfuss asserted to the specter. "She is the one that conjured you up! I, unfortunately, had the mishap of breaking some of the items on her table. If I knew then what I know now, I would never have entered that horrid chamber of depravity! I thought I had destroyed you!"

"There have been many others like myself with evil intentions, perhaps," the lone peeper admitted. "Master, don't you see? I am only your loyal servant! And, being so, I am only capable of whatever emotions dwell deep within the heart of my master. I was a good person most of my lifetime. I am as much a part of *you* as your very name! Thus, *I* am not evil! *Please,* Master. You have waited so long to avail yourself of my services! Please accept me as your loyal, faithful servant *now*! I promise you will never be disappointed!" The glowing orb blinked again, hopefulness apparent in its expression.

It continued. "Many of the spirits you released were indeed evil, and they are the ones possessing that madwoman. They know her corruptness and have more power over her than she does them. She just isn't aware of that fact. Some of them have continued to follow us in your adventure. I am sure you know of which events pertaining to them that I speak!" Dorfuss nodded, beginning to connect the dots.

"For example, the statuary at various places that talked and even moved were possessed temporarily with evil. You have not been entirely incorrect in your perceptions. When Hilda began to raise all of us sorry souls from the dark pit, she raised us *all*, both good and bad! Spirits can be either good or evil, as you should well know by now! You, Master Dorfuss, have a good, kind spirit." The vermilion eye bobbed up and down slowly in the darkness, still with an imploring look about it.

Dorfuss didn't know what to think. He looked again at the orb, which only held sadness and yet seemed to seek approval. If he accepted this apparition's services, would it later turn on him and wreak Hilda's vengeance on not only him but the children? And how could he ever trust something that was the ultimate result of such evil?

"Don't worry, Master. As I have already told you, it is not possible for my spirit to be filled with hatred when the heart of my master only lives for good! Please accept my services. If you are not pleased, then if you asked me to leave, I would! I promise you that!" the specter informed him, even though Dorfuss did not voice his thoughts.

Dorfuss was astounded! "How did you know what I was thinking!" he demanded harshly.

"Because, Master, as I have told you, I am part of you! I know all of your innermost reflections as well as emotions!"

The cat considered the specter's offer for a few more long minutes. He believed the touch of magic dwelling within him was enough already. He certainly never asked for anything of the sort. He also knew a large part of his inner self had always felt uncomfortable over that unasked for gift.

Dorfuss observed the apparition objectively one last time. Finally, he spoke to the bobbing eye. "I'm very sorry. I never asked for any of this. My sole ambition has always been to protect the children and keep them safe. And that is all I have ever used Hilda's magic for! I have no interest in delving any further into Hilda's wretched wickedness."

The red peeper glowed sadly and began to retreat. Dorfuss watched with an oddly lightening heart as it began fading from his view.

"Go find someone else to haunt!" he commanded, feeling even better yet. "I do not wish to be your master. I already have the most important job of all and that is my responsibility to those three children out there. And I have done quite an efficient job, I might remind you! Without your help!" Dorfuss was back to his eloquent, articulate, and lighthearted self! "Go now! Certainly there must be someone else just waiting for the chance to avail themselves of your services. Perhaps they will be wicked, as Hilda is, or perhaps they will be good. I release you to search out another master on your own!"

The scarlet orb began to fade away from view, appearing to be filled with utmost despair. Just before it disappeared, it turned once again to Dorfuss, blinked with obvious sadness, and then it was gone.

With that, Dorfuss strutted from the darkness of the great building into the warmth of the sunlit day.

An immense burden seemed to rise from his very being, as if the weight of the world were lifted from his shoulders. Suddenly, he felt free, very free!

That's when he knew with absolute certainty that he had just done the right thing. He had unwittingly acquired some of Hilda's witchcraft. He supposed he could live with that, at least for the time being until the children were delivered into safety, sometimes with its aid. Once they were safely there, he never intended to use it again. Also, he knew he did not wish to delve any further into something holding the potential for evil to take over and possibly consume him, as it had the wicked Broom Hilda!

A small chipmunk scurried past him in an effort to escape down into the safety of its hole before its natural enemy, the cat, could catch him.

Instantly, Dorfuss pounced, catching it easily and with agility before the rodent disappeared into the ground.

Dinner now awaited him. Feeling satisfied with both his decision and the ample catch he had just made regarding his dinner, he sat down on the ground in contentment, forgot about the ghostly eye, and began his meal.

The farmer and his wife were kind enough to offer dinner to the children if they agreed to stay until just before the sun went down. They hungrily accepted. Everyone had worked up huge appetites with the strenuous work they'd performed all afternoon. The food was absolutely delicious, and it was the first home-cooked meal the children had eaten since they ran away.

While everyone ate, the woman talked almost nonstop. She yammered away, asking numerous, prying questions. Jon managed to bluff his way through them for the most part, not giving away too much information.

The farmer sat and ate silently, not contributing to the conversation at all. Inside, he ruminated about the destruction that had befallen his farm and what it would take—not only labor, but also expense wise—to get things back in tip-top order.

Impatient to get away from this nosy farm wife, the children ate quickly and went back outside to resume their chores. Dorfuss arrived back up at the farmhouse. His stomach was full for the time being. He was happy to see the children had been lucky enough to obtain real meals for a change and sat near the porch, waiting for them.

Just before the sun began to set the farmer paid the children, thanking them, and they promised they would return in the morning to help again. The kind man waved as the little group made their way out to the gravel road and chuckled at the goofy-looking cat that seemed to follow them everywhere.

The children hoisted their belongings and trudged back out toward the road, waving to the old farmer in turn. Once they knew they were well out of sight, they doubled back and made their way to the farmer's junk heap. It was nearly dark when they arrived.

Jon and James strained and heaved and lifted the old shed roof section until it was leaning up against other odd junk. They tested the whole thing for sturdiness and then slid the loose boards underneath it onto the ground. Now they had a place to lay their sleeping bags and duffels to keep them from getting wet. The ground was still damp from the earlier storm.

Their makeshift shelter was cramped, and the floorboards were hard, but no one cared. Their tummies were full, and they were exhausted from all their hard work. Also, the nerve-wracking memory of the horrifying storm they barely escaped earlier in the day had taken its toll. Now the weather was much cooler than before the storm. They scooted a few other large items up to their temporary lean-to for security against marauding animals and then unrolled their sleeping bags. Dorfuss cuddled close to his beloved Jenna, and soon everyone was sound asleep.

That evening in her vile vault, Hilda observed with corrupt delight as the magical ball revealed to her the deadly events of the children's day. *So there was a tornado wherever they were! Another clue! Finally!* Mother Nature had helped her out!

None of the children appeared to have been injured. Now she could let the police know they were staying at a farm that had been heavily damaged in the twister's path!

Eagerly, she headed to the telephone in the parlor.

A tired-sounding officer answered the phone at the police station. Hilda gushed and informed him that she just knew the children had been in the vicinity of a tornado earlier that day. She stopped short and began to stammer, realizing just how insane that must have sounded to the man.

On the other end of the line, the man rolled his eyeballs. He leaned back in his chair and placed his feet on the edge of his desk, stretched, and sighed audibly. Did the woman actually believe she possessed the powers of extrasensory perception? Or perhaps did she know more about the children's disappearance than she had previously let on? Having been a police detective for decades, he had learned to suspect *anyone* and *everyone*. He paused a moment after she finally shut her mouth and quietly informed her there *had* been a break in the case of sorts. Just that afternoon, Ralph's old beater mobile had been discovered parked behind a barn on a vacant farmstead. He informed her it had been noticed by a neighboring farmer who kept some of his equipment stored on the property. It was close to twenty miles away from the Walters farm. Astonished by this additional discovery, Hilda temporarily found herself speechless. The officer paused for a pregnant moment for effect and then gruffly let the wacky woman go.

Back at the farm where the children and their cat were spending the night, the farmer and his wife were preparing for bed themselves. While they turned down their bed, the woman continuously yakked at her husband, irritating him. "Kenny," she said with a knowing look on her middle-aged face, "something is not right about those children. I can feel it. Why are they carrying big duffel bags and sleeping bags around with them if they are visiting at the farm up the road? They look so dirty! Something also seems familiar about them. I just can't quite put my finger on it!"

The farmer merely shrugged. He was not one to pry into other people's business. He climbed into bed and turned out the lamp on his side. His wife kept nagging him and blithering on even as she scooted down under the covers and began to get comfortable in the soft down mattress on the bed. All he could think of was how greatly his weary bones ached. Minutes later, his wife still had not shut up. He rubbed his eyes in fatigue, yawned deeply, and then sighed to himself with frustration.

Finally, he turned over to face her. "Mabel," he scolded with uncharacteristic irritation, "I am exhausted after such a long, awful day! I want to go to sleep now! If the children seem familiar to you, it's probably because they *do* live nearby, we *have* seen them before, *and they are!* If they don't live down the road, then what do you believe they were doing with a tractor and wagon? If you need to know so much about those children, who to *me*, seem to be very kind and helpful, ask them yourself!"

Mabel promptly shut up, not used to her husband taking charge in such a way. She lay next to him in stupefied silence. Her eyes were wide with the shock of her husband actually having the nerve to speak up. Finally, realizing she had forgotten to turn out her bedside lamp during her rant, she sat up, reached over, and shut it off. Kenny rolled over away from her, and within seconds, he was snoring.

Bright and early the following morning, the children consumed their breakfast sandwiches inside their little rickety shelter. Hopefully, while they worked at the farm, the farmer's wife would be kind enough to feed them lunch and dinner. At least now while they remained, they had a small shelter to leave all of their belongings in.

They made their way back to the road and headed on down toward the farm. This day was bright, cheery, and still somewhat cooler than recent days had been, with a gentle breeze.

They worked side by side with the farmer all day long. Occasionally, his wife came outside and chatted all their ears off. Then, having exhausted her useless statements and questions, she disappeared and resumed her wifely chores.

She fed them all a delicious lunch, which made her incessant chatter at least relatively tolerable, and also served them dinner that evening. Since the children had started work much earlier that day, they left shortly after dinner was finished and headed back to their crude shelter after the grateful farmer paid them each again. Dorfuss was already waiting for them there. He had remained behind for the day to catch up on his rest and search for a stream for water. He had been lucky enough to come across one not too far off.

He was glad to see the children arrive back home and told them about the stream. They were all relieved since they had not had an opportunity to clean the dirt and dust of the past couple of days off. One by one, he led them there to take care of their baths.

Finally, they were all ready for bed, and even though the sun had not quite set, they all wearily slid into their sleeping bags. They were exhausted, sore, and stiff from their hard labors and within moments were sleeping peacefully.

During the night, coyotes howled in the distance, and the children and Dorfuss awakened briefly. They laid in wait for the sounds to come closer, all of them frightened. But eventually the noises faded, and before they even realized it, everyone again drifted off into a contented slumber.

PURSUED

Wednesday morning was much the same as the last. Everyone awakened bright and early to the cheerful chirping of birds in the trees nearby. The weather seemed unusually mild again for that time of the summer. Soon they finished up their picnic breakfast and made their way back to the farm for another hard day of work.

Quite a visible dent had been made in cleaning up the debris. The kind farmer seemed happy with the results of everyone's hard labors of the last couple of days and was much more cheerful as a result. Jon and James spent the day taking repeated trips to the junk pile in the back forty and occasionally patted the patiently waiting Dorfuss on the head when they encountered him.

Other than the buildings around the farm showing just how much damage they had sustained during the storm and the extensive repairs they awaited, things were slowly beginning to shape up.

The charitable farmer let them know bright and early that either

this day or the next would be the last he would be in need of their help. Carpenters were due to arrive and begin repairs within the next several days. He was looking forward to having the patching up completed, everything painted, and his place looking as good as new.

The children didn't mind terribly much that their work at this particular farm was nearly completed. The work had been difficult. They hoped perhaps if they stopped at other farms in the area they would possibly be able to pick up some additional temporary work. Jon, in particular was satisfied with their accumulated earnings of the last couple of days. Dorfuss cheered them on in that respect. He was certain himself that within a day or two at the most, the children should have earned ample money to obtain train fares to Davenport.

Again, that day he remained behind at their shelter to investigate, curiosity always being an instinctive trait in a cat. From time to time, Jon and James appeared with yet another load of debris and petted him for a few minutes before returning to their work. It felt good for him to catch up on some much-needed rest.

At the end of the day, the farmer generously paid the children their wages and waved them on toward home. Shortly before telling them good-bye, he let them know he probably still had at least the next morning's work cut out for them. He kindly told them he would be happy to compensate them for a full day's work even if they finished before the day was over. The children were all especially glad for his offer.

Soon the children returned to their makeshift shelter, tummies full of two good meals prepared by the appreciative farmer's wife. Of course, they were wearied from all of their labors, almost to the point of exhaustion after three full days of work. Each of them had now earned six dollars.

Jon added it all up in his head on their trek back to their shelter. That meant they already had eighteen dollars total. When he added that to the several dollars still remaining from the commencement of their trip, he figured each of them should soon have more than adequate money for an honest fare on a passenger train.

Dorfuss *had* been right when he suggested they help the unfortunate farmer several days before. Jon was much obliged he had listened to their wise protector.

At their temporary home, they took turns washing up at the stream. With all of them feeling much cleaner afterward, they quickly retired to their shelter and abruptly let unconsciousness overtake them.

That evening up at the farmhouse, Mabel was tidying up the house after several days of letting the disliked chore go by. She grumbled and ruminated as she tackled the job. *Kenny always has had such a bad habit of leaving things lying around and not returning them to the spot he retrieved them from! Throwing disposable items such as finished newspapers into the trash when he is finished with them would be nice*! His untidiness had been an endless source of aggravation for her all the years she had been married to the man, and she resented it!

She waddled about the house in her faded farm dress, apron, white ankle socks, and shoes, picking up the coffee cup that had somehow made its way into the living room. It had been sitting there for at least the last day or two. Likewise, she grabbed two dirty plates with utensils plopped on top of them sitting nearby. She returned that ink pen back to its holder on the desk in the den and set the notepad back near the telephone. Next, she scooped up the dirty, stiff pair of socks her husband had wadded up and tossed next to the recliner in the television room. While muttering away to herself as she did everything, she spied several days' worth of old newspapers hiding on the other side of the recliner up next to the wall. As usual, they were carelessly tossed aside when he had finished with them. He could have been considerate of her and placed them in the wastebasket.

Kenny was upstairs taking a forever shower and probably using up all of the hot water again to boot, she ruminated as she worked, irritation building. Surely when she followed him, there wouldn't be enough hot water left, and she would have to rush through her shower before the water turned nearly freezing. That was an almost nightly occurrence.

Wondering how she had ever allowed herself to become trapped into marriage with such a careless slob of a man, she grumbled when she returned to retrieve and discard the unwanted newspapers. She scooped them up and headed for the trash can in the kitchen. One section of a paper fell from her arms. Complaining to herself once more, she leaned down with some effort to reclaim the errant section. As she bent over her plentiful girth to pick up the newspaper, something familiar caught her eye.

Her eyesight was beginning to fail her in her middle-age, and she squinted as she looked at the large picture right on the front of what was a several-days-old newspaper. *Perhaps I should locate my reading glasses!* She held the paper slightly closer and blinked in an attempt to focus better. *So I was right*, she thought with triumph. *I have seen those children before and just couldn't place exactly where until this very moment!*

She looked at the headline above the large photograph. It proclaimed, "Linn County Fair Kicks Off!" with a smaller subtitle underneath stating, "Annual Fair Parade First Event of Fair Celebration."

Glancing back at the photograph of the children, one only needed to assume they had been participants in the parade. *Why, that was last Friday, wasn't it?* It was now Thursday. The fair was most likely nearly over with.

Mabel looked harder at the picture. There were the children's telltale sleeping bags and duffel bags sitting in the middle of a junky trailer. And there was Jon, driving the tractor she had observed twisted beyond repair in the drive when she had arrived back home that day just after the storm.

Next to Jenna and James on the trailer was plopped the stupid cat she had seen tagging along after them frequently here at the farm. *It has to be the same children. I know their faces too well by now!* "Huh!" she exclaimed to herself and ran hastily to the kitchen to dispose of the rest of the papers. She would just go upstairs and prove to Kenny that she *had* known what she was talking about the other night! She only wondered why the kids appeared to be on their own! *Are they runaways?*

That question lingered in her mind as she became more excited. She hefted her large form up the narrow staircase quickly on chubby legs.

"Kenny!" she called out. "Oh, Kenny?"

Kenny sighed within the confines of the steaming bathroom as he toweled himself off. His wife sounded like a herd of elephants coming up the staircase! *So what does Mabel want with me now?* he wondered with vague irritation. *That woman will certainly be the undoing of me!* He didn't doubt that for a moment! *She's probably here to nag me about my untidiness as she is apt to do so often in the evenings. And just when I am always looking forward to a bit of quiet relaxation! Why, the woman never seems to shut up!*

Wrapping the towel around his waist, he sighed again and opened the door of the small bathroom, letting a burst of steam escape into the hallway. Mabel was just outside the door, fist raised in her readiness to pound on it. She was holding something. An I-told-you-so look filled her expression.

Without saying a word (for once!), she victoriously handed him the section of newspaper and held her head proudly high. She was barely able to contain her excitement as she waited for her husband to observe the children in the photograph.

Kenny was nearsighted too and had to briefly set the paper down while he wiped the steam off of his glasses that were sitting near the sink. Mabel fairly squirmed with the urge to spill the beans before he had a chance of his own to look at the picture, but somehow she managed to compose herself. Her thoughts were racing a mile a minute.

Kenny read the headline, not bothering to look at the picture below it. With annoyance, he handed the paper back to her, saying, "So what? So there's a fair going on back in Cedar Rapids! We live just outside Iowa City! Certainly you don't expect me to haul you there now?" he queried without disguising his irritation.

"No, Kenny!" she excitedly replied, unable to hold herself back any longer. She tapped at the article with a pudgy pointer finger, wrinkling the paper. "Look at the photograph below it!" She poked at the photo in emphasis. "Those are the children and their cat! You know, the children that have been helping us clean up the mess from the storm these last couple of days!"

She handed the paper back to her husband, who was still not in a receptive mood for her babbling. "Look at the picture, Kenny!" she insisted again.

With resignation, he did.

He didn't want to admit it even to himself, but his wife did have to be correct on this one. There was Jon, driving the tractor and wagon he had pulled into their drive just three fateful days before, right before the twister hit. With him were Jenna and James and that confounded cat of theirs in the wagon that had blown away with the storm!

"Remember, Kenny? Remember Monday evening when I told you something seemed familiar about those kids? Well, now we both know why, and that was because we had seen them on the front of that day's newspaper!"

"All right, Mabel," he conceded. "Those definitely are the same children. But how on earth does that affect us, and what difference could it possibly make? They've done an excellent job here helping us around the place!"

"Well, yes, dear, they have!" she agreed with a whining tone to her voice, feeling deflated. "But why do they appear to be on their own, and why again, are they carrying their baggage with them wherever they happen to go? Answer me that at least!"

"I don't *know*, Mabel! And speaking of that baggage you say they always have with them, I haven't noticed that since the first day they came here when we had the storm! *How do you explain that?*"

Mabel hesitated. But not one to be proven wrong easily, she persisted. "Well, Kenny, I say that those there children are most likely runaways. The least we should do is inform the sheriff's office about them! Those kids probably have parents somewhere, miserably distraught over their disappearance! I think it's our duty to at least let the authorities know!"

It was Kenny's turn to hesitate. He rinsed off his razor blade for the final time, having completed his shaving, and set it inside the medicine cabinet. He mulled everything over in his mind for a few minutes while patting his face dry with his towel. Then he reluctantly agreed with his meddling wife they should probably telephone the sheriff.

However, he made it plain to her he wished to wait until first thing in the morning to take care of it. After that, he told her bluntly, he intended to wash his hands of the nonsense for good. He was not one to pry into other people's business. If those children had seen fit to leave their home, then in his opinion, they most likely had a very good reason to do it! They seemed like good kids to him!

For that evening, he was not about to let a bunch of commotion the sheriff's office was likely to inflict on them both ruin the peace and quiet and relaxation he had so anticipated all day, and he deserved it! This business involving the children could wait until morning! He firmly stated that very thing to his wife, who appeared to be about to burst with excitement. Her rotund face collapsed with disappointment as he walked past her on his way out the bathroom door.

After sitting by himself downstairs in silence and relaxing with the current newspaper for about half an hour while Mabel bathed, Kenny set that aside on the floor next to the wall. His eyes were tired from reading. He briefly watched the remainder of a show on the television set with Mabel sitting silently nearby, looking as if she were about to explode.

Afterward, the farmer and his wife turned in for the night. Kenny slept like a rock, exhausted after his days of labor outdoors. Mabel tossed and turned the whole night through. She was still having extreme difficulty containing her excitement at her discovery.

Finally, after a nearly sleepless night for her, Mabel rose at five o'clock in the morning, went downstairs, and immediately telephoned the sheriff's office.

Someone was always there day or night, she reassured herself as she dialed the phone. Sure enough, a kind-sounding young man answered. She filled him in with all the information she could think of and asked him to please do some checking into whether any runaways had recently been reported in the area.

Forty-five minutes later, the young man called her back, affirming that yes, a group of children with a cat matching the description she had given had been reported missing from their own hometown of tiny Laurel nearly three weeks before. They had also received another call several days before when a guardian notified the local police of the children's appearance after she too saw their photograph in the Cedar Rapids newspaper.

Almost boiling over with excitement, she hung up the phone. The young man promised they would send a patrol car out to investigate. Mabel nearly flew up the stairway despite her girth. Into her and her husband's bedroom she hurled her obese form, opening the door with such force that it banged against the wall behind her. Immediately, she went over to their bed. Kenny lay there, still snoring soundly. She began shaking her husband, waking him out of sound sleep and causing him to grumble loudly at the rude interruption.

"*What,* Mabel?" his slightly garbled voice asked her as his consciousness began to surface. *This woman never gives me any rest!* He rubbed his eyes with aggravation and then glared at her.

"Kenny, you need to get up now! I waited until morning like you asked me to, but I've already telephoned the sheriff's office, and they have someone on their way out here. Most likely they will want to question the both of us! Get up, and I'll fix you a good breakfast before they get here!"

"Oh, for heaven's sake, Mabel. Couldn't you have waited until a little later?" he asked in sleep-induced irritation. "It's still dark out!" he exclaimed. With annoyance, he glanced at the glow-in-the-dark alarm clock on his side of the bed. Its face faintly said it was almost six o'clock. *Well, I probably only would have stayed in bed another half hour or so anyway,* he ruminated as he grumbled for his wife's benefit again. He made his way out of bed, pulling his pajamas off and his jeans and work shirt on.

He sputtered and muttered all the way down the stairs. There, Mabel was already frying up eggs and pancakes for their breakfast. Realizing right then just how hungry he was, Kenny was suddenly grateful, and his irritation began to fade. Mabel's cooking was always delicious.

They ate their breakfast in relative silence while the sun rose gloriously over the horizon, shining in through the green gingham curtains in the kitchen window.

It was still patently obvious that Mabel was about to burst in her agitated state. Kenny silently shook his head. *Granted, the boring life we live on this farm does not usually offer much excitement, but gee whiz; her current frenzy is pretty much uncalled for!* One would have thought, upon casual observance, that Mabel had just discovered a buried treasure on their property with the way she was behaving!

While Mabel began clearing the breakfast dishes away, a squad car appeared in the driveway. Mabel immediately abandoned the job she normally would have insisted be completed before beginning anything else. She rushed to the doorway and onto the front porch, holding the porch door open widely as the sheriff slowly got out of his car.

He ambled on up to the house in an unhurried way and greeted them both. Then they invited the officer inside, where they directed him to sit down at the table. Hastily, Mabel cleared away the remains of the breakfast dishes and threw them into the sink without caution. She quickly wiped the table clear of any remnants of the food they had just consumed and poured everyone cups of coffee.

With everyone finally seated then, Mabel proceeded to tell the sheriff everything they knew and also said the children would probably make their appearance on their doorstep within the hour. The sheriff frowned absently as he filled out his report. He looked at his watch and decided it would probably be wisest for him to just wait and simply let the children come to them. He was still filling out his report and had taken the newspaper clipping also for a reference. Mabel sat at the table, chatting about nothing in particular while her husband sat nearby, clearly annoyed with his rambling wife.

The children rose cheerfully, this time packing all of their belongings carefully and rolling up their sleeping bags. Jon and Dorfuss decided it would be wisest for them to be ready to be on their way as soon as their work was finished. The little group ate a quick breakfast of sandwiches and apples while Dorfuss went off briefly and foraged.

When they were done, they hauled everything out nearly to the road, leaving their possessions hidden at the corner of the field and next to the fencerow.

They would still need to search out a new place to spend the coming night. The farmer had, after all, told them they probably only had half a day's work left at best. Now, they would be completely prepared to immediately head on to the next town and seek out the coming night's accommodations.

Relieved of all their baggage, Dorfuss strutted alongside of them proudly, following them happily back to the farm. All were in a cheerful mood at the prospect of finishing up a job well done and receiving remuneration for it besides. It would be good to be on their way. Dorfuss particularly was eager to see his mission accomplished.

However, bright moods suddenly turned to dark worried ones when, as they approached the long drive, they all saw the sheriff's car sitting way up near the house.

They stopped and began agitatedly whispering with trepidation, trying to decide what to do. Should they proceed and possibly end up in a hornet's nest, or could the officer merely be friends with the older couple and visiting with them?

Finally, after mulling everything over himself, Dorfuss interjected. "Children," he said hurriedly, "you probably already have enough money saved up to get us onto a train. I believe we should proceed posthaste along to the next town. What awaits us all inside that house could most definitely be a trap, and then what would happen to us? We would be sent back to the loathsome Broom Hilda and her horrible magic tricks and evil spells! Everything we have been through these past weeks will have been for nothing! We are so close to reaching our final destination now, especially with the money you have earned. I say enough! It is time to cut and run!"

The children wavered briefly, then finally agreed with Dorfuss. He had almost always been right so far. So, in reluctance they hurried back to the corner of the field and retrieved all of their belongings. At almost a run, they headed toward Davenport. For the next hour or so, they scurried along the road and remained undetected.

Then, they observed dust in the distance behind them on the gravel road and heard the sound of a car approaching. Quickly, they scurried for the cover of the thick corn in the fields. As they waited and watched from a safe distance, the same sheriff's vehicle they had recognized back at the farm very slowly made its way past them. They could see the officer inside, just barely. He appeared to be taking an inordinate amount of time, gazing to and fro, apparently looking for something in particular.

They waited for several minutes after the car disappeared from sight before resuming their trek along the gravel road. Jon's insistence that they stick to the back roads and take cover in the fields whenever someone happened along had paid off again.

So they pressed on, growing weary and hungry as lunchtime approached. They were nearly out of food. At lunchtime, they took cover along another fencerow some distance away from the road and made the remainder of their bread and peanut butter into sandwiches. They had hoped for at least one more home-cooked meal before hitting the road again, but it had not been meant to be.

Silently and sadly, they sat and ate what remained of their food. Hopefully toward late afternoon they would be lucky enough to find another place to stay in the middle of nowhere, and Dorfuss would be kind and search out more wild game for them. They clung to that thought with optimism.

As they were finishing their meal, up at the road, another squad car slowly approached, gravel dust billowing around it. The children quickly dove from the grassy strip along the fencerow into the cover of the corn and waited with worried anticipation for the sound of the wheels rolling slowly on gravel to dissipate. Finally, they could hear it no more. They were fairly sure the farmer and his wife had figured out who they were, and now the police were in pursuit of them. They waited several more agitated minutes and finished packing up the remainder of their items, and soon resumed walking.

As they moved along the edge of the road at the quickest pace possible, Dorfuss promised he would keep his keen ears alerted to any sounds of approaching vehicles.

It wasn't long before another vehicle approached, and the group once more took cover in the fields. This time, it was merely a regular car with ordinary people, and soon there were more cars. Later, another squad car passed them by while they hid in the safety of the corn.

It was becoming obvious to all of them they were approaching another town due to the amount of traffic that appeared to be consistently increasing.

However, for the unfortunate group, they did not make it into Iowa City that day. Due to the numerous times they were forced to take cover in the tall corn of the fields, they lost hours of traveling time. Toward evening, Jon observed a stand of trees a distance into one of the fields along another fencerow. They made their way to it and spent the night under the stars. Dorfuss was lucky enough to obtain two rabbits for their dinner, which they skinned and roasted and consumed with great hunger.

The next day dawned clear and bright, and the little group was optimistic as they walked along, getting ever closer to the city. They were all hungry again, but no one complained. Toward late afternoon, a sign for Iowa City came into view, informing them it was only two miles away. "Yes!" Dorfuss proclaimed with mounting excitement. "Iowa City is big enough we shouldn't have any trouble coming across a train station!" The children just shook their heads in amusement. They had no idea how a cat could know such things.

Before long, true to Dorfuss's word they were within the city limits. They trudged along. Their only worry now was the difficulty they might have taking cover if the police happened by. However, there were many more people about, so it was a little easier to blend in.

Eventually, streets lined with residences became city streets. Evening was approaching, and the little group decided it would be wise to search out a place to spend the night. Finally, they found a vacant, shoddy factory building along the main thoroughfare going through town. It was large and dark inside the rundown structure and a little scary. But it was certainly better than trying to spend the night outside, where they might be discovered and then sent back home!

Their voices echoed about in the gargantuan place as they searched for a secluded area inside the building suitable to rest their heads.

They stashed their belongings in one corner with relief. Then they came to the conclusion that since they were out of food, perhaps it would be best if they stopped at a nearby eatery and paid for their first meal ever on this long, tedious journey. Dorfuss decided to follow along and scare up his own meal in the meantime.

While they sat at a booth in a small family diner nearby, the children enjoyed their meals with gusto. They talked happily about what tomorrow might bring when they should come upon a train station, and then be on their way to Davenport via train. Dorfuss remained outside, hiding beneath the well-manicured bushes surrounding the place.

Many other folks were enjoying their meals in the diner. As the children were finishing up, two police officers walked in the door. They scanned the entire place with interest. Jon noticed them first and hunched down in his seat, bending over his nearly empty plate with intensity as if something particularly delicious resided there.

"Pssst!" he whispered, elbowing James, who sat next to him, and then getting Jenna's attention next. They too adopted his pose of extreme interest in their nearly empty plates.

The officers continued to stand up front, conversing quietly with the cashier near the door for several minutes. They glanced around the room one more time and then finally left the establishment. The children sighed in relief. Jon and his brother and sister sat in silence for several minutes longer, hoping not to attract attention to their little group. All three of them saved some food for their beloved kitty waiting patiently for them outside.

Then Jon stood and craned his neck in an attempt to see if a police car was still parked outside. He couldn't see anything, so he figured the officers were gone. The sun was beginning to set outside, lingering a few more minutes before it said its farewell until dawn.

They asked the waitress for a small container for their left-overs and their check and then paid their bill and began to leave. They were just outside the door when, with chagrin they realized the squad car with the two officers was still in the parking lot with both men seated inside. One appeared to be communicating on his two-way radio. The officers had not gone anywhere; they were only parked toward the back corner of the parking lot, where their car was out of sight. Suddenly, from the street another squad car swiftly pulled in directly behind the children as they began to hurriedly cross the street.

"Run, guys!" Jon urged with haste as they hightailed it in the direction of the vacant factory. Even louder, he yelled, "Come on, Dorfuss!" Dorfuss quickly emerged from the bushes, scampering across the street closely behind them.

Suddenly, Dorfuss thought better of it. In a hoarse voice, he urgently instructed the children to run the opposite direction. Soon a police car was in pursuit of the hapless group, lights flashing and sirens wailing. The frightened kids swiftly picked up speed, running away from the vacant factory, down a grassy hill and close to a river. A second police car joined the first.

The kids cut across several empty lots to evade the pursuing vehicles. Eventually, the group approached an enormous lumberyard, which consisted of several huge open buildings. Quickly, they scurried inside one of the dark buildings in hopes of finding cover. Luckily enough, by now it was almost dark outside, and they disappeared into the darkness before the police cars had a chance to catch up.

They remained inside for what seemed hours afterward. They were huffing and puffing to begin with from their exertions, but eventually they lay flat on the ground underneath a large stack of plywood and waited silently and watched. Jon whispered right to begin with they would probably need to stay there for a long while to make sure the police were gone, and it was a good thing he had.

The squad cars parked near one of the buildings at the end of the cluster. One by one, the police began to search all of the structures with flashlights. It was totally dark. The children remained silent but shook with fear when the officers finally entered the building concealing them and their cat.

They gazed at Dorfuss, wide-eyed with fear. Quietly, he shushed them. The children watched fearfully as the three officers thoroughly combed the large structure, shining their flashlights into every dark corner and crevice, surveying the entire building.

The kids and Dorfuss were terribly afraid they would all be discovered. Dorfuss knew he must do something quickly! Purring for only a few moments, he raised his paw and crooked his tail, as he had done so often on this journey. Without warning, a dark, magical shield enveloped them all. Light shone from his eyes. He spoke quietly to the children, reassuring them while they gazed back at him with wonder in their eyes. "You are shielded from the light. Have no fear, for the officers will not be able to see us. Remain silent!" Dorfuss instructed.

For several long minutes more, the officers searched, yet they came up with nothing. Several times they shined their bright spotlights directly on the children but miraculously did not see them!

They eventually left and searched the one last building, finally returning to their squads. Yet, they remained in them for quite a bit longer, presumably communicating with their base and likely waiting to see if the children would be foolish enough to leave their hiding place.

"Thanks, Dorfuss, I don't know what you did, but apparently it worked!" Jon finally whispered to the crouching cat. Jenna and James agreed, and Jenna reached out and ruffled his furry little head. Dorfuss's eyes took on a proud demeanor.

"No problem, children," he offered modestly.

Several times while they remained waiting, Jenna became impatient, wanting to leave, and Jon hushed her up. "No!" he admonished both her and James. "We are not leaving this place until the police have been gone from here at *least* ten or fifteen minutes, and that's final! We've gone through too much to get this far, and we are not going to take any chances now!"

Finally, the squad cars turned off their colorful, flashing lights, and then they slowly pulled away. The sound of tires rolling on the gravel drive finally faded into the distance.

After waiting for several more minutes, the children and Dorfuss decided everything was safe for them to return to the vacant factory building. Only a sliver of a moon and a few stars and street lamps lit their way.

Returning to the hulking structure, they unpacked their belongings to prepare for bedtime. Jon discovered a large, old sink in the back of the building in the shape of a half circle. He tested the knobs, and it *worked!* There was an old rubber stopper for the drain. Both hot and cold water flowed from the spigots. And so, with appreciation the children took turns at their first real, hot baths since the beginning of their journey.

Of course, after relaxing in their baths, they were all wiped out from their endeavors of the day and couldn't wait to slide into their welcoming sleeping bags.

Dorfuss cuddled again with the already dozing Jenna in her sleeping bag. He too was exhausted and grateful they all had managed to escape the police who were in pursuit of them. He knew they would all have to be extremely careful from now on. Now that word of their sighting had gotten out, any stranger might recognize them, and then their incredible, arduous adventure would have been for naught! At that very moment, he was thankful for the unasked-for gift of magic he had somehow acquired on the Fourth of July. Even the abhorrent Hilda might have been proud, albeit resentful, if she had known of his ability to temporarily make their small group become invisible.

In the final moments before he dozed off, however, he knew that once he delivered these three children, who he loved so very much to safety, he never ever intended to use his unexpected and unwanted powers again!

DISAPPEARED

Friday evening at the Walters farm, not long after the children had escaped the police in Iowa City, Hilda paced anxiously about, awaiting any kind of news about the children. *When will that blasted sheriff's office ever call me back?* she thought angrily! She was nervous and irritated! Earlier that morning, the sheriff had telephoned and let her know the children had definitely been sighted at a farm only a few miles north of Iowa City. The farmer the children had been staying with and helping had corroborated that they definitely belonged to the faces and furry cat in the newspaper article they had come across.

Hilda waited patiently for hours, with great disappointment and frustration and nothing more. Because of that telephone call, she did not open the library at all that day. Certainly her daily patrons had been upset to find the doors locked. And she was forced to miss work and call in sick because of those stupid children! She had also forfeited her daily salary.

Finally, in the late evening, the telephone rang. Hilda practically jumped out of her own skin when it jangled intensely. It had been the only perceptible noise in the huge and otherwise empty house since morning. *Perhaps my jitteriness is also due to my shot nerves*, she reasoned with herself as the phone rang again. As she picked up the receiver, a feeling of dread overwhelmed her. Deep within, she knew with certainty that she really did not want the children to be located. For, if they were they would be sent home to her, and she just didn't know if she was capable of dealing with that disruption in her life anymore.

Her hand trembled as she placed the phone against her ear and answered in a weak voice filled with trepidation, "Hello?"

It was indeed the Iowa City police. The kind gentleman that spoke with her now sounded vaguely discouraged. He had been one of the patrolmen that spotted the children in Iowa City that evening at the local diner only to end up losing them all. "I'm sorry, ma'am," he apologized to her profusely. "Those three children of yours are slippery little devils, I'm afraid!" he quipped with ill humor in an attempt to lighten the moment.

"Well, I never!" Hilda mimicked a huff, secretly experiencing great relief deep inside. "Those are children you are referring to, young man!" *My life will not be disrupted by those children this night at least*!

Again, the young man apologized profusely, and Hilda abruptly lost patience with the wimpy fellow and slammed down the receiver while he was still in midsentence.

She resumed her pacing. Back and forth she moved in agitation, between the kitchen and the parlor for endless moments, muttering to herself uselessly. Hilda was consumed with worry. It was becoming obvious to her that the children and their stupid cat were headed in the direction of Davenport. Her sister, Ruth, and husband, Tom, resided there, along with their children. Was that what the kids had in mind?

Should I telephone the sheriff's office and perhaps suggest that motive to them? What if the children actually made it there unharmed? Ruth would surely question the children's reasons for having done such an outrageous thing. And if she discovered they had been all on their own, completely at the will of fate and away from Hilda for longer than three weeks, Ruth would be appalled!

Hilda continued to pace, arriving back at the desk and peering through her glasses at the phone. She reached out to pick the receiver up, hesitated, and then drew her hand back sharply, as if the telephone was terribly hot. *Best not warn Ruth or the sheriff just yet. Why expose anything? It might turn out to have not been necessary, and then I wouldn't be able to take it back!* The beans would be spilled! Certainly there was something she could do to stop them from arriving at their destination. But what?

Then it struck her! *I should attempt another magical spell!* She had engrossed herself in her witchcraft these recent days with a vengeance since her date with Thames. She had not heard from him since, and it was already Friday night. Apparently a date this weekend was not to be. *What must I have done to repel him? Certainly there was something! After all, no other man has even shown that much interest in me before!*

Most of her thoughts the past week had centered on trying to somehow make her beloved Thames fall equally in love with her. She spent many laborious evening hours bent over the magical accoutrements on her low, round table. Nothing but her small attempts to scare the daylights out of the children had worked on the several occasions that she had fiddled with the nonsense. She had not been successful in forcing them to return home. She hadn't really accomplished anything of worth, even after all of the hours and money she invested into her magical tomfoolery. Hilda knew Thames would be completely shocked if he knew what she had been up to. He was a decent man. If he were to find out, most certainly he would lose interest in he once and for all! Yet, any embarrassment she had known several weeks ago over her brief dalliances with the darker side had subsided. Her conscience had faded away; her mind was totally corrupted. A voice deep within its recesses contradicted and confused her thoughts. *How would he ever find out anyway?*

Even after all of Thames's obvious interest in her, unfortunately Hilda lacked the confidence in herself necessary to simply leave things between herself and Thames alone. She was beginning to feel increasingly possessive even though she still barely knew the man. That too had added to many of her recent jitters.

The fantasies of spending her golden years with a man she loved and could finally call her husband always seemed to lie just outside of her reach, taunting and mocking her with vengeance. If only she could prove, once and for all to her sister Ruth, that she was just as good as her!

To add to all of her frustrations, Hilda lately heard voices telling her awful things about herself that she feared could possibly be true! "No!" she screamed at them loudly in a vain attempt to get them to shut up. Her only answer was a resulting, resounding silence. And eventually the mocking voices always resumed, chipping away at her mind and soul and making them weary and even more so receptive to their evil.

She heard them again now, calling to her sinisterly and loudly. She stopped pacing and without really thinking, followed their wishes and went into her bedroom. Her magical ball was sitting there in the darkness, already glowing brightly as if it had been expecting her. She approached it cautiously. *Lately, this thing has begun to take on a life of its own*, she mused, and she involuntarily shuddered. She peered into it in the hopes of envisioning the children and their cat. She still hoped vainly for some clues as to their whereabouts.

She waved her hand over the glowing orb and chanted a few words over it, beseeching the contraption to finally give her the answers she had so unsuccessfully searched for all of these past long weeks. Deep inside, an enchanting image of the children materialized. They were satisfying their appetites at what appeared to be a diner, corroborating what the useless officer had told her just a short while ago. The blockheaded cat was nowhere in sight. *Why, oh why, won't this thing give me a name, a location, something to go on that I could give the police?* Most likely, if the children *were* indeed staying in Iowa City, there were at least half a dozen more little establishments just like this one! She snorted in frustration.

Trying to ease her mind from its nervous frenzy, she decided to distract herself with something else in the meantime. Perhaps later she could consult the magical ball again, and perchance it would allow her to envision a road sign or something more tangible than what she was given.

The atrocious Hilda lit several candles on the table to facilitate searching her spell books for some proper spells. She particularly wished to retry the one pertaining to "Attaining Heretofore Unrequited Love" and marked the page for it. *Oh, Thames, I do love you so!* she swore silently, practically swooning. She had spent the entire past week obsessing over him.

The more she mulled things over in her twisted state of mind, she knew she was leery of attempting to bring the children back home. The sheriff was getting frighteningly close to finding the miscreant threesome, the corrupt voices within her mind reminded her. The last thing she needed right now was to have bold, splashing headlines in all of the area newspapers proclaiming that Ralph's children had been found.

What would Thames think? Certainly the reporters for the paper would do their jobs, and insist on interviewing her! And even if she refused to grant them such an interview, they would probably still name her since she *was* involved in all of this. Besides, she knew she had never told Thames of their disappearance. She just couldn't let him know *now* about all of this! *I can't!* It was far too late to tell him. He would certainly be very dismayed with her, as he put great stock in close, loving families and loved his own very much! She knew he believed she'd been a motherly figure to Ralph's children. *Oh, this is all so very confusing!* The inner voices taunted and laughed at her! She clamped her hands to her ears in an unsuccessful attempt to quell their insipid noises.

The murmurs quieted somewhat as, laboriously, Hilda paged through the large, yellowed volume while she searched her ravaged mind and the infectious book for answers that refused to be revealed.

Her mind raced a mile a minute as her eyes scanned the yellowed pages, wishing for a definite answer to her problems. Then, all at once, there it was, calling to her. The title at the top of the page appeared to speak directly to her innermost being. *Or is it perhaps just those irritating, condescending voices yet again*? This was the chapter regarding *Disappearing Objectionable Individuals.* Yes!

In her dementia, a brief paragraph underneath its headline sucked her in completely. In smaller letters, it asked, "Having problems with certain unsavory individuals in your life? Don't know what to do about them? Make them disappear once and for all, and all of your troubles will be history!"

Yes! Her excitement built rapidly. This has to be it! While she was at it, she was going to extinguish that idiotic vermin the children called their pet. *That moronic cat has somehow successfully stolen my magic! Trespasser!* What *did* they call him anyway? *Umm... Dorfuss... Dorfuss Bubblebutt; that's it!*

She shook her head with renewed disgust at the ridiculous name and then reflected back to the newspaper photograph she had come across just the other day. That confounded creature was still with them! She remembered with contempt the stupid, cocky appearance the critter had about him, as if he somehow perceived himself to be intelligent! Why, of all the ludicrous things she had ever encountered in her lifetime, he had to be one of the most! And how *had* he been so unlucky to be blessed with those outrageous buck-fangs? Exhilaration coursed through her veins. Something told her that she *would* be successful with this spell!

Wild, evil cackles resounded within her mind, encouraging her. Soon she was giving actual voice to them.

She read the entire chapter thoroughly, from beginning to end twice, to make sure she definitely understood all of the steps exactly. *No use botching things up again!* Other times, she had not paid particular attention to every single detail or let something that seemed useless slide. Perhaps that had been the reason for her numerous failures in the beginning. She did not know for sure. A nagging voice within taunted her again, asserting perhaps she was just a lousy witch! She fought back the impulse to believe it! Stubbornness overwhelmed her.

This time, she did not intend to fail! After all, she had accomplished several other lesser spells she had tried to date. The most important one had been releasing the spirits and gaining mastery over them. She beckoned to them in her demented, twisted state.

She went throughout her ghoulish room, lighting each and every candle while beginning to vocalize the recommended chant that accompanied this certain spell.

Next, she began to assemble the required ingredients for this particularly virulent sorcery. She reached the most important ingredient. Bats! One bat for each individual would be required. Her little covered aquarium only held three! *No!* What would she do now?

Finally, she shrugged. They would just have to do. The spell book specified all the bats had to be alive. Their lives would be consumed into her magical ball once she was successful, having acquired each of her objectives' souls. *Then none of those pesky children will ever be heard from again!*

She reasoned to herself a bat should not be necessary for the cat anyhow. There was no soul there to possess; animals don't have souls! She chuckled wickedly at the sick humor and irony in this! "Hee, hee hee, hee!"

She continued to lay things out very carefully. The bats, she saved for the very last. She was to tie their little legs together and then hang them all upside down from a special, magical stick, suspending them over a low, burning candle. As they began to writhe in a futile attempt to escape the heat, she was to begin a new chant. Part of her began to become queasy at the prospect of the innocent bats' impending fate, but she shrugged the nauseous feeling off. After all, they *were* only bats! The immoral voices inside her head cheered, encouraging her to continue.

This would undoubtedly be the trickiest part, she reflected, as she then worked to truss up the bats. Holding them down in order to tie their little legs together did not appeal to her. Somehow though, she prevailed. They struggled and flapped their wings, hissing crazily and baring tiny fangs and snapping at her bony fingers in a vain attempt to escape their doom. The depraved murmurs within her brain began to chant. Then one of the little critters had the gall to bite her. She gasped over the stinging pain, which destroyed her concentration. Two tiny beads of blood appeared where its fangs had pierced her skin. Upon observing the little bat's fangs, she was overwhelmed with the spite her heart held for the obnoxious cat named Dorfuss Bubblebutt. How dare he acquire the magic that she had worked so terribly hard to achieve. And how dare he stand in the way of her laborious endeavors to make the children return home. *I'll fix him!*

Finally, all three of the little creatures were secured and tied to the magical stick. She placed the stick in its special holder, suspending the bats over the flame. Hilda grinned with delight, perceiving that her success was only minutes away. She rubbed her skinny hands together in anticipation and began her perverse chant. Hers joined the insane voices within her reasoning as the poor bats began to struggle valiantly in an attempt to free themselves from the ever-increasing heat of their inferno.

Her chanting advanced then to a fevered pitch. She began gyrating wildly around the low, round table. Her eyeballs rolled back inside her head in her festering frenzy. She could feel it all beginning to happen. *Yes! Oh, yes!*

Suddenly, something startled her from her demonic reverie. She opened her eyes, which had adopted a brilliant red and possessed glow, to find the magical stick had fallen off its perch. As she picked it up to place it back where it belonged, one of the bats' little legs somehow unwound from its bonds. It suddenly came free and flew straight for her face, scaring the daylights out of her and causing her to back up swiftly. It hissed at her menacingly, unseeing eyes glowing brightly red also. Then it disappeared somewhere high up into the shadows and cobwebs in her room.

She was left dazed, and her eyes were briefly blinded, as if she had just peered directly into the sun. She blinked her scalded eyes to regain proper focus and searched the ceiling without success for several minutes. *Oh no!* Now she only had two bats left. What was she to do? "Oh, the injustice of it all!" Hilda cried out into the empty room with anguish. She would now need to specify which two individuals she most wished to have out of her life once and for all.

After wringing her bony hands for several minutes, she resolved her quandary. Jon was her first choice. He was old enough he would be capable of telling anyone who might inquire of all of her iniquities. She certainly didn't wish to worry about any chance of that happening. Then, she deduced that James, even with his rather simple mind would also be a good choice for elimination. Jenna was not even eight yet, and people would likely assume the little girl had been fantasizing if she did spill the beans.

She rubbed her emaciated palms together. Concentrating, she replaced the magical stick on its holder. The pair of remaining bats resumed their attempts to free themselves from the increasing heat of the candle, and she again renewed her corrupt chanting. Afresh, her body recommenced its gyrations with almost no will of its own. The moans inside her mind began to revel in their frenzy. And once more, another bat somehow managed to free itself, this time without her knowledge until it too pelted itself in fury against her bewildered face. It then disappeared into the darkness and cobwebs on the ceiling, presumably joining its companion.

"Noooooo!" she screamed. "It's not fair!" she caterwauled as the remaining bat continued to twist and turn over the flame on the table, hoping to become as lucky as its mates and find freedom too.

Finally, in frustration, Hilda forced herself to settle down. The calls inside her head quieted briefly. Collecting her insane thoughts, if that were possible, she specified the individual she wished to have out of her life most of all. That confounded cat! Why, he had been the bane of her existence for long enough already. He was the one, the one she wished to vanish from the face of the earth forever! Somehow she just knew he had been responsible for the children's disappearance. Almost underneath her breath, she began chanting his name. "Dorfuss Bubblebutt! Dorfuss Bubblebutt! Dorfuss Bubblebutt!" Along with her voice, the evil demons in her brain repeated the cat's name also. They also began wildly repeating Hilda's name, cheering her on in her demented toils. Hilda's excitement began to rise.

The lone bat continued to seek its freedom while swinging wildly from the tenuous prison of string that stubbornly clung to its tiny legs. Obviously, it was terrified. Hilda observed this and reached to still the diminutive thing over the flame so that *it* didn't get loose.

With no explanation, hot wax sputtered and spattered from the candle as her hand neared the tiny, terrified creature. Some of the scalding wax from the candle beneath the flame splashed onto Hilda's unprotected hand. It left behind a long, red streak on her wrist that appeared instantly as the wax began to cool. "Hilda, Hilda, Hilda!" The fiendish voices continued to encourage her obscene obsequies.

"Aaaggghhh!" she yelled, shaking her emaciated hand furiously with the unexpected pain. Some of the wax had also landed on the bat, making it struggle even more valiantly with all its might. As Hilda quickly withdrew her hand in discomfort, she bumped the magical stick carelessly, and it fell once again from its perch. The bat landed head first in agony into the hot, melted wax in the center of the large candle. The poor thing perished from suffocation almost immediately as the flame extinguished the instant the bat struck it. The wax, without delay, began to cool and harden.

"Nooooo!" Hilda caterwauled as she feared her spell was ruined. "No, it can't be!" She wrung her bony hands together as disappointment loomed.

Suddenly though, and inexplicably, a weird spiral of light slowly began to emanate from her magical ball, which had remained glowing ever patiently while she toiled so feverishly over her spell. The odd spiral picked up speed, humming quietly at first and then becoming steadily noisier, transforming into a wickedly wondrous, diabolical intonation. The musical notes and hum of it became more stunning, magical, and immorally awesome by the second.

Transfixed, Hilda turned completely toward the amazing sight and gazed with wonder at her accomplishment. She had never seen anything of this sort take place before! She was successful once again, of that she was certain. Even after so many of her bungled attempts of the past and the tiny accidents that also took place during this try, somehow everything had all worked out. She had achieved success. This was an extremely difficult spell and she, Hilda Walters, had mastered it!

Her heart leapt with joy as she watched and waited, completely awestruck, as the uncanny swirl grew larger and larger, and its cacophony grew greater. *Oh, how beautiful!* A marveled smile of wonderment filled her evil face. *Is this what twisters look like from the inside out?* she mused with awe and wicked detachment as the cyclonelike form began to encompass her!

With total astonishment, she bided her time and observed the eerie, fantastic scene as it played out before her. Dorfuss Bubblebutt would disappear from her life once and for all, of that she was absolutely certain. The demons within her mind were ecstatic. "Hilda, Hilda, Hilda!" they continued, singing with encouraging, evilly gorgeous voices. She was still reeling with all-consuming delight when to her great dismay, it occurred to her that the ominous, gyrating glare had completely surrounded her! She was now inside of the tornadolike radiance! *Is this how the spell was supposed to turn out?* Hilda wondered.

Suddenly, her heart and mind became consumed with dread as she realized too late just what had happened. Deep within the center of the spiral, there appeared a dark, seemingly endless tunnel. First, her head began to be sucked into the giant vortex of doom. Hilda started to scream in futile desperation as next her arms disappeared and then finally the rest of her body. The swirling vortex continued, and Hilda's final utterance of "Aaaagggghhhh!" vanished along with her. Next, all of her witchcraft implements, gadgets, powders, liquids, and the remainder of the whatnots on her corrupt tabletop were sucked inside the dusky swirl. Following were every heavy candlestick, book, and any other evil item that remained, except for the magical ball itself.

Inside the churning swirl contained within the magical orb, pandemonium spawned and spread. Evil spirits floated here and there in the enormity amongst Hilda, laughing and scorning her with ruthless, lewd abandon. "Hilda, Hilda, Hilda!" they continued to chant in between bursts of giddy laughter and insipid pointing. They were laughing so hard they were holding their sides! She gazed about at the debauchery circling around her, and for the very first time in her entire existence, the atrocious Hilda felt genuine terror.

"No!" she called out to anything willing to listen. "This wasn't supposed to happen to *me!* A mistake has been made! Please, someone, help me to reverse this! I wanted that dunderheaded cat to be removed, *not me!*" she caterwauled with the full knowledge of her imminent yet unwanted surrender beckoning to her. Hollow, morbid faces taunted her, laughing without restraint or remorse, holding their rotund sides in spite of their own, sorry predicaments. It was the same plight Hilda was about to share for eternity with them!

A particularly gruesome apparition floated past her, glowing ruby eyeballs and nostrils oozing with a pestilential, greenish slime. It surveyed her with particular, noxious interest even while it mocked her fully. Hilda's gaze focused on it, not knowing whether it would be wisest to attempt to befriend or escape the wicked form as soon as possible. Deciding she could use all the friends she could make at this horrible, hopeless point, she attempted a smile that instead took on a desperate distortion of a futile grin. The apparition began to float away from her, but still its gaze remained fixed upon her desolate countenance. Utterly despondent, Hilda called out to it in one last, vain attempt. "Help me, please! This wasn't supposed to happen! This wasn't what I wanted!"

The gruesome phantasm began to laugh with wicked abandon, returning to Hilda's side swiftly, and its glowing eyes nearly sucked her inside of their own, separate demonic vortexes. Hilda, consumed with complete, overwhelming terror, attempted to back away from the demon with absolutely no success. Then the wicked mouth of the poltergeist opened, revealing decaying, rotting fangs. Horrid flames deep inside its chasm could be viewed flickering insanely. A putrid stench emanated from the fearsome pit.

Finally, the monster spoke with an insidiously grating voice dripping with absolute sarcasm. "Well, guess what, Hilda? *It isn't all about you!"* The specter finished the damning sentence with a shriek, laughed at her hideously and scornfully one final time, and swiftly it left her side, abruptly disappearing forever into the dark center of the swirling, maddening vortex.

Hilda could see everything then as plainly as the daylight she would unfortunately never again witness. Of course! The cat possessed no soul! She had known that all along, but in her zeal had temporarily forgotten! Therefore, the only soul that remained had been her own! She had ruled out the children in favor of the cat, after all! Her wish *had* come true; she would never set eyes on the preposterous feline again! What had she *done*? What had she become? And what, dear Lord, what would *become* of her now? Depraved faces without bodies beckoned her, and detached hands motioned with twisted, grotesque fingers for her to come join them. Obscene laughter ruled and beckoned, deep within the pit of never-ending torture and horror she finally appeared to be descending into herself. Demons mocked her, repeating her earlier cries of "No!" They made fun of her, screaming horridly, "Oh, the humanity!" over and over again. They were no longer her minions. She was instead an equal slave to the enormity she had created.

Deep inside the swirling mass, Hilda was battered about like the human debris she had become. In the end, the heavy brass candlestick she had hurled at the children weeks ago struck her soundly against the side of her head, and she lost all consciousness. Who knew what unspeakable horrors awaited her when she ultimately reawakened into her eternal nightmare and the dark abyss of never-ending, tormenting doom?

Hilda's sanctuary of sinfulness, nearly empty of every last tangible trace of her, suddenly began to lose its morbid, chilling darkness. Her multitudes of formerly released demons were swiftly consumed one by one into the mystical orb. The cobwebs in her room disappeared. With a burst of energy, the room was filled with a resplendent, purifying light radiating from the orb in every direction as every evil presence and object continued to be sucked inside. The room-darkening shades were ripped from their moorings and also swallowed up into the tornado-like funnel continuing to emanate from the magical glass.

Dresser drawers, as well as closet doors, were sucked widely open, and all of their contents followed the doomed Hilda into the abyss of her enchanted ball. Soon the room was entirely empty of every last item Hilda had ever owned. Yet the magical orb on the low, round table remained.

The vortex of revolving light began to subside and darken, and then it shrank swiftly. Finally, it became only a tiny, circling mass above the magical glass ball. With a huge sucking sound, the coil dissipated and vanished into the spherical object. Then, with almost a sigh of relief, the orb imploded upon itself, disappearing into its ornate brass base.

The brass base melted and pooled into a shiny, golden puddle that would forever seal Hilda's fate, pit of darkness, and unspeakable depravity inside.

Ultimately the tawny puddle shrank, and, in the end, it evaporated from sight, disappearing forever into thin air. The table upon which it had resided for so long suddenly began to crumble, gathering into a small, dark pile on the floor. With a barely discernible poof, it exploded into a tiny fire, which quickly extinguished itself. The few ashes remaining finally vanished in a minute wisp of smoke. The radiant light that had filled the room sparkled and glowed, twinkling and diminishing and finally fading away into the darkness of the night.

Not a trace of Hilda was left in her room or the old farmhouse, nor would any remains of the atrocious woman ever be discovered.

It was as if she had never existed at all!

Dorfuss the Stowaway

The children wakened early again on Saturday morning. Dorfuss approached them before they were even out of their sleeping bags. He suggested they wait a bit until the hustle and bustle of the city was in its glory by midmorning or so before leaving their cover. He felt it would be easier to blend in with other folks while they searched for the train station and then again at the station itself.

So, following Dorfuss's suggestion, everyone got comfortable in their sleeping bags and slept in a bit.

Later, when they did rise, they were all hungry. Jon felt it best they evade public places as much as possible even though they knew eventually they would be in a very public train station. They decided together it would be best if they waited until they were safely situated on a moving train before endeavoring to eat again. Dorfuss told the children it would be likely that a meal would be served on the train.

They carefully packed up all of their belongings, this time shifting some of the items in one duffel bag into the other to make room for Dorfuss. They had all discussed it after Dorfuss expressed concern that the conductor might not allow pets on the train. Also, they knew their little group would not be as conspicuous without their cat present.

They all decided to conceal him inside one of their large bags. It took a bit of time to rearrange everything. Jon decided to throw out a worn pair of shoes. After that, there seemed to be adequate room.

They let Dorfuss crawl inside and zipped the duffel shut most of the way, leaving a small portion open at the end where Dorfuss's head was so he could breathe.

When they left the vacant building the hustle and bustle of the city was widespread, and they were able to blend in easily.

They walked along the city streets. It was your typical busy weekend day. People were everywhere, going to and from their jobs, doing their shopping and other daily business. The closer the children got to the center of town, the thicker the hustle and bustle became. A lot of cars moved about in the city, which trembled as if it were fairly alive with the rumble of traffic and daily life.

It wasn't much longer before the little group came across a road sign pointing the way to the train station. They were so glad to see it, and quickly headed that direction.

Things were even busier at the train station. The children observed a few police officers milling about here and there, but in the commotion, the officers did not seem to notice them. The children, likewise, didn't glance their way often, not wishing to be recognized. Dorfuss reminded them again, from the confines of the duffel bag, to do their best to appear inconspicuous and blend in with the throng in the station. The place was alive with the commotion of commuters and weekend travelers.

Jon decided it would be prudent for him to attempt to purchase their tickets alone. He instructed his brother and sister to sit and wait on one of the many benches in the humungous building. They did so, clustered near several other families with their own children.

At the ticket counter, Jon was forced to wait in line behind several people. Finally, it was his turn. He approached the older woman behind the counter and asked to purchase three passenger tickets to Davenport. She hesitated, appearing to size him up first, then inquired why an adult was not there with him to purchase the tickets.

He replied that his father was just over there on a bench, pointing vaguely, and asked her again if she would please sell him the tickets he had requested. She pruned her lips into a disapproving pucker resembling something Aunt Hilda's ugly face might have effectuated. She then denied him, telling him to bring his father with him when he came back.

Jon headed slowly back toward his brother and sister with his head hanging. *What are we going to do now?* he wondered. He doubted any adult in the building would be willing to purchase their three tickets for them. He began surveying the room just in case someone looked like they might fit the bill. Unfortunately, there appeared to be no one.

There were many businesslike looking people about, appearing impatient and dressed smartly, carrying briefcases. Three rather dirty country children would not fit in with them. Then there were families with plenty of small children and aggravations of their own. And Jon doubted any of the older folks would agree to temporarily fill in for their lack of a parent. He didn't know what to do.

He reached his brother and sister, head hanging low, and told them sadly what had happened. He was frustrated and angry. After everything they had been through together and all of the hard work they had done to be able to ride the train, now the old prune behind the ticket counter was determined not to sell him their passages. He was afraid they would have no choice but to travel the remainder of the way to their Aunt Ruth's on foot.

Dorfuss, inside the one duffel bag and listening to the children's conversation, began to squirm. He stuck a fuzzy paw outside the zippered air hole, imploring the children to notice him. "Jon, I have an idea! Pssst, Jon! Open the bag a little so I can talk to you!"

Jon reached over and unzipped the bag just wide enough to see Dorfuss's eyes glowing in its shadows. "What do you want, Dorfuss?" he inquired sarcastically. "Here we are, stuck in this train station! Maybe we should see if we can get a taxi instead!"

"No, Jon. That would most likely cost much more than we could *ever* afford. It is still many miles to your Aunt's house! Besides, I have a much better idea! I would be more than willing to turn myself into a suitable adult, with your permission, of course!"

"Oh, exactly what do you have in mind, Dorfuss?" Jon was becoming angrier. "Are you going to turn into Pappa or something? Because that old prune up there behind the ticket counter said I would need a parent before she will sell me any tickets!"

"Well, actually, Jon, now that you've suggested it, why on earth not?" Dorfuss chuckled inside the duffel at the novelty of the idea. "I was simply going to turn myself into an ordinary adult, but actually, the idea of me resembling your Pappa is an even better one! Can't believe I didn't come up with it myself! Your wish is my command!" Dorfuss poked his face a little way out of the bag, and his fangs sparkled. "Take me into the men's room and then let me out, Jon!"

Since the hustle and bustle in the train station was so great, Jon did as he was told. He just hoped the ornery woman waiting behind the ticket counter was busy selling tickets and would not notice what they were up to. He picked up the duffel bag and instructed James and Jenna to wait for them.

In the men's room, Jon made sure the room was otherwise vacant and let the cat out of the bag in one of the stalls. He whispered to Dorfuss, "Come on. Let's get this over with before anyone else comes in here!"

Dorfuss climbed out. Grateful to be free from the confines of the dark bag, he shook his fur with gusto, stretched long, and yawned a bit. His eyes began glowing their telltale, oddly lit green color. Making use of his magic, he commenced purring loudly, crooked his paw, and bent his tail oddly as it consumed him. He stood and waited with his fuzzy head held high. Long, downy, sparkly cat hair loosened into the air and began to circle and glisten around him, in nimbus effect. And then, before Jon's very eyes, Dorfuss was transformed into a likeness of Pappa so very close to the way Pappa had always been, even in his mode of dress. Jon was completely dumbfounded. "Dorfuss, how did you do that?" he whispered, astonished.

"Just taking advantage of a bit of your Aunt Hilda's magic as usual, that's all *son*!" Dorfuss teased.

"Well, that's amazing!" Jon asserted as he shook his head. They left the restroom and began to head back into the large waiting room of the station. Soon they approached James and Jenna. Dorfuss and Jon were both smiling broadly.

Jenna, observing this latest miracle, suddenly began to cry. "Pappa!" she began to wail loudly, jumping up from her seat on the long bench and running toward him.

Dorfuss strode toward her on his human legs. "No, dear girl, I'm afraid not. But if you want to imagine that I'm him for a little while, that is fine with me." Then he leaned toward her and whispered, "I *do* love you, just as he always did!" and picked her up easily with his muscular farmer's arms and held her close.

Jenna buried her head against her "pappa" for several minutes and continued to cry. Finally, she settled down and rubbed the tears away from her eyes, leaving dirt streaks on her face. James stood next to them and also hugged his "pappa." His eyes too brimmed with nearly shed tears. Even Jon developed an emotional lump in his throat, although he never would have admitted it to any of them.

After this brief "reconciliation," Jon told James to watch over Jenna while he and Dorfuss went back to the ticket counter.

When they neared it, the prune-faced, disapproving woman was still there. She observed Jon and his father with skepticism as they approached. They waited their turn in line patiently, finally reaching the counter. The older woman's eyes bored right into both of theirs. "And will you be traveling with your children, sir?" she demanded harshly of Dorfuss. Astounded, neither Dorfuss nor Jon knew at first what to reply.

"Because we do not allow minor children to travel on our trains without an adult present! We are not babysitters, mind you!" she rudely finished, squeezing her lips into another unbecoming prune.

Dorfuss thought fast, calculating things in his head. That meant he and Jon would need to buy four tickets instead of three. Well, so be it! They had enough money saved. He knew he would never be able to convince this obstinate woman otherwise. "Yes, ma'am, certainly I will!" he replied eloquently with a commanding, pompous tone to his voice. Yet, he was also rather endearing as he grinned and winked at the offensive woman in a flirtatious manner. It was his plan to either intimidate the woman in the same way she sought to intimidate the two of them or catch her completely off guard, whatever worked.

The woman was startled at the obvious English accent of the charming farmer clothed in worn overalls but did not comment. She blushed at the blatant flattery, seeming a bit confused, and her demeanor softened. "Three tickets then?" she asked, remembering Jon's earlier request.

"Well, ma'am," Dorfuss answered back with confidence, "originally, I had hoped to send the children on to their aunt's alone, but if you require an adult to ride with them, then I will need a ticket too, so make that four tickets to Davenport, please!"

The woman gazed briefly at Jon and his father, still summing them up. Dorfuss looked upon the disagreeable prune one more time in a flattering manner. A flustered look materialized on her face, and she blushed. She must have decided everything appeared to be on the up and up. She turned around, did the necessary paperwork, dropping items in distraction while continuing to blush, and then brought four tickets to the counter. "Your train will leave in an hour and a half. Lunch will be served during your trip. Sixteen dollars, please!" she said with a much more compliant tone to her voice.

Jon was forced to dig into his own pocket for the change while Dorfuss stood next to him feeling a little bit useless. He hadn't thought about that part of it! Jon paid the disparaging woman as Dorfuss winked at her one final time. She handed them their tickets without further comment, and finally reciprocated to Dorfuss with an awkward, toothy grin that also displayed an ample amount of gums. She batted her eyes at her supposed admirer, and then they were on their way.

"Whew!" "Nice way to distract the horrid old bag, Dorfuss," Jon teased. Dorfuss's false flirtations had not been lost on him.

"Yeeesh!" was all Dorfuss replied.

They resumed their wait on the bench with James and Jenna, listening for the conductor to call for them in the meantime. Immediately after Dorfuss sat down, Jenna climbed up onto his lap. She buried her face into her "pappa's" chest, hugging him to her with all her might. After time, she relaxed and laid her head against him, gazing absently at the commotion in the station. She sighed, saying, "Pappa!" in a whisper.

Dorfuss smiled and hugged her back, glad to give the dear girl a few brief moments with the pappa she had so dearly loved and missed so greatly. James also leaned against him, just absorbing the peace and love emanating from the cat's heart.

Police officers strode here and there in the station, obviously looking for something while the hapless group continued to wait and worry. The officers appeared to be somewhat thrown off with an adult being present with them. The uniformed men glanced the small group's way several times. The description of the missing children they had received had been so similar to these kids. They finally shook their heads, assuming these children could not be the ones they were looking for. Obviously, *these* children had a father.

Finally, the conductor called out their train number. Quickly, they all rose from their seats and gathered their belongings. Soon they were seated comfortably on their train, and everyone became excited. Only an hour or so of traveling time ahead, and then they should be in Davenport!

Dorfuss felt it would be best if he remained in his father mode until they reached their destination. The last thing they would need would be for train officials to observe the three children traveling alone. That could cause questions which he did not want the children to have to answer, particularly after encountering the rude woman behind the desk in the train station.

Soon all the passengers were settled, and the train slowly began to roll. It wasn't long before it began to pick up speed, and they all relaxed. Jenna remained next to her "pappa," and Dorfuss gladly let her cuddle with him. *Let her enjoy these few brief moments while they last.* Frankly, he was enjoying all of this himself! He did love these three children so!

As the train chugged along, Dorfuss thought back to the spring night that seemed so long ago now, when he had dreamt of their pappa's death. That had been the point when he had miraculously realized just what his purpose in life was to be.

What a sad way for their father to have departed this earth! Surely, there was a God in heaven, for a miracle *had* occurred, and Dorfuss had come to understand just how the children came to be orphaned. He had then realized just what he had been called to do. He was proud of not only these three beautiful children, but also of what he had accomplished for them. It wouldn't be long now, he knew, before they finally reached the destination they had longed for, for so many weeks.

Once the children were safely delivered to their aunt's, Dorfuss was looking forward to returning to his former life of just being a cat. He knew from the knowledge he had gained that wondrous spring night that Ralph's sister Ruth would be a good, loving parent and her husband would as well. When everything came to fruition, he would no longer be in need of this magic he seemed capable of. He did not care for it, did not particularly trust it, and was frightened of the apparitions that had shadowed them for much of their journey.

He shuddered with the memory of the corrupt night when he and the children had witnessed Hilda's attempt to conjure up demons. He knew, deep within his heart the magical powers he possessed were not a good thing. Otherwise, those evil spirits would not have continued to harass them all so persistently, obviously hoping to wear them down!

Time passed, and the little group was served a delicious early supper, which they enjoyed tremendously. The children perked up, grateful for the food and "Pappa's" welcome company. They were also excited with the knowledge that possibly this very day they would reach their aunt Ruth's home safe and sound. They were thrilled at the prospect, in fact.

Dorfuss enjoyed eating a human meal in a human way for the first time ever. Soon he had the children talking boisterously as everyone relished their food. Now and then while they ate, Dorfuss inserted a particularly funny quip in his usual, proper-sounding English accent, and the children giggled while they chewed their food.

After their meal, they all felt relaxed, just grateful to be on the last leg of their journey. Everyone was exhausted.

The knowledge and hope that their troubles should soon be over made them all feel wholly thankful.

The train moved along at a steady, relaxing pace. Again, Dorfuss began to reflect. Perhaps, in a strange way, accidentally ending up in the wrong city had been a good thing for them all. Jon had grown up considerably since the beginning of their trip.

He observed Jon slumping in the seat facing him next to James with his eyes closed.

James was silently gazing out the window, enjoying the passing landscape. Dorfuss said a silent prayer for James, imploring the God in heaven to keep helping James with his learning difficulties. Throughout their long journey, James had changed a lot. Dorfuss no longer considered the boy to have a simple mind. He had watched him grow and change, and Dorfuss felt proud. Although James would perhaps never be as bright as his brother, he had a quiet, confident air nonetheless. He also was blessed with the gift of common sense. Both of these boys would grow into fine, young men, of that Dorfuss was certain.

Then Dorfuss glanced down at his side at dear Jenna, who seemed to be taking a bit of a snooze while wrapped in the warm crook of her "pappa's" arm. Her birthday was coming up soon also, he reflected as he gazed upon her pretty, peach-colored and freckled face. Her fiery hair framed her face softly, and she looked just like an angel. She was young yet and would need the loving nurture of a set of parents who would only want what was best for her, along with her brothers. He just knew if they all could find Ruth that everything would be okay for all of them.

Dorfuss hadn't been aware that he'd dozed off himself until he heard the loud calling of the conductor announcing that Davenport was approaching. He shook his head to clear the cobwebs. Suddenly he realized that during his brief nap, he had resumed the form of a furry, tortoise-marked cat. Acting fast, his eyes glowed, and he purred and crooked his tail and paw in an attempt to resume the human form of Pappa he had taken on earlier, but he was unsuccessful. He *was* still rather weary. And each time he performed his unusual feats, the magic left him feeling somehow drained. Perhaps that had something to do with it. He simply couldn't seem to muster up the required energy right then.

Quickly he nudged Jenna, urging her to awaken and open up the duffel bag that Jon's legs were draped over so he could resume his status as a stowaway. The only thing important to him anymore was making sure the children got off the train without attracting any undue attention. If they were to be seen with him in this state, there most certainly was the potential for someone to recognize the little group. And now there was no adult to accompany them!

"Pssst, Jon!" he whispered loudly as Jenna began rubbing her eyes. He jumped up onto Jon's lap, stirring the slumbering adolescent.

Irritation was apparent on Jon's sleep-consumed face. He shifted a bit in his seat, got comfortable and resumed his low snore. Cautiously, Dorfuss moved into the crook of Jon's arm, rubbing against him as he often did with Jenna, in an effort to wake him. "Jon!" he implored.

Jon moved again, raised his hand, and patted the cat absently in his sleep, muttering, "I love you, Dorfuss." He gnashed his teeth, smacked his lips, and recommenced snoring.

Dorfuss's heart was moved, but he hesitated and glanced up at Jon's dozing countenance. During all of their travels together and of course before, the boy had never once expressed affection of any kind for him. He had mainly acted irritated with Dorfuss, although as the days and weeks had passed, the boy *had* adopted at least a semblance of respect for him, a mere cat.

But now to hear that Jon actually *loved* him, well, it was almost too much to bear!

Dorfuss's heart swelled in that instant, feeling almost as if it were becoming twice its size. Finally, he replied softly to the sleeping teen. "I love you too, Wrench!"

Jon did not acknowledge the statement but only continued to snooze.

Dorfuss looked at Jenna. "Sweetheart," he asked then, "would you please awaken your brother? I simply do not know if I have the capacity to do so at this very moment." Unshed tears glistened in the corners of both feline eyes, and Dorfuss rubbed at both of them with a furry paw.

Jenna and James both observed Dorfuss with amusement and astonishment. James reacted with a broad smile. Jenna giggled girlishly. Never in their whole lives had they actually witnessed a cat with the ability to form tears or display emotion. Dorfuss had never failed to surprise either of them!

Jenna complied with Dorfuss's request. She rose and shook Jon gently at first and then harder when he still refused to budge.

"Mmmm? What?" Jon finally muttered.

James shoved his brother gently. "Jon! We are almost to the train station! Quick! Move your legs! Dorfuss wants you to return him to your bag!"

Jon finally began to awaken fully, noticing the other passengers as they began to rise. He started suddenly, realizing Dorfuss's transformation back into his former feline form.

"Jon, quick, put me back in the bag!" Dorfuss implored as Jon, rather perplexed, quickly complied. He unzipped the duffel bag and hastily rearranged items within to make room for the large cat.

Passengers were moving about, becoming noisy and conversing with each other while getting their baggage and other possessions together. They paid no attention to their little group, Jon observed. He relaxed as Dorfuss quickly disappeared into the bag's confines, and he carefully zipped it shut most of the way. Now, all they needed to do was mingle with the other passengers and make their way off of the conveyance as hastily as possible.

Soon the train came to a grinding halt, and the doors opened. Sunlight streamed through the opened doorways as people began to make their way down the steps and out onto the platform. It was early evening, summer was beginning to fade, and the days were becoming noticeably shorter. The sun glared brightly in their faces. It hovered just above eye level as it made its gradual descent toward the horizon. Soon it would disappear for the day, not to return until the fresh new dawn.

The children stuck close behind a man and woman that appeared to be married, blending in as if they were part of their family. It wasn't long before they reached the platform and were *finally* home free. Quickly, they headed away from the train station, all of them thrilled to have nearly reached their destination.

Final Night on Their Own

They resumed walking, all with a spring to their step. Once they were out of sight of the large train station, they let the patiently waiting Dorfuss out of the duffel bag. He stretched and yawned in contentment and then began to prance alongside the children in the direction they were heading. Dusk had nearly arrived, and streetlights and inside lights in structures could be seen coming on for the night. There were many large industrial buildings just outside the train station. The weather was nice, but things were beginning to cool with the approaching nighttime.

After searching with the kids for a long while, Dorfuss gazed about. "Well, children, it looks as if we may be forced to spend one more night camping out. I am, unfortunately, not entirely sure of the exact direction we need to travel. If we should become lost, it would be difficult to read the street signs in the dark. I believe it would be wise, as we are all worn out and not sure exactly where to head, for

us to look for some out of the way place to spend our night once again!" he commented.

Naturally, the children were not terribly happy about the prospect of yet one more night on their own, and they all groaned a bit. On the other hand, they *were* feeling rather wistful over the prospect of having their awesome journey come to an end. In many ways, it had been just glorious being all on their own!

Jon was the first one to speak. "Well, Dorfuss, you have always taken excellent care of all of us. And I know we will probably never get to do anything like this again! Direct us, dear sir, to wherever you think would be the best place for us to spend the night!"

James and Jenna agreed with Jon, both also wishing suddenly for just one more night of this wondrous, magical adventure they had all nearly completed. Dorfuss felt proud to be in charge of leading the children their last evening together on their own. He continued to strut haughtily beside them as his fangs sparkled brightly in the illumination from the streetlights above.

They walked along together for some time searching for an appropriate hideaway as darkness fell. Finally, they arrived at a large, grassy clearing that sloped down toward a wide river. The lights from area buildings and businesses, as well as the streetlights, glittered and glowed in reflection, duplicated in the steadily moving water some distance below. It was a picture perfect summer nightfall—warm but not too hot. The stars in the sky were so numerous and radiant in the cloudless sky that it was astounding. One almost felt as if he could reach upward and simply grab one out of the indigo heavens. Hanging low above the glistening river, surrounded by the countless stars, Mr. Moon was full and huge and yellow, and he smiled down at them in welcome.

Everyone in the group took one look at the beautiful picture before them, and together they all decided this would be it. This beautiful, splendorous place was to be where they spent the very last night of their marvelous adventure. It was as if this special setting had been chosen for them and awaited to celebrate a journey well done!

So, without any of them uttering a single word, they merrily began to run down the hill toward the river. The grass was long and full of glowing wildflowers in this nighttime meadow. The bright moon lit their way, almost as brightly as day. Cheerfully, they all scampered down to where the land leveled out just by the water's edge.

Out of breath, but still feeling on top of the very world, the children began unpacking their sleeping bags for the final time. And for the very last time, all three children took turns bathing in the river behind the privacy of several large willows, whose leafy fronds hung low along the water's edge.

Dorfuss, as he had done so many times on their amazing adventure, took it upon himself to forage for one last meal of fresh fish for the little group. Jon gathered together some firewood along the river's banks, and soon had a small fire crackling.

A short time later, the little group of three children and their cat enjoyed the last delicious meal of their long, shared journey together. Everyone was in a cheerful, mellow mood. Dorfuss promised them all in the morning they would begin the final leg of their journey and it wouldn't be long before they had all been delivered safely to their aunt Ruth's home.

Eventually, after everyone's tummies were full, the three children scooted down into their sleeping bags, fluffed their pillows, and made themselves comfortable. The amiable atmosphere between the four in the little group reminded them all of the times back at the farmhouse after Pappa had passed away. There they had chatted for hours in the boys' shared bedroom before going to sleep every night. Dorfuss curled into the warm crook of his beloved Jenna's arm and began purring contentedly, rumbling loudly.

For hours, it seemed, as the fire began to burn low, everyone reminisced about their fascinating, sometimes frightening, but mostly wonderful and astounding journey. Everyone in the small group began to feel a bit wistful at recalling all of it. All three of the children had matured greatly during those past few weeks, though none of them really realized it. Dorfuss, however, *had* noticed. He was so very proud of all three of them! He contributed tidbits to the conversation here and there of all of the memories of their amazing trip. As they all continued to talk late into the night, eventually everyone's eyes began to grow heavy and sleepy with contentment.

Without even realizing it, everyone drifted off into a satisfied, joyful sleep, each to mull over in dreamland the wondrous events of their journey and what might lie ahead. Mr. Moon beamed directly down onto them with his large grin for hours afterward.

Morning dawned. The sky was filled with the radiance of the morning sun just as it began its return over the horizon. Birds began to chirp cheerfully, fluttering about in the rainbow-colored hues of the sunrise. The sunlight streamed down into the tall meadow grasses, and gradually, the little group began to awaken. Yawning and stretching with pleasure, they began packing up all of their belongings for what they hoped would be the final time. The sun sparkled on the water of the river, dappling it with brightness. Everyone was full of cheer and optimism over what this new day would bring, and they all chattered lightheartedly.

Finally they were all on their way. No more would there be worries over modes of transportation or long, difficult journeys ahead that would need to be traveled on foot.

Dorfuss strolled proudly alongside his three charges, head held high and preposterous buck fangs twinkling. He informed them all which street they needed to search for as they made their way through the large city. The children happily complied, very appreciative of the fact they all had nearly made their way successfully to their aunt Ruth's place. Gradually, industrial buildings began to change into stores and then a downtown area. And eventually the downtown area began to fade away and be replaced by large, gracious homes.

It had been a long, arduous journey for all of them. They had actually come to enjoy all they had shared together on their trip and knew they would miss all of it to some extent. Yet they realized it would be wonderful to have a good, decent place to call home if only their aunt Ruth and her husband didn't object to taking them all in. That would be the final hurdle to overcome. Dorfuss, however, seemed very certain that everything would be all right, so they tried not to be too apprehensive as they walked along, getting closer to their final destination by the moment.

DISAPPOINTMENT

Thames Fulton arrived at the library Saturday morning just before noon. It was a sunny, fair August day. *A slight sense of the coming fall is in the air today*, he observed. He pulled up to the library in his car, parked it, and turned off the engine, sighing. He was looking forward to seeing Hilda's friendly face.

To his extreme disappointment, however, when he reached the front of the large brick building, he was greeted by locked, glass doors, and an official-looking note taped to the inside of one of the glass panes.

He bent closer to read it, dismayed.

It read, "Closed Until Further Notice." Underneath this large caption, in smaller letters, it went on to say that due to the inexplicable absence of their one and only librarian, the library would remain closed until Hilda either returned or a new person was hired to take her place. It implored patrons with any information regarding Hilda's disappearance to please call the police. *Disappearance!*

What might that mean? It also asked that patrons either patiently hold onto any checked-out books in the meantime or return them to the Township Hall until the matter had been resolved.

Confounded and distraught, Thames swiftly made his way to the township hall. There, he was met with a stern but sympathetic mayor who apologized to the poor salesman for traveling to Laurel for nothing. The mayor himself seemed rather baffled over the whole situation regarding Hildegarde Walters.

He offered to take the upset Thames's phone number and call him if Hilda materialized anytime soon. The mayor was not at all happy about Hilda's absence. He expressed hope that Hilda would return soon. He informed Thames she had called in sick just the previous morning, which was something she had never done. And then, this morning, she had not even bothered with that. The mayor indicated that perhaps their librarian had simply been too ill to telephone him this morning and would return bright and early on Monday. He also complained to Thames that patrons had been stopping by the town hall all morning long, wondering why the doors to the library were locked. Finally, he had taken it upon himself to post the note in the doorway for folks' information.

Hilda had been the town's faithful librarian for so long that everyone just assumed she would always be there. It was totally uncharacteristic of the woman to behave so irresponsibly.

Thames reluctantly left the mayor his business card, making the man promise to call him as soon as he heard anything. The mayor promised and then shook his hand grimly in farewell.

Unfortunately for Thames, it had already been a particularly grievous and frustrating week. His best friend, a former colleague he had known since his college days, had unexpectedly suffered a severe heart attack and passed away early just the past Tuesday morning. The poor man had only been fifty-four years old, the same as Thames. All of that upsetting news had gotten Thames to dwelling morosely on his own mortality.

He seemed healthy enough at the moment, he knew, but then so had his dear friend Andy. Poor Andy had left behind a grieving wife,

children, and grandchildren to boot, as well as many close friends just like Thames himself.

He had kept in close touch with Andrew over the years, but an empty hole now existed in his heart that would never again be completely filled. They had shared so much of their lives so often that he felt utterly lost. Andrew would be irreplaceable.

It had been with great anticipation he had traveled to the library that morning. He had attempted to telephone Hilda there, yesterday afternoon at her work and again in the evening but with no success. The telephones at the library and also the one at her little home in town had only rung and rung. He had even tried the farm number later last night but with no results there either.

Not one to be easily put off, Thames had assumed she was out when he attempted to phone each place. He craved the comfort of her friendly face and the ease he always felt with her, especially after the recent and tragic loss of his best friend. He was hoping she might be kind enough to accompany him to an early dinner in nearby Marshalltown that evening.

Just yesterday morning, Andy's funeral had taken place, and Thames's heart was still heavy with despondence. And since that had taken up so much of his day, he had only assumed perhaps he had somehow missed Hilda each time he attempted to phone her.

Nothing had prepared him for this odd news. What on earth had happened to her? She did *seem* to enjoy their date last Saturday evening, as well as the kiss he had so gently placed on her lips when he bade her farewell. There had been no indication, none whatsoever, that she had been less than pleased with their evening together or with him when she bade good-bye to him in return.

And then Thames had been through the past horrible week, and he had not been able to find the time or the heart to call her until yesterday. Apparently, his bad luck had not yet changed.

Completely lost as to what to do, he sat in his car for several minutes more next to the township hall trying to gather his wits.

Suddenly, he had a stroke of inspiration. His car was about due for a fill of gas anyway, and he wondered what harm there would be in inquiring about directions to the Walters farm. Perhaps something had happened out there, and Hilda had been unable to leave. Maybe she had been injured or perhaps left evidence of some sort as to where she had gone. Maybe, as the mayor had suggested, she had just been too ill. *It is at least worth a try*, he thought to himself, feeling slightly encouraged.

Briefly, Thames ventured to Hilda's quaint little house in town. He knocked and knocked on the front door with no result. He peered into the graceful picture window but only viewed several lovely, antique lamps, and a few African violets through the lacy, ruffled curtains.

At the gas station, Thames obtained directions from a nice young man behind the counter in the building. The man was very helpful but full of gossip, just as most of the folks around there seemed to be, and wasted Thames's precious time. *How empty folks' lives must be,* he mused, *to have nothing to do but worry about what everyone else is up to!*

He knew Iowa people were famous for their kind ways, always there to help another farmer or neighbor in need in times of tragedy and such. Unfortunately, the flip side of the coin seemed to be meddlesome people who needed to get lives of their own.

He remained politely listening to the clerk behind the counter for several moments more, struggling to pay attention to the useless chatter in the vain hope of deriving some important but previously undiscovered information without results. He finally made a lame excuse to the man that he was in a bit of a rush and doffed his hat at him and made his exit out the door.

While driving to the Walters farm on the dusty gravel road, Thames's mind played back to him the afternoon he and Hilda had fist met. He recalled that quiet, serious woman, and again he found he missed her terribly. There weren't too many women like her around. Most of the women he had encountered since his lovely wife had passed away had been the same sort of shallow, uninteresting people he had only minutes before scoffed in his mind at. Thames had always avoided ladies full of gossip and useless details and unbecoming personality traits. Hilda had displayed none of those traits, only a serene intelligence and an almost childlike wonder at his interest in her.

She was the kind of woman he might one day consider asking to marry him if things worked out right between the two of them. But now she was missing and apparently hadn't left a clue as to where she had gone! *Well, I will find her*, Thames promised himself.

He arrived at the Walters farm, which did appear to be deserted. He got out of his car and knocked on the front door of the house for many long minutes, calling Hilda's name, with no answer. Then he wandered about the vast grounds for a bit but discovered no one.

Finally, in frustration, he got back into his car and drove to a neighboring farm. An older woman holding a plate and dishtowel greeted him on the front porch. She kindly told him that her husband, Harvey Jensen, had been tending the farm since poor Ralph Walters had died. She insisted that Thames was welcome to come inside until her husband returned from his trip into Marshalltown to pick up a part for their tractor.

Grateful for the kind offer, he went inside and was treated to a slice of fresh-baked cherry pie and a piping hot cup of coffee. The woman was friendly and chatted with him while they waited.

Thames inquired whether the kind woman knew anything about Hilda's reasons for not showing up for her post at the library. The woman adopted a vague look on her face and then informed him she had never really gotten to know Hilda. Hilda had always kept to herself, she told him, and even when Harvey was over at the Walters farm, they rarely spoke with each other unless there was something important pertaining to the farm.

Everywhere he had gone, Thames had run into stumbling blocks. Apparently this was going to be just another one. This had *not* been a good week.

Eventually, the jovial Harvey returned from his errand, and he came into the house as soon as his wife informed him they had a visitor. Thames Fulton was sitting at the table, absently glancing through the day's edition of the newspaper.

"Mr. Fulton, is it?" Harvey inquired.

"Yes, sir! And you are Mr. Jensen? The good caretaker of Hilda's farm?"

"Yes, I am. How can I help you?" Harvey offered.

Thames filled him in on the details of his day, starting with the note taped to the front door of the library. Then he told Harvey about his trip to the mayor's office and his subsequent, fruitless discussion with the attendant at the gas station.

Harvey was sorry to inform Thames that he really knew nothing more than Thames did. He had not even realized Hilda had not been at work for the last two days. Hilda had always been vague about her personal activities at the farm and never very friendly with him. Inwardly, he shook his head. *Hilda has always been an oddball.* Harvey then went on to expound on the virtues of her brother, Ralph, his deceased wife, Edith, and their three lovely children. He expressed dismay at the fact they had all been missing for over three weeks.

Thames was astounded taking in this new information. No one, not even Hilda herself, had ever mentioned their disappearance. It struck him as quite odd, as she had led him to believe just these past weeks that they had been in her care for the entire time he had known her. She had not even mentioned this new revelation the last couple of times they had been together.

As he spoke with Harvey, he began to wonder gravely about this woman who had struck his fancy so. Perhaps he had not known her quite as well as he'd thought!

Very disconcerted at this new information, he inquired if Harvey would be so kind as to follow him back over to the farm and perhaps let him in the house. It was his wish to see if Hilda had only taken a few days off of her job or had left behind any clues. Harvey kindly agreed.

Later, after searching the farmhouse thoroughly for any evidence of what might have happened to Hilda Walters, both men came up almost entirely empty-handed. The room Hilda had stayed in for all of those long months appeared to have been completely packed up, cleaned, and vacated.

Harvey suggested to Thames perhaps Hilda had decided to leave on her own. What other reason could there possibly be for all of her personal items to have disappeared along with her? The only question in both of their minds was why. Unfortunately, no one ever was to discover just what had happened in there only the day before.

The corrupt, magical spell that the evil Hilda Walters had so victoriously accomplished had been quite thorough in its mission. Virtually no trace of her or her existence had been left behind.

The only thing the men came across in the house was the address book in the parlor. It had been left opened to the page with Hilda's sister Ruth's address and telephone number listed. Harvey pointed it out to Thames, remembering fondly the attractive sister of Ralph's that had married and moved to the city and even her married name.

That evening back at his home in Des Moines, in desperation, Thames telephoned Hilda's sister. He hoped to either find Hilda perhaps visiting with Ruth there or at least discover something tangible that might lead him to her.

But what startled Ruth during their conversation even more than Hilda's disappearance was Thames Fulton's inquiries as to whether she knew of Ralph's children's whereabouts. She had known nothing of her brother's death, the fact that Hilda had been taking care of his children, or the children's disappearance. Upon hearing this news, she became distraught. Perhaps, she reasoned to herself as Thames waited on the other end of the line, the disappearances were all somehow related and everyone was together safely somewhere. It was all she had to go on for the moment.

Thames became more than a little disturbed during this stilted, uncomfortable conversation to discover just how ignorant he had been regarding Hilda. Although she had mentioned her brother's death to him and the fact she had been the children's caretaker, she had never discussed her living sister with him! Obviously she had not been on good terms with the poor woman. Why, Hilda had never attempted to inform her own *sister* of their brother's death!

Ruth had been left totally in the dark and had not even known that Ralph's children had been orphaned!

How could Hilda have let something like that go on without telling the people who certainly deserved to know the facts anything at all? Most definitely the woman must have been mentally disturbed! Perhaps even sociopathic! And here he was feeling bereft and left to deal with a poor, distraught woman on the other end of the phone line. She was discernibly crying and obviously upset over all of the revelations Thames had brought about! He certainly didn't care to be the harbinger of such bad news, particularly to a stranger who seemed to genuinely be a good, caring person.

After Ruth regained her bearings, she thanked Thames sincerely for calling her and promised to let him know if she heard anything from Hilda. He apologized to her for upsetting her so with not only the news about Hilda, but the children and her brother, Ralph, as well.

As he said a few more parting, consoling words to the poor woman, Thames's heart began to implode. *How could I have been so easily and completely fooled by Hilda Walters? And how could she have led me to believe she was a sincere and virtuous person?* In reality it was now obvious to Thames that she had been nothing of the sort! Families just didn't *do* this sort of thing to one another; it just was *not right!*

And besides, what possible reason could Ralph's children have had for taking on something as dangerous as running away from home? His stomach curled itself into a tight, sick knot. A feeling of overwhelming foreboding began to overtake his soul. He kindly apologized one last time to the poor woman on the other end of the line and wished her and her family well. Thames placed the receiver back on its base and felt the sickening taste of bile in his mouth.

After she let the kind-sounding Mr. Fulton go, an extremely upset Ruth telephoned her husband, Tom. He was working at his post of head physician at the nearby hospital, and she filled him in with a trembling voice as to what had taken place. He was equally distraught and mystified with the news of Ralph's death and also Hilda's and the children's disappearance. He rushed home to console his wife and telephone the police, making what was to be the first of many inquiries regarding all four missing relatives.

Destination Finally Accomplished

It was midmorning on Sunday. The clan of children and their cat were merrily walking along the shady streets of a residential area in Davenport. It was a beautiful August day with a slight coolness in the breeze. This was the first day during their travels they noticed the change in the weather. There was an ever-so-slight sense in the air that autumn was on its way.

Feeling greatly cheered at having almost reached their destination, their walking became casual. They observed the quaint neighborhood they were strolling through with pleasure as they walked along.

Grand, old Victorian houses graced the block. Huge shade trees lined the streets and filled the yards.

Beautiful gardens abounded. Wraparound porches on many of the homes contained large plant pots or flower boxes overflowing with brilliant blooms. The homes had a welcoming manner about them.

Plushy, cushioned wicker furniture resided in the shade of the porches, inviting a person to come and relax in their make-yourself-at-home softness. Birds flitted about happily between the large trees, chirping with joy. Beautiful butterflies fluttered about here and there.

The whole neighborhood looked like the kind of place that would be absolutely wonderful to grow up in!

The mood of the little group as they walked along the tree-lined streets was joyous. Dorfuss proudly led the way in all of his pompous, fuzzy glory.

Finally, they reached a stately, old Victorian. Dorfuss stopped, turned, gazed happily at the children for just a moment, and then proudly announced that they were home! The children hesitated a bit. Jon removed from his pocket the faded and worn paper that contained Aunt Ruth and Uncle Tom's address and checked it over. Indeed, the house number matched it, and they were on the correct street!

The children began to jump up and down for joy! Finally, they had completed their journey! Their worries were over! They were home!

Then, after their brief celebration, they quieted somewhat. Thoughts of rejection suddenly filled their minds, and it occurred to them perhaps their aunt and uncle would not be any happier at the prospect of caring for them than their Aunt Hilda had been. They never considered something such as that before.

Their worries were soon to be quelled, however. With apprehension, they climbed the gracious stairs of the lovely old porch with Dorfuss leading the way, set their belongings aside, and then Jon rang the doorbell. Dorfuss moved and waited apart from the children, off to the side.

Only moments later, a kindly but distraught-looking woman grasping an embroidered hankie answered the door. Her eyes were reddened, and she looked as if she had recently been weeping. There were traces of their Pappa's and Aunt Hilda's looks in this beautiful lady's appearance. This had to be their aunt Ruth!

Apparently, however, she did not recognize them! "Yes?" she inquired kindly. "May I help you?"

It was Jenna who spoke up first, breaking the silence of everyone else. None of them were sure what to do or say. "Are you our auntie Ruth?" she blurted out without preamble.

The middle-aged woman immediately adopted a look of relief and utter astonishment on her lovely face. For an instant, she could not muster the power to speak. Then finally she returned, "Are you Ralph's children?" She had not seen them for several years and was so perplexed and yet suddenly thrilled at having them turn up on her doorstep with absolutely no warning. She only learned less than a day ago that they had all been missing for weeks, and she didn't trust her eyes just now.

Without warning, she burst into tears once more, and then she bent down to scoop up the precious little redhead. "Oh my God!" she said aloud to no one in particular. "So you're all safe then! I was worried sick, absolutely sick!"

Jon and James stood nearby, the beginnings of broad smiles developing on their faces. Aunt Ruth vainly began to swipe at the tears that flowed freely down her face. At that moment, a distinguished-looking man appeared in the doorway, surveying the odd scene with a questioning look in his eyes.

Now, it was Jon's turn to speak. "Are you our uncle, Tom?" he questioned with a wide, crooked grin on his inquisitive face.

The astonished man stepped out onto the porch, evaluating everyone there for just a moment, and then realizing these were Ruth's brother's missing children, he gave a huge sigh of relief. "So," he inquired also, "you are Ralph's three children, am I correct?"

Ruth cut in then, composing herself enough finally that she was able to speak. "Yes, dear, here they are, safe and sound! God surely has answered our prayers!" She set Jenna, who began to cry with joy also, back down on the porch. She hastily welcomed them all, along with their furry, tortoise-marked cat, and ushered them inside the grand old house.

There would now be lots of catching up for them all to do!

In the hours that followed, Ruth fed them all a delicious, hearty meal while the children filled her and their uncle in on all of the unknown details. She was so thankful that she and her husband had only been forced to fret about the children's disappearance for less than one short day before the children had miraculously turned up on their front porch! The ravenous children filled their stomachs while they surveyed the welcoming kitchen and dining room. This was more than just a house; it was a home, and already they felt as if they belonged!

Ruth was so upset to learn of the treatment they had all been subjected to by her sister, Hilda. While the children talked, inwardly her heart filled with utter disgust at the injustice Hilda had inflicted on these dear, innocent, and unfortunate children.

She and her husband were both equally mortified to learn that Hilda had been practicing witchcraft, albeit mostly unsuccessfully. The children told them of how Hilda had slowly but steadily lost her mind over the long months she had cared for them.

They spoke of the evil that appeared to lurk about the farm after one rather unsuccessful attempt of Hilda's. They also told them of the subsequent day when she seemed to completely lose her mind and hurled the large, brass candlestick directly at them all.

They went on to discuss their ultimate decision to run away, leaving out purposely the details of Dorfuss's magical transformation, how humanlike he was, or that he'd had such an important paw in everything they had done. Dorfuss was very content to leave the victory and accomplishment of the whole matter solely with the children. He never once spoke, for obvious reasons, instead choosing to sit quietly in the corner of the dining room, comfortably purring and cleaning himself after also being heartily fed.

He knew it was no longer his place to take charge over the children. Even though he would miss their great adventures, he hoped to quietly live out the remainder of what he perceived would be many good, long years ahead in the security of this wonderful, new family.

After their early dinner, two of Ruth and Tom's children returned home for the evening, and the children were introduced to them. They, just like their parents, were very welcoming and accommodating and made Ralph's children feel as accepted as their parents had.

That evening, Ruth arranged the spare bedroom for the three

children, promising them that as soon as she had the time she would provide more permanent and appropriate bedroom accommodations for all of them.

Their two older children had just gone away to college, and she promised to see to it to rearrange their rooms for Ralph's kids within just a few days.

Jon, James, and Jenna were worn out after their journey and so appreciative to slide into the welcoming, soft beds Aunt Ruth and Uncle Tom provided for them. As they drifted off to sleep that night, their minds were filled with the joy of having completed their arduous travels safely. And they had been welcomed so very lovingly into this new home that would be theirs as long as they wished!

A Brand New Home

The next few months passed with the children and their new parents and siblings adjusting well to all of the new changes that took place. School began, and the children were enrolled and attending every day. They quickly all made many new friends, and soon it felt to everyone involved as if things had always been this way.

Memories of the abhorrent Aunt Hilda quickly faded, replaced by the love of two parents who doted on all three of Ralph's children as if they had always been their own flesh and blood.

Their aunt and uncle almost immediately observed Jon's unique talents for tinkering with motors. They enrolled him in the nearby college in a special class designed for young adults that taught him everything there was to know about repairing engines. He greatly enjoyed attending that class twice a week. It made him feel even more grown up, as there were several adults in the class also.

Jon also began to develop an interest in girls. A very pretty girl named Sophie was in his grade at his new school. She in return, also seemed to notice him.

James's special talents with animals were soon discovered, and his uncle and aunt found him work at the local veterinarian's place of business. There, he helped care for animals of all different sizes, making sure they were fed and that their pens were cleaned out on a daily basis. The kind veterinarian spoke to his aunt and uncle, encouraging them to see to it that James maintained the best possible grades in his schooling. He felt James's unique ability with animals would eventually serve him well and that perhaps he too could become a veterinarian. This had come as a huge surprise to James, who had always known a vague fear that the simple mind he had been told he had as a child might limit his abilities in his adult years. However, James's teacher assured his aunt and uncle that he was not simple. His only real drawback was a vision disorder that made reading words and numbers difficult, scrambling the messages sent to his brain. She had been working with him closely to overcome the problem.

Jenna became useful to her aunt and uncle, helping them around their home by cooking, cleaning, and gardening also. She also found at her new school that she greatly enjoyed art, something she had never before known. Her previous school in Laurel had never offered anything other than the basics.

And Dorfuss, dear Dorfuss, he was content to easily revert to normal life as an ordinary cat. He spent long, languorous days exploring the neighborhood and making friends with other area cats. Next door, he discovered the love of his life: an exotic-eyed, slinky, black and white tuxedo-marked female cat named Cleopatra. Often, together they would explore the backyards of the lovely, gracious homes in the neighborhood.

He took great pleasure in lounging around in the afternoons in the delightful sunroom off the back porch of the grand old home he now also thought of as his own. His days of wild, crazy adventures, long journeys, and responsibility for the children were over, and he was pleased.

Evenings and weekends when the children were at home, he still spent closely by their sides. However, he reverted back to normal feline ways in this respect also. Only occasionally did he speak now with the children. One day soon, he believed, there would be a time when he wanted to speak and would no longer be able to. But that was fine with him. He knew the new members of their family would never believe it if he was heard speaking!

Hilda's accidental and unasked for magical traits also seemed to be gradually disappearing. That too was okay, as he knew they had only been a part of that brief miracle: his remarkable, heavenly endowment of protection and responsibility over the children. He had always been uncomfortable with those unusual talents, knowing they could easily be used for corruptness just as well as good. The glowing red eyes that had persisted in following them throughout much of their journey were gone. Likewise, the haunted statues, evil, poisonous mushrooms, unusual and frightening screaming faces on possessed tree trunks, and other unusual happenings had long since faded away since the day he had rebuffed the single-eyed spirit on the tornado-stricken farm.

His worries about using up the final of his nine lives nagged at him no more, as the days of perilous living on the road were now behind him. Never again would it be necessary for him to conjure up dangerous modes of transportation or frighten off wily coyotes bent on eating not only himself but the children for late-night snacks.

He reflected back many times to the wonderful, and sometimes frightening adventures he and the children had all shared together. He felt much older than just the mere year old that he was. He was certainly much wiser than he had been only last spring when he discovered for himself on that strange, beautiful spring morning just how the miracle of his own life had come to take place.

He hadn't asked for any of it but was so very thankful for the supernatural occurrence of his unusual blessings. *How many other cats,* he wondered, *have been able to do what I have accomplished? Cer-*

tainly there haven't been many, if anything of this sort ever took place before! He knew irrevocably that his life had been a special kind of miracle, unique in its very own way, and it would most likely never again be repeated.

His purpose had been to protect and watch over Ralph's children and to deliver them into safety, and he had done just that. He looked forward to many long, lazy years of just living as a housecat with no other requirements for his existence than eating from his food bowl, drinking from his water dish, roaming the neighborhood with his beloved Cleo, and cuddling with the children when they so wished. That was the best part of all and what he lived for now. *Love* was all he needed and what he most definitely had found!

The End as the Beginning

In late fall, the children began to beg their aunt Ruth and uncle Tom to let them visit their beloved farm. They had all settled readily into their new home and school and were very happy.

After she and her husband discussed the best time to take them there, they agreed on Thanksgiving, as they would have a four-day weekend with no school or other activities to worry about the children missing.

The children awaited the date with anticipation, talking excitedly about it before bedtime in the boys' room at their new home, as they had grown so used to doing back at the farm after Pappa had died. They would spend Thanksgiving down on the old farm and knew this one was sure to be much more joyous than the last year's had been.

Finally, the big day arrived. Everyone, including Dorfuss, packed themselves into their aunt and uncle's large station wagon early in the morning with a huge turkey and all the fixings stashed in a cooler in the back. Soon they were on their way to visit home—their farm, the wonderful, old place they had grown up on!

The children realized things would never be the same there again. Mamma and Pappa, of course, were waiting for them up in heaven, and the fate of Aunt Hilda had never been determined. No one knew what had happened to her, not even Thames Fulton, who had been left wondering just what had become of the woman he had begun to become so fond of. He was never to be entirely sure if he had ever really known her at all.

The children had long since learned from their aunt and uncle that a gentleman had called their house in desperation just the day before they had arrived. Ruth and Tom had not been aware of Hilda's disappearance, the fact that the children had run away, or their father's death until Thames's call! Ruth grieved over that awful news for weeks, even while rejoicing that the children had made their way safely to their place.

Hilda had lived her life as a loner and would most likely spend the rest of her existence, if she were even alive anymore, as a loner. Perhaps that was how she preferred it.

After nearly two hours on the road, everyone arrived just as excited as could be. Harvey Jensen was there, waiting with a wide grin to let them all in and give them a key to the house and a few minor instructions before he left for the day. Then he wished them all well, waved cheerfully, and was on his way.

Even Aunt Ruth was happy to visit the old place. It was much as she remembered it from her childhood. So many memories of life with her parents and her brother, Ralph, and her sister Hilda began to swirl through her mind the minute she walked through the door. She prepared the turkey, getting it all trussed up with Jenna's and her daughter's help, and placed it into the oven. It would be hours before it would be ready.

As she walked slowly through the house with her husband, she pointed to various objects that brought back certain memories and told him the stories associated with each and every one. Sometimes the memories were enough to bring tears to her eyes, and Tom squeezed her to him compassionately. She was the only one left now. It was up to her to see the legacy of love their parents had left behind be continued with her newfound responsibility and love for Ralph's children.

The kids were having a blast outside, running around the barnyard with their cousins. They were busily introducing them to all of the old standbys, as well as the new animals that had taken the place of old ones that had passed away. They also showed them the many other changes that had taken place in their absence.

Another litter of kittens cuddled with Mamma Kitty again, born just a week or so before. James once more occupied himself with helping her, reminiscing about last year's litter and the miracle of Dorfuss.

Jenna petted not only the newborns but all the other loveable kitties. Dorfuss strutted about the farm, proud to see the children returned to their place of birth and the only true home they had ever known until they ultimately made it to Aunt Ruth's place. He was also particularly glad to visit his dear Mamma Kitty and also his brothers and sisters. Some of the cats had remained on at the farm, and others had gone, hopefully to the safety of other farms in the area. He had missed them all so very much.

The family enjoyed Thanksgiving dinner together that evening, laughing happily and telling jokes while enjoying the delicious meal that Jenna, Aunt Ruth, and her own daughter prepared together. The atmosphere was now joyous at the old farmhouse, something the children had not known since their Pappa had been killed so tragically that fateful early November day the past year. It had been over a year since he had passed, but they all still missed him deeply.

Nonetheless, memories such as those did nothing to suppress the joy they all felt at that instant. Instead they only served to deepen everyone's contentment at their newfound closeness as they shared their delicious meal of Thanksgiving.

Before bedtime, the three children and Dorfuss spent more than an hour talking with each other in the boys' shared bedroom, just as they had done after Pappa died. Of course, as always, Dorfuss reserved his voice for only when he was in the children's presence. Lately, in fact, he hadn't had much use for it at all. It was wonderful to be back at home in *their* rooms again, and they delayed the inevitable until Jenna began falling asleep in the overstuffed chair with Dorfuss already sound asleep in her lap.

"Better get that girl to bed now, Dorfuss!" Jon suggested to the loveable cat, poking him gently to awaken him. "She has obviously stayed up past *her* bedtime!"

Dorfuss yawned, stretched, and jumped down off of Jenna's lap. "Come on, dear girl," he told her gently. "Time for bed."

Yawning widely and stretching too, Jenna rose, said good night to her brothers, and then disappeared around the hallway corner into her own room with her cat.

Soon everyone was sound asleep, perfectly content to be back at the wonderful old farm in the beds they had slept in for so many years. There was no place as good as home, indeed, and for that they all gave thanks!

Daybreak came—a new, typical late November day, blustery and cold. A few stray snow flurries whipped about in the relentless wind. Dorfuss woke earlier than the children to the chilly wind rattling the windows. He peered at Jenna in the dawning grayness of the dark room, cuddled warmly with him and sleeping soundly in her soft bed. She always looked so angelic when she slept. She stirred a bit in her sleep and then rolled over and away from him with a sigh.

Soon Dorfuss, with his keen feline hearing became aware of some movement downstairs, and also out in the barnyard. The animals were beginning to stir, and suddenly he felt the urge to cuddle with Mamma Kitty and his siblings, as he had once done every morning when he was very young.

After all, he had been so busy behaving like a human for so long that suddenly what he longed for was the ordinary enjoyment of just being a cat, the smell of the barn, the taste of freshly drawn warm milk, and the comfort of those like himself.

He rose carefully so as not to disturb sweet Jenna and jumped down onto the large rug beneath her bed silently. He padded away noiselessly and headed downstairs.

Aunt Ruth and Uncle Tom were in the kitchen, reading the morning paper and enjoying steaming cups of coffee. The furnace was turned up for the day, and the house was warming steadily.

Dorfuss went and stood at the front door, scratching at the wood trim on it gently and meowing plaintively a couple of times to get their attention. Aunt Ruth rose and opened the door and let the sweet cat outside with a quick, affectionate ruffle of his fur.

The wind whipped a few flurries wildly around Dorfuss as he trotted on down to the barn. There were several frozen puddles in the gravel drive. It was a very cold morning. Obviously, it wouldn't be long before the snow really began to fly. He shivered, thinking about the coldness of winters in these parts. Soon he reached the barn and went inside to its welcome warmth, eager to cuddle with all the other warm cats in the hayloft.

He began to ascend the ladder leading to the hayloft, as he had done hundreds of times before. His toes were numb from his short time of being out in the cold. *I am just not used to being outside often in this type of weather anymore*, he reflected. He had become a pampered, and perhaps spoiled housecat!

He was nearly to the top of the long, tall ladder, sinking his razor-sharp claws into each board securely as he made his way up there.

The few top boards were shinier and harder than the rest and appeared to be newer. *These are the boards Harvey replaced last year*, Dorfuss noted absently. Apparently Harvey Jensen had decided to stay on top of such things so he himself wouldn't meet the same fate as poor Ralph.

Unfortunately for the cat, when he was only one rung away from the plywood floor of the loft, one of his paws slipped. In the split second when he realized what had taken place, his sharp claws were unable to penetrate the board to grasp it. It startled him so severely he overcompensated and made a wild attempt to grasp the board firmly with the other paw. It was all in vain. He meowed loudly with terror.

As fate would have it, he began to descend the long distance down to the dirt floor of the barn, much as poor Ralph Walters did only a little over a year ago.

Suddenly, the memory of his dreams that fateful spring morning just over six months before flooded his mind. As his body twisted and turned in his plunge to the ground, everything seemed to be playing out before him in an unreal, slow-motion effect, mingling with what was taking place inside of his own mind presently.

Again, Dorfuss pictured the middle-aged farmer as he had perceived him in his dreams. He remembered how one of the boards had given way from dry rot when the man had placed his full weight on it. He watched everything act itself out in his mind as the farmer reached out in vain with his one free hand to grab onto another board, only to miss it completely, just as Dorfuss did only a split second before.

He felt all the emotions once again that ran through the mind of the children's poor pappa as he made his descent toward certain death. "What will become of the children?" rang through his mind over and over, echoing in resounding waves in his head, pounding repeatedly as Dorfuss's furry body plummeted to the ground.

He felt terror as his head moved toward the barn support beam and then connected with it sharply. Pain exploded into his brain in a thousand points of blinding light, just as things had come to pass for the man in the dream. And then Dorfuss blacked out entirely.

Minutes, or perhaps hours later, as he would never be certain of exactly how long he had been unconscious, Dorfuss's awareness began to emerge. He was aware of a horrible coldness pervading his furry body. He quivered violently from his absence of warmth and the bleakness of his future. He blinked several times, attempting to gain focus as the familiar sights in the barn began to gradually come back into view.

He attempted to turn his head, but with the way it was cocked up against the side of the support beam, his neck hurt too painfully for him to move it. He attempted to survey his furry body next to his head. It appeared to twist grotesquely. It looked useless. He could not feel the lower half of his body at all. He trembled again from the enveloping coldness; it seemed to be worsening, and suddenly, for the first time, he feared he was dying.

The vague remembrance that this was his ninth spent life suddenly filled his thoughts fully. *So it is true then. Cats have nine lives! And I'm afraid I have just consumed all of mine! Well, that is certainly more than most living beings get!* Despite realizing his impending death with certainty, he found himself to be instantly thankful. They had been a very good, actually wonderful, nine lives!

Reflecting on the past year, he was reassured, for he knew with absolute faith he would not leave this earth with *his* heart deeply troubled over who would watch over the children and care for them. He knew with all confidence they would be perfectly safe and happy with their aunt and uncle always as their caretakers. The children would grow up well, never doubting they were fully loved. Their new parents would be able to provide for them in ways that never would have been possible for a cat. The children would receive good educations in his absence and all go well prepared into their adulthoods. Dorfuss would not die as the children's father had, uncertain of what would befall them in *his* absence.

He lay there for many moments longer, waiting for the inevitable to happen. Death! He wondered what it would be like. Would it be dark and empty or full of light and filled with joy? He knew not what eternity held in store for him, being only a lowly cat, but he had faith that everything would be all right. He knew he had lived his life well.

Without warning, something moving into the field of his again blurring vision distracted him from his thoughts. He blinked to clear his sight once more.

Sweet Mamma Kitty, who had given birth to the miracle of his life, as well as countless other babies in her lifetime, approached him hesitantly. She reached him, imploring "Meow!" twice. She licked his furry head in affection, worry radiating from her dear green eyes. He closed his eyes, enjoying this last tiny bit of warm, comforting pleasure before he departed this earth forever.

Mamma Kitty had seen this sight once before. Something was all too familiar about it, and she knew her beloved Dorfuss did not have much time left. He felt terribly cold to her as she continued to lick his furry forehead.

Dorfuss barely had any energy left in his battered form. It took every last ounce of effort remaining in his dying body to open his eyes the final time. Finally, he forced them open and looked deep into his mother's eyes, knowing he would never see them again or her sweet, beloved, tortie face. He smiled at her as she gazed back into his eyes and similar tortie face with growing distress.

With his last dying breath, he opened his mouth and spoke for what was to be the final time. "Don't worry, Mamma!" he whispered. "I love you, Mamma Kitty. Always remember that! I *will* see you again; I promise. *I love you!*"

He gazed upon her a few concluding moments, etching firmly into his being forever the feeling of love encompassing him just now, along with the memory of his mother's beloved face.

Mamma Kitty began yowling with despair. A glistening tear escaped one of her eyes, rolling down her furry cheek, sliding onto a whisker, and then plopping off the end of it onto the dirt barn floor, where it was quickly absorbed, fading entirely from view.

In that very instant, Dorfuss's head slackened, and then slowly his loving green eyes closed in sweet finality. Just before life departed his furry body forever, he glimpsed the dear children all smiling happily at him in his fading mind. Then their beloved images also lost their luster and vanished.

In eternity, a messenger of the angels delivered a joyful message to their dear brother Ralph and his much-loved wife, Edie. "Your children are safe!" he exclaimed with jubilation. "The miracle we provided to see them all to safety has accomplished his mission! Jon,

James, and Jenna will live out the remainder of their childhoods with their aunt Ruth and uncle Tom watching over them with love!"

Ralph and Edie rejoiced at the marvelous, long-awaited news.

The heavens thundered, resounding with applause and cheering. Every soul residing within shared now in Ralph and Edie's jubilation. Trumpets sounded, and soon every imaginable musical instrument in the heavens joined in.

And God, in his heaven, from the vantage point of his eternal throne, surveyed the jubilant, brimming-over-with-love-filled scene taking place before him ... and smiled.

PROMISE ME

A poem
By Cynthia Jean Mueller

We will meet again, you and I,
Somewhere, somehow, far off in the sky.
Know the peaceful flutter of angel's wings,
Experience the undying joy of eternal springs.

Life cut short, way too soon,
Our time together now gone, under a crying moon.
Who was to know how it all would end?
Who was to know death was just around the bend?

Under the sun we have shared our lives,
And over the rainbow our hearts will still thrive.
You have been my most dear, treasured friend.
My solemnest wish was for you, God would never send.
Promise me after you've entered through heaven's blessed door,
You will wait patiently for me there evermore.
Search for me until one day soon, I gladly join you
Where the clouds are purest white, and the sky is radiant blue.

A poem dedicated to the memory of Jacob Steven Gordon